The Year of the Rat

The Year of the Rat

Lucille Bellucci

Writers Club Press
San Jose New York Lincoln Shanghai

The Year of the Rat

Writers Club Press
an imprint of iUniverse.com, Inc.

For information address:
iUniverse.com, Inc.
5220 S 16th, Ste. 200
Lincoln, NE 68512
www.iuniverse.com

ISBN: 0-595-14895-6

Renato, I remember us

Preface

So many said Mao Tse-tung would not change the China they had always known. It was only a civil war; business would resume, China would absorb this alteration in its government to fit and continue to be as good to its taipans as before. Later, the phrase "How The Far East Was Lost" would resound in the halls of the United States State Department, and in endless articles on the phenomenon, for good or ill, that the revolution had wrought.

Acknowledgements

I owe so much to my sister Maria and my brother Victor for their patient instruction of what occurred in the years when I was too young to remember all of it, and my friend Emily Chung for supplying me with the name Ming Chu, which means Bright Pearl, a perfection of choice for the woman she was. I am grateful to my friend Paul Fletcher for his knowledge of insignia and uniform, his reminiscences of the Jeep known to the troops as the Double Deuce, and for connecting me with the U.S. Army Military History Institute in Carlisle, Pennsylvania; and always, as in my entire life with him, my husband Renato for his devotion in helping me.

I

The house was full. That is to say, five of the
nine tables were occupied, the best showing since
The Camellia opened six months ago. Maria Conti
had objected to that name the moment Zoya had
thought it up. A night club that was really only
a hole to drink in, called The Camellia? Could
they hope to attract the American servicemen who
threw their dollars around like funeral paper
money in genuine night clubs like the Lido, Del
Monte, Delmonico's, Eventail, Merry Widow,
Ciro's, and the splendid Metropole? Not to speak
of the Palace Hotel, where they hired the best
bands and acts?

Zoya was stubborn, and her friend Galia, who
sympathized with her sentimental fancies, sided
with Zoya. Oh, by all means, let's keep her dreams
alive, said Maria, And of course as our partner
she's going to share in our zero profits from running a nothing place called The Camellia with
pink walls and a bandstand big enough for two
infant mandolinists. In reply, Galia had uttered

one of the imprecations that sounded twice as menacing in Russian and kissed her cheek.

Maria was outvoted, regardless. Her money covered ten percent of the startup costs; Galia and Zoya owned the major shares. Yet she worked the same hours, helped with the books, helped with the bar, and helped with the kitchen, where the sole dish produced by their chef was a dubious sort of club sandwich. Yung made his own mayonnaise with peanut oil. For bacon, he had found a cheap substitute, a Chinese ham whose origins only he knew.

She also served as hostess. When necessary, she emerged from behind the stubby little bar and took orders from the customers. The cotton dress she wore clung like silk because of frequent washings; it was nothing she could help. Her father had never visited here and so cherished a belief that Maria worked in the office as full-time bookkeeper. Her mother, Maria knew, had understood from the beginning what she did because she understood her daughter.

A rating from the HMS *Amethyst*, berthed across the Whangpo River at Pootung, whistled as she crossed the floor. She knew she possessed certain physical assets. They came from both parents: her Italian father, a tall man whose hair, when he had had any, was auburn; her Soochow mother, a slender woman with a fair complexion and delicate features.

She asked the rating if the drinks and his meal were to his satisfaction.

"Not so you'd notice. Then the view improved things," he said gallantly. He was sweet, with his clipped hair and baby's mouth. Maria was twenty-four, and often she was amazed she was not older. The war had wrought powerful lessons during the Japanese occupation. In fact, the American assaults on the city to drive away the Japanese had hardly been much easier on the people of Shanghai than the Japanese soldiers had been.

"Another drink?"

The rating turned to his companion, the Russian who had brought him here. Maria's partner Galia disliked her compatriot, particularly his habit of escorting enlisted men around town. The sailor appeared to be no older than a schoolboy, a fact that worried Maria. The Russian's name was Grigory Gromeko. Galia said he had been a spy for the Japanese, then he had been a pimp when the Americans had taken back Shanghai, and though he no longer pimped—as far as Galia knew—he went regularly to all the night spots in Shanghai. Oh, then we are officially a night spot? Maria said. Galia laughed. Don't be a wise ass, malenki, little one.

Gromeko smiled, showing neglected teeth, and said politely, "For me, cointreau. My friend will have another Johnny Walker, Black Label, no ice."

Maria nodded and reminded them to pick up their drinks at the bar. She was a hostess, not a waitress. The Camellia, she told the customers, was still interviewing for the post of waitress. This information was often taken for the joke it truly was, for the city overflowed with women of a dozen nationalities who were out of work and would have taken the job for twenty American dollars a month. The Camellia budget concentrated on stocking the best whiskies and brandies, now that these were available again. The partners were fully agreed on that. Quality spread the word for itself and would attract quality spenders. In Maria's private opinion this was as likely as her other partner Zoya getting her dream husband and house with camellias in the garden.

She collected more drink orders. The civilians were Portuguese, Filipino, and perhaps a Frenchman who looked as though he were out of work. All asked for Tsingtao beer. It was good beer, but not profitable.

The record on her father's old gramophone lapsed into hisses. She put on another one, "Blue Heaven," and caught an incredulous grin from the British sailor. Well, it was old, and she was old. She held out her arms to him and smiled. He got up at once, the grin pulling down at the corners. She knew that look. Assailed by groin and armpit aromas of sexual arousal, Maria held him a staid six inches from herself. Zoya's beloved pink walls, cloaked in dim lighting, whirled gently around them as they foxtrotted to the clomping beat. Sometimes Maria was almost convinced that this illusion of a night club was working.

"I don't want to spoil your evening," she murmured into the rosy ear of the sailor, "but do watch your pockets around Gromeko, would you? Perhaps you should get together with some of your own shipmates before you leave our club."

Before the sailor, pulling back to look at her, could respond, Galia appeared behind him; her pale face, broad of cheekbone and balanced by a long upcurved nose, was unaccustomedly flushed. She tapped the sailor on the shoulder. "I always cut in on the good-looking ones." To Maria she said softly, "Go and see what Yung's moaning about. I don't know what the hell he wants."

As soon as he saw Maria, Yung burst out in the Shanghai dialect, "Upstairs, *hsiao-tzia*. The landlady wants you up there. Something terrible has happened!" Maria saw blood on his apron, smelled something burning and scanned him up and down and then around the kitchen. Had someone attacked him? Had he attacked someone?

Understanding, Yung said, "No. Not me. I only cut my finger, the landlady gave me such a fright. Go upstairs. She's waiting for you."

The stairs behind the kitchen led to a second floor. The moldy treads gave no one privacy, singing their news to the world: steady creaking—a woman; a lopsided creak along with a screech—a woman and her man of the moment. Galia did not trust the shaky structure and always trod on the edge, near the wall. On the first landing, Maria saw the landlady standing in a doorway, her hands clamped over her nose and mouth. The smell of burning yet not burning was strong, a smoky bluish gas of a smell that made Maria cough.

The landlady pushed Maria inside the room. "Look at this disgrace," she said harshly. "Your dirty foreigners can never be trusted. I don't care what her trouble was, just get her out of here by tonight."

Maria took in the figure on the bed and the charcoal brazier beside it. She ran to the window and flung it wide, then bent over the girl. "Tasha," she said, shaking the shoulders and knowing the girl had gone beyond this room. She tried to lift her, but the inert weight was too much. "Help me get her away," she panted.

The landlady did not move. She looked tired. "You know it isn't any use. She must have started that thing burning yesterday. One night will do what she wanted from it."

"Could you fetch Zoya for me, Chen Tai-Tai?" As she asked this, she realized there was nothing to keep her from going to find Zoya herself. But the landlady turned and walked to Zoya's room, two doors down. The middle room belonged to Galia. Mrs. Chen tapped on the door, then again, harder. Zoya's voice, high-pitched and annoyed, told the knocker to go away. Mrs. Chen continued rapping with her knuckles. At last Zoya opened the door, tying the sash to her flowered robe, her hair a black tangle. "I need to sleep," she complained.

"Last night was awful, the customers were awful. You know how tired I get."

At the door of Tasha's room, Maria beckoned. "Over here, Zoya. You're needed tonight."

"What's that smell?" Reluctantly Zoya advanced to Tasha's room. "Oh, my God." She began to wail. At the age-old tones of lament, heard everywhere outside on the streets, coming out of demolished doorways, from heaps of rubble where refugees made their shelters, from mothers rocking dead babies to shrunken breasts, until Maria dreamed that she was the one uttering these cries, she felt her control begin to crumble. She had listened to enough nightmare shrieks of pain and grief and loss during the war. The respite had been brief after the surrender of Japan and Germany. Three years afterward, the sounds of anguish had begun again all over the city.

Zoya clung, weeping, under Maria's chin. "You have to get Galia. I can't go down like this."

"I know. Get dressed as quick as you can." Maria detached herself from Zoya and went downstairs.

Galia was dispensing drinks. Several more customers had wandered in; unbelievably, all the tables were taken. Of all nights for business to pick up, thought Maria. "Tasha is dead," she told Galia. And she had done it the Chinese way; the newspapers no longer considered killing oneself by coal gas news.

"Over to you," Galia said, and left.

Maria finished making up the drinks.

A short while later Zoya appeared. Dressed and powdered, her hair swept up over "rats" in the current popular fashion, she looked nearly herself. Her pink walls were kind to the hung-over swelling of her eyes. "You'd better go up and help her. I can't do it."

Zoya's tender heart. If Galia coddled her, Maria could do no less.

Mrs. Chen had gone; she had set the charcoal brazier, perilously balanced, on the win-dowsill. The fumes had thinned but not by much; a muggy August breeze barely stirred the short curtains. Wearing rubber gloves, Galia stood over Tasha. A huge wad of cotton wool sat on Tasha's stomach. Her dress had been pulled over her hips, her panties a little heap at the foot of the narrow bed. Her bare feet and pretty ankles turned outward, an attitude of helpless-ness that made Maria want to weep.

"We have to hurry," Galia said, all nurselike. Well, she had been a nurse, that was why she was the one they all had thought of right away.

"What do you want me to do?"

"Turn her over. Here, we'll do it together."

She was forced to lean over Tasha's face as she slipped her hands under the body and pulled and heaved her over in concert with Galia. In muted horror Maria saw that Galia had stuffed cotton wool in Tasha's mouth and nostrils. The girl's flesh had hardened; her right arm thumped against the wall like a stick of firewood. Only nineteen, Maria thought, staring at the smooth skin of

Tasha's averted jaw. There were parents, who lived in Frenchtown in a decent enough apartment. Tasha spoke good English, having graduated from the British School. She had enjoyed advantages few Russian emigres ever attained.

As Galia worked, she cursed men. She wished unspeakable disease upon the universe's race of males, their male offspring, and upon the male get of those offspring. Had Maria not known her well, the ferocity of her curses would have convinced her that Galia hated men. The true Galia loved them at the same time she despised them; she kidded them while she pitied them. She had a lover, a Norwegian sea captain who put into Shanghai twice a year and each time asked her to marry him. Seeing you twice a year is enough, Galia said. Any more would make me dislike you.

Maria had found a comb on the dresser and busied herself with Tasha's hair at the back of her skull. This is stupid, she thought, but kept on tugging at the matted hair. Anything to keep from looking at what Galia was doing. She felt grateful for the obliterating smell of coal gas. The charcoal must have been mixed with cheap coal briquettes, for the carbon monoxide from pure charcoal was almost odorless. They had not found her soon enough; the sheet beneath her body was already stained.

"Is…was she pregnant?" she asked.

"What else?" Galia said, busy packing cotton. "About three months, I'd say. Those parents of hers think they are still in Russia. The mother acts more like an aristocrat than she ever was in Russia. A lousy baroness. Did she expect Tasha to find a prince?"

"Was he that sergeant? The one who came downstairs with her sometimes for a drink?"

"Of course. It was Love, darling," said Galia in a good imitation of Zoya's breathy style. Maria had never heard her make fun of Zoya before.

"And he left with his unit," guessed Maria. "And she never heard from him again."

Galia shrugged. "We'd better turn her onto her back again." When they had done so, she picked up the soiled panties and put them back on Tasha and pulled her dress down. Then she stripped off her rubber gloves. "Do I call the police, or will you?"

"I'll do it." Galia would never manage it right, with the broken Chinese that she spoke.

"All right, I leave it with you. But tell them to be careful taking her down the stairs or they will crash through that rotten wood. And before you do that little thing," Galia said, her dark eyes large and glistening, "send me up a bottle of the best, would you? A nice, full one, Black Label. And a big glass."

Maria was exhausted when she chased the customers out at two o'clock and closed up. Normally she let them stay as long as they were buying, which they were doing tonight. Daniele had been sitting at the near table the last hour, his haughty countenance as usual out of place in an atmosphere of tipsy conviviality. The glass of water in front of him remained full. Though Maria kept assuring him that Yung always boiled their water supply for twenty minutes, Daniele only pretended to drink it, for her sake.

When she had locked the door, he took her arm and they walked toward Garden Bridge and the former International Settlement. Across the street, lights showed at only a few windows at the Astor House Hotel. The Astor was moldy with age and not located in the center of life downtown. Next to the Astor stood the Japanese Consulate, and next to that the Russian Consulate. Their people seldom dropped in at The Camellia. On the corner opposite The Camellia stood the sixteen-story structure of Broadway Mansions. At this hour, people still came and went; the building housed a good restaurant and bar (an excellent reason why The Camellia got only the enlisted men along with the usual down-and-out Europeans). The Foreign Correspondents Club occupied some of the floors and she knew that American military personnel did mysterious things on some of the others.

Daniele said, "I hate it when you get so tired. It makes me feel like a pimp, to see you pandering to all those men."

How would he feel if she told him what had happened upstairs tonight? She had no intention of telling him anything. One word, and he would start in again about finding a respectable job

in the Settlement. He had told her last night
there was an opening for a cashier at Jimmy's
Cafe on Nanking Road. Cashier! She could never
explain in a hundred nights that working for
herself was better than committing her future to
the drudgery of a job behind a cash register.
How long could Jimmy's survive when the Reds
broke through to Shanghai? Jimmy, the owner, was
an American; he would get out with the rest. She
and Galia had worked for that epitome of
American might, the petroleum company Caltex,
which shut up shop and let them go to scramble
for themselves. How long, for that matter, could
The Camellia keep open? Her owners were two
Russian emigres with no passports and one
Italian citizen with no cash. It was all the
same. The Reds would level everybody as they saw
fit. Daniele dealt from a position righteous as
it was unjust; he received a monthly pension
check from the Italian Navy via the Italian consulate. And he was free to go home anytime he
pleased to his wife and two children in Bari.
Maria did not insist on sending him away because
his presence, abrasive, confining, often tire-
some, was still that of a man who loved her. It
was a comfort in a world of rare comforts.

"I love walking with you, Dani, it's such a
peaceful night and it's finally cooled off,
but could we please catch a pedicab now? My
feet hurt."

"Not until we get over the Bridge." The pedicab
drivers always wanted more money on the Hongkew

side because of the hump in the center of the
Bridge. You either held a loud, long, bargaining
session, or you walked to the other side.

Perfectly aware that Daniele thought he was
disciplining her by making her walk, Maria
laughed, and as expected he stiffened and
snapped, "What was that for?"

"Nothing, caro. You're sweet, you really are.
There's a rickshaw. I'm going to get him."

And she did, giving in at once to the man's
outrageous price while Daniele stood by no doubt
seething. When they were settled in the narrow
seat—rickshaws were built for one—Maria snug-
gled against him and Daniele, unwillingly
pleased, put his arms around her. Males had
their uses; their strong arms felt wonderful
when you had need of them. For a little while
tonight she would draw strength from Daniele,
who loved her. She was fond of him, and sometimes she did love him, especially when he
helped her father.

On the other side of Garden Bridge they passed
the British Consulate at the head of the Bund. A
single light burned, on the ground floor. Foreign
nationals (her own father included) still
believed the fighting between the Communists and
Chiang Kai-shek's Nationalists had nothing to do
with them. Despite the refugees flooding into the
city, despite the hasty evacuation of foreigners
from the major cities of Peking to the north and
Chungking to the west, people who were not

Chinese refused to believe anything was really going to change for them.

China has had so many revolutions, they insisted. The foreign nationals are needed here, for business and the routes to the West, you know.

The bobbing of the rickshaw went on and on, off the Bund to Nanking Road, then into Bubbling Well Road, passing a late tram, mostly empty, at the corner of Yates Road. Home was at the opposite end of the International Settlement, on the western edge of the French Concession which everyone called Frenchtown. Grayish lumps of bedding, ten thousand watchers in the night freeholding their bits of sidewalk, lined Maria's route home. She fell asleep.

When the rickshaw finally halted, near three o'clock in the morning, in front of her lane on Route Magy, Daniele pushed away her hand holding the money and paid the coolie himself. Round two for him, and he was welcome to it. She was glad that he did not have the coolie take them two blocks farther to the room he rented in a house on Tifeng Road. Rather than physical love she longed for a soak in a tub and to wash her hair. He had not commented on the smell in her hair, probably having lumped that in with all the cheap cigarettes smoked in The Camellia.

The lane of stucco row houses was cluttered with garbage, as usual. Yesterday's rain had backed up the drains at the last house, which belonged to the Contis, so that she had to hop over the puddle to the doorsill. Out of habit, she stamped her heels down noisily going past the door of the Wong apartment, then tiptoed up the stairs to the Conti apartment on the second floor. Their living quarters consisted of two rooms, a bath and a kitchen. Her parents occupied one room, and she and Nola shared a bed in the rear portion of the dining room. Curtains divided their cubicle from the eating section. Amah slept in the kitchen on a pallet. Maria teased her about her snoring, calling them roars, and Amah always protested that the *hsiaotzia* was exaggerating.

In the bathroom, Maria pushed the open window wider, turned on the gas to the pilot of the ancient gas water heater, lit it with a match, then stepped back as far as the door and waited for the loud fwoom! of the gas jets coming alive. Twice in the past year the steady gas leak, though infinitesimal, had blown the hood off the heater.

Bathed, weary, her hair at last free of coal fumes, Maria lifted the mosquito netting and crawled into the double bed and found her sister sprawled on her face on Maria's side of it. She felt for a small hip and pushed. Nola responded by humping on her stomach, like a caterpillar, a few inches east.

Maria sighed. "Nola, my child, one of these days I am going to...." She leaned over, but Nola knew what was coming and ducked before Maria could blow into her ear.

"Were there lots of customers tonight? Did you get any dollars?" asked Nola professionally.

Maria stretched out and stared at the dim white canopy of their mosquito netting. "We did all right," she said.

2

A decade ago, Leopoldo Felice Conti, known to his friends as Poldo, had been a man of means, a business force within the international community. He had owned two freighters, which carried woven silk and raw flax and cotton, wicker and rattan furniture, and wheat and rice to Hong Kong, Singapore and India. In exchange his ships steamed back with manufactured goods, radios, refrigerators, automobiles, European furniture, the latest American films made in Hollywood, and electric cables for Hungjao. Hungjao was the burgeoning country enclave of foreigners west of the Settlement.

His glory days. A handshake sealed a contract. Not one had ever been dishonored.

His old Chinese partners, for all he knew, were either still flourishing, or had journeyed the slow, humiliating slide to poverty, as he had. It was possible they survived better than he; their ships had not been sunk in the Whangpo on Pearl Harbor Day. Perhaps his friends were

safe and prosperous in Hongkong; he hoped so.
Unlike him, they would have had the acumen to
know when a good thing was over even when the
war ended in 1945. If they could see what he was
doing now!

Peering at labels—his eyesight not what it had
been—he measured out, into a large glass pitcher:

    1.3 oz. Butyric Acid
    2   oz. Acetic Acid, 66% by volume (he was
           still experimenting with the propor-
           tions)
    1/2 oz. Acetic Ether
    1/2 oz. Butyric Ether
    24   drops Oil of Caraway

The door opened and Nola came in, home from
school. This second child of his and Ming Chu's
always caused a a hurtful twinge of the heart
when he saw her like this, unsmiling, her thin
arms laden with books. She seldom went out
again. The scenes of scourged humanity along her
daily routes caused Nola to dive deep into the
well of her books. It was not right, Poldo
thought. She should have a gaggle of girl
friends, play games, whatever little girls did,
and above all have decent food to eat. What she
seemed to do was eat up those books of hers. One
of Maria's Russian friends ran a lending library
full of English-language books. Poldo had seen
some of the titles she brought home. He did not
object to selections of Rudyard Kipling's

stories and poems. But having scanned a few
pages of *The Well of Loneliness* and *Ethan Frome*
while Nola was away at school, he had suggested
that she return those books unread. Nola looked
puzzled. Why, Daddy? They are only stories in
books, not real things that happen here in
Shanghai. What can be wrong with them?

Poldo found himself at a loss to explain. He
already knew that the reins of guidance over this
child had somehow slipped out of his hands. If not
for Ming Chu, this household would be Bedlam.

Nola wrinkled her nose. Butyric acid at its
purest smelled like rancid butter.

"Pew! Did you get an order for whisky? And the
color's all wrong. Here, let me taste."

Poldo removed his glass stirring rod from the
pitcher and allowed two drops to fall onto her
extended tongue. She rolled them upon her
palate, separating flavors, considering. Her
eyes, closed now, resembled her mother's dark
ones, with eyebrows like gentle strokes of a
calligrapher's brush. He felt a foolish qualm
about her hair: it grew so thick and long; perhaps it depleted her bones of growing food. Both
his daughters resembled their mother, for which
he was grateful. They possessed comely lips,
unlike his wide ones, and well-shaped noses,
unlike his big one. Nola's cheeks lacked the
normal blush of youth. Poldo resolved to tell
Ming Chu to reserve for Nola what good meat they
managed to get. The others would eat the fatty
bits. Oranges and apples, her raw materials of

sun and vitamins, he could not buy in the quantities she needed.

For God's sake, man, he told himself. Do something useful, or die and let your family get on with it. They will do a better job without you.

"You put in too much caraway, Daddy. That's strong stuff. Cochineal could make it redder without the taste."

"I'm running short of cochineal. My last order from Bush House didn't get through." The company in London had probably written off Shanghai as a market. Cochineal was a red dye made from the dried bodies of insects. He would have to find a safe substitute. A vegetable dye? He suppressed a bitter laugh. Why bother to make it safe? People died eventually, and a lot faster this year than last.

"Don't add the alcohol yet," Nola said. "I'll help, as soon as I change."

Her precious blue serge uniform. The nuns at the Loretto School would be deeply suspicious of a student who turned up reeking of the seamen's dives in Blood Alley.

To avoid disturbing Maria still sleeping in the cubicle, and because the girls' closet was only big enough to hold a few dresses, Nola kept her clothes in her parents' bedroom. He could hear her and Ming Chu speaking in the room next door. No matter how his wife asked about school, the substance was always the same. Did you learn?

Ming Chu's anxieties for her younger child felt like reproaches to Poldo that she never voiced. She did not say outright to him what was on her mind: She must learn to save herself. She isn't even twelve, yet, Poldo thought. Ming Chu asked too much.

"The Wongs are setting up to wash their clothes today," Nola remarked, when she came back.

He knew what she meant. Poldo had once made the error of calling down to ask if they couldn't be less noisy. The result had been a tumult of banging of washtubs and loud talk in the small yard below the Contis' windows.

Nola held the funnel in place while he poured the contents of the glass pitcher into a clean five-gallon demijohn. Without being told, she began uncapping a gallon bottle of distilled water. The grain alcohol went in last. The supplier of alcohol, a Chinese grocer who ran a still in his home, swore that the alcohol was pure; he had never topped it up with any other kind. Poldo had to trust him though he heard stories of deaths from wood alcohol. These occurred among the emigre population, usually Russian and a few incautious Frenchmen.

As he rotated the demijohn, gripping its neck with both hands, Nola got up on a stool and surveyed his shelf of essences. "Maria says there's a Frenchman who keeps asking for pastis. Isn't absinthe the same? Let's make up some for her to take tonight. She says he gets homesick and starts crying when he's had a few."

The curtain of the bedroom cubicle parted, and Maria came out, yawning. "'Had a few'? Is that a proper way to talk?" Poldo's old pongee bathrobe was large on her, but Maria refused to have it cut down, for in the winter she was able to wrap it around almost twice. "Did you worship Sister Maureen today? She used to be mean to me, you know, so you ought to show a bit of loyalty to your own sister. Hello, Daddy. Did Amah save me something to eat?"

Mulling over her essences, Nola said, "You shouldn't say 'worship' about anybody but God. Amah has noodles in a pot, but you have to help yourself. Mama sent her out to buy up cooking oil with our old dollars. And I took your stockings to the mender. She wants six million old dollars or five new ones. She always says afterward there were more ladders than I showed her. I think she cheats."

At the end of every month Poldo hated his existence more than at any other time, yet doggedly he made the rounds as surely as the tides flowed in and out at the Whangpo's mud flats. It was not a small matter of pride. He wanted it known that Leopoldo Felice Conti had not given up his right to demand rightful compensation for what was his.

He climbed the stairs to the top landing. Of course the Samoyed, the whited hound from hell, knew it was he. Dog claws scrabbled upon flooring that had become splintered grooves; the dog throat emitted roars that had frozen Poldo in terror the very first time he met the animal.

Porcupine-ruffed, the Samoyed threw itself to the limit of its chain again and again. The invisible other end of the chain was hitched to something inside the half-open door. Poldo thought it appropriate if that something happened to be grandmother Bordokoff/Krichevsky.

Poldo stood just out of reach. He cupped his hands to his mouth and shouted above the roars, "Bordokoff or Krichevsky, whatever your name is this month, I have come to collect your rent! You are thirty-two months in arrears. Show me you have self-respect. Begin by paying for this last month."

He paused. The dog, as if awaiting a directive from within, subsided to a growling.

Poldo pronounced the Russian words he had taught himself, his ritual closure: "Kak nde beni stedna." Shame on you. Indifferent now, the dog allowed him to walk within inches of his nose as Poldo approached the second door and knocked.

Almost at once it opened, and Leon Kwilecki's apologetic brown eyes confronted him. The man's embarrassment enraged Poldo as much as the Bordokoff/Krichevsky flintiness did. Kwilecki always had an excuse. There was never a political action in the most obscure corner of the government that did not affect Kwilecki's fortunes. A minor functionary deep within Shanghai's public works department who happened to change the hour for garbage-collecting from eleven o'clock to noon somehow managed to disrupt Kwilecki's budget. Kwilecki and his wife were the most trouble-prone individuals Poldo had ever known. Obviously he was an educated man—an engineer, he claimed to be.

Poldo pitied Kwilecki's wife, a physical spec-imen of dramatic contrasts: dead-white skin, tar-black hair, and tragic eyes. Further, she suffered from a disease no one could name. One might be speaking to her and suddenly she became a heap on the floor at one's feet. She did this several times a day; Kwilecki alone earned their keep, such as it was.

"You see, Mr. Conti, the labor union kept back a big part of my salary this month," said Kwilecki in his accented English. "I can give you a quarter, and maybe next month I can make it up." He proffered a sheaf of paper currency. Naturally, the money was old Chinese dollars, which as of the beginning of August everyone was frantically trying to convert to the new "gold" dollar before the rate depreciated fur-ther. Yesterday's rate was four million old dollars to one new gold dollar. Today, one American dollar was worth either five million Chinese dollars, or two cans of sardines, or one can of evaporated milk, or a stick of mar-garine. The world had gone mad. Kwilecki's handful of paper had extra zeros stamped over the original denomination.

Poldo accepted the paper. He did not say Yes, do try next month. He did not offer a Good day. Dispirited beyond speech, he turned and walked down the stairs.

For this, he had sold the big house in the Hongkew district. He had exchanged twelve rooms, servant quarters, a landscaped garden, a garage that once had housed a Fiat, and Maria's horse for the Plan. The Plan, since his ships were sunk and his offices had shriveled to two rooms in a godown, had been to buy income property. The Plan would provide rents for the Contis to live on; they could manage in two rooms for a little while, until Shanghai had recovered its old commercial powers.

Poldo had met the previous owner of this hell-house briefly. He was French, liquidating his assets, as he put it, so that he could repatriate to his country. Jovially, he wished the Contis good fortune and departed the next day. Poldo had not appreciated the cause of his happiness until the Contis had moved in and met the Bordokoff/Krichevsky sisters and their grand-mother. One B/K was easily the equivalent of ten million Kwileckis. Print that on your banknote, Chiang Kai-shek.

On the ground floor, before Wong's door, Poldo consulted with himself. Could he go through with this today? He lifted his hand and knocked.

To his surprise the door opened and Wong stood there. Then he fell to the floor. Bewildered, Poldo wondered if Mrs. Kwilecki had infected Wong with her disease. "AYAAAA!" screamed Wong, clutching his stomach. His wife came into view and dropped to her knees beside the writhing Wong. "Police! Police! This man is beating my husband!" Their daughter Grace was right behind her mother. The combined noise of all three made Poldo's ear canals crackle. He did not hear his wife come down the stairs, nor his daughters. Ming Chu touched his arm; he turned. He said, "I don't know what happened," and could not hear himself.

Then Grace Wong dashed past them and ran down the lane.

Ming Chu said, "She is going to fetch the police."

"Not if I catch her first," said Maria. Followed by Nola, she ran after Grace.

Wong continued to scream. After a while, since no policeman had yet come, his crying diminished. He said conversationally, "You shouldn't have beaten me, you know. The police don't like foreigners anymore."

Ming Chu said, "They do not care for liars of low quality, either. Leave them here, Poldo. If the police do come we will deal with them in our own home."

Mrs. Wong laughed. She had pulled at her hair and torn open the top button of her cotton dress. "Oh, listen to the grand Mandarin! Her own home! They live like mice in a miserable nest, and they treat us like persons of no background. Frankly, I am tired of you snooty foreigners, and I do include you, Ming Chu Conti." The Wongs occupied the best unit in the building, two bedrooms and a living room in addition to the cement-paved yard.

"Do not speak to her, Ming. Come away." Poldo took his wife's arm and they began to ascend the stairs.

Multiple footsteps clattered up the lane. At the entrance a policeman, a young man of about twenty-five, stood peering at them. Poldo saw a revolver in his hand. Maria's voice, sounding bored, said, "The scene of the crime is right before you. Isn't there a lot of blood? I wonder who really beat whom?"

Wong recommenced his cries, and his wife returned to tearing at her hair. Grace Wong shoved past the policeman and shouted, "There. There. Do something! This foreign landlord has been forcing us to pay twice as much rent as anyone else, and he just raised it again. He won't listen to reason! When my father opened the door the foreigner began beating him. He fell on him without a word!"

Poldo said, "They have not paid one dollar in rent in three years, and that is why they are acting this way." His Shanghai was quite good, and he saw this surprised the policeman. The young officer holstered his sidearm; he glanced at Ming Chu, who stood above him on the stairs. She said nothing, her bearing straight-backed, disdain in her lifted chin. He turned back to Wong and snapped, "Shut your howling," then in the sudden quiet, said wearily, "I suppose I have to take both parties in to the station."

Maria descended the few steps to her father. "I'll go with you, Daddy. Nola, you go upstairs with Mama." Nola opened her mouth to protest, looked at her mother, then nodded.

The policeman's glance flicked to Ming Chu's tiny bound feet; all knew she would not keep up with them, not unless she rode a pedicab or rickshaw to the station. "Get off the floor," he told Wong. To Mrs. Wong he snapped, "Button up your clothes."

The sound of leather soles clicked in the lane. Everyone turned to see who it was.

Daniele appeared in the doorway and stopped there. Uncertainly he said, "Buon giorno." He looked around at the still figures: the policeman; Wong upon his elbow on the floor and Wong's disheveled women; the Contis, distributed along the hall, up to Ming Chu on the stair, as though counting each one to make sure their numbers were intact.

"He is my friend," Maria told the policeman. "He will come with us."

The station house on Avenue Petain had once been staffed by French police. The French had style as well as palate. One entered the station grounds through a handsome wrought-iron gate, and then walked upon cobbles patterned in diagonal T's. Poldo and Maria Conti, Daniele, and the three Wongs filed into the station house and were told to wait. As far as Poldo could tell, very little of the motion and talking in here appeared to concern the business of policing. Men wearing uniform trousers but without their jackets, and some in civilian clothing, loitered sipping tea and talking. "...fifty thousand trapped in Changchun...Chiang can't supply them anymore... Hsuchow won't last much longer." Hsuchow was the corridor to the Yangtze River, three hundred miles from Shanghai. In Mao's path, Nanking lay before Shanghai. There were rumors that the Chinese police had been deserting; a Communist purge would not overlook leavings, however minor, of the Nationalist government.

Wong had limped all the way to the station, now and again rubbing a hip, an arm, his stomach. He too, had overheard the gossip in the room. He glanced at Poldo and said, "Things are changing fast. Foreigners no longer have any power over us Chinese. And when you leave China, be sure and take those half-breed girls of yours, especially the whore."

Poldo felt the blood leave his face. He looked down at his hand, which had become a fist. "You may say what you wish about me, Wong. You will keep your dirty mouth shut where my children are concerned." He had never struck anyone in his life. A small pain jabbed below his windpipe.

Uncomprehending the exchange in Chinese but seeing Poldo's anger, Daniele asked, "Has he insulted you? I'll drag him out of here by the neck and deal with him outside." Though not a large man, he was physically strong. He had been first officer of the Italian gunboat *Lepanto* and personally saw to her sinking to the bottom of the Whangpo River. Allies no more of the

Japanese, the Italian crew had been rounded up
and interned.

Maria inserted herself between her father and
Wong. She topped Wong's bushy locks by three
inches. They grew in a crest, like a rooster's
comb. Bending to his egg-shaped face she said,
"Do you know something? If you aren't careful
you'll find yourself with a half-breed grand-
child. I've nearly broken my leg a dozen times
stumbling over Grace and her Portuguese
boyfriend saying good night."

Poldo shook his head, Do not stoop to their
level. Grace flinched from her mother, who began
to speak to her in a fierce whisper. Grace was
pretty, though like her mother's the outside
corners of her eyelids were severely pinched.
Upon Ming Chu's first sight of the two women she
had remembered a Chinese proverb: Beware the
hidden eye; it takes what it wants and gives
nothing away.

Their young police officer brought them a
ledger and a pen. "Write down your names here,
and your addresses. We'll look into this."

Wong heard the lack of conviction in the
man's tone. "But shouldn't you make an arrest
now? He cannot be allowed to gouge tenants the
way he has."

At this, the officer seemed to lose patience.
"Mr. Wong. Do you want to know something? No one
in this police station has been paid for two
months. We have ration cards that get us one
catty of rice per week. Our captain walks or

takes the tram because there is no gasoline for his official car. Chiang's war has requisitioned every resource there is. Now, if you want to take your case to the Central Station on Foochow Road you are free to go there." He walked away from them and joined a group talking hotly around a desk.

Maria said, "Goodbye, Wongs," and left the station with her father and Daniele. Hesitating, the Wongs consulted among themselves, then followed, a few yards back.

As they walked home Poldo's fatigue felt like death approaching. He could not care properly for Ming Chu and Maria and Nola, his family. He should have taken them home to Italy at the first shot of the war between the Japanese and Chinese in 1937. Instead, he had stayed on for the second act, World War II. Wong was not entirely mistaken. The foreigners were, indeed, greedy fools.

They walked down the lane to their house, the Wongs a hostile rear guard. At the foot of the stairs Maria paused. Poldo continued up; he heard Maria say, "The gods hate a liar. I'm doing you a favor, you know," and he turned to see Maria smack Wong on the head with her purse. It was Mrs. Wong who screeched and tried to attack Maria; her husband grabbed his wife and daughter and opened his door and shoved them inside. The door slammed.

Ming Chu was tallying the few purchases Amah
had made in the markets. They were meager: four
catties of rice—about six pounds, two tins of
cooking oil, a lump of meat which looked to be
pork, and some carrots. Amah, a stout woman who
seldom smiled in public for fear of revealing
to thieves the gold in her teeth, recounted for
the third time how she had inveigled her way to
the front of the line at the bakery, only to
find they had run out of bread. "When my husband visits next month, Tai-Tai, he will bring
fresh vegetables and a couple of chickens. You
will see. He will not let us starve." She
returned to her mistress one bundle of old dollars that she could not unload on the wary merchants. These bundles were called "bricks," an
apt term for a currency so unpliable in the
chaos marking this year.

Why do you stay with us? Ming Chu often wanted
to ask. It would be easy to get on with your
daughter-in-law as long as you had enough to eat.
But Amah was stubborn. Let her husband truckle to
her daughter-in-law, who acted as if she and
their son had already inherited the farm.

Poldo came into their bedroom, and Amah said
she hoped the police had given the Wongs their
due. Flashing a smile full of gold, she rapped
her fists upon her head to show what she meant.

When she had gone, Poldo said, "Maria gave him
his due with her handbag, just now."

Ming Chu made a gesture denoting exasperation.
Her older daughter had too lively a spirit. She

liked to think she was tough, and perhaps she was; Ming Chu hoped so. "I almost wish Daniele would take her away with him." She knew he would not keep her if he did; Maria would leave him when she pleased. Ming Chu had searched her conscience and found it tolerant of considerable tarnish where it concerned the safety of her children. If a man who was not free to marry nevertheless wished to possess a woman, he suffered whatever consequences came of it. She supposed she had changed her views; in these times, who had not?

They must have gone to his place, she thought. Nola was next door, doing her homework at the dining table. The little routines to attain privacy were carefully observed. Poldo had switched on his shortwave radio and was tuning in to the Voice of America. She hesitated, then said, "Amah heard some rumors." These daily doles of anxiety were punishing, yet they all had a need to know. "People are saying the Americans are not going to help us."

Bent to the radio, Poldo did not reply. The radio's antenna, a complex device comprising mast and boom with driven elements set into the boom, had been rigged by Daniele. During thunderstorms, Poldo dismantled what parts of it he could reach outside the window. One never knew what lightning would do.

Reception at sunset was always poor. Volume as high as it would go, the broadcaster said, through static, "The United States Department of

State confirms that no support, directly or indirectly, will be given to a coalition government in China with Communist participation. Secretary of State George C. Marshall reiterates that the United States has no intention of again offering its good offices as mediator in China. Earlier this month he declared that it was not likely the situation will make it possible for the United States at this juncture to formulate any rigid plans for our future policy in China. This policy directive was issued to the staff of the American Embassy in Nanking."

Ming Chu could not follow this rapid and official English. She waited as long as she could bear, and then asked if Poldo had heard anything important.

Slowly, as though he had aged a hundred years within a minute, Poldo turned to her. "What Amah heard was correct. President Truman is pulling out."

3

He was suffocating, but without the handkerchief protecting his mouth and nose Leon Kwilecki fared worse. Chaff and fine powder from the rice, plus burlap lint floating about his head got into his eyes. He knew how he looked. The men working beside him and across the long flat metal table all sported caked runnels of moisture from sore, weeping eyes. Lifetimes past—centuries ago, his sympathy for Metzenbaum's dry coughing had given way to a desire to strangle him. Though Metzenbaum did not know it, he owed his life to the foreman. Any interruption in the shoveling of rice from big burlap bags into small bags was punished with a cut in pay. Kwilecki could not afford a cut in pay while he took time to kill Metzenbaum. I may kill him on our break, Kwilecki thought. He would, gladly, work twice as fast to make up for the loss of Metzenbaum's labor.

The prospect of violent release sustained him for another hour.

The mountain of burlap sacks containing rice dwindled too slowly for the pleasure of their elderly foreman. Roaming up and down the cavernous godown, with frequent detours to one of the open windows for fresh air, Hsung exhorted, prodded each of the twenty men with a stick; sometimes he called the foreigners insulting names. Kwilecki's special designation was "turtle dung."

Hsung was not a bad man. The size of his daily pay depended upon the same shadowy powers that produced jobs for people such as Kwilecki and Metzenbaum.

Kwilecki finished transferring the contents of his burlap sack and went to fetch another. Warily, he reached for two corners of a sack and pulled it to the edge of the tier, a foot above his head. When it tilted and began falling he pushed at the same time to keep it from hurtling, unchecked, to the floor. One of the newer men had allowed his bag to hit the concrete too hard; Hsung had made him sweep up every single grain of rice that had burst from the bag. A hundred pounds of loose, raw rice had cost that man half a day's pay.

The large stenciled letters on the burlap sacks spiraled in Kwilecki's brain in lunatic song: SIN-RAH, SIN-RAH, SIN-RAH RAH RAH, I LOOOOVE YOU. Thank you, Chiang Kai-shek, I suppose. The letters were actually CNRRA and stood for China National Relief and Rehabilitation Administration. The American people donated food to the starving people of China, and the Nationalist government sold it on the black market. Well, they did need the money for the war effort, didn't they? The one-catty cotton sacking bags had nothing stamped on them, but any fool on the street could tell they contained rice.

I'll slip a few grains into my pocket every hour or so, Kwilecki thought. In a week he could save up enough to pay Mr. Conti his rent in rice. Two pockets' worth was food for two days for him and Zina. But he never did it. Hsung watched too closely.

Metzenbaum's wife, everybody's wife or sister or girl friend except Kwilecki's poor Zina, shuttled between the men's big table and their own big one, where they sewed up the one-catty bags. Hsung refrained from speaking to these women if he could possibly avoid it. Shame, embarrassment—Kwilecki could not decide, or could it even be compassion?—flitted over Hsung's wrinkled features when he had to look at them. Perhaps it was resentment, for the jobs could have been filled by the Chinese women in his family, which would be a large one, given Hsung's age.

Then why did the SIN-RAH people allow the hire of foreign men?

Because we work even cheaper than Chinese men, Zwilecki thought. He was the only Pole among the Germans here. The German and Austrian Jews lived in the Wayside district across Garden Bridge, in

the waterfront section of Hongkew. In the late
thirties, 50,000 refugees built a community of
small factories, tailor shops, and kosher butcher
shops. They had a good, working wharf, too.
Hitler would have admired their industry, though
it was the Japanese who created the ghetto.

Hsung rapped the table with his stick. The
skilled drumming suggested that Hsung had once
been a dumpling chef. One heard the strumming
spatulas inside a doorway and knew at once the
specialty of the shop. Thinking of that,
Kwilecki's dried-up mouth moistened a little.
Such delicious dumplings, sprinkled on top with
sesame seeds and stuffed with meat and fried
golden on the bottoms. His very first time, he
had eaten two before noticing Zina's stricken
expression. "It's pork," she said. "But I am so
hungry." We couldn't have known, he and Zina
told each other. But that was partly a lie. The
aroma and cheapness of the dumplings had overcome their caution. When they spoke together, it
was always in Yiddish. Talking in Yiddish about
having eaten the pork made Zina feel worse about
their sin.

In the godown, Hsung's dumpling-shop rattle
signified the lunch break.

The break lasted twenty minutes. Kwilecki at
once drank the boiled water Zina had put in a
bottle. He managed to chew and swallow two
pieces of black bread and longed for more water.
He thought that drowning must be a delight, to

be swallowed up by more water than he in turn could ever hope to swallow to sate his thirst.

Metzenbaum and his wife, their faces turned up to the overcast sun, were sitting among the weeds in the back lot of the godown. I give him three months, Kwilecki thought, listening to him cough. He'll die without my help. Tuberculosis had cleared out half the inhabitants of Metzenbaum's flat in Wayside. It was too bad the Metzenbaums weren't going to live to enjoy the extra space. The wife had a bad color, too; her skin wore a prickly pink sheen. Kwilecki thanked God that Zina could not work. Zina, instead, cursed herself for doubling her husband's burden. Never to worry, *libe*, he told her when she cried over his cracked hands. Once he had come home reeling on his feet; a tire rim had popped off its mounting with force enough to knock him out and he had nearly lost an eye. He blamed his own lack of experience as a mechanic, though he had done quite well assembling bicycles for CNRRA, better than scooping rice in this godown. Once, for two weeks, he had put together film projectors, a commodity that someone in the bureaucracy deemed vital to the reconstruction of China's economy.

His own noonday meal finished, Hsung bellowed "Chi leh! Chi leh!" Kwilecki knotted his handkerchief in place and walked into the gloom of the godown.

At six that evening, the day's pay in his pocket, Kwilecki trudged out to the lot with the

rest of the work gang. The group, automatically
stringing out into a rough column, crossed the
dirt path to the pocked wall of the godown where
Harry Truman waited for them.

This area of godowns in Pootung, on the east
bank of the Whangpo River, was arid as the Asian
steppe; the village of Yangching lay a few miles
inland, where there were farms and rice paddies.
Kwilecki had heard the countryside was pretty;
he and Zina had never enjoyed the luxury of an
excursion outside Shanghai.

The line formed; Kwilecki took his place in
it. His SIN-RAH song hummed in his head as he
shuffled forward.

The Chinese who called himself Harry Truman
spoke good English, and even Kwilecki with his
English acquired secondhand recognized the
man's university education. The workers knew he
called himself Harry Truman because it amused
him; the money made a round trip, so to speak.

As always, he nodded pleasantly. The men and
women who had worked that day filed past
silently and one by one handed him their "union"
dues. Kwilecki took his pay out of his pocket
and divided it exactly in half. He was receiving
the new gold dollar now; the number of banknotes
felt disturbingly thin in his hand, even though
its value was no more than it used to be. Harry
Truman accepted the money with a polite thank-
you, and Kwilecki walked on. He no longer ques-
tioned the system. No tribute to Harry Truman,
no jobs.

Zina would take the money Kwilecki had left and buy bread and some vegetables. The remainder went for tram fare. Kwilecki felt a detached pity for Mr. Conti, destined never to receive his rent money. He dared not explain about Harry Truman. What if Conti talked about it? What if that unfathered son of his mother, Wong in the ground floor unit, heard and worked some mischief? They'd had clashes before. No. Kwilecki's only recourse was to dig in and play on Conti's sympathies.

I used to be an honest man, Kwilecki thought. And I have lost my humanaity. I no longer feel anything for anyone else.

The workers re-formed, husbands with wives, men with their girl friends, and shambled to the launch tied to a small jetty. The ride across to the Bund took twelve minutes, and it was free, courtesy of CNRRA. Today, Kwilecki got himself aboard the first of three runs the launch would make. The late October wind was cold, but felt good in his lungs. He scooped a little of the water in his palms and rinsed his face, then he dusted his shirt and trousers before donning the jacket he had kept folded inside out. He took a comb from his jacket and tried to get the dust out of his hair. Each time he washed himself with Whangpo river water he was careful not to let a single drop pass his tightly compressed lips. He did not mind dying of cholera; it was Zina he minded leaving, to fend for herself alone.

The launch made an arc, churned toward the
landing jetty below the huge Custom House and
its clock spire. To the right of the Custom
House ranged the imposing panorama of Shanghai's
commercial might: the squat, thunderous bulk of
the Bank of Communications, the airier Central
Bank of China under its two-tiered roof, the
narrow Bank of Taiwan mounted on four pillars,
the taller North China Daily News topped by twin
spires, the broad, solid Chartered Bank. Then
came the two hotels, the Palace and the Cathay,
facing each other on the corners of Nanking Road
at the Bund. The Cathay was queen of them all.
Built by Sir Victor Sassoon and converted partly
into a hotel, its size, height, and towering
spire made it the tallest building in Shanghai.
The man's history fascinated Kwilecki. Sassoon
made so much money in opium for the British
Empire that he had been knighted.

With Zina, Kwilecki had once gone inside. The
Russian doorman, festooned in gold braid and
crowned with imitation cossack hat, moved toward
them with that unerring instinct that doormen
have about unsuitable types. But Kwilecki
(because Zina was there and he was so tired of
being nobody) had stood his ground. He and the
burly, blue-eyed doorman had stared at each
other for a full minute; then Kwilecki turned
leisurely, Zina on his arm, and strolled around
the lobby looking at the pictures on the wall.
They did not leave until Kwilecki was ready.

A small victory of no importance. He was much more familiar with the seedier quarters of down-town Shanghai. When he was new here he had gone to the big taipan-run companies to apply for work. He had heard of their histories. The giant Butterfield And Swire, a distinctly Scottish operation and engaged in shipping, began life as an importer of opium; Jardine, Matheson And Co., another shipping firm first established in Canton, cleared a million pounds sterling in twenty years of importing and distributing opium. These two were the biggest; there were dozens more, most British but some American. Money flowed by the ton until the opium trade ended by official agreement in 1917.

And the irony of it, the beautiful irony of his position was that none of these opium-run-ning newly respectable tycoons thought he, an educated professional, was good enough to work for them.

Alighting on the Bund, Kwilecki parted from the other workers and walked three-quarters of a mile to the offices of IRO, International Refugee Organization, on Avenue Edward VII. The building was old, situated one block from the notorious Blood Alley, and bracketed by small tradesmen. In the Chinese custom, the stores had living quar-ters above and were open to the street: the hot-water seller steamed himself all day over his boiling cauldron and served green tea at a few tables inside; candy shops displayed their sug-ared ginger and dried, salt-sour-sweet prunes, plums, and mangoes in glass jars. Kwilecki liked these bits of China more than he did the big shopkeepers on Nanking Road.

He was not surprised to find the waiting room in the IRO offices filled; those who had no seats stood along the walls. After he signed the register, he found a spot to stand. He saw his next-door neighbors sitting across the room. One of them, looking around at the competition, noticed him; Kwilecki nodded curtly. He wondered which surname the women were using on their applications. Irene was prettier than she was plain, with frizzy blond hair and light blue eyes; Tanya had the same features, but hers were scarred by smallpox, and she was taller. Both were physically strong, with calves muscular from whatever it was they did in their night club skits and from carrying their bicycles up and down the stairs. They sang as musically as wildcats in heat.

Typewriters clacked in the various offices branching off the waiting room. Kwilecki had worked in an excellent office in Krakow. Once he had worn a good suit and his fingernails were clean and clipped; some people at work actually asked for his opinions. He remembered, with amazement, that women had flirted with him because they thought him good-looking. One had compared him to Henry Fonda, the actor. He doubted any resemblance was left.

A case worker emerged from an office and called, "Bordokoff, Irene and Tanya."

So they were Bordokoffs now. Irene had once told him frankly that using the Jewish name Krichevsky had gotten them extra rations from the relief people. Therefore as Bordokoffs, thought Kwilecki, they were laying claim to nobility in the hope that IRO would process such persons faster for immigration.

Kwilecki found this amusing. The Reds wouldn't care what they found when they got here. Foreigners, Jew or Gentile, stank in their nostrils. Chiang's northern front was crumbling. On September 24 Tsinan, the capital of Shantung Province, had fallen. And two days ago, on October 20, Changchun, the capital of Manchuria, had collapsed. If the Communists reach Shanghai before the Bordokoffs get their tickets out, Kwilecki thought with bitter humor, the women might well find their good White Russian name worthy of a firing squad.

Kwilecki's case worker was a Russian named Subarov, and he was a genuine prince.

"I have some news," Subarov said, wearing an expression of pleasure. Kwilecki knew it must be mostly relief. The Kwileckis represented an especially sticky problem for the IRO.

Subarov opened Kwilecki's folder. "Because you took away your birth certificates from Krakow, we have been able to obtain passports. You are no longer stateless, but have been reinstated as citizens of Poland. You may embark on any ship bound for Europe and go overland to Poland. The organization will, of course, pay your fares." His greenish-blue eyes beamed upon Kwilecki. The prince's sparse white hair still had some blond in it. His face was narrow and long, with a chin that would have exactly bisected the high collar of the brilliant dress uniform of the Czar's Imperial Hussars. Kwilecki had no trouble envisioning him, splendid in evening dress and silk sash denoting his station, seated at a banquet table dressed with silver and crystal. Under the glitter of stately chandeliers there would have been music, champagne, beautiful and spoiled Russian women wearing gloves over their elbows while their gowns showed the tops of their breasts.

"The Dutch liner *Boissevain* is setting aside berths for evacuees. You may register for two places with us now, if you like." When Kwilecki did not reply immediately, the lines of optimism on the prince's long face slowly faded, as though he knew what was coming.

Kwilecki almost felt sorry for him. "My wife and I are most grateful. But we will not return to Poland."

The other option hung between them, unmentioned. Since the partition of Palestine on May 15 this year, Subarov had been urging him to consider moving to the new state of Israel.

In so doing, Subarov had bumped into a conviction, born in a turmoil of emotion and now hardened. Kwilecki's credo was this: he renounced his

Jewishness. He did not want to live amongst Jews in Israel wallowing in their history, history, history; anything to do with being specifically a Jew, past, present, or future. He had, simply, resigned his place amongst their ravaged numbers. He did not, yet, disbelieve in God. These thoughts he kept from Zina, and he practiced without qualm the rituals that comforted her and left him unmoved.

"Things have changed in Poland," Subarov protested. "Attitudes are no longer the same. Many people in Poland did not approve of what happened to Jews there."

"An acquaintance of mine, Mr. Metzenbaum, does not wish to return to Germany," Kwilecki said gently. "And if you will pardon my impertinence, you yourself officially reside in the United States."

Subarov inclined his head; he could not dispute Kwilecki's observations. "Then we must put you on a list for openings wherever they turn up. All the quotas of the countries willing to take in refugees have been filled, you know."

"I do know. My wife and I appreciate everything you are doing for us. I will return in a week."

For many minutes after he left the IRO office, he stood on the sidewalk testing the limits of his exhaustion. A chill wind blew in gusts, not so welcome this time. Kwilecki shivered and put up his collar. He smelled rain on its way.

Were he and Zina to end their lives in Shanghai, far from home? For himself he did not care. Their families were gone, incinerated in Oswiecim. But Zina yearned to touch the soil of her forefathers, though he told her often and emphatically—the only time he ever raised his voice to her—that when he was dead she could set foot in Poland, not before.

He began to walk to the tram stop.

4

Pedaling west on Avenue Edward VII, Irene and Tanya passed Kwilecki crossing the street.

"Stupid Pole," muttered Tanya. "Thinks he's better than us. Did you see the way he brushed us off in the IRO office?" A coolie toting two baskets slung on a bamboo pole got in her way and she swerved. "Pew! What the hell is he carrying, corpses? They didn't used to allow that kind of traffic on the main roads in the old days. Now they even let peasants like Kwilecki walk here."

Irene let her rant. Though younger than Tanya, she knew she was twice as smart, which she had proven by hiding that fact from her sister. It was she who got them out of Harbin, Northern Manchuria, where the sisters grew up. Harbin swarmed with refugees from Russia. They had made her ill, all those upper-class Russians moaning for their lost Russia while doing their best to build a new one in exile. She and Tanya had laughed and laughed at the sight of Chinese New

Year parades clanging gongs and rattling their
colored dragons past the Russian Orthodox
churches. Those gilded onion domes looked like
noses stuck in the air.

Unlike the fretful aristocrats, Irene understood where the tide was turning; the Japanese
army garrisoned in Mukden to the south would
never stop hungering for complete conquest of
Manchuria. She counted the thousands of emigres
riding through Siberia on the Trans-Siberian
Railroad to the Russian port of Vladivostok on
the Sea of Japan. From there they took ship for
China. Irene tucked the route of escape away in
her mind. That was Number One. The prospect of
entering Russian territory once more made her
uneasy, so she figured out a Number Two—the
railway south to Port Arthur, though they would
have to pass by Mukden to reach the port.

Risk entering Russia or risk a brush with the
Japanese? When the time came to run to Shanghai,
she would make up her mind

She did not mention her mistrust of Manchuria
to either Tanya or their Babushka.

She had got them out and here to Shanghai, and
Shanghai delivered on its promise. Irene did not
dwell upon the things they were forced to do to
survive in this cosmopolitan and utterly corrupt
city.

They made a right turn onto Yates Road. When
they first arrived from Harbin they lived on
this street in the British Concession, above a
tailor shop. Yates Road was famed for its tailor

shops. Foreign women brought their fashion magazines here and had their tailors copy the most complicated outfits Paris could design. If a woman said she needed something from "Pants Alley" she meant Yates Road.

Gromeko was at home. His room above a yardage shop was like himself, unadorned and functional. It was unimportant to him that he shared a bathroom with six other roomers. He drank ceaselessly. The syrupy liqueurs he loved colored his teeth with whatever he happened to be drinking at the time. He had never had enough sweets when he was a child, he told the girls.

Unshaven, clad in a sweater without shirt underneath, he offered them a swig of anisette from a brown bottle.

Irene said, "I prefer something true with no color, like vodka."

Gromeko shrugged. He disdained vodka.

"Grigory, you should quit drinking this garbage," said Tanya. "Your eyeballs look like hell. And it's bad for business. People can smell you before they see you."

He laughed. The sound of his mirth suited the appearance of both the room and the man. "And you, my darling cow, should stop eating before you crash through the stage one of these nights. People will wonder how you stay so healthy in these hard times, hmm?"

Tanya was not insulted. They were lovers once. Grigory had not been bad looking fifteen years ago. He had been a common soldier, like

their father. The night he visited Rosinka's
house of joy in Love Alley he asked for a
strong Russian girl and got Tanya. If not for
him, the sisters might have ended their days in
Rosinka's establishment.

Irene got to the point. "The night's take is
always locked in the office safe. When H.C. goes
home, a guard comes in and sleeps in the office.
H.C. locks him in, and—oh yes," she added humor-
ously, "he leaves a chamber pot with him." She
and Tanya were working on Chekiang Road at the
Race Club, a night spot owned by a Chinese man
who despised Russians. His miserly salaries
failed to attract the few classier acts in town.
The sisters pretended to be grateful for their
jobs; in private, they found their boss's scorn
quite amusing. "One thing, though. The captain
skims thirty, forty American dollars a night. He
hates H.C. and is always making fun of him
behind his back for being so stingy. Once, he
showed us the dollars in his pocket, and said
he'd give us some if we went to bed with him.
He's Filipino, and he goes straight home after
work. I followed him." From her pocket she took
a paper with an address scribbled on it.

Gromeko glanced at the slip; then he got up
and walked three steps to his ice box. An enamel
basin, placed beneath to catch melting ice, was
nearly full to the brim. Its smell of decay was
milder in autumn and nearly undetectable in winter. Rummaging, he asked, "He has a family, I
suppose?"

"Oh yes. The full thing. Wife, three children." She answered Gromeko's unspoken question. "He says he's saving his money so they can go home to Manila. The man talks about his wife and kids all the time. He'll be easy. You can make him help you get into the office safe without saying a word."

"I know my business," Gromeko said. He took a package out of the ice box. From the soft thump it made on the table, Irene guessed the package contained meat. He rooted under the bed and dragged out a bag of oranges. "By the way. Did you know the ratty hole they call The Camellia is doing better and better? All those American servicemen coming down from the north and hanging around Broadway Mansions and the consulate. The place is in an ideal spot. I hear Galia Galinova is getting the walls knocked out so they can expand."

Irene smiled and looked at Tanya. A grin began to spread over her sister's pocked features.

When they left Yates Road, night had come down, and with it a light rain. Pedaling fast, they crossed Avenue Edward VII and entered Frenchtown. Irene allowed Tanya to forge a rough path through the congested traffic. On Avenue Joffre she noticed that the elegant Gascoigne Apartments had barricaded itself with private security guards. So many store fronts had erected plywood shields over their plate glass windows that only regular customers knew what goods were inside. The architecture and commerce

along Avenue Joffre were more westernized than
any in Shanghai, therefore one felt, passing
these blank-faced businesses, that a truly serious change in the city's fortunes was imminent.
Irene called to Tanya to look at the boarded-up
front of Madame Greenberg's fashion boutique.
Tanya shook her head and said, over her shoulder, "Dead, or gone." Every day the traffic got
worse, people carrying baskets and bundles of
bedding jostled you and you had to watch your
belongings. The package of meat was safe inside
Irene's buttoned coat. Tanya had the oranges.
Her big bosom was ideal for items that bulky,
for the overhang created a large cavity under
her sweater.

When they got home to Route Magy, the women
picked up their bicycles and carried them, shoulder-high, through the lane to the last house.

On the first landing they encountered the
glowering and slightly stooped form of Leopoldo
Conti. Irene held a special contempt for him; a
man who could be held at bay by a house dog
deserved all the bad luck visited upon him. The
lawyer that Conti hired the year he became their
landlord had lasted only until Gromeko paid him
a call. A dog and a bear, thought Irene. Best
friends a woman can have.

"I hope you break your necks," Conti said.

"Don't worry, we won't," Irene replied, calmly.
On the top floor, they were greeted by a whining
and wriggling Ivanka. The bitch lavished her wet
tongue over their ankles and stood on her hind

legs to be petted. "Good girl, good girl," crooned the sisters. It was Tanya's turn to take her out for her daily run; the dog was never let out until at least one of the sisters was home with Babushka.

Their grandmother had set the table and was in the kitchen grating carrots to cook with fish. Their neighbor Zina Kwilecki usually stayed out of Babushka's way until she was finished in the kitchen. The same system applied to the bathroom. The ascendancy of Babushka and her girls over the Kwileckis had been established early.

"You both smell like Ivanka," she said, as Irene and Tanya walked in shedding their wet coats.

Babushka was tall, taller than Tanya, and weighed two hundred pounds. Her bulk was shapely and she was strong for her age, which was seventy-seven. She wore her white hair in short braids, pinned astride the nape of her neck. Although she could not sew, she started a dressmaking shop in Harbin after her granddaughters found jobs on the railroad. Calling herself Madame Luba she had, at first, earned enough to pay her sewing women and the one woman who could design dresses. The commissions poured in: silk tailleurs for countesses, woollen coats trimmed with Chinese mink to wear against the frigid winter, skirts and blouses and riding habits, and even ballgowns for the annual ball on the Czar's birthday. After the first down payments, the money stopped coming in and Madame Luba

found herself in debt for the materials she had
purchased to make up the orders. She went to
speak to her clients. You will hear from my mistress, said the young maids who shut the door in
her face.

Though a little money trickled in every month,
the accounts were never fully settled. Madame
Luba had to let half her sewing women go.
Eventually, she closed her shop.

That day, on September 18, 1931, a Chinese bomb
exploded on the railroad tracks near Mukden, and
the Japanese army attacked the Chinese National
troops. The fighting in the south sent Russian
society in Harbin into a panic.

Armed with a broken rifle stock she always
kept behind a curtain, Madame Luba strode out
into the night alone. She went first to the
house of Countess Sofie Alexandrovna and smashed
the window of the parlor, then went on smashing
windows until she had made a full circuit of the
house. There were screams from within, but no
one appeared outside. Next, Madame Luba walked
to the house of Nikolai Prudoff, whose wife owed
her the most money. Again, persons inside the
house shouted in alarm but were too afraid to
come outside. When Madame Luba had finished off
the windows of six more houses, she dropped the
rifle stock on the ground and returned home.

Her granddaughter Irene was already directing
Tanya in the packing of their belongings. "We
will take the early train to Vladivostok. A ship

leaves for Shanghai late this week," Irene said, without preamble.

Within a year, long after the three women were safe in Shanghai, the Japanese controlled Manchuria and changed its name to Manchukuo.

Though Babushka mourned her dead son (never his wife, whose hysterics had caused the delay that led to their deaths), she often felt that Irene more than made up for his absence. It was Babushka who had scooped up the children and fled Russia, barely in advance of the Bolsheviks who by then scarcely distinguished soldiers from officers. She did not mind their cramped living space here on Route Magy, where they slept and ate in a single room. Since Harbin, their possessions were kept to whatever could be carried in three suitcases. Keeping this home was a simple task for the old woman, who had raised her granddaughters by cleaning houses.

When they sat down to their evening meal, Tanya made little smacking noises with her tongue and lips. "Ummm, fish with carrots, my favorite. I think this calls for some *pivo*." She fetched beers from the kitchen and poured for everyone.

Through the wall, Zina Kwilecki could be heard crying. Irene said, "The IRO people must have told Zwilecki off."

"And what did they tell you?" Babushka asked. Her voice was deep and rather loud.

"The usual. The quotas are filled, and we should wait for a vacancy if someone changes his

mind or dies." Irene dug into the food. Her
Babushka had made good bread, and there was an
abundance of kasha. The rich grains filled her
stomach as rice never did. She spread butter, a
quarter-inch thick, on a bread slice. There was
dessert as well, a jam tart heavy with crumbly
pastry. Good old Gromeko. He always produced,
for the family.

"And if no one does, or if three vacancies
don't turn up…"

Irene shrugged. The cigar box hidden in the back
of their cupboard was stuffed with their savings,
eight thousand American dollars. Babushka and
Tanya nodded. In a crisis, and only in a crisis,
they would apply the money, like grease, to
smooth the way.

The hen squatted there, its left eye nearly
pressing against the window pane. It seemed fascinated by its reflection. The slashing rain had
sent its mates in the yard next door into hiding, but this one, this silly bird, had taken
fright for unknown reasons and flown up to the
windowsill of the Conti dining room.

"Chickens aren't supposed to be able to fly,"
Daniele said.

At the advent of the bird, Maria had frozen
where she stood. She said in a low voice, "Who
cares whether they can or not? Nobody move,
please. Dani, open that side window, just sort
of glide over the floor, slow, slow! All you do

is slip your hand through the crack and grab a leg. Come on, now. That's it. Thaaat's it."

In the act of unlatching the window, Daniele said rigidly to the glass, "This is not right. I can't go through with it."

"Yes, you can," Maria said fiercely. "Or get away from there and I'll do it. Nola, get off your chair to the floor."

"What?"

"I said, crawl on the floor so the bird won't see you moving and take off. Go to the door and lean on it in case someone tries to come in. We don't want anybody marching in here and scaring it."

Nola did as she was told. She began to giggle and Maria laughed, but softly. Daniele's head wagged stiffly in disapproval.

"Now, do it," ordered Maria.

The latch slid along its path, its slow progress maddening to Maria, who whispered, "Yes. Yes. Yes. Oh, come on, yes." At last it was freed. Daniele eased the window open. The hen blinked, undecided, not yet affrighted. Danielo's hand drifted down from the latch. It darted and caught a leg. In a moment the bird was inside the room, squawking and dangling upside down from his hand.

Maria dashed to the window and shut it. At the sight of the chicken struggling and flapping in Daniele's reluctant clutch, Nola let out a shriek of laughter. Maria staggered over to Nola and collapsed on her; they held each other, shaking with laughter.

On the other side of the door, Ming Chu's voice called, "What is going on in there? So much noise. Is anyone hurt? Let me in."

Instead of getting up, they rolled aside and allowed the door to open.

Their mother looked at them on the floor, ascertained grief was not the cause of their scarlet faces, and then saw the chicken hanging from Daniele's hand.

"Don't ask how. Just call Amah," Maria gasped. "Oh, Mama, your face!" She wiped her eyes on Nola's sleeve.

Amah did not ask how. She rushed the bird off to the kitchen; in less time than it took for Maria and Nola to rise from the floor, the squawking was silenced.

At dinner, however, Nola turned stubborn. Amah had stewed the bird with oddments stored in her cupboards: gingko nuts, dried bamboo shoots, some chestnuts, some green beans and a potato. There was rice. "I won't eat it. It's a sin to steal and it's a sin to eat something that's stolen." Nola said. The food steamed on her plate; she held her nose.

Daniele had said he was not hungry but accepted a little rice. Poldo added a gingko nut to his plain rice. Ming Chu, declaring such scruples were foolish since the deed was already done and wasting food was worse, took a small portion of chicken. Only Maria, after heaping Nola's plate, freely helped herself.

"I won't tell Sister Maureen," Maria said, forking up chicken and rice, "Um, this is good. Nola, don't be silly. God won't mind, I guarantee."

Ming Chu considered her younger daughter. "If your father and Daniele have some chicken, will you eat?"

Nola thought this over. "I will, and if Maria does something for me."

"Oh, kid sisters are a pain." Making a bow, Maria said, "Your wish is my command. Only make it quick. Your vitamins are getting cold."

"Promise?"

"Lord be merciful and send Sister Maureen back to America! Do you realize she's an evil woman? Promise, promise."

"Will you—" Nola glanced at Daniele, then whispered in her sister's ear. Maria grimaced. She became aware of curious stares. "I promised, didn't I? Now eat!"

Nola waited until her father and Daniele spooned chicken onto their plates, then picked up her fork.

"You two were trying to set an example for nothing. The kid is a born terrorist," Maria said.

The chandelier began to sway. Transferred from the house in Hongkew, it was too big for this room; also, the ceiling was lower than the lighting fixture's old habitat. The great, tarnished silver wheel of hundreds of crystal drops hung

five feet above the table. Three twenty-five watt
bulbs nested in a thicket of empty sockets.

Heavy footfalls resounded overhead; the pounding ran in a roughly rhythmic pattern, as though
someone on crutches were stomping in circles.

Female voices could be heard singing.

> The stars at night
> Are big and bright (CLAP CLAP CLAP CLAP)
> DEEP IN THE HEART OF TEXAS
> The prairie sky
> Is wide and high (CLAP CLAP CLAP CLAP)
> DEEP IN THE HEART OF TEXAS

The Bordokoff/Krichevsky sisters had commenced
their nightly rehearsals.

5

For a man with so many inhibitions, Maria thought, her head pillowed on his bare stomach, he was remarkably nice to make love with. Although he was the first man she had known sexually, she felt she could hardly do better when it came to being satisfied. The agreeable weariness, the peace of sleep; a snatch of a dream was already carrying her away.

"Some of these men are ruffians," Daniele said. "The bigger you make the place, the more ruffians you will attract."

"As long as they keep coming and spending, I don't care how they act. They don't all behave badly; most just want a good time. Better our place than some other."

She riffled the tips of her fingers through his chest hair and traced the odd joining of the hair down his abdomen. The furry growth collided in the center and made a beeline to his pubic patch. Even limp, the size of his penis was impressive. Maria compared it with one other she had seen, a specimen pulled out of its trousers by the owner and offered to her, as though it were a hand for her to shake. There were so many incidents at The Camellia she would never share with anyone.

"I spoke to Galia yesterday about it," Daniele said. "If you are going to make a success of The Camellia, you have to maintain higher standards. Then a better class of people will start coming around."

Maria swung her legs off the bed and stood up and glared at him. "You spoke to Galia? Who are you to speak to Galia about anything to do with our club? And how many times have you done it behind my back?" Barefoot, wrapped loosely in his dressing gown, she marched into the bathroom and slammed the door. In a second she opened it again and returned to stand over him. "While you are worrying about your standards, Shanghai is falling apart. There is no better class of people, Daniele, for your information. At least, that kind are not thinking of bars like ours. They've got their own crowd, that bunch on Amherst Road and Yu Yuen Road and Seymour Road. The Brits entertain at home or they have their Country Club and the Amateur Dramatic Society. The French like Ciro's, they've got the French Club. And the big men have their precious Shanghai Club to drink in. Even if they had no place to go they wouldn't come near The Camellia. We're lucky to get the Yanks in uniform while there's still something to get." She threw off his dressing gown and began to dress. Why don't I ever have a robe of my own? she thought, pulling on her stockings. She was quite tired of small deprivations like that.

He sat up and tried to draw her to him. "It's just because I care. I'm frustrated that I can't do anything more for you." His black eyes, set wide apart, were sad.

Let him be sad, she thought. I have too much to do.

"Do you remember your crew from the *Lepanto*? The night they got leave from internment camp and my father invited them over?"

She could see his suppressed wince. The family were still living in the big house in Hongkew. The men had gotten very drunk on her father's hoarded stock of good wine. Two had begun crying, three cornered Maria and began groping her. Daniele had hauled them off her and thrown them into the street. The *Lepanto*'s captain was not there to see the debacle, having stayed behind in camp as hostage to the men's return.

"Now, weren't they a classy bunch. Why didn't you go back to Italy with them?"

"You know why." He got up and began to put on his own clothes.

Maria finished with her garters and checked the seams in her stockings. "But I still don't understand why you hang on. I mean, don't you care about seeing your daughters grow up? Doesn't your wife miss you?"

"Don't." The sadness in his face deepened. He sat on the bed to put on his shoes, then dropped them and held his face between his hands.

"Do you see, Dani? I have to go my own way. You've put four years into me, and neither of us has much to show for it."

"Nothing? How can you say, 'Nothing'?"

Oh, Maria thought. Now he's going to get maudlin. I thought women were supposed to be the ones who got sentimental and hysterical. Dani's emotions were the sort she thought of as typically female. Bereft of purpose, his life had narrowed to a very few interests, all of which had to do with her. He was thirty-one and living in a sort of time capsule and he seemed to want to shut her up in it with himself.

Shouldn't she have fallen in love the day she first saw him? All the ingredients must have been present: the handsome dark man in muddied whites, hunted by the Japanese enemy. Rather than surrender the gunboat to them, he had scuttled the *Lepanto* with his own hands and sunk her to the muddy bottom. The Italian Consul General had called, asking her father to give temporary asylum until he could decide what to do.

Daniele should have gone home at the end of the war. He refused to admit that, because if he did then four years were lost. The concept of love awed her.

"Dani," Maria said gently, kneeling between his thighs, "Next to my father, you are the best man I know. That's why I don't want you to waste any more of your life on me. I'm an awful, terrible person. I don't care what's right or wrong, only what's necessary. I'm even capable of killing, you know."

At that, he smiled. "Don't be absurd. I also love you because you're so dramatic, because you are a child."

She felt a genuine surge of love for him, then. It was not so bad being called a child. Sometimes it was nice to be petted as though she were one.

    5   grams Tartaric Acid
    1   gram All Spice
    1/4 gram Extract Gentian
    1-1/2 gram Caramel
    10   drops Essence Grape
    10   drops Essence Sage
    4   drops Oil Orange
    8   oz. Sugar
    48   oz. Water
    16   oz. Alcohol

The grape essence was finished, so was the gentian. It was a miracle he could get sugar at all. Of course its quality was terrible. Nola's job was to sift the dirty brown grains and, because her eyes were sharp and her fingers nimble, pick out the impurities. In a couple of months the only liqueur for which Poldo had ingredients would be cherry brandy, which consisted of not much more than tartaric acid,

cherry essence, and coloring. Amazingly, The
Camellia was proving to be a brisk outlet for
Poldo's products. Maria told him the Europeans
who hadn't much money but who liked to drink in
the company of Americans ordered his Imperial
Brand of liqueurs.

As a result of this quickened demand, Daniele
often delivered as many as two cases a week to
The Camellia. He also supplied the Russian Cafe,
the Bubbling Well Restaurant, and the Race Club.
At the latter, one night, he caught fifteen minutes of the Bordokoff/Krichevsky act. How were
they? asked Maria. Like they sound rehearsing
over our heads, he replied.

The tart odor of chemicals made Poldo's eyes
water. He noticed Daniele blew his nose once
every five minutes. All windows were open while
the two worked. The dining table was stocked
like an assembly line: bottles, a box of metal
caps, a supply of Imperial Brand labels, and a
sponge in a dish filled with water. Normally,
Nola applied the labels, after Daniele or Poldo
put on the caps and crimped them tight with a
device like a stationery embossing clamp, except
that the handles worked horizontally. She was
with her mother and Maria; the tailor had come,
and they were busy next door.

He would miss Daniele if he left. Not for his
labor, which he contributed free of charge, but
for the fellowship that kept Poldo's perspec-
tives from becoming wholly skewed. Daniele represented the world outside the daily agonies of

China, though he seldom talked about Italy. The subject of his abandoned family lurked in his very avoidance of mentioning them to Poldo.

The Voice of America three nights ago had announced the re-election of President Truman. The president's triumph at the polls was yet another blow to Chiang Kai-shek's government, for a Democrat victory was expected to cut off the flow of aid to Nationalist China. President Truman then told Congress that "many difficulties" were involved in making aid to China effective and that Americans had to oversee constantly how funds were expended. Upon that cautionary word, the United States had released a meager five million dollars to Chiang for the purchase of arms.

It isn't any use, Poldo thought, rotating the demijohn full of chemicals, the Americans are throwing that money down a well. His friend, Simpson Sung, once a banker and now denizen of a shabby flat on Weihaiwei Road, thought so too. His distress embarrassed Poldo, who knew he had asked for too much. Why, even if it were within Sung's means, should he want to buy an apartment building full of nonpaying tenants?

From his friend's home he had taken the tram, then walked the rest of the way to his office on Honan Road, near Soochow Creek. Poldo's gray pinstripe suit, pressed that day by Amah, collected beggar children like a whirling vortex of leaves, with him at its center. Their faces beseeched, their hands plucked. He saw death over their shoulders, and he wished it would be merciful and come for them soon.

The keys he used to unlock the door, then to open the padlock, did not feel as though they belonged to him. As he walked inside the darkened godown, the very silence of ghostly abandonment rejected his presence. A graveyard would have felt friendlier. He walked past the bank of filing cabinets, dusted off the oak swivel chair and sat down. He opened the biggest drawer and pulled out file folders and laid them atop the moldy blotter on his desk. These were the companies with which he had done business in the United States. Many, he knew, had changed ownership; a few—no more than three—were still engaged in trading with Far Eastern countries, but those countries no longer included China. Why invest in a cause their president had virtually declared lost?

The godown belonged to Sung, who charged no rent. Was that a sliver of good fortune? Poldo needed to believe so.

Go, man, Poldo said to Daniele silently. Get out while you can.

Ming Chu did not like asking these favors of Mr. Liu, for what he did for them were surely favors. What must it be like to get nothing but old garments to pick apart and piece together the odd sleeves and collars and trousers so that he could fashion a new garment out of them? Nola's growing posed special problems for Mr.

Liu. He attended her physical changes almost as closely as her mother did.

They had just solved the matter of her serge school uniform, which was too short again. Mr. Liu, pale, undersized, patient, said he could add a band of cotton fabric inside the waist and thereby gain an inch-and-a-half in skirt length. He specialized in foreign styles, and Ming Chu knew he had several customers on Amherst Road where many of the British lived. She did not doubt they gave him new fabrics to work with. It was possible he was sorry for the Contis; from their long association they were friends, as well. He had once sewn for her sumptuous dresses, tiers of air-light, gauzy georgette, for which she had matching satin shoes made with French heels. He tailored fine woollen suits for traveling to Macau and Hong Kong on her husband's ships. For Maria he made the pleated skirts and the blazers that she wore with knee socks, until she grew older and insisted on silk stockings. Ming Chu no longer wore western clothes. From the moment Japan conquered China, she had gone back, proudly, to wearing Chinese gowns.

Ming Chu brought out the long pink dress he had created for Maria's sixteenth birthday. Maria smiled when she saw it. Her parents had thrown a party at which she shone in that dress, her first long gown.

Her mother spread the silken folds of the full skirt. "Mr. Liu, there is so much material here that, for once, you will think you have been given a bolt of new material. This will be for Nola's birthday next month."

Immersed in the fables of King Arthur, oblivious of everything said over the materials laid out on her parents' bed, Nola's consciousness returned to the present. "Mama, I don't like pink. Couldn't Mr. Liu dye it some other color. Light green, maybe?"

"I don't like pink anymore, myself," Maria said. "Can you do it, Mr. Liu?"

"The color will not come out even, and in any case it would not be a light green. Would you care for a dark green, *hsiao-tzia*?"

Nola did not hesitate. "Navy blue."

"So old for you, *hsiao-tzia*." Mr. Liu had known Nola since she was born. He looked to Ming Chu, then Maria. They spoke almost in unison. "It's her dress."

They began scanning dress styles in a copy of Vogue borrowed from Galia. At last Maria cried, in exasperation, "Why don't they have any designs for kids in Vogue?" Nola paid no attention; she was back in the world of Camelot. But when Maria was being measured for a new dress for herself, Nola looked up from her book. Her steady scrutiny made Maria uncomfortable.

"I'm too big to have anything cut down for me," she said. "And I have to have nice clothes to wear to work."

Ming Chu was amused. A discomfited Maria was a rare creature.

"I don't care about that," Nola said. "Do you remember your promise?"

"Oh. That. Of course I do."

"Then when?"

Neither had confided in Ming Chu what passed between them that night at dinner.

"When I'm ready! I won't forget, naturally, because you're not going to let me."

"Please hold still, *hsiao-tzia*," said Mr. Liu.

A half hour later, materials folded away in the large square of cloth whose four corners he knotted up to make a bundle, he took his leave.

"Nola, would you please make sure Amah has got all the tea things ready?" Ming Chu's aunt from Soochow was expected at five. She was both pleased, and nervous. Visits between them, constrained by distance (although Poldo used to drive there in his Fiat), became more infrequent after the Contis sold their automobile and moved to Route Magy. The journey by train to Soochow was expensive.

When Amah knocked and opened the door to admit Ho Yin, Ming Chu came forward quickly to take her hands. In the Chinese style, they did not kiss, but bowed rapidly several times as their hands expressed their pleasure at seeing one another. Aunt Yin had turned sixty this year, her complexion still fine with wrinkles only at her eyes. Her hair, more black than gray, was skimmed back in a chignon. Like a practiced ice skater, she stood upon the blades of her bound feet without a wobble. They were bound tightly in white cotton and

shod in black cotton shoes. Ming Chu, on the other
hand, had long ago learned to wear western shoes.
The black leather pair she wore came from the
children's department of the Wing On Department
Store. Unsupported by bandages, her feet—doubled
under at the toes, the arches bent unnaturally
high—ached badly by midafternoon. It was a living
fact she accepted because she could not change
it. Sometimes she did feel bitter about being
crippled, a word that would have been alien to her
mind had she never married a Western man. On the
other hand, Ming Chu had learned for herself that
Western women, in their own way, were just as much
at the mercy of men as Chinese women.

Maria took her Aunt Yin's hands, bobbing her
head, and spoke words of welcome. All of a sudden, she was very Chinese, the model of sub-
missiveness. The imp, thought Ming Chu,
wanting to laugh. Secretly she had always
wished she could be like this daughter, who
blithely did as she pleased, and reacted like
a lioness when threatened.

Now Nola performed her courtesies. Being a
child, she was not required to be effusive, so she
merely shook Aunt Yin's hand and said "How are
you, *Yee Bo*, Great Aunt?" very nicely in Chinese.
Aunt Yin put her hands on each side of Nola's
face. "How fair and delicate," she said approv-
ingly to Ming Chu. No, Ming Chu thought. Not fair
so much as pale. Aunt Yin is being tactful.

Amah came in bearing a tray of refreshments,
and Maria and Nola made their excuses and left.

Ming Chu took her aunt's coat and hung it in the big mirrored wardrobe. The square rosewood table and two matching chairs, inlaid with mother-of-pearl, had also come from the old house. These items of furniture overwhelmed the boxy room; there would have been a black hardwood drum table and matching stools, filling every niche, had Ming Chu not sorrowfully agreed with her husband the room could hold no more. At least they had fetched a good price. Ming Chu seated her aunt in one of the chairs and took the other. She refrained from apologizing for the condition of the plumbing in the lane, the streaked paint on the staircase, and for receiving her in the bedroom. Once she started, she might never stop. There was no shame, at least, in the quality of food she could offer. Poldo was selling five cases of cherry brandy and gin per week.

Aunt Yin asked after Poldo's health, and they reminisced about the last visit, three years ago, of the Contis to Soochow. Acceptance of Poldo had not come about immediately. Although situated close to Shanghai, Soochow people thought the metropolis too Westernized, corrupted by the influence of foreigners. They traded, yes. They did not mingle. The foreigners remained entirely unaware of the reverse snobbery of which they were undisputed practitioners in Shanghai. The Ho family treated Poldo with no more than correct politeness; they could not converse satisfactorily, for Poldo in the early years did not yet speak Chinese well. Poldo asked Ming Chu to teach him some Soochow phrases.

One day, he said to Aunt Yin, his accent tilting unmusically in all the wrong places, "I may be foreign, but I will not remain a devil for long, if you give me half a chance."

Aunt Yin and her husband were too well bred to exchange glances, but Ming Chu, proving once and for all that her careful upbringing had been enfeebled by foreigners, spoke up in her turn. "If you will give me the other half chance, I will help him succeed."

How curious is the will of heaven, Aunt Yin was given to saying to Ming Chu, that you should meet Poldo on the day before your betrothal to that cotton merchant's boy. Poldo had come calling on the Ho family to enquire about the supply of silk textiles, and there in the courtyard had glimpsed Ming Chu. She was seventeen.

Twenty-seven years ago, thought Ming Chu. Why is it the affliction of human beings to believe their luck will never change? She grieved for Poldo in his defeats, and she realized that she was really very Chinese after all, for she could not bring herself to impose her will over his.

She urged Aunt Yin to try a custard tart and asked how her niece was doing in her work.

"She has got a position at the Southern Kiangsu Technical Institute," Aunt Yin said. "You recall that as a child she was interested in silkworms? She is studying ways to improve their breeding and quality. She speaks of reorganizing the farming of the silkworms, and also of planting a variety of mulberry tree from the east coast of America. The tree is said to be more resistant to disease, so the worms will not starve in a blight. Perhaps the…Communists will let her continue." Aunt Yin's hands, slightly marred with liver spots, clasped each other in her lap. The Ho family owned large tracts of land in Soochow; besides that, her husband collected rents from tenant farmers who raised silkworms and cultivated the mulberry trees whose leaves fed them. Thus, the Hos were landlords of prominence, a class the Communists vowed to exterminate in blood. Their armies marching to Shanghai would reach Soochow first.

Ming Chu lifted her aunt's restless hands and soothed them between her own. The two women stared at each other, their tea cooling on the table.

Had her aunt come to say goodbye? Please save them, she prayed to the Catholic god of her adopted religion. Please save Aunt Yin, her mother's younger sister. Ming Chu had no other reminder of her mother left.

Drifting in a boat on T'ai Hu Lake, surrounded by fields greening in the new-born spring; that was what Ming Chu remembered best. And the hills along the eastern shore, jubilant with pink, red, purple wild azalea. So many canals wound this way and that, a child could not wander far, nor think of what lay beyond. The rivers led

away from home, and busily bore their human
cargo to and from places of which she had heard
and never expected to see. For a girl, Ming Chu
was privileged. She was allowed to learn to read
and write. The only child of her parents felt
her powers burgeon, but that proved to be illusion. Her feet became as the canals, and she was
imprisoned.

Ming Chu lay in bed staring at the single star
visible through the window, thinking of azaleas
and the surprise of the occasional rhododenron
blooming like a host of happy trumpets.

The door whispered open, and Nola crept to her
side. Ming Chu lifted the blanket and covered as
much of Nola's shoulders and torso she could
reach.

Nola said softly, for her father was asleep,
"Before all my silkworms hatch in the spring,
should I send the eggs to Aunt Yin? I'm going to
need all the leaves in the neighborhood to feed
four hundred worms."

"Aunt Yin may be to busy to take care of your
silkworms." The black night weighed her down and
colored her sadness. This was not the first of
the thousand half-truths she would have to tell
this child.

6

The stars at night
Are big and bright (CLAP CLAP CLAP CLAP)
DEEP IN THE HEART OF TEXAS

Tanya bent her knees, and Irene hopped aboard her thighs, placed her hands on Tanya's shoulders, and with a grunt (heard only by Tanya) leaped into a headstand. The tops of their heads together, they sang,

The Prairie sky
Is wide and high (CLAP CLAP CLAP CLAP)
DEEP IN THE HEART OF TEXAS

Irene had difficulty opening her mouth to sing in that position, upside down. Upon the word "wide" both spread out their arms, except that Irene also spread her legs, while Tanya performed a few cautious dance steps on the platform. Both clapped, on cue; that always threatened their precarious balance. H.C. Ping, their boss, primed

some of the customers to clap along, but few did.
The Chinese customers seemed not to have a clue
when they were supposed to do it.

Irene smiled; below her, the red bow of
Tanya's mouth smiled. The hem of Irene's short
skirt fluttered around her breasts as Tanya
moved. All eyes were fixed upon Irene's crotch.
The G-string and shaved pubis brought them in,
night after night; these Chinese had obviously
never seen a blond one, shaved or not. Naturally
they missed the meaning of the next line,

Reminds me of
The one I love (Tanya alone clapped, while
Irene fondled her crotch)
DEEP IN THE HEART OF TEXAS

On the final word, Irene placed her hands on
Tanya's shoulders and vaulted to the floor.
The Filipino drummer hammered a few riffs and
finished simultaneously with a loud chord from
the piano.

"Throw money, you clods," Irene muttered
between smiling lips. Few did, although the
Texas number, saved for last, always received
the most applause.

Sweating heavily, they exited through a side
door to the little dressing room next to the
kitchen. They stripped and began to towel their
torsos. Neither ever used the flimsy plywood
screen, which H.C. had supplied for purposes of
modesty. There was no shower. On H.C.'s orders,

a single bottle of orange pop was placed there for their refreshment. Muttering imprecations upon H.C.'s head, Tanya opened the bottle and drank half of it. She pinned her hair up and poured water into a basin to wash her face. "You're getting heavier," she complained. "I almost turned an ankle and went down."

"Let's do it tonight," Irene said. She never paid any attention to Tanya's complaints, but she made a note to cut down on bread and butter.

"You mean, go to The Camellia?" Tanya made a face. "I hope I don't put my fist through Miss Maria's face. I wanted to, the last time I met her on the stairs. 'Why, it's the Thundering Swan Lakes,'" she mimicked in a mincing voice.

"This is business. Gromeko will take care of them. Do you doubt our Grigory?"

Smiling, Tanya stood sideways to the floor-length mirror and cupped her big breasts. Their lusty heft always gave her a pleasant tingle between the legs. Once the makeup was washed off, she never looked at the pits in her face.

Maria stepped back and devoted several minutes to a careful inspection of the mahogany shingle just put up by the workman. She had painted the new name of the club herself, copying the forward-sloping English script from a dictionary. Zoya admitted THE CAMELLIA ROOM sounded better, though she was dubious about the letters being in silver paint. Okay, Maria said, and took the sign back home and painted a pink camellia with three leaves. The stem of the camellia twined through the big capital C.

The shingle looked rather nice on the canvas awning, added last week. What was more, the club owned a bit of landscaping, a single mimosa tree growing through a crack in the sidewalk. Maria decided to have the workmen widen the crack into a circle to make the presence of the tree appear less accidental.

A lot had been done to spruce up the club. Mrs. Chen, the landlady, had allowed them to take out a dividing wall and nearly double their interior space. The bar had been extended. The bandstand was now big enough for a band, if only they could find one that wasn't composed of three parts violin and two parts drum. Disliking the lumpy plaster facade, Maria had wanted to panel each side of the new double doors, then realized that would be like handing firewood directly to the beggars who roamed the streets.

The Broadway Mansions on the opposite corner was full of incoming American service personnel, who flocked to The Camellia Room and made it their own. The club's new prominence also attracted another element, the fringe industries of the Wayside district on the lower end of the boulevard known as Broadway.

And here came Mr. Katz, shuffling toward Maria. He was perhaps eighty years old, his moldy coat held together in front with safety pins. No damn side door, thought Maria. Was it worth the expense? Probably not. Every bright

side of the coin had its obverse gloomy one.
She greeted Mr. Katz.

"Beautiful Miss Maria," he said, indistinctly.
He was toothless, and he had a strong accent.
"Today I bring three bottles of my best."

"Come inside, Mr. Katz. I was just making some
tea, so let's have some together."

He nodded, pleased, and followed her inside.
She led him past the bar into the little office in
the back. It was early; only two of the regulars
had dropped in so far. The Marines who had come
down from Nanking acted as messengers between the
American Consulate and the U.S. Military Advisory
Group occupying Broadway Mansions. The U.S. Navy
was busy as well, evacuating American civilians
from Shanghai. She wasn't sure any of the servicemen should be telling her what they did, but
they were sometimes so artless that she had twice
told them to shut up. She could not imagine a
Japanese soldier talking so much. Their lack of
guile, however, imparted to her a startling
insight into the basic American character. How
secure their lives must be at home. One would
think America was one wide prairie of gimlet-eyed
straight-shooting, black-hat, white-hat men,
their women by the natural grace of America The
Beautiful imbued with virtue and all the right
instincts of hearth and kitchen. Maria understood
that separation from home enhanced that vision;
hard service in the war for many had cemented it.
Still, the occasional sour character seemed more
normal to her.

She invited Mr. Katz to sit down and made tea and served it in a large mug, with plenty of sugar and milk. From one of Galia's desk drawers she brought out a box of cookies baked by her mother. Mr. Katz's expression was blissful as he dipped cookies into his tea and consumed the soggy mess. When Galia walked in, he put down his cup and attempted to rise. "Sit, sit," Galia said, pressing down on his shoulders. She went out, returned with a bottle of brandy. Mr. Katz wrestled with his manners: "No, no, a little, so, so," he murmured. Galia kept pouring until the mug was filled to the top.

"Stay and rest, as long as you like," she said, and excused herself to tend to business in the front room.

Warmed by food and alcohol, Mr. Katz's pores, augmented by his ancient suit and coat, released their unwashed odors into the little room.

In fifty years this could be me, Maria thought, and then fiercely rejected the idea. Never, never, never would she allow herself to live this way. She would choose the time of her own dying. God would not be consulted.

Maria stole a glance at her watch. "You say you brought three, Mr. Katz?"

Mouth full, he nodded. A clanking of bottles sounded in his pockets as he shifted to get at them. "You have empties, please? I need them, to make more to sell."

"Of course. Be right back." She went into the kitchen and told Yung she wanted his empty bottles. Yung, on his own initiative, had taken over the disposition of Mr. Katz's homemade Kvass. Whether he drank it, sold it, or traded it, Maria did not know. Kvass had a powerful alcohol content; from its murky tan color, topped by a soapy scum, she guessed Mr. Katz brewed his from stale bread.

Yung pointed, "Under that table. Those are the washed ones." He was busily slicing sandwich bread. The Camellia Room now featured several kinds of sandwiches; branching into a dinner menu was a headache none of the partners was ready to face. As it was, bread alone was hard to obtain. The partners had no intention of spending any of their hard-won dollars and ster-ling on the black market for foodstuffs. They were content with the current formula that seemed to work.

Her father's Imperial Brand labels were on half of the empties. Most of his products also fell in Yung's domain. Maria accepted whatever income Yung was inclined to share with her and asked no questions. The arrangement satisfied the Chinese passion for collecting "cumshaw"—tips, commissions—anything beyond mere salary. In her turn, Maria paid her father a fair sum in American dollars for what he supplied. A small deception with momentous results: to see him smile, stand taller, busy himself purposefully—she had seldom felt so glad about anything since before the war.

She chose a half dozen one-liter beer bottles, some brown, some clear glass, and took them back to Mr. Katz. He distributed them in coat and suit pockets, accepted thirty gold yuan, and with a gummy smile offered his raspy old hand. Anytime, Mr. Katz, she said. Look forward to more Kvass. He left, shuffling and clanking, by the front entrance.

The night's rush was beginning. A huddle of white sailor caps with their boyish ribbons proclaimed the British were in port. These were new faces, hardly older than the cadets from the frigate *Amethyst*. The men spotted Maria and smiled, beckoning. She smiled back, gestured she would drop by but that she was busy right now. The new ones had not yet found girlfriends; otherwise, Shanghai's stock of eligible women were well represented here. How many were Russian? It was easier to count the ones who were not. The club's one waitress, a Portuguese woman named Amalia, was striding about with trays of drinks. Galia worked the bar. Evgeny, whose name the customers had simplified to Gene, was wandering among the tables plucking "Down Honolulu Way" on his ukelele and singing in a falsetto:

Come where the moon is always shining
Down Honolulu way;
Come where the palm trees sway,
Night-time is just like day
And, while the sweet guitars are ringing
We'll dream the night away,

Where the moonbeams play on the distant bay
Down Honolulu way

For a baritone Gene did a creditable job in the region of his nasal passages, which were hidden behind bushy mustaches. A classical violinist, Gene had taken to the ukelele because he was sick of playing gypsy music. Galia approved. She had blanched at the sight of the violin case he brought for his audition. No classical music, she told him. Do you want to ruin us?

"Hey Gene," an American called, "Do you know 'Alabamy Bound'?"

Gene, his deep-set eyes perpetually sad, shrugged and plinked another chorus of "Down Honolulu Way."

"Shoot," the serviceman said disgustedly, "you call that a mew-si-shun?" He got up and walked to the bar. "Hi doll," he said to Galia. "Look what I got for you." He came around the bar and set a paper sack in front of her. Galia looked inside. There were two bottles of bourbon and two cartons of Camels. Swiftly, Galia made the items disappear under a shelf.

The serviceman helped himself to a beer from the ice bucket. "You two are the prettiest ladies in this big old town," he said. "Would you both marry me? Aw, never mind. How 'bout twenty bucks, then." Relaxed, beer bottle in hand, he leaned on his elbows and surveyed the room. "Look at those limeys over there, offa the cruiser *London*. Musta been born this morning on their way up the Yangtze. If I'd seen those kids alongside us in the war I'da surrendered to the Japanese to save time." A Marine corporal, he had a lean, dark face with a combative jawline.

"You leave them alone, Dean," Galia said. "The Shore Patrol only gives a club three chances before they post us off limits. Twelve dollars."

"Aw, come on baby. The Eventail will gimme thirty and dinner on the house. Eighteen. What you got to say, Maria? Your friend here gives me a hard time every time."

"The Eventail is on the other side of town," Maria said. "Feel free to go. I hope you get there before curfew. Last offer is fifteen."

But the corporal wasn't listening. "Holy cow. Who's that babe coming in the door?"

Heads were turning. Maria had been stunned the first time she saw this woman. The body was big, it was tall, wide-shouldered, the hair deep auburn, waist-long and springing wildly from a face boned like a warrior Mongol's. The cheek-bones were broad, high bumps, the lips thin. And the eyes, Maria thought. She could never decide about the eyes. They were slitted and green and became truly inscrutable during laughter. The complexion was that of a typical redhead, pale and creamy. Genghis Khan in United States mili-tary PX nylon stockings.

"That is Liudmila," Galia said. "She is very nice."

"Oh, man. I ain't sure I want to find out." He leaned over the bar and spoke in a stage whisper,

"I think I'll go over and take cover under those limey kids."

Galia laughed, handed him fifteen dollars, and patted him on the shoulder. The cigarettes were as good as, often better than, American currency on the black market, and he knew it. Luckily for them he chose to feather his nest at their club, apparently his second home. Now and then he sold them cases of Toddy, a malted milk drink that Nola adored.

After he had given Maria a handful of Milky Ways for Nola and gone back to his table, she said, "You're looking prosperous, Galia."

Her friend, always well groomed, smoothed her upswept dark hair. She had a good figure and fine legs, clad in nylons. Gone, until the new crisis, were the days of relying on street stocking menders to tack together hose past due for the garbage bin. Three partners in sleek dresses and upswept hairdos, never to look the same in the future fast coming around the corner. In the still of some late nights Maria thought she could hear the booming of guns north and west.

"You look good, yourself," Galia said affectionately. "Who needed Caltex, huh? I got tired of examining hemorrhoids in that medical department." She gestured, encompassing the room. "This is okay, but you are thinking ahead, Marusha? Has that man proposed yet?"

"What can he propose, with a wife and two children in Italy? Do you know what I hate, Galia?

That women have to depend on men. Everywhere I turn I'm looking at women depending on men, using them. Look at Liudmila, over there, everybody's chum. She can read and write English; she speaks French. What happened to thousands of women like her because of politics? We were supposed to rely on our daddies, and look at us today. At least you've got a profession."

"A daddy, and he wasn't mine, paid for my nursing school." Galia's tone was matter-of-fact. Her mother had died when Galia was ten. She had lived six years in Mukden with a foster family and moved with them to Shanghai. At eighteen she married an American in the Fourth Marines, who then left to go to war. She did not discover that he already had a wife in the United States until she applied to the consulate for a visa to the United States.

What did you do then, Maria asked. She had taken to dropping in on Galia in the little clinic on the third floor of the American petroleum company. Galia opened her eyes wide comically and replied, I found a man to keep me, of course. Few things managed to crack her hard-candy glaze; one of them was her yearning for babies. Galia adored children; perhaps that was why she indulged Zoya, who was thirty-seven and older than Galia by two years.

The noise of a good time being had in The Camellia Room thickened in swirls of tobacco smoke, cheap and de luxe. A sailor's girl got up to sing "In The Chapel In The Moonlight" to

Gene's accompaniment, then on a sour note collapsed in giggles to hoots and cheers. A Marine sergeant came up to the bar and asked Maria if there were rooms for rent upstairs. "Sorry, there aren't," she said. He was new here, or he would have known. As a matter of fact, bitten by the money fever, Mrs. Chen the landlady had suggested that Galia and Zoya turn over their rooms and take a flat elsewhere. If we go, the club goes, they told her. There were plenty of choice sites lying vacant on Broadway. More important, they had no intention of paying four to five thousand American dollars in key money for an apartment. The term key money meant exactly that. Money up front to get in was more desirable to a landlord than any monthly rental that might never get paid.

On the other hand, living over the shop was forever causing misunderstandings among the customers.

Before the Marine turned away he glanced speculatively at Maria, his gaze roving over what goods were visible above the bartop. Anticipating, she shook her head. I may be Eurasian but can you believe that I am not available? She did not care if she might be doing him an injustice. That old, old yardstick of social inferiority set by the British colonials was alive and well in Hong Kong, even if it was disintegrating in Shanghai along with their own standing.

Balancing a tray on the palm of each hand Amalia, a thin tense woman near middle age, came and went; currency changed hands. Galia stashed the dollars in one drawer, the yuan in another.

Why was Zoya sitting with a local?

"That's Amalia's brother," Galia said.

"He's not rich, he doesn't look it. He can't give her what she wants."

"No," Galia said, "of course not. He's her ticket out."

"I see. How much does he want?"

"Two thousand dollars in cash, or the equivalent in gold bars."

"My God, Galia. Who does he think he is? Tell her to try the French. They don't think they're God or even American." Zoya had been married to a Russian, the man of her dreams, as she persisted in telling everyone. Sad through her irony, Galia told Maria they had a perfect marriage for one week, and then he had died, killed by an American bomb during an air raid in 1944.

"If he will marry her, a Portuguese passport does the job as well as any other," Galia said. "After that, who knows?"

"And what about you? When are you going to say 'yes' to Eric? He's coming in this week isn't he? Galia, I wish you would. You keep telling me to do something about a man."

"I know that, *malenki*, don't worry about me. I'm going to milk this cow for as long as she lives, then I'll think of something else."

Maria believed it. She was fond of Galia and she admired her, two emotions that Maria didn't often feel for the same person.

Her hands performed mechanically, making change in two currencies, reaching for glasses, seltzer bottles, corkscrews. An occasional request for her father's vermouth or cherry brandy pleased her, though she disliked the man ordering the liqueurs. Gromeko here again. Among the rough elements who frequented the club he was the crudest, if one could separate crude from rough. Yes, there was a difference. The man had fought his war a long time ago and passed on to an uglier dimension. He did not seem to care that the soldiers and sailors also disliked him and left him alone. As though he heard her thoughts, Gromeko looked around and met her eyes. Maria did not adjust her unfriendly expression, but he smiled as if she had sent him a kiss.

Galia nudged her. "Some new blood. I've never seen them before."

Maria looked toward the door. "My God. The nerve of them." Irene and Tanya Bordokoff/Krichevsky, unescorted, stood looking curiously about the room, then walked to the bar.

7

Irene spoke first. "I told Tanya we should see the club. Everybody says it is very nice, and it is." She was too clever to smile with the compliment, to make it ingratiating. Maria appreciated that display of intelligence; a gorilla might not have done so well in such a touchy situation.

Maria had tersely identified them to Galia. She needed no more explanation; she knew everything else about the B/Ks.

Tanya said, "We thought...." She shut up as her sister shifted impatiently.

Irene said, simply, "We need a job. They cut our pay at the Race Club, and we are only working three nights a week. You don't have an act yet, do you? Tanya and I can work something out to suit you." Lacking a response, she went on, "I can get a combo to come with us, the same one we have at the Race Club." Turning to Galia, she spoke briefly in Russian, her hands spread in a sketch of ruefulness, an appeal to sisterhood, not quite supplication.

Galia snapped, in English, "Don't talk to me. It's entirely up to my partner."

The waitress Amalia came up and slapped her tray on the bar, "Three rye and ginger ale, one Scotch-no-ice, two Tsingtao beers, are we out of peanuts?" She left for the kitchen to give Yung his orders for sandwiches.

Automatically Galia and Maria poured and mixed, rummaged for beer in the ice bucket, filled bowls with peanuts, found crackers that were harder to come by in the shops than peanuts. The B/Ks waited. Zoya came behind the bar and started collecting the dirty glasses. She smiled at the B/Ks and said hello. Amalia returned, picked up her drink orders and scooted away. She needed this job and the tips, which made up the bulk of her income. She was probably supporting a family, including her brother, Zoya's suitor.

Maria noticed Irene's narrowed, speculative observation of the bar activity and felt her anger get away from her.

"Well, I'll tell you," she said, the words drawn out so that Irene, alerted, stiffened. "We could use a doorman, somebody in a clown costume. Tanya can be…let's see, our bouncer. Perfect. And I'll give your dog a job, too. Why not stuff the bitch so we can use it for a doorstop." On hearing her name, Tanya turned from staring around the packed room, where somewhere in the depths of the smokescreen Gene could be heard plinking on his ukelele.

Irene spat one word, "*Bliyd!*" and walked away. Tanya's nostrils flared; she scowled, seeming to imprint Maria, Galia, and Zoya on her mind. Then she went after Irene.

Galia called after them, "Best regards to your Babushka, too."

"What did she call me?" Maria asked.

Galia smiled. "Whore."

"Well, we are at whore, aren't we? She noticed." She leaned back on the bar, chuckling. To the bewildered Zoya, Galia said only, "Those were the famous B/Ks."

"Oh," said Zoya. "I guessed but I was not sure. They are exactly as Marusha described them." She was wearing one of her many new flow-ered print dresses and the latest Carmen Miranda platform shoes. Chinese shoemakers, as well as tailors, could copy anything depicted in a mag-azine. She had ten new dresses to Maria's one. Obsessed by uncertainties and because she owned but ten percent of the club, Maria was chary with money. She squeezed her needs to the barest essentials, her wants to nothing. And still what she managed to save was a mite compared to what the Contis needed to get away and survive. Two hundred fifty American dollars barely covered two berths on a tramp steamer to Hong Kong. Once there, where would they stay, what would they do? They were not British subjects, and so nei-ther she nor her father could get work permits.

"How are you tonight, ladies?" All three turned. Gromeko said pleasantly in heavily accented English, "You know, you should add nice tall stools here. You get more customers, and then also they have a chance to talk to you. Not everyone has a lady friend to keep him company." The hands resting on the bar were large and callused. Maria remarked later that the size and length of his thumbs struck her as gruesome, as though he had been strung up by them.

Just as pleasantly, Galia replied, "We like to choose the time to talk, because we are always so busy. That is why we did not put seats along the bar." They had tried it for a few nights and gotten too much attention. Zoya had liked it, though. She enjoyed the badinage from the men, and as a consequence mixed up the drink orders and made a mess of the exchange rates for dollars, pounds sterling, and local gold yuan.

"Those two women who were here," Gromeko said. "I saw them singing and dancing at the Race Club. Are you going to hire them? It would be nice to have a nightclub act at your Camellia Room."

He has too many suggestions, Maria thought. He was so obviously a man who was unused to smiling that he could not know the disagreeable effect it had upon others. Did he always wear that three-day stubble on his face?

"They are not going to work here," Galia said. "Drink, Gromeko?"

"Oh…yes. You have cherry brandy? That is very good." As Galia poured, he said, "But I thought the act was excellent. All the customers liked it. The men here will like it, too."

"Really?" Maria said. "Are you sure you know what they like? You don't seem to get together with anyone very much."

"No. But men are men. The act is very sexy." The thumb of his right hand hugely extended, he tossed down the cherry brandy. Over the rim of the tumbler his red-rimmed eyes swiveled in her direction. He winked. Galia walked off without speaking.

Go away, you jerk. The G.I. slang word did not do him justice. Maria was glad to see another man approach the bar. He was wearing civilian clothes, but his haircut and his shirt and gabardine slacks clearly marked him as an American. The scuffed brown leather jacket he laid on the bar was only confirmation of that fact.

Gromeko looked at him and moved back to his table.

"Evening. Can a fellow have a conversation with you? You're always moving around, so I thought I'd catch you while I could."

"What do you want to talk about? Can I get you a drink?"

"This and that. Nothing in particular. You know, conversation, as in getting to know each other." He seemed to realize she was waiting patiently for his order. "I'm not much of a drinker. Two is my limit, and I've had it. I guess this is dead time for you unless I'm drinking." He pondered awhile. "How about…can you come up with a soda pop?"

"Why not? Have you tried this?" Maria poured a slug of cherry brandy in a tall glass and filled it with soda water from the spritzer. The reddish-brown fluid swirled and blended nicely; for a moment there was even a soda-fountain foam on top before it subsided. I may have invented something, Maria thought. It was too bad the club didn't have a big enough freezer for ice cream. She set the newly invented cherry brandy soda in front of him. "We're out of straws tonight. Sorry."

Gingerly, he tasted it. "Very…uh, what brand was that liqueur you used?" She showed him the bottle. "Imperial Brand. Local, I suppose. Has it killed anybody yet?"

She did not smile with him. "Not so far. You may be the first." It annoyed her that he took her father's label as a joke.

"Some ice might improve it. Have you got any?"

She felt like taking it from the ice bucket that cooled the beer but took pity on him. The average visiting American's stomach was notably feeble. She put two cubes of safe ice into his glass.

"Much better. My name is Thaddeus Huell." Maria nodded and went on with her tasks. "You're supposed to complete the ritual," Huell said. "What's your name?"

She did not give her name away freely, and seldom did she look the customers directly in the eye. The men usually misunderstood when she did and pressed their advantage; didn't bargirls

come as part of the package of good times? A
cheery sweep of a glance sufficed; in a group
she was relaxed, bantering, elusive.

She studied this man, whose name struck her
ear with a curious rising and falling harmony of
syllables. Light-to-nearly-blond hair cut short
but not shaved up the sides like that of soldiers, blue eyes, flat cheekbones, a curved
slightly hooked nose, and an attractive mouth.
He was, she thought, about thirty.

"My name is Maria Conti." She felt a pang of
nervousness, as though she had entrusted some
part of herself to the unknown.

"Thank you. Is that Italian? There's Chinese,
isn't there? I've been looking for a chance to
meet you without a pack of guys baying around. I
wondered what you would really be like, without
the hostess disguise."

"And now you have met me. I am not a princess."

"We don't have those in the States, either.
But I think you come close."

She would not fall for this one line of so
many thousands she had heard, but there was no
harm in continuing to talk to him. Perhaps it
was because he was so careful to keep his eyes
above her neck. The man was either very experienced or shy. No, he wasn't shy. A sensitive
military man? She smiled to herself. "You're an
army officer, aren't you? That's why you're in
civvies." Overwhelmingly patronized by enlisted
men, the club was not one in which officers
would feel welcome. Of course the EMs would know

what he was, but the shirt and slacks neutral-
ized him. "What made you come in here? Don't you
have your own mess and bar in the Broadway
Mansions?"

He looked uncomfortable. "You're assuming a
lot of things. Suppose I work at the consulate?"

"With that haircut?" She said, half-playfully,
"I think you're G-2 Intelligence, therefore
you're army, because all the troops these days
are navy or the United States Marines. Broadway
Mansions is your G-2 base."

"What else do you know? What makes you think
you're right about anything?" He drank off his
cherry brandy soda, and held out the glass. "Now
I need a chaser to help keep it down. Plain
soda, please. And now, we were saying, or I was,
something about princesses."

"You're changing the subject, aren't you? Did
I get too close?"

Huell straightened up and looked very stern.
"Young lady, have you ever been spanked?"

"Not by G-2 Intelligence." But she knew she
had taken flippancy too far. Huell was dead
serious, while she had gotten into the habit of
treating the military as a joke. "More soda?"
When he shook his head, she excused herself to
attend to Amalia's demands. He did not move
away. For no reason that she could think of she
stole a glance at his thumbs. They were ordinary, the nails clipped and clean. In a lull, as
she sorted currencies—there was some Canadian,
and twenty Mexican dollars in silver as well—she

was keenly aware of being watched. Galia and
Zoya were in the kitchen, helping Yung.

"It's getting late," Huell said. "When do you
get off?"

"I go home around midnight."

He nodded in understanding, a rare military
man whose limit was two drinks and who heard the
message in a simple sentence. "Would you go out
with me some day when you're free? Maybe a
drive, a date if you want to call it that. I'd
really like to forget about guns and politics
for a while. Is that possible in Shanghai?"

"I no longer know." Wry, in mourning for her
lost Shanghai, she said, "You'd have to wear a
blindfold and put glue in your ears, and ignore
your sense of smell. It would help to wear
armor plating, too. Other than that, nothing
has changed."

His sudden laugh startled her. It was a happy,
exultant sound. "See? We are having a conversation. We cut through that bar business and
became real persons."

"Don't you know any real persons?"

"I don't know if I do. I think I've forgotten
what they're supposed to be like. But I made a
bet with myself about you. I said to myself,
Thaddeus, if you can't connect with that lady in
ordinary, everyday terms, you are washed up for
what rest of your life you've got."

"A bet." She did not like the sound of that.
"Am I supposed to be an especially difficult
challenge?" A saloon hostess of mixed blood in

a Shanghai dive. "Are you sure nobody egged you on?" She was going to be disappointed in him, and she was angry at him but more with herself. What else could she have expected? He gestured, contradicting, and she recoiled before they touched. "Another drink? Scotch? Bargirls make the most from doubles," she said, bright and hard.

Huell said, "Nobody put me up to it. Do you want me to swear on my mother's head? Then I will. May my mother know her oldest son is a liar to women and children and never speak his name again. I don't have to raise my right hand. That was a true oath."

A stillness came over Maria, and she stared at him as though she could read signals in his skin, the pulse in his neck; she wanted to tear open his shirt and feel the treacherous pace of his heart. He was solemn under her scrutiny, a wrinkle forming between his eyebrows which, she noticed, were darker than his hair.

"Don't make me sorry. Don't talk, don't tell your serviceman's jokes about me." No childhood playground pact had ever meant more than this one; she was so tired of not trusting anyone in this place, this grown-up tainted playground she had helped create.

"Maria ma'am, I will try to proceed like any other person in a peacetime situation. That is to say, no less, and maybe more, because I am a red-blooded male. I won't kid you on that."

She did not respond, but involuntarily she
looked at his lips. She was fastidious about
men's mouths, their shape and personality and
cleanness. "Do you want to know what I was just
thinking a while ago, before you walked up to
the bar? That I don't like myself when I work
here. I mean...." She decided to stop explaining.
Let him take it anyway he cared to.

He did not ask what she meant. "Hazard of war.
I've been around this city. There are more ways
of dying than being hit by a bullet." He pushed
back his cuff and checked his watch. "I have to
march. I can't tell when I'm going to be free,
but can I take it that we are squared away on a
possible future date?"

"I have a question. Are you married?"

"The answer to that, ma'am is, ah, 'Negative.'"

After he left, Maria's attention returned to
her job. Only then did she notice Daniele sitting three tables off. For a long, long minute
they stared at each other, Daniele's face drawing into lines of bitterness as she watched.
Graphic as a self-discovered cuckold, that twist
of a smile. She fetched her coat from the
office, looked in on Galia in the kitchen and
said, "Going home. Good night, Galia."

Galia nodded. "He's very handsome. Did any sparks
strike there?"

"Is he? I don't know about sparks, Galia." She
walked out to Daniele. "Shall we go?"

Silent, he got up and helped her on with her
coat. As they emerged through the double doors,

two ragged figures carrying a long object darted across the street and disappeared in an alley.

Maria looked up at the awning. Her handpainted sign was gone.

"It didn't last long, did it. Well, I hope they cook some good meals with it. I hope they have food to cook. The awning will be the next to go. Twelve square feet of canvas makes a pretty decent house for those people. Why worry? The customers will find the club in an air raid blackout, if it comes to that." She hoped they would not cut down her mimosa tree, though; she would miss it.

She put her hand in his arm; he let it lie loosely in the crook of his elbow. They walked for a few minutes. A thin sleet moistened her warm cheeks. The cold, condensing in their breaths, did not quite mask the odors of garbage and human wastes in Soochow Creek. The sampans along the sides had been battened down for the night; here and there candlelight glimmered through an oilskin flap. The Soochow, a busy artery of commerce, flowed under Garden Bridge and joined the Whangpo River, which harbored its own sampan population. Above it all presided the square head and shoulders of Broadway Mansions, every floor lighted up: G-2 and the foreign correspondents at work.

"You should have worn your coat, Dani. At least a hat."

A slap rocked her head back.

"*Siete tutte puttane!*" His eyes in the dim
lighting no shape but a swimming black, Daniele
flung around and strode away.

You are all whores. Her left ear ringing, she
hardly noticed the pain. Emotions too complex to
sort rushed through her. For the second time
that evening she had been called a whore. She
ran after Daniele, the drumming of her heels
like a stampede of staves, clubs, rifle stocks,
broomsticks and knitting needles, a motley army
troop passing over the silence of the sampan
families. Near the crest of Garden Bridge she
overtook him.

Her fist caught him in the side of the head.
Daniele staggered, then righted himself. At the
sight of him weeping, she held back a second
blow. "Dani," she said. How tired she felt all
of a sudden. But she put her arms around him and
held him as he heaved silently. The sleet thickened, enveloped their two figures so that she
could see no farther than a few feet. They began
to walk, her arm around him. She shivered; her
hair clung to her temples in wet strands.
Daniele didn't even have a coat. She unbuttoned
hers and tried to cover his back with half of
it. So this was how the end was to come. She had
tried to picture its coming, and the means,
someone perhaps in the shadowy guise of a
Thaddeus Huell, though Huell was no more than a
bearer of the inevitable message.

Every bone ached as she climbed in beside Nola. A sleepy protest from her sister, "Ugh, your feet are like ice."

"Well, warm them up, then." She tucked them under Nola's calves and encountered stiff cardboard on the far side. "What's that in bed with us?"

"…eggs."

"Eggs? Are you hatching chickens or something?"

"Amah said s'too cold in the kitchen. Won't hatch in the spring."

"Won't hatch in the...." It dawned on her then. "You mean your silkworm eggs? You have your silkworm eggs in bed with us?" She sat up, ready to flee. "Nasty little black wiggly things crawling all over me. Get them out of here."

Fully awake now, Nola explained patiently, "I said they won't hatch till spring. And the eggs are in a shoe box, anyway. They can't climb out of the shoebox. If I don't keep them warm the eggs will die."

Sighing, Maria slid back under the covers. She was too tired to fight over silkworm eggs. "I'm still so cold. I'm never going to be warm again."

Nola squirmed over and plastered herself to Maria's side. Her sister's small warm body felt boneless and somehow nourishing, like milky porridge. Her muscles slackened. Poor Dani, with no one to warm him up. He had asked her to stay with him and she had almost given in and said yes. He was penitent for striking her, and sweet; had she

agreed to go to his room they would have made love
and tomorrow he would have assumed everything was
the same. He would accommodate, and adjust, and
pretend, and never never acknowledge, as tonight
at the last he began to dismiss as imaginary what
he had sensed at the club.

She examined her feelings. She pitied Dani.
And yes, she was a little frightened to be cut
loose from him.

She began to croon a song she made up when
Nola was seven years old.

    Nola, Nola,
    Not a capi-to-la
    Just a little town

"Maybe it was little, but it wouldn't surrender to the Romans," Nola said. "Daddy said Nola
was the bravest town in Italy. Can we go to
sleep, now? I have a test tomorrow."

8

Chilly and overcast, this was not a day for an outdoors excursion. It was, however, free. Kwilecki could actually hear the wind whistling through the weave of his jacket as he curbed his pace to match Zina's. He had bundled her up until she protested, laughing, that she could not breathe through the muffler he wound around her neck and half her face.

Visiting the zoo in Jessfield Park had been her idea. Not a good one, as they walked past cage after cage. Those not empty held starveling inmates who crouched in corners on moldy straw, or else stared with dulled eyes. The monkeys were piteous, though no more so than the single tiger whose every rib could be counted. Zina kept saying oh oh, what is happening, I can't look anymore, Leon, make them do something, at the same time clinging tighter to him. No custodians were in sight. If he had a gun—if he had this or that—he could do something, put these creatures beyond the reach of mankind's cruelties.

He steered her away to the grass and found a spot under a tree. It was a spruce, at least seventy feet tall. Winter buds like rough yellow darts bristled over every inch of its generous spread, their robustness not at all dependent upon Chinese Nationalists or Chinese Communists. Kwilecki thought a living tree that looked happy would be good for Zina, and she did settle back against its trunk with a sigh of pleasure. Such simple small pleasures were theirs.

She began to unpack their picnic. A thermos of hot tea, heavily sugared, four slices of black bread spread with carrot jam—a product of Metzenbaum's numerous cottage industries—and, behold, a surprise for Kwilecki, two chicken legs, an attempt to make up for her night-long weeping when he came home from the IRO. Kwilecki's personal prince, Subarov, the director of IRO who also handled the Kwileckis' case file, had nothing to report. No openings anywhere. The stout-hearted country of Belgium, accepting stateless persons until its seams were bursting, could not take another soul within its portals.

Kwilecki would have preferred to spend his day off in bed sleeping, but an expressed wish of Zina's always merited indulgence. She seldom wanted to do anything; when she did, Kwilecki thought it was a good sign. A desire however modest staved off depression.

They were not the only visitors to Jessfield Park. Chinese families used the city's nearly dozen far-flung oases of greenery with enthusiasm, winter or summer. Even today, the humming of wooden tops roamed and swooped over the meadow. Young and old, the spinners held contests to see who could keep the tops balanced on their cords the longest. The tops were shaped like a spool, two large flanges connected by a thin spindle. A wooden grip in each hand, the artist seesawed the cord with delicacy, sometimes tossing the top into the air and then catching the spindle again on the cord. The gusty weather only presented a challenge to the good spinners. A true champion could balance a top with one flange removed.

A few yards from the Kwileckis an elderly man, bulky in padded cotton tunic and pants, practiced his slow-motion dance of the tai ch'i, the Supreme Ultimate, the primary source of all reality.

I live among humble philosophers, thought Kwilecki, and I will never find the serenity to endure as they do.

They began their picnic, Zina urging Kwilelcki to eat most of the food. Triumphing over cold winds, the hot sugared tea brought a becoming flush to Zina's cheeks. Normally so white, her complexion the past weeks seemed faintly rosy to Kwilecki. Perhaps she was getting better and would stop her fainting spells. He took to asking her, making a joke out of it, Any dives today, my swooning dove? The answer was usually disappointing. There was no change there.

He fingered the flying jet ends of her hair. "Let's do this more often. If it's really cold, we'll make sculptures in ice. All you have to do is throw water over me. Very easy."

Zina giggled. The sound of it was startling. It was miraculous what an outing away from their room could do.

"More tea, Leon?" She poured, proud of their Chinese thermos with the bright red flowers painted from top to bottom. No doubt about its efficiency. The Chinese liked their tea kept hot.

"Leon." The single, tentative note halted him in mid-sip. He watched her watching him. She looked—what was it—fearful. "I know I haven't been much help, crying like a spoiled child. It isn't your fault the IRO can't give us visas. I decided it is my turn to be brave, that's why I want to tell you this, here, in a nice green place. Leon, don't be angry. We've been careful, but these things happen. Imagine if we were still trying to cross Siberia."

When he frowned, trying to get the drift, she took his hand and placed it on her shapeless coat, over her stomach.

Oh, God, he thought. Help me. Help us. Near them, the elderly Chinese man remained oblivious, rapt in his tai ch'i discipline, the principle of the universe.

The crab season, open at the onset of cold, rainy weather in late October, had been underway for some weeks. Foreigners do not know this type of crab, which comes from a specific lake in Hangchow, about 150 miles southwest of Shanghai. This lake, in the past an imperial summer resort of audacious luxury, is fed by numerous large adjoining lakes. It is called in Chinese the West Lake. Its water is clear, and twenty to thirty feet at the bottom the living delicacies may be seen walking about. The West Lake crab, the *doo zah har*, is so famous throughout the land that rich men as far away as Hong Kong will contrive to have quantities shipped to them. Its consumption always engenders merriment and messiness, for one has to roll up sleeves and wear aprons, and there is much teasing about who ate the most and who took more than his share of females. The abdomen of the female crab yields a treasure of orange roe that is deliciously crumbly and fatty, compared with food of the gods. The use of sauce is optional, but nothing has been invented to improve upon the traditional blend of soy sauce, white vinegar, some sugar and water, and minced ginger. To begin, one plucks off the broad carapace, to which some of the roe adheres, adds sauce to its contents and spoons the shell clean. That is the first tasting of crab. The carapace is then used as a dipping receptacle for sauce. Next comes the part eagerly anticipated: the bulk of the roe in the abdominal cavity. The flesh of the female is thin and somewhat watery, for all the nutrition has gone into the making of roe. The flesh of the male is rich and robust, but then in place

of roe there is only a teaspoonful of fat.
Consumption proceeds: the cleaning and eating of
the carcass, cracking of legs, spilling of
sauce, jets of juice squirted inadvertently in
someone's eye, laughter, quaffing of beer and
zoshing wine, and finally, droll disbelief at
the mound of debris accumulated on table, in
bowls, buckets, whatever.

In the ground floor apartment at Route Magy,
the Wong family had been feasting on crabs. Day
by day, the Wongs carted the remains out to
their backyard and threw them into a large
garbage bin. Each time they did so, they looked
up toward the windows of the Contis and uttered
an insulting comment or two, accompanied by
laughter. The rubbish accumulated; by mid-
December the bin was full to the top, the stench
of its contents multiplying and mounting to the
bedroom windows of the Contis. Even with windows
shut tight the smell seeped into their rooms and
permeated curtains, clothing, and the Contis'
eiderdown quilts.

During nights of torturous wakefulness Poldo
lay beside Ming Chu wrestling with visions of
violence. What would he not sacrifice to give in
to primitive animal instinct! A bomb, dropped on
the stinking garbage bin, kill whom it may downstairs, upstairs, his whole family and himself,
Amah in the kitchen. A satisfying cataclysm of
shattering glass bottles and demijohns, never to
be used again. His recipes burned to flakes of
black ash. Let the blast bring down the B/Ks,

not forgetting the damned dog, and crush them in
broken masonry. He could make such a bomb, he
knew he could. All the ingredients could be
bought and assembled.

Though he had not moved, Ming Chu whispered,
"Shall I make you a cup of green tea, husband?
The jasmine flowers are very soothing."

"Nothing will help. Nothing but total annihi-
lation."

"We will go down and talk to them tomorrow. Or
better—we can bribe the police to enter the
place and make them clean up the yard. The
police will act if they get paid."

"I will not spend our money on those apes. I
am going to do something about them, Ming Chu. A
man cannot take much more of this." He got out
of bed and paced the intricate paths of their
bedroom floor. "The trick is to be like them.
Who's going to care? I don't, not any longer. At
last a blow for our side! Is there a more satisfying way to finish this joke of our lives?" He
paced faster.

The stifled rage of her husband frightened
Ming Chu. What did he mean, "finish this joke of
our lives"? It was one thing for herself to cast
her angers about in the dark, for she could not
sleep either, and another for Poldo to talk
about killing and dying. He breathed as though
he were running. This life is killing him, she
thought. A mother always has someone to hope for
while despairing for herself. It hurt her to
remember the times she wished she were dead. The

hours of the night took away every tenacious grain of resistance one had and left nothing but terror and weariness.

"Get into bed before you catch cold. We will do something when morning comes. Please." When he went to the window and stared down, she rose and pulled the quilt off the bed. "Here. Help me, Poldo," she said, when he ignored her attempts to wrap him in the quilt. "I wonder all the time how the smell does not bother them? And how can they hang up their laundry near the garbage bin?"

"It does not bother them because they are apes. Besides, the smell rises. Am I a coward, Ming Chu? Do you all laugh at me behind my back?"

"Never. You are a loving husband and father. A good man bred with gentleness." He seemed not to hear. On the other side of the house, the one with the flock of chickens, a cock crowed. Sharing the quilt, Ming Chu stood at the window, waiting for morning.

At nine o'clock Maria, groggy with interrupted sleep, shuffled into their bedroom. "My God, my God, what's going on. Daddy, what on earth are you doing." She looked for explanation from her mother, tense on the edge of a rosewood chair.

"Apes, pigs, die in your own filth! Yes, jump and jabber, you hairless ape! Can you read? You are more worthless than a noseless leper! Everyone on the block knows you have no honor. Thieves, filthy offspring of thieves a thousand generations back! Why don't you choke to death on the next crab you crack?" Poldo's head and shoulders, shaking with passion, leaned out the window; his hands manipulated something. Maria leaned beside him and saw what it was: a string. A string with a sheet of paper attached to its bottom. In the yard, Wong stood looking upward shouting curses. Poldo teased him with the string. Whenever he lowered it within reach, Wong jumped and tried to snatch the paper. Poldo laughed when he did that. The sound of it was harsh, a bit mad, booming back in echo from the concrete-enclosed yard.

In consternation, Maria looked at her mother.

"Insults," her mother said. "Your father had me write terrible things in very big characters for Wong to read."

"Words won't make any difference to them," Maria said. "They've got hides like gravel."

"This is for your father. He must take some kind of action or he will go mad. Those people are dev-ils, or they must hate foreigners very much."

"Both, I'm sure. Are you all right, Mama? You look tired and sort of desperate."

Her mother rose. "I am going to stay in the kitchen for a while."

Nola burst in and cried, "You should hear the commotion outside their door! The wife is screaming about burning the house down. Grace's boyfriend is in there too, and he's telling Wong to stay inside, not to give Daddy any satisfac-tion. I could hear Daddy shouting right through

their front door!" She turned to go out again,
but her mother caught and held her.

"Nola, you are not to go anywhere near them.
This is not a game. Those people can be very
dangerous if they catch you. You either stay
here or come with me to the kitchen." She left
the room. The smell of rotting crab detritus,
fainter in the kitchen, was overlaid with the
perfumed aroma of tung oil.

Amah was grooming her hair. Once a month she
purchased shavings of the wood in the market and
prepared a sticky sap by pouring boiling water
over them. The ritual was careful and slow: a
dipping of a bone-handled brush made of stiff
pig bristle into the oil, then a thorough curry-
ing of her long black hair. "Those Wongs are
nothing but trash, they wouldn't even know how
to work on my man's farm," she said.

And my man has lost all his dignity, Ming Chu
thought. There was no help for it. She hoped
this ugly brawl worked as a dose of medicine for
the sickness in his soul. Resting on a kitchen
stool, watching Amah perform her toilette, she
tried to shut out the noises of the conflict.

Finished with her hair, which she bound in a
coil at the neck, Amah next picked up her mirror
and proceeded to tidy up her upper lip. Instead
of tweezers she used two coins with which to
pinch the hairs. The work went swiftly, for all
the thickness of her work-coarsened fingers.

Ming Chu heard the bedroom door open. Her husband strode past the kitchen to the dining room,

Nola at his heels. Seconds later he strode back, bottles of alcohol in his arms. The bedroom door slammed after him and Nola. Constrained by Amah's presence, Ming Chu resisted an urge to put her fingers in her ears. Nola's voice piped excitedly, Here's some newspaper, Daddy, let me hold it. Poldo's voice boomed, Take this present from heaven, Wong, then Nola's laughter. Angry shouts from the Wongs, audible via the stairwell. A new smell—nauseating, greasy, fishy smoke—reached the kichen. A shriek from Nola, Daddy, the curtains!

When Nola ran into the kitchen, Ming Chu was already at the sink filling a large pot with water. "Here you are," she said. Nola took it and ran out. Ming Chu found another pot, filled that, and gave it to Maria. "There is nothing to laugh about," she admonished, but Maria gasped, "Oh, Mama. You should see the scene down in the yard. The whole gang of them are running around dumping water on their laundry and screaming. The laundry caught fire from the garbage bin. They broke one of their own windows swinging a pot of water."

And what of our own curtains and shutters? Ming Chu followed Maria into her bedroom. The shutters had not caught. She was in time to see Maria tear down the flaming curtains and drop them into the yard below, then dump her pot of water after the curtains. "There! I'm helping you put out your fire," she called.

Ming Chu looked down. Maria had aimed her water nicely. Wong was looking up, for once speechless, his face and clothes begrimed and quite drenched.

At dinner that evening Nola insisted on recounting the morning's events to Daniele. She flung her arms high to show how the flames from the garbage bin leapt; all alone she demonstrated the Wongs and the boyfriend scuttling about their yard with basins and cooking pots. She was adept at mimickry, a gift Ming Chu had not noticed before. Her father said little, but there was a peace in his face that assuaged Ming Chu's perturbed heart.

While Maria seemed to enjoy Nola's performance, Daniele only nodded and smiled. Not once did he break into laughter though her drollness certainly merited a chuckle or two. Finally, sensing her audience lacked enthusiasm, Nola directed a disappointed look at her father, her partner in the adventure, and settled to her dinner.

Daniele ate in silence. He did not stay afterward to chat with Poldo but before leaving stood talking with Maria on the landing. They spoke in Italian, but even so Ming Chu, helping Amah in the kitchen, heard the strain in his voice, then a stretch in which he sounded pleading, and finally a bitterness tipping into anger. Through it all, Maria was equable, like a mother keeping her temper with a difficult child.

Ming Chu was aware that Daniele was prone to fits of melancholy, yet this time she sensed a difference in Maria. How often had Ming Chu heard her joke and tease when he was in this mood. There was none of that tonight.

"You can't come home alone from across town," Daniele said. "You're not going to stop me."

"It will be dangerous whether or not you're with me, Dani. I have to do it alone sooner or later. Do you understand?"

"It's that American, isn't it? You've got something on with him. Bitch. All women are bitches." The lighting on the landing was indirect, coming from the open kitchen, but it was enough to reveal the dead paleness of his face. Pale, but not calm; Dani was like tinder awaiting the torch. Oh, what did she know? She thought she could handle him and his moods.

Dani was not going to help her get free of Dani. This Dani perhaps no longer even loved her; a sickly obstinacy had taken over. Loss. Ego. Fear? Yes, she detected fear.

The dining room opened and her father emerged. He said, "Pardon," and quickly went into the bedroom. Rapid thumps beat above their heads, the dog scratching itself.

"Dani, think over what you're saying, and understand why you are saying those things. You can't keep a woman against her will. The American just happened by last night." Sadly, for her own loss, she said, "We were nice together, but that couldn't last, Dani."

"Nice. You call it nice." He took a step, his face falling into shadow. Instinctively, Maria reached out and gripped the handrail. The air between them seemed to push at her. Then Daniele whirled and clattered down the stairs.

9

Nola and her friend, Elizabeth, were in the kitchen counting silkworm eggs in the shoebox. "Why aren't you girls in school?" asked Maria. She opened cupboards, the fridge; the gas stove-top was bare.

"In the oven," Nola said. "Amah saved meat dumplings for your breakfast. And it's Saturday, is why."

Maria made herself hot tea and bit into a dumpling. She closed her eyes as the ginger-flavored pork juices flooded her mouth. She loved this food, and Amah indulged her as often as she could.

She had spent most of the hours she should have been asleep thinking about Dani. Her ties to him, she was discovering, were set deeper in her heart than she realized. The relief she felt when he didn't appear at the club was supplanted by worry. An exhausting act of will kept her from telling the pedicab driver to stop by his place when she came home at two o'clock. Last

night on the landing he could easily have
snapped her neck. Dani would have been as surprised as she. Oh look, Poldo. I've just killed
your daughter.

"Four hundred and twelve," Nola said.
Elizabeth, a pretty girl whose mother was
Japanese and father was Danish, said, "I counted
four hundred eighteen." The eggs, laid by a single moth early in the fall, dotted the bottom of
the shoebox like pinhead-size egg yolks.

"Remember that business you've been pestering
me about?" Maria said.

Nola looked at her. "The promise, you mean?"

"I didn't forget, you know. It just wasn't, ah,
convenient. I could do it today, if you like."

Elizabeth had plum-dark eyes and a high,
rounded forehead. Nola's best friend since third
grade, hers was a presence of few words. Her
mother made her wear a gauze mask in the
streets, as though it could save her from
typhus-bearing fleas and lice. The refugee-beg-
gars were a rich source of both. The device made
her eyes huge, her unlined forehead vulnerable.
She looked alertly from Nola to Maria. When
Maria was eleven she thought of nothing but
clothes and film stars. She would have ignored
anything said over her head. Whatever happened
to childish children?

Calmly, Nola told Elizabeth that she was going
to be busy today, that she would drop over
tomorrow. Elizabeth nodded, didn't ask why she
couldn't stay, and left.

"I don't suppose anyone will be around there at lunchtime," Maria said, hopefully.

"I'll find somebody. Don't worry."

"Why should I, with a little bulldog like you to handle things." She went to get dressed.

On the way down the stairs they ran into Tanya striding noisily up with the dog on its leash. Nola had to step behind Maria, who nodded to Tanya. Tanya's glance flashed from her and then to the dog straining at her collar. Her foot paused on the step. In minute rapid shifts her clumsy features gave away her intentions: hand and mouth commands to the dog, barely begun, when Maria said coldly, "Try it, and I will kick the throat out of the bitch, and you down the stairs."

Nola at her side, she continued down without looking back. "If you meet her by yourself, Nola, just keep on going. Pretend she's invisible. You don't need to worry about Irene. She's a lot more devious than that clod back there."

The parish of St. Columban's on Rue Maresca was a short walk from Route Magy. The beggars on the edge of Frenchtown were less aggressive than downtown; they seemed mainly to want a peaceful place to camp. There were several private mansions on this block. On their high walls the notices Post No Bills were tattered and smeared with excrement. When she was little, until her father explained, Maria thought the posters were an instruction to the postman to deliver no bills. The owners of these

mansions were sometimes European, but most
were Chinese. One of the more famous million-
aires was a night watchman from the province of
Ningpo who had made his fortune with an opium-
tinctured medicine for cholera. No one knew
whether the drops cured the cholera, but they
calmed and comforted the sufferer so well that
the ex-night watchman soon had his millions in
American dollars and forty rooms, a graveled
drive, twenty servants, and a dozen automobiles. He also acquired several wives, each
installed in a separate household.

Set apart from the property of a more humble
millionaire, long fled to Taiwan, stood the
structure of St. Columban's. Of brick and stucco,
the parish encompassed church, sacristy, library,
a dining hall, an office, and living quarters
upstairs. The secular order of St. Columban's
originated in Navan, Ireland; Nola knew every one
of the five priests in residence. They allowed
her the use of their modest library, from which
the rector, Father Bowles, had banished every
work written by an Englishman or Englishwoman. He
was prone to become fiery on the topic of the
English.

She went to the office and rounded up Father
Liam Carnahan. Maria was already in the
church, so small it was really a chapel. She
knelt in a pew near the confessional booth.
Father Liam entered with Nola, at whom Maria
glared. Give me some privacy, you pest. Nola
pretended not to understand, crossing herself

and genuflecting, but then relented and went
out to the hall. Father Liam ensconced himself
in the confessional and Maria moved to kneel at
the screened window. A warm moisture ringed
her neck; she cleared her throat. The dark head
and boyish features of the priest inclined
toward the screen. She saw him once a year at
Christmas Mass.

Father Liam spoke a blessing, his Irish lilt
overpowering the Latin.

She crossed herself herself and began, "Bless
me Father, for I have sinned. It has been four
years since my last confession."

"Yes, my child."

"I...uh, sinned with a man many times." Did you
call it adultery when you weren't the one married? "He was...is a married man."

"Yes."

"I have taken the Lord's name in vain, many
times." After making love with Dani hundreds of
times, apologizing for saying God or Jesus
seemed the height of silliness. But when the
confessor bent his head that way, waiting to
hear more sins, you found yourself thinking of
more things to say. I stole a chicken. That was
really stupid.

"Yes."

"I can't think of anything else, Father."

"Very well." His hand lifted, two fingers
signing the cross. "Ego te absolvo in nomine
Patris, et Filii, et Spiritus Sancti. Amen. Now

say an act of contrition. For your penance say
three Hail Marys and three Our Fathers."

Without conscious voliton, the words of the
Act of Contrition came from her lips. Removing
herself to a pew and amazing herself further,
she recited faultlessly the Hail Mary and Our
Father. They were the official warrant of the
end of her affair with Dani. She looked at the
altar, draped in a plain cloth, the mystery of
the Host enclosed within the gilt portals of the
Tabernacle. If God weren't God he would lose his
own faith because he heard so many less-than-
pure reasons for penitence. Except for Nola, He
certainly got puny satisfaction from the Contis.
Her father never went to Mass, nor her mother, a
convert upon her marriage. She rose, stepped out
of the pew, genuflected, and at the door dipped
her fingers in holy water and crossed herself.
Nola materialized from the library next to the
chapel. She gave Maria a big smile, angelic now
that she had got her way.

"Are we quits on that promise?" Maria asked.

"For now," Nola said.

Maria shook her head. When she was eleven
going on twelve, her shrewdness had to do with
bargaining for candy, permission to go somewhere, stay up late.

She and Nola returned to Route Magy to pick up
a three-gallon tin of kerosene, and then rode a
pedicab up the Avenue Joffre to the corner of
Avenue du Roi. The Mexican-dollar trade rose to
its height around midday. Up and down the street

men clinked silver dollars balanced on their fingertips. A clear, sweet ring denoted the purity of the coins. Maria took her kerosene to a spot on the sidewalk and waited. Presently a Chinese man jingling a handful of silver approached. He looked at the tin, inquiry in his expression.

"The best kerosene from Caltex," she said. "What's your offer?"

Promptly he answered, "Five silver dollars."

"Ten. All Mexican." She wondered why she even bothered to say that. No one had seen any other kind since 1934, when greedy banks shipped tons of silver coins abroad to be sold as bullion. They had made huge profits. The Great Depression did not touch Shanghai because of that silver horde, the largest in the world. Only a few hundred thousand Mexican dollars were left and were the only hard currency anyone trusted. The Mexican dollar was equal to about forty-five U.S. cents, the current rate of exchange; you dealt Mexican dollars as you breathed without thinking.

"Seven," the man responded. He looked at Nola, a gold tooth flashing. "Your sister, hah?"

Maria ignored that. "Nine."

"For you, and your pretty half-Chinese sister, I make it eight." Upon her nod, he counted out eight coins into her hand. Nola continued to sit on the kerosene tin while Maria did the clink test. "All right," she said, and Nola got up.

"Velly smart young ladies," the man said in pidgin. "Do business again, hah?"

One-tenth of eight Mexican dollars equaled eighty Mexican cents, or thirty-six American cents. Her share of the proceeds at the club. And that was before expenses were taken out. This wasn't worth the trouble. She resolved not to accept anymore commodities in payment for drinks. A Dutchman had once offered a sack of tea for a jigger of Scotch.

A hundred eyes watched her put away the silver coins inside her coat. Squatting on the curb, a woman with a child at her breast scratched at Nola's leg, her deep-socketed eyes challenging Maria: Money or.... Sometimes they spat on you before you got out of range. Nodding acquiescence, and telling Nola to get away from her, she put a few paper notes in the woman's dirty hand. "Did she break the skin?" Nola shook her head.

Perched on a three-legged stool on the sidewalk, her back against a shop window, a little girl mended stockings, her hand a blur of speed as she plied the thin metal hook down a ladder in the hose. She was younger than Nola, about nine.

"How about a spot of lunch? At the Chocolate Shop?"

"No, really?" Nola glowed. This was a treat.

Free of the heavy tin of kerosene, they hopped a tram, alighting at Nanking Road on the corner of Honan Road. Nola made a straight line for the soda fountain, no table for her. She climbed on a stool that Maria had sat on dozens of times when she was a teen-ager. After-school sodas and

sundaes, boys teasing and affecting sophistica-
tion. Bob Madigan, where are you now? Dead at
war, or safe in America?

Nola knew what she wanted, a club sandwich and
a chocolate ice cream soda. Maria told the
Chinese counterman she would have the same. He
wore a white fore-and-aft cap, like the soda
jerks in American films. The emporium of sweets
always did a prosperous business from expatriate
Americans avid for malted milks, banana splits,
cream pies and the illusion of being back in
Waukegan, Chicago, New York City. A generation
of Shanghai-born Americans was inducted into the
culture of the ice cream parlor at the Chocolate
Shop on Nanking Road before they ever saw their
home country.

The club sandwich placed before Nola was as
genuine as Yung at The Camellia Room could never
make it. Carefully, she removed the toothpick
from a four-inch segment and took a juicy bite.
Mayonnaise bracketing her lips, she said dream-
ily, "It's a fine dish for an empty stomach."

"Why is it that everytime you go near St.
Columban's you talk like an Irishman for days?"

"Do I?" She chewed for some seconds. "Deedh
Faderr Liam geeve you tventy Ourr Faderrs forr
penance?"

"And that's a terrible Russian accent. Don't
try it in front of Galia. She likes kids, but
not smart-alecks."

"I'm not. It's on account of what I'm reading.
The story makes me sad. This beautiful woman

Anna Karenina falls in love but she's already married and she can't marry him, so they run away and everybody despises them. It's an awfully long book, so I peeked at the ending. She's very unhappy and throws herself under a train. I hate sad endings like that. Um, look, there's still loads of chocolate ice cream in the soda."

"That book is too old for you. Why do you pick those things, anyway? You didn't get it at St. Columban's."

"Of course not. You have to know where to get what. Yuri's library has the best grown-up books. But he's always drunk when I go now, so I grabbed *Anna Karenina* without looking through it first. I thought it was a love story, and it is but not the kind I thought. I liked the last one better." The remaining half-inch of soda burbled at the bottom of her straw and she lifted the glass and drank it off. A rim of watery choco-late garnished her upper lip, where mayonnaise and a bit of bacon already clung. "I loved *Lady Chatterley's Lover.*"

"Oh, my God," said Maria.

10

Grigory Gromeko ordered another anisette and
waited for the girls to finish their number. He
had a toothache; several days of nonstop pounding
in the region of his molars on the right side had
put him in a hellish mood. Also, the Filipino captain had given him the worst table in the house,
near the swinging door of the kitchens. Gromeko
refused to give him the usual cumshaw for a better table; each time he came here it was the same.
No cumshaw, no good table. You are next on my
list, friend. The Filipino was going to catch a
surprise soon. Gromeko caressed the picture in
his mind. The wife would be locked in the bedroom,
the brats in another, a wonderful way to keep
everybody off balance. Do you want to see Manila
again with your whole family intact? He was a generous man, he would leave him a bit to live on or
to get out. He surmised the man would go home to
Manila.

As for Gromeko, he knew how to disappear. No
one knew where he lived, and his connection with

the girls was a profitable secret they had kept for fifteen years.

The drum hammered a ruffle and Irene vaulted to the stage. The two stood side by side, their arms upraised as the spectators applauded. Thirteen or fourteen customers rose, laughing and talking; Irene's crotch-stroking number always got everyone very animated. A few men stayed on for another round of drinks. Usually these were not regulars; they didn't know the high point of the evening had passed. The Filipino captain was busy settling up bills, bowing good night. The girls had left the stage and gone through the curtained doorway to their dressing room. Gromeko left money for his drinks and mingled with the crowd. Three men headed for the bathroom on the side of the stage. The girls' room was next to it. Gromeko went with them but veered off and entered the dressing room.

Already stripping, Tanya said petulantly, "You didn't applaud very hard, Grigory. We need lots of support out there. H.C. keeps saying business is bad, which means a cut in pay."

Gromeko didn't want to talk to her, to either of them. The pounding in his jaw made the act of speaking unpleasant. "Get me a chair," he said. Tanya took the only one there was, a kitchen chair, and placed it behind the plywood screen. Gromeko removed his good wool jacket, handed it to Tanya, and took from her the sweater she had brought tonight. Then he sat down behind the screen and tried to make himself comfortable on the hard seat.

On the other side of the screen: elastic snapping, the metallic tune of zippers, rustle of clothing.

Tanya said, "Always the same old answer at the IRO. I'm getting worried. You'd think somebody would die once in a while and make room."

"I know," Irene said. "But we have a card or two to play, yet. I hear Subarov is tough, but nice."

"How tough?"

"Well, we'll find out, won't we?" Irene said softly, "We're going now, Grigory. We have to turn out the light now, or H.C. will come in here. See you later."

Gromeko grunted. He wanted to get this over with; his toothache had just given him a nasty jab.

The laughing and talking in the outer room seemed to go on for hours past closing time, though by the fissured light between the curtains and the gap in the screen, Gromeko's watch showed it was only one o'clock. The toothache jabbed him with the devil's own forked tail; he could not stop gasping at the immense pain of it. A bear snuffling in a cave, that was how he sounded to himself. Tomorrow he would see a dentist, a Chinese who lived on his street. He hated doctors and he hated dentists, he hated anyone to touch him with needles or knives. He did not plan to allow the dentist to lance the abscess that was killing

him, just to pull the teeth and Gromeko would
take care of the rest himself.

To take his mind off the pain he dwelt on the
flawless execution of his job on Yu Yuen Road
last week. The wife of the British banker had
nearly peed on her lovely carpet when she felt
his knife at her throat. He had never actually
cut anyone in a job; the quarrelsome man he had
stabbed in a bar in Mukden who called him a stupid *mujik*, peasant, had paid for it. In his
trade, knives were preferable to guns, which to
him were clumsy weapons as well as noisy. If you
were too far from your target to use a knife,
then you were too far to do the job correctly.
His tool was a Schrade switchblade, its three
inches whetted to a gleaming edge during solitary winter evenings. The point was especially
wicked, honed for slashing. She hadn't said a
word to him, just whimpered, "Basil, do as he
says, please," as though she wasn't sure her
husband was going to exchange his money and silver spoons for his wife.

A good haul. Greedy pigs.

It really was their own fault for not getting
out. They had the money and a place to go to,
while Gromeko had no papers and no country. He
despised the IRO route. Once you were resettled
in a new place, the IRO passed you over to the
local authorities. Here is a list of jobs, Mr.
Gromeko. If we can help further, let us know.
Citizenship will be granted after we deem you
have met all our requirements.

Obscenities upon them and their requirements! And nobody was going to slink back to Mother Russia, wagging his tail. Since '45 the truth had filtered back to the stateless Russians in China. The returnees became prisoners; they were treated like criminals. Might as well be a damn good one right here, free and on his own. Maybe he would marry Tanya, acquire a ready-made family—with Babushka doing the cooking—and all of them would become obedient Communists.

He groaned softly and pushed his fist into his cheek. The pain was making him half crazy.

At last, at last, no more sounds of jollity. Footsteps of tidying up. The captain and two bartenders should be going home soon; the girls said they left almost right after closing. Gromeko sidled around the screen and moved aside the curtain one inch from where it met the jamb. Only two waiters, collecting glasses and dirty tablecloths. H.C. Ping walked out of his office, having a last look at the waiters doing their work. The most delicate part of Gromeko's timing was near. H.C. never counted the night's take until everyone was gone. He let in the armed guard only after he had locked the money in the safe. In the morning H.C. removed the money and took it somewhere, but not to a bank, never a bank these days.

"All right, go home," H.C. told the waiters. He was a short man with a short neck, and broad in the chest. The silk scarf knotted over the open collar of his silk shirt made him look as

though he had no neck at all. He watched the
waiters go out, then locked the door after them
and switched off the main ceiling lights.
Another quick scanning around the club. He came
toward Gromeko, who tensed and reached into his
pocket for his knife. H.C. walked hurriedly,
began unbuttoning his fly, and Gromeko relaxed.
The bathroom next door. He leaned against the
wall, cupped his jaw, and moaned as H.C.
splashed into the toilet bowl for an eternity.
The bathroom door opened; Gromeko watched his
back retreat and disappear into the office.

He took a woman's stocking from his other
pocket and pulled it over his head; it went
scratchily over the stubble on his cheeks. Its
effect was terrifying, he knew that from his own
mirror; that was why the British banker's wife
and all the others nearly died of fright. He did
not especially enjoy frightening people; he was
just a workman doing an efficient job. For a
moment he stood, gathering himself, his panting
shallow and rapid. He had to rouse the dentist
from his bed after he finished here; he could
not endure this agony until morning.

On rubber-soled shoes he walked, blade open in
his right hand, to the office and looked in. His
jacket off, H.C. was seated at his desk separating gold yuan from American dollars swiftly, like
a card dealer. A metal box on the desk was filled
with silver coins. Behind him the door of the safe
stood open. The shoulder holster strapped over

H.C.'s shirt surprised Gromeko, who knew at once he had to be fast.

As Gromeko strode in H.C. looked up and bolted from his chair, drawing his pistol as he did. The first shot hit Gromeko in the right biceps, the second caught him alongside the ribs. Gromeko turned, bent in a crouch, and fled through the club to the front door. H.C. ran after him and kept firing. Gromeko had dropped his knife when he was hit. He rattled the knob, remembered it was locked, and ran for cover in the dimness of the club, throwing tables and chairs out of his way. The shots boomed in Gromeko's ears like explosions. Firing away at the dodging form, H.C. shouted curses in Chinese. As soon as he heard the pistol click on empty Gromeko straightened up and sprinted back to H.C., who fled into his office and tried to slam the door. Gromeko's left shoulder smashed against it and flung H.C. against the desk. Paper currency and silver coins spewed in all directions, some of the coins hitting the safe and rebounding in a hurricane of jangling metal. Two or three coins spun on the floor, twirling musically, before collapsing. The only sound in the final silence was a liquid pattering—Gromeko's blood streaming to the floor.

Stunned, his nose squashed and bleeding, H.C. lay motionless on the desktop.

Gromeko became aware of someone banging on the front door and Tanya's voice screaming, What happened, are you all right, Grigory open the door. The banging went on and on, underlaid with Irene's voice telling Tanya to come away, this was no place to be if Grigory was dead.

Panting, assaulted by pain from every inch of his body, his jaw a mass of fire, Gromeko looked at H.C. The man was conscious; even if he didn't understand Russian he knew it was Tanya and Irene shouting out there. Gromeko thought over his situation. The wounded arm needed a tourniquet, and he had to have help to get home.

H.C. stared straight into Gromeko's stockinged eyes. Terror spread over his bloody features; he struggled to get up.

Gromeko made his decision. He picked up the knife where he had dropped it and swept it across the ridiculous foulard at H.C.'s throat. H.C. gasped, "*Umah*, Mama," and slumped back, his eyes locked to Gromeko's until they no longer saw anything. For want of anything handier, Gromeko wiped the blade on H.C.'s trousers, feeling the plumpness of flesh, then pressed the blunt edge against his own thigh to close it.

The banging continued, or was it inside his head? The key must be somewhere in H.C.'s pockets. Gromeko fumbled in one pocket after another, finally pushed H.C. off the desk to look there, and heard metal tinkle to the floor. Wearily, Gromeko bent himself and picked up the key.

When he unlocked the door, Tanya screamed at the sight of him.

"It's just a stocking," Irene said impatiently. "Take it off, Grigory." She pushed Tanya inside and shut the door. Tanya blubbered, Grigory, you're hurt, let's go, let's get out, but Gromeko said, "Get the money first. You'll have to do it. In there. And find something to tie off this arm." He righted a chair and sank onto it.

Tanya darted about, hunting, brought back napkins, rolled one up and tied it too tight as Gromeko cursed; she worked it loose, tried again. Irene yanked the stocking off his head and elicited another curse as it chafed his pounding jaw.

"Is he dead?" Irene asked. But she was walking to the office already. Gromeko waited, panting and feeling a chill creeping through his limbs, the sweat on his face ice atop fire. Exclamations of disgust from Tanya, clanking of silver coins in the office; they returned, the silver knotted in napkins, the paper money stuffed inside their clothing. Between them they lifted Gromeko, a hand in each armpit.

The night was cold and darkness nearly total; the utility company no longer replaced broken street lights. The glowing end of a cigarette almost touched Tanya's face before she stopped with a shocked "Oh!"

They had all forgotten about H.C.'s armed guard.

"Was it a good haul?" he asked, his Shanghai tinged with the soft r's of a Northern accent. "You made me wait a long time." He stepped back a few paces. A faint shine came off the large service revolver he was pointing at Tanya's

middle. "What's that in the napkins? Must be
the silver. I will make a trade with you. You
give me the silver, and I let you go."

Gromeko croaked, "Give it to him."

Tanya and Irene handed him the bundles, which
he stowed inside his padded jacket.

"Very good. I see one of you got hurt. Since
it's quiet in there, I think H.C. must be dead.
So I'll have to go to the police, and they'll
tell me someone will come by in the morning. Or
maybe I won't report anything and just go home
myself. Nobody will care about H.C. except his
family. One thing is sure. I'm out of a job. I
used to be a policeman, you know, a good one,
too. I earned a commendation from the British."
He sucked on his cigarette, consuming it in one
draw, and tossed the butt away. "Go on, get out
of here."

They did, Irene and Tanya walking Gromeko as
fast as he could go. His weight fell more and
more on the hands under his armpits. Grigory,
Tanya kept saying, Grigory don't faint. Their
trek out of Chekiang Road, leaving Soochow Creek
at their backs, took ten minutes. On Peking
Road, a larger thoroughfare, they found a pedicab, whose driver refused to accept three riders. Irene thought she would be more useful to
Gromeko, but all the same let Tanya ride with
him. She did not want to have to worry about a
hysterical Tanya on her own. The pedicab started
off, Irene trotting after it. Nearing the corner
of Tibet Road she shouted at the driver to turn

left. At least, on Bubbling Well Road, she might catch a tram to Gromeko's street. And she did. Her tram passed the pedicab, an oblivious Gromeko in Tanya's embrace. When the tram stopped to pick up two passengers, the pedicab overtook Irene and turned the corner at Yates Road. She got off at the next stop and walked quickly to his flat and up the stairs. Out of breath and sweating heavily, she knew her superb physical condition had made this much possible.

Tanya was just helping him into a chair and babbling about fetching a doctor.

"No," Gromeko said. Its color bluish, half his face was swollen, the whiskers spread apart by the stretched skin. "Get the dentist. Over the European Lady Tailor shop."

When Tanya hesitated, confused, Gromeko said again, the words slurring, "Dentist. Dentist. Tell him to bring forceps."

"Go on, then," Irene said, flinging off her coat and rolling up her sleeves, "I'll see to him." She had no experience with wounds but supposed the first thing to do was to wash them. He had no bathroom attached to his room, only a sink with running water. She rummaged his cupboards, looking for alcohol. Ah, Saint Vladimir, she thought, Nothing but the usual sweet liqueurs. Live by anisette and die by same. Using a worn paring knife she found on the window sill, she cut off, sawing with difficulty, the sleeves of his sweater and shirt, then opened the sweater on his side. The holes in his arm were plugged with blood; more seeped out as she looked. The damage to his side was shallow. She dared not untie the tourniquet until she had done something for the wounds.

Gromeko panted shallowly, faster and faster it seemed since they first found him at H.C.'s place. There was a washcloth, not too fresh, draped on the edge of the sink. Irene rinsed it out with soap and used it to wipe the skin as close as she dared around the wounds. Then she opened a fresh bottle of anisette and poured it over the holes in his arm. She did the same to the torn skin in his side. The smell of licorice permeated her nostrils; his sweater and trousers were soaked with the cordial. What did you put on top of bullet holes? She opened drawers in the splintery pine dresser next to his bed and found useless things: tarnished brass buttons embossed with a sheaf of grain, a torn pocket flap of coarse gray wool material, a cartridge crusted with dirt, a yellowed photograph of a couple holding a child (Gromeko and his parents?), pencil stubs, shaving articles and—too late for her purpose—a pair of scissors, and a cracked leather belt with no tongue or buckle. Finally she found boxer shorts and cotton knit undershirts full of holes. She tore up an undershirt and placed strips around his arm. Over the strips she wrapped more of the undershirt and tucked the ends under. His arm was the same color as his face, perhaps bluer. The tourniquet had to be removed, at least loosened. She had an idea.

"Come to the bed, Grigory."

She pushed his two pillows against the white-washed wall—there was no headboard—and helped him from chair to bed. Wordless, panting, he sank onto the bare American army blanket. She pushed his upper body against the pillows.

"Now we put your arm up, like this."

She propped his wrist against the edge of the dresser, as high as his arm would go. At eye level, his big thumb looked huge. Cautiously, holding her breath, she undid the tourniquet. She watched the bandage. Slowly, blood darkened the cotton stuff; only a little overflowed and dripped. That was the main thing. As she went back for another undershirt to do his side, she heard Tanya running up the stairs.

Tanya burst in, looking wild, her hand clamped around the arm of an elderly Chinese with long white chin whiskers. "He's all right, don't worry," Irene said, to forestall more hysterics.

Gromeko said, his Shanghai harsh, "Pull out these teeth. Quick. Quick." When the dentist only stared, Gromeko roared, "DO MY TEETH, NOW!" and opened his mouth, pointing inside, panting and sweating, a picture of pain going mad so that the two women and the dentist all stood frozen. The reek of anisette enveloped everyone, candy gone berserk in the senses. Then Tanya pushed the dentist toward Gromeko.

With trembling hands, the old man opened his kit. "Injection?" he asked, pantomiming a syringe

as though Gromeko had not just spoken to him in
Chinese.

For answer, Gromeko grabbed the kit, flung
tools left and right, until he found the forceps. This he thrust into the dentist's hand,
growling "Do it do it."

Irene did not think there was that much
strength in the old man's arm, but of course he
was also practiced and moved by a desire to
leave as soon as possible. Within a few seconds,
a blackened molar with jagged bloody roots
emerged in the grip of the forceps.

"*Bokh*, God," whispered Tanya. "Poor Grigory."

Gromeko had not made a sound; he opened his
mouth again and pointed. Back went the forceps,
and soon a second molar was gone from him.

"Done," the dentist said. "Now I have to clean
the abscess. It's a big mess in there." He
uncapped a small bottle of alcohol and soaked a
wad of cotton wool.

Gromeko took it from him; he also appropriated
the bottle of alcohol. "You're finished here.
Leave more cotton. Pay you later." He pressed the
cotton against his gums and hissed with pain.

The dentist was already at the door and letting himself out.

"Better, Grigory?" asked Tanya. When he did not
answer, she said, "It's hot in here," and seemed
to realize she still had her coat on. When she
unbuttoned it, Grigory's good wool jacket fell
from its niche under her breasts to the floor. She
stooped to retrieve it. "I forgot all about it,"

she said. "What a night, eh, Irene?" When she and Irene had left the Race Club after their show they walked three blocks across Soochow Creek to an all-night noodle stand. The soup was good and hot, making them sleepy, but then they had to walk back to the club. To avoid running into the night guard they waited in an alley behind the club. Gromeko was to find them there. Instead, they heard the horrible racket of gunshots and furniture crashing inside.

"More than that. I've been thinking about tomorrow," Irene said. She was tying off the underwear bandage around his side.

"Well, yes. Without H.C. there won't be a club, or will there? Maybe someone in his family will manage it."

They had worked out a story in case H.C. suspected them of hiding Gromeko in their dressing room. They would accuse the bartenders. They could have been bribed to let him crouch under the counter; perhaps the waiters had let him stay in their smelly bathroom. And there was the toilet cubicle reserved for customers. One way or another the Filipino captain was going to be blamed.

"We have to act worried about our jobs, you know." With H.C. dead, Irene thought they had a better chance of escaping suspicion.

This annoyed Tanya. "Of course I know that. Sometimes you think too much of yourself, Irene." Gromeko finished mopping his gums and settled himself lower on the pillows. He reached across himself, fumbling with his good left arm, and opened a drawer of the dresser. He laid his wounded arm on the drawer. "How does your arm feel, Grigory?"

Eyes closed, Gromeko said, "Bugger the arm."

II

When Huell arrived at eleven o'clock, Maria was waiting for him outside the lane at Route Magy.

Huell was driving a civilian car, a squat Morris Minor that seemed to be missing a cylinder. The Morris was British-made and had a right-hand drive. "Do I look like a local?" he asked. "I keep trying, but all I do is make people suspicious."

"Is that why you asked me out? To help you look like a local?" This was the first time she had seen him in the light of day. The profile was hawkish, the eyes a brighter blue than the club's fluorescent lighting allowed. He wore his leather bomber jacket, so obviously American Army that he could not have been serious about camouflaging himself.

"Of course that's why," Huell said. "Why else would anyone want to be with you? Such foolish questions."

Maria smiled. She was in a somber mood. Daniele had dropped in last night at dinnertime, refused a meal, and afterward, walking up and down Route Magy at a heel-thudding pace, he kept saying, After four years, is this it? Can you say goodbye just like that? And she, Not just like that, Dani. It starts somewhere, doesn't it? It's time, can't you tell when it's time?

Huell was driving west. They had already left Frenchtown, the houses more and more separated by stretches of open field. The fields were cultivated; women with babies slung on their backs were hoeing and hauling water. For a change this rainy December the sun was out, though Maria was not yet ready to open her coat. The Chinese walking toward the city seemed to be wearing everything they owned on their backs, layers of cotton and quilted silk jackets piled one over the other. Grandmothers surrounded by pots and boxes rode on three-wheel carts hauled by men bent almost horizontal as they struggled to gain ground.

"Where are we going?"

"I have to go to Hungjao Airfield. There was no way I was willing to give up the day with you, so you're coming with me like it or not."

"Shall I tell you what I think? I know that you know important secrets, even if you deny it, but I don't know anything else about you. That's the real secret." They bumped over a rock, and something pinged under the hood. "Is this car going to make it? I thought Americans got the best of everything."

"Don't worry about the noises. Nigel, from whom I borrowed this car, says they never mean anything. About the other...." Huell glanced at her, "You've just opened a very profound, seldom discussed topic of the post-war period. Do you want to go on with it, or shall we save it until we get everything else under control?"

Instead of answering, she said, "I haven't decided on your name. I mean, should I call you Thaddeus? It sounds so formal. How old are you? What state are you from? Did you fight in the war?" I sound frantic, she thought, surprised at herself. She wanted to know everything. Was this attraction what they called a rebound?

There were no more sidewalks. Broken by few trees, the land was flat. The foot traffic grew denser, appearing to be pushed from behind by a canopy of dark sun-glanced clouds. The crops were both blue and green from heavy rains, which swelled a creek meandering on the Morris Minor's side of the road. A naked dead baby lay on the bank. Though rapidly passed, the image of the muddy body remained. It was the size of her old Shirley Temple doll, except that the exposed limbs were not pink.

Huell drove in silence for a minute. "In college they called me Thud, after I fell out of a window. My parents call me Thad. My grandmother calls me Tad. Take your pick."

"You fell out of a window?"

"Too much beer. The obligatory rite of passage. Do you have any idea how many stupid things young men are expected to do to earn respect from their peers? And all of it was for nothing, because the war came along, the real rite of passage."

"So you've been in combat, and you're still in the Army."

"Let's say I'm in it, again. Recruiters lie, you know? They tell you anything you want when you enlist, which I did just before I graduated from law school. I said I wanted to go to China, and they said sure, so they sent me to Europe."

These bits and pieces amounted to a day's work for Maria to absorb, yet they did not present the whole of Thaddeus Huell and only raised more questions. She decided she had asked enough.

The Morris Minor was the only motorized vehicle heading out of the city. Humanity poured toward Shanghai. The women were trussed like pack mules. They carried babies slung on backs, bundles in each hand and dangling from the crooks of their arms; many bowed forward against extra weights supported from bands on their foreheads.

Maria muttered under her breath and trained her look upon the sky. Sorry, murmured Huell, as though all of it were his fault. They began to pass stretches of walled estates, enclaves of wealthy foreigners, some of whom had lived here for decades. These were proud to call themselves China hands, their occupations fed off the commercial bounty that China offered. As her father's had. Was that opportunity what

Huell sought to reconnoiter when he asked to be sent here? A future China hand hoping for the good life?

The last time she had been in Hungjao was exactly one year and two weeks ago, when she had driven with a couple of Caltex employees to a party at the home of their departing boss. The man had actually wept, while his erstwhile employees made awkward and insincere remarks about keeping in touch. Until that moment, jollity reigned. Not once did anyone mention the stark fact that the guests were out of work. The drinking was hard, liquor virtually flowing like gasoline from a filling station. Two Chinese house boys, faces expressionless, circulated constantly with trays of bottles, soda and ice.

After three double highballs, Maria stood up and told her ex-boss, "Shut up. I don't want to hear about your troubles. Tell them to the Caltex president in his cushy office in Texas."

A hand was on her arm; one of the locals, an accountant, tried to pull her away from the shocked silence around her. Her former boss wore a blush, either whiskey-induced or caused by her. He would remember her, she did not care in what way. Back in Texas he would think twice about bragging of his exploits in "old" Shanghai.

Huell slowed the car. Ahead, gray sandbags were piled on either side of the road. Behind the barricade, tops of helmets moved; one emerged, a Nationalist soldier, his rifle pointed at the approaching vehicle.

"Of course you have your papers," Huell murmured, in a questioning tone. "A small matter I
meant to ask when I picked you up at your house.
It went clean out of my head when I saw you."

"Nobody goes out without them," Maria assured
him. His remark made her terribly happy. A giddy
sadness was perhaps more accurate. Poor Dani,
the specter at her feast. Ships and planes left
everyday. Trains were still running, untram-
meled, to the south. Soon he would be on his
way, she hoped.

As Huell came to a stop, she handed her pass
to him. He got out and began to speak Mandarin
to the soldier. Maria did not speak Kuo-hua,
Mandarin, but knew that his was not fluent. The
phrases lacked connectives, the sort of Chinese
some foreigners who had lived in China for years
spoke, I go out, Bring baby bottle, Pay him
check; the equivalent of pidgin English spoken
by Chinese.

An officer, wearing a shiny-billed cap, came
from behind the sandbags and scanned their
passes. The soldier lowered his rifle and peered
into the car at Maria. In Shanghai, the officer
said, "The American likes his comforts while he
goes around on business." The soldier laughed
deferentially.

Maria opened the door and, motions leisurely
and graceful, exited from the Morris Minor.

Huell said, "I didn't quite get that."

Arm resting on the top of the car, she looked
first into the eyes of the officer, then at the

soldier—a mere flicker for him. "I guess your mother would know all about things like that," she said to the officer. For a moment or two, Maria's hazel eyes engaged his hot black ones, before smoothly she reinserted herself in the car.

The soldier did the wisest thing, retreating from his superior. He went behind the barricade. The officer was silent. Huell got in, slammed the door, and drove on.

"I think I got it," he said. "You handled that very well. Does this sort of thing happen often?"

"I don't know how often is often to you. There are different ways people like to let you know they think you're inferior. A British woman ordered me to get out of her way on the side-walk, once. She was huge, with a red face and pop eyes. I was fifteen, I think. I thought she was the most frightening thing I'd ever seen."

The concrete buildings of the airfield ahead were painted in camouflage patches of olive-tan-yellow; an array of antennae bristled on the roof. Two large airplanes painted olive drab were parked on the skimpy grass beside the run-way. A man holding flags stood on the strip, watching the sky to the south.

"The glory days of colonialism, gone for good with India," Huell said. "The French are going to lose theirs in Southeast Asia. They sure have made some beautiful children, though. They would give anybody like that woman an inferiority complex."

"Is that what it was? Annam," she said, using the Chinese name for Vietnam, "is tiny, compared to China, but they are a tough people. We have lots of Annamese in Shanghai. They won't speak French."

"But you speak English," Huell said. He stopped at the gate, handed over their passes once more, and waited, fingers tapping the steering wheel, as the Nationalist guard scrutinized the papers. They were returned and Huell was waved on. He drove to the administration building and parked under the lone tree, a scruffy acacia. Turning to her, he said, "I really apologize for dragging you out here. Other than that, I'm glad I did it."

It's much nicer seeing him straight on, Maria thought. He had a lean face and a marvelous complexion, fine-grained as a girl's. She was not yet used to being gazed at by those blue eyes.

Perversely, she said, "Am I supposed to say, touche?"

He looked perplexed. "About what? Oh, back when I said something about your speaking English? It's a habit of mine, pointing disparities out. I was trained as a lawyer," he said, with discernible wryness. "That makes the tedious side of a person even more obvious. I'll only be gone ten minutes, maybe fifteen." He reached behind his seat and lifted a briefcase from the floor. He left the car and walking fast entered the building. The windows were opaque glass, and behind them hung wooden venetian blinds to ward off the sun in the summer. A Nationalist guard at the entrance watched her suspiciously.

Yes, I am a spy, Maria said without moving her lips, but she turned her face toward the field downwind of the administration building. A farmer and his wife labored, their figures hunched and slow, their methods both ancient and ingenious. The stripped-down bicycle he pedaled in place drove a waterwheel, a cumbersome wooden device that scooped water out of a homemade ditch and sent it along homemade irrigation channels. Enduring as the broad field at her back, the wife chopped with a short-handled mattock to deepen the channels. They paid no attention to the migrating hordes on the road, nor did they look up as a plane approached rapidly and swept low, roaring over their heads, to put down its wheels on the runway. Another military aircraft, perhaps one of General Claire Chennault's Flying Tigers of the war, painted over in olive drab. A truck painted the same color drove onto the field.

The Nationalist guard was still watching Maria. She opened the car door and got out. She stretched, filling her lungs with country air alloyed with the human ordure fertilizing the crops, and began to stroll back and forth near the car. There was no need to look directly at the soldier to realize his stance had stiffened.

Give the poor man a respite.

Wishing Huell would hurry back, she got back in the car. A minute passed during which she felt displaced; the sensation was quite physical, as though a giant hand had dropped her in this spot at random. Everything she knew, everyone in her life, receded from familiarity. It was because of being in the open, she thought. The smell of panic in the closeness of the city was different from the same thing in the country.

The car door opening startled her. Huell flung his briefcase behind his seat and got in, saying with relief, "Duty done. Let's hit the road." His presence brought a wind with it, a flurry of legs and arms, a whiff of leather, his face and features that she hadn't yet had time to absorb. "Are you all right?" he asked, when she said nothing.

"Yes," was all she could say for the moment. She didn't know him. She would have to start all over again.

Huell edged the car onto the road, calling out Sorry, excuse me, sorry, to the refugees. "Do you want us to give anyone a ride?" he asked.

Maria said, helplessly, "Which ones? They come in groups." But she called, through the window, "We can take two or three," repeating herself as Huell drove slowly on the wrong side of the road. There was no correct side going toward Shanghai, only where he found a hole to pass through. A young man, a hale specimen, came to her side, smiling and saying "*Hsieh, hsieh*, Thank you.

Maria said, "We have a customer."

Huell scrutinized the young man, taking care to inspect his footwear, and said flatly, "No, I don't think so."

"Why not?"

He did not stop, and Maria again asked him why not. She too preferred to take the old ones, but they already had rides on the carts, perched on their family quilts.

"I don't want him at my back," Huell said. "I'd have to body search him first. He could be a Red soldier. Those were boots on his feet. They may not be army, but I'm taking no chances."

Maria hadn't thought of that. "Then I'll talk straight to the women with babies.

"We can take two women with babies, two women with babies, two women with babies," she called.

A woman not yet thirty turned her exhausted face to her man, who might have said, Yes, go, or who, judging by his quizzical expression, might have said, How will we find each other in the city? In either case the woman did not bother to answer Maria but plodded onward.

Maria rolled up her window. "It was nice of you to think of it, anyway."

"I wasn't being nice, exactly. Just trying to justify my next officer's club steak dinner."

They did not speak again until Huell reached the edge of the city, where he swung right, detouring south to Avenue Petain. As they drove up the wide, tree-fringed boulevard, passing the green lawn of the Shanghai American School, Maria relaxed the precise placement of her feet on the floorboards. Huell's shoulders dropped, and he settled back in the seat. They agreed lunch (Huell said he liked hearing her call it "tiffin") was the ticket, and Maria decided to take him to a good restaurant on Nanking Road, the Dah Ning.

The Dah Ning had seen more prosperous days, yet still starched its napery and set a table with fine porcelain. They sat at a window table on the second floor. Maria ordered for both, a first course of white chicken to be dipped in sauce, then a steamed yellow fish, and greens.

"I would have chosen eggplant, but are you one of those....?" Little things to discover. Dani liked it roasted, recoiled from it cooked any other way. She wondered if he had dropped in at Route Magy today. No one knew about Huell, but Nola had noticed the care with which she dressed. There's one hair hanging down at the back, she teased. You look a terrible mess. Better pin it up.

"You did right. I hate eggplant. I'm suspicious of anyone who doesn't." He asked, "I need a beer badly, whether or not it goes with what you ordered. Am I a barbarian? I need something cool in my throat." He looked down at the glass-muffled pandemonium on Nanking Road, his gaze unfocused. "Those people may have walked from Nanking. I was there to see them leave. They might as well have stayed. Chiang or Mao, China will get them."

Maria watched him, discovering that his eyebrows were on the nascent edge of shagginess. He would be a hawk-nosed old man with great brushes over piercing blue eyes. Allowed to grow, his fair hair would be unruly, but always he would keep that marvelous complexion.

Soft-voiced, musing, Huell said, "He had opinions about everything, you know—I'm talking about General Stilwell—he despised the bureaucrat types in the British army, ditto the Indian army, he liked the French, but he said something about Chiang Kai-shek that has stuck in my mind. 'He's a vacillating tricky undependable old scoundrel who never keeps his word.' That was old Vinegar Joe, he didn't survive his retreat out of Burma to keep his mouth shut about fools and snakes. But General Claire Chennault said, 'The Generalissimo is one of the two or three greatest military and political leaders in the world today. He has never broken a commitment or promise made to me.' Take your pick."

"General Chennault is married to a Chinese," Maria said. "His Flying Tigers were Chiang's pet American volunteers in his war with the Japanese. The American Volunteer Group was terribly glamorous in China before Pearl Harbor. Did you ever see 'Flying Tigers'? John Wayne helped Chiang Kai-shek more than he knew with that film of his. My father agrees with Stilwell. Chiang and his family and friends cleaned out the till. And they are going to get away with it."

Speedily delivered, the beer, a liter bottle, was uncapped. The waiter poured from on high, achieving a foaming head in each glass four inches deep.

Huell sighed. "He should have given us straws, too. Do you have both parents? Can I meet them? Have you got a big family?"

Maria thought, I have a lover whose heart I have broken. Ask me about that.

Huell reached over and plucked her hand from where it rested against her cheek.

"You've been looking sad all day when you thought I wasn't looking," he said. "Maybe I should have picked you up on my way back from Hungjao. Nasty sights on that road. Next time, we're going to stay on the Bund in some rich, artificial lounge without a view."

A wiry hand, with strong fingers.

"Feels good," Huell said. "No serious rings on these pretty fingers."

"You said you were trained to be a lawyer."

"I wish I hadn't told you that. I can tell it's going to come back and haunt me every time I try to dig information out of you." He sighed. "After I mustered out I went back to law school. I was a real lawyer for about three days—my father couldn't be in court so he sent me. It was a personal injury case. I won it. My father said he couldn't have done better, that he'd be giving me more of the same if I wanted it. I'd been clerking for him while studying for the bar exam, so working as a lawyer was the next logical step. That night I went to him and asked if I could take a long leave of absence, like for two years. I hated to tell him. It was like putting out a light."

"You must have been thinking about that leave for a long time. How did you get the army to do it right the second time?"

"I wrote my Congressman, then collected the hardware the army handed out, not forgetting the Good Conduct Medal, and went to see the director of the Asian Affairs Desk in Washington. I showed off my Mandarin—don't laugh—he thought I was fluent as the devil until the expert he called in told him I was at the level of Foreign Languages 101. I told the director I had two years to give the Army in Peking or Nanking, where I knew the U.S. had a significant presence. I can't believe how I lectured him, but I was fresh out of winning my first court case and that's my only excuse. Instead of telling me to go back to kindergarten, he let me sound off about what we could all expect in the conflict with Mao. Something new was coming around the bend, I told him, something old, really—you just needed to read up on Russian history to figure out what was going to happen when Mao got into power. I didn't tell him the original China was what I wanted to see before the big change.

"They must have needed to recruit some bodies, with or without smart mouths, because the Army took me back."

"So you came to China. The stink, the poverty, the high and the low? What's so wonderful about that?"

He shook his head. "The whole thing awed me. The Mongol conquest of China started by Genghis Khan and finished by his grandson in the thirteenth century. I did a paper on Kublai Khan in college titled 'Cult Of Heaven.' Amazing thing was the Mongols never forced the Chinese to adopt their religion. I thought that was so smart. Think of the waste of energy trying to convert eighty million people to your religion. You'd never get anything else done if you were their ruler. The Christian missionaries set out to convert no less than seven hundred million! And they'll be set back to zero after Mao takes over. So I sat there working on my paper, thinking about huge territories and feudal warlords, the intelligence, cruelty and the—"

"Romance," said Maria. "Did you really hate being a lawyer that much? I notice you said Peking and not Peiping. Peking has the old, glorious sound of romance, doesn't it?" A momentary illusion, she knew, but she felt older than Huell. He was so open about his infatuation with the idea of China. But she shouldn't have interrupted him; Huell must not have talked like this to many people, if any. His parents, certainly, wouldn't have understood. To come back safe from one war and volunteer for more, possibly hazardous service?

He had relinquished her hand and was drinking his beer, perhaps annoyed with her. He was right; she sounded patronizing. She smiled.

"You're crazy, you have brains, but the wrong ones for lawyering. Is that better? That's what I meant."

"A whole lot better. Let's dig in, I could eat the plate and tablecloth. Wonder what makes our waiter think I can't handle chopsticks?" But he used knife and fork to tackle the white chicken. "You eat so daintily. How do you strip the meat off the bone? In goes the package, out comes just the bone."

"After all your research on China, you don't know our big secret?"

"Here it comes," he said, resigned to being tweaked. Controlled, good-natured, the minor essences of Huell revealed. "Okay, what is this big secret?"

"Chinese teeth," Maria all but whispered, "are prehensile."

Huell dropped her off at Route Magy at about five o'clock. Again she did not ask him in. She waited until the Morris Minor was out of sight, then walked to Tifeng Road to Dani's rooming house.

Foreign Languages 101. The meaning had come clear some time later, while he told her more about his resistance to charting his academic courses toward a career in law. He took her comprehension of purely American terms for granted,

not knowing that she learned as she listened. He
was twenty-nine years old, she also learned. He
had been in the beachhead invasion at Anzio. His
unit was the 15th Infantry Regiment of the 7th
Infantry   Division,   commanded   by   General
Stilwell. The 15th had a long, honorable history, Huell told her. It was stationed in China
after the 1911 revolution, when the emperor Pu-
yi was retired and Sun Yat-sen became China's
first president. The Regiment's motto was "Can
Do," derived from Chinese pidgin. Huell idolized
Stilwell.

Reluctant to talk about his combat experiences
in Europe, he showed her a photograph of his
family, parents, younger brother, and grandmother. The Virginia sun shone brilliantly on
the smiling Huells, standing in front of their
home. His parents were primly clad, he in a
business suit, she in skirt and long-sleeved
blouse. His brother slouched a bit, not quite
turning away as he smiled for the camera.
Huell's grandmother wore a blue dress and shoes
that seemed to have little heels; her hand was
caught in the act of waving to him. Huell resembled his father. There were two more grandpar-
ents, cousins, and an uncle and aunt, Huell
said, in the Midwest. They had lost track of
other relatives. Maria thought of the house in
the snapshot. It was white clapboard, seemed
large from its most visible portion, a broad
door with brass knocker. Flagstones and shrubs.
Straight curtains in the window, a large lamp.

Of his family she told him, Very nice (meaning how normal they look). There was a dog at his brother's feet, an elderly black Labrador. Rover? Fido? Marco Polo, Huell said. The unlucky pup came to them when Marco Polo's adventures cast the first germ in Huell's brain.

She walked more slowly, aware that she did not want to arrive at Dani's. The building in which he lived was once a three-story family home owned by a Russian. Unlike Maria's father, Emma the landlady collected a fair income in rents. Emma's own apartment was filled with treasure; she owned works of art both inherited and purchased. They would be valuable in any regime, she often told Daniele; she would always live decently by trading on her fine things. Maria suspected none of it would leave her possession. Russians clung to things, giving them up only when they were starving. The entrance had the distinction of a bit of landscaping, as well. A broad-leaf laurel flanked the low step.

Long ago Maria was given a key to the front door; when she entered, Emma was talking on the telephone at the little table by the stairs. She waved, and Emma nodded. She flirted with Daniele, was inclined to offer him physical solace that he tactfully spurned. He was engaged, he told her one night in the first month of his occupancy, Maria was the jealous type. You told her what? Maria shrieked. The Contis had recently sold their Hongkew house; until then he had occupied two rooms in its spacious attic.

She went up the polished stairs, familiar as her own shabby ones. Except for Emma's loud accents on the telephone, the house was silent. A hooked rug, made by her devoted hands, sat before Dani's door, a good solid piece of Chinese mahogany.

Maria had a key, but it seemed wrong to use it now. She raised her hand and knocked.

12

Maria waited a minute before she knocked again. She called, "Dani?" If he wasn't in, she would leave him a note and go home. She used her key.

The shutters were partly closed; she caught the smell before she made out his figure in the deep rattan chair. "Oh, Dani," she whispered. She knelt at his knee, trying to read his face, but the light was poor. She got up, not touching him (already remembering he was lifeless, no longer Dani!) and went to the window and opened it; the shutters she flung out all the way. The action recalled another like it, and she remembered Tasha in the room over the bar.

She charged her lungs with three deep breaths before she turned back to the turbid odors of death. The coming evening's dusk equaled the gloom inside, but it would have to do; she could not bear an electric light glaring upon the forlorn flesh of Dani.

Kneeling again, she laid her arm on his knee. The bullet had entered at his right temple.

There was no exit wound, unless it was at the back. She did not look. A small caliber pistol lay on the floor, beneath the chair; his dangling right arm seemed to point to it. He sat low, tilted to the left, his head fallen slightly forward.

I am very tired, his bowed head seemed to say, his gaze locked to his thighs. Let me sleep.

Their faces were level. Maria smoothed a lock of his black hair, absently noting his skin was clammy. She could not tell if his body had stiffened, and did not, really, care to know. Blood turned blackish, she also noted. But she knew that, from the bombings in the war. First there were the air raid warning sirens, rising and falling, rising and falling. The Americans came overhead in waves, droning with a ferocity that shook one's heart. Armageddon, Dani said once, speaking low to himself, holding Maria close under the dining table.

"Remember Nola's peanut snacks under that table, and her *Bobbsey Twins* books?" Maria asked Dani's dead face, straightening his shirt collar. He had put on a fresh shirt, tied a Windsor knot so meticulous that a vertical groove dimpled the necktie below the knot. His shoes were glossy, their laces looped in precise lengths. She found her handkerchief and scrubbed away the drool from the corner of his mouth. Then she placed her fingers on his lids and closed his eyes. With that, he was truly gone. "I have to leave you for a while. We won't be together anymore, afterward.

Goodbye, Dani." She kissed his cheek. The cool flesh did not yield.

Maria rose to her feet and went downstairs to the landlady's apartment. She knocked, calling, "Emma, it's me, Maria."

Emma's heels thumped, muffled, on her nice Chinese carpet. Evidently she had been redoing her hair; the "rat" plumping up her pompadour was half-pinned, brown locks seeded with gray tumbled about her shoulders. "Yes, Maria? What is it?" She put a hand to her mouth, her slightly veined eyes big. "You are so strange. Something happened...Daniele?"

On the far side of Emma's living room wall hung a Russian icon, the holy figures embellished with much gilt. Their nimbuses glowed with gold leaf. Maria stared at it. "I am very sorry, Emma. I hope they don't disrupt your house too much."

"Who, Marusha? Who will disrupt the house?" She gave Maria's arm a little shake.

"Yes, it's Daniele. He's dead."

"Ayyy...God, God." Tears rushed to her eyes. She fell against the doorjamb, sobbing; her "rat" dangled by a pin over her forehead.

"He shot himself. I am so sorry, Emma," Maria said again. "I have to go and notify the police."

"But I didn't hear anything! He must have done it this morning when I went out."

"I couldn't say, Emma. I am so sorry."

"Poor Daniele. He was a lovely, lovely man." Emma stopped crying and looked at Maria with hostility. In her youth, she often declared, she

had been a beauty; the flame of that girl blazed
at Maria, "Why did you treat him so bad?
Sometimes he was so down, you must have quar-
reled with him. He was too good." Hands on hips,
"rat" jiggling, she shouted, "I would have married him if he'd asked me. Now look at what
you've done! And how am I going to rent that
room again? Everyone will talk about it. Don't
turn away from me, you!"

Maria didn't answer; she walked to the front
door and let herself out.

Raindrops pattered on the broad-leafed laurel
shading Emma's window. She had gone half a block
before she remembered that Emma had a telephone.
A call to the police might have been sufficient,
though one never knew anymore. She kept walking.
The rain thickened, slapping her cheeks and
sliding coldly down her neck. A Chinese man
walking past under an umbrella muttered, "Crazy
woman." She walked toward the station house on
Avenue Petain. She had passed it today, with
Huell, and hadn't given it a glance.

The gate to the station house was shut, the
small courtyard deserted. On the other side, a
soldier wearing a rubber poncho leaned against
it. She pushed at the gate, which would not give.

"What do you want?" The soldier turned and
peered at her through the bars.

"I have to report a death. Can I come in?"

"What for? There's nobody here. I'm not likely
to stay here much longer, myself."

"But somebody died," Maria said. "I must see a police officer."

The soldier shifted his rifle, dropped it with a clatter on the cobblestones and cursed. He was a southerner who spoke bad Shanghai. "Thousands die in the city every hour. What's special about your death?"

My death, Maria thought. "This person was shot. He shot himself."

"I see." He looked closer at her. "Maybe you shot him. Do you want to turn yourself in?" He chuckled. "Too bad, *hsiao-tzia*, nobody's home. I'd arrest you if that was my job. Why don't you go to a funeral home, then? There is a cheap one on Tifeng Road. All it takes is money, never mind the cops."

Maria was already walking away from the gate. The soldier shouted, "Do you want me to handle it? I'll do it for five Mexican dollars."

She walked along Avenue Petain until she met a solitary rickshaw, its canopy pulled up against the rain. The oilcloth panel was clipped on, but she could see through the gap that the rickshaw was empty. "Avenue Haig," she said, and without discussing price climbed in. The oilcloth panel closing her in made her think of coffins. She pushed aside the panel a few inches, ignoring the rain hitting her, and looked at the living, laboring figure of the rickshaw coolie. She watched his wide-brimmed straw hat and straw cape and naked, trotting muddy legs all the way to Avenue Haig.

Everything about the building was the same. The mock Greek columns bracing the double doors of the Greater Shanghai Funeral Home needed paint; perhaps they already did when she worked here briefly, after Caltex let her go. Sleepless in her quarters above the embalming rooms, she tried to find solace in her regular weekly paychecks. The red bulb by the telephone possessed her, shone through her eyelids. It was meant to be a convenience, the red bulb, so she could locate the telephone in the dark without switching on the light immediately. Calls frequently came in the night. Maria's job was to send out the driver and wake up the embalmer; in the humid Shanghai summer bodies could not wait until the morning. Cries over the telephone wire by night; tortured widows clutching at Maria by day. She gave her notice at the end of a month.

Mr. Heller answered the doorbell. He did not recognize her at first. "What can I do for you?"

When she gave her name, Maria knew he was wondering if he should fetch his wife; Mrs. Heller was skilled in dealing with the difficult living, while Mr. Heller exercised his skills on the speechless dead.

"I need your services, for a friend."

"Oh, I see." Heller opened the door. "I am very sorry," he said. "Come in and rest. Clara will bring you a cup of tea."

He invited her into his office, where once she had sat listening to familial storms and applying the occasional smelling salts. Now she heard herself, explaining, her voice impersonal with name, address, circumstance of death.

"Ordinarily," Mr. Heller said, his German origins strong within the irksome syllables of the word, "you should go to the police first."

"Ordinarily. Yes."

"That is no problem these days. I will send Ling out. You remember Ling?"

Was she supposed to smile because she recollected Ling? "Yes. Will you ask them to be quiet and not upset the landlady?"

"Do not worry, Ling knows what to do. What we must do now is select a coffin. What kind of service do you wish? If you need to think these things over, there is no hurry."

No. In the winter there was time. No one need hurry out there to collect Dani, but that was not what Heller meant. He meant that Dani could lie on a slab here until she made up her mind about the coffin and a service. There was a padlocked shed in the back yard, stacked with coffins. The Chinese consulted horoscopes for a propitious day of the month for burying their dead. There was that luxury in the winter.

She realized Heller had got up and was standing by her, patting her shoulder, murmuring, "Now, now, relax, Maria. Where is Clara? I am sure she knows someone is here. Take your coat off, rest, rest." He hurried out, a man in need of his capable wife.

Maria lurched to her feet. She did not want Clara Heller fussing over her. "Mr. Heller, I will come back tomorrow to talk about the details. Just have Ling go out there. Thank you. Goodbye."

She noticed the rain had stopped. Her shoes squished, her coat felt heavy and cold on her shoulders. She rode home in a pedicab.

Dinner was on the table, and there were two place settings empty and waiting. "Take off your shoes at once and dry your hair and feet," Ming Chu said, and then she saw Maria's face. She did not speak, merely waited. This was so like her mother, Maria thought. She did not ask useless questions, which would get answered in time. There was first the need to brace herself for the inevitable.

Nola said, "The front of your hair is flat as a plate," then she, too, was silent.

Wearily, Maria sat down, shed her shoes, and began on her coat. "It's Dani," she said. "He's dead."

"*Madonna*," her father said, reverting to Italian as he always did in moments of severe emotion. Her mother flinched, but still she waited. Abruptly, Poldo rose and went to the sideboard, found the *Shanghai Evening Post and Mercury*, and sat down again and picked up one of Maria's shoes. The only sound was the crumpling of newspaper as he stuffed it in.

Nola silently cried. She's too young to hear these things, Maria thought. But she'd been too young for everything for years. "He shot himself." Her mother sighed, and at last moved to fetch towels.

It was very good to be ministered to, her father massaging her feet while her mother toweled her hair. They helped her gain minutes in which she did not have to deal with the hard core of pain, like an apricot pit, which had formed in the center of her breast. The seed was planted, ready to sprout. If she was clever, she would not let it get big enough to suffocate her.

Amah entered with a pot of tea, frowned with misgiving, and was reassured by Ming Chu, "Nothing terrible, don't worry." Maria looked at her mother. Cornered by necessity, Ming Chu rated tragedies by their starkest immediacy to her family. Poor Dani was relegated outside that circle. I must try to see it her way, Maria thought. But she knew that was impossible.

"Is there something I can do for you?" Poldo asked. "Things to do, arrangements…?"

"All done, for today. But you could come with me tomorrow, Daddy. Thank you for not asking questions," she said to her father's lowered face and her mother's still one. "We'll talk about it tomorrow, all right?" She got up and padded to the curtains dividing her bedroom from the dining room. "I have to change and get off; I'm already late."

"But you must eat your dinner first," Ming Chu said. "At least drink some hot tea. Maria, I wish you would go to bed. I will bring you the tea and a hot water bottle for your feet."

"I have to go, Mama. They need me. There are no holidays except for...." Except for the dead. She brushed aside the curtains roughly. She should have telephoned Emma to tell her to expect Ling. Now it was too late. Ling and his henchman would have collected Dani (the body, not Dani) and gone their way, back to the Greater Shanghai Funeral Home.

The curtains parted and Nola came in, her eyes red and still tearing. "Was it because of what I did?" she asked.

Maria unzipped her dress and pulled it over her head; it snagged on her hairpins. "Help me, will you?" she said, caught within its folds. Small fingers tugged, tickled in her hair; their touch in her blindness stirred the apricot pit embedded in her breast and nearly broke her open. "What are you talking about? What would you have to do with it?"

Released, the dress slipped from her shoulders. She flung it on the bed. Nola picked it up and gave it a shake; this was the other good dress Maria owned. "You know," she said. "What I made you do at St. Columban's. Daniele must have been mad because maybe, maybe you didn't like him anymore. Was it my fault?" She sat on the bed, holding the dress draped down her front to keep it from wrinkling. At least ten sizes too large, the dress hung over her legs to the floor.

"It's nothing to do with you, at all," Maria said. She dressed rapidly, brushed her damp hair, assessed its limp mantling of her shoulders and decided to leave it down. "I've got to rush, but when I get home and you're not sleeping we'll talk some more. I promise." She had picked up a bit of energy at the prospect of seeing Galia. Her friend was exactly the person for this sort of thing; already Maria felt cheered at the prospect of walking into the club and slipping on the guise of hostess. For a few hours she would know what was expected of her. "Stay with Mama, or read one of your books, but don't think too much. 'Bye now," she told Nola, whose shoulders drooped like those of a small tired adult.

Ming Chu was waiting at the dining table, a cup of steaming tea in her hand. Seeing her mother's implacable expression, Maria obediently accepted the tea and drank it standing up. Strong, heavily sugared, enriched with precious evaporated milk, this brew was one of Ming Chu's special restoratives; she had others, much less palatable ones involving roots and tree bark from the herbalist's shop on Tifeng Road. This tastes like tiger claws, Maria would say, her throat closing up, I'd rather have my stomache ache.

It was raining again. For the third time that day she ignored her budget and took a pedicab instead of the tram. She was hidden behind the oilcloth like a doll in a box, she thought. She

didn't have to act or say anything, and that was
marvelous. But then she began to feel smothered.
It was so dark under the oilcloth. The pedicab
tilted upward; she peeked out and saw the driver
was laboring over Garden Bridge. Broadway
Mansions was visible; all sixteen floors were
lighted. Was Huell up there? Don't let him drop
in tonight, she thought. Don't.

As soon as she walked in, Galia said,
"Marusha, you are smiling like a crazy woman.
And you have lipstick on your teeth."

"I like it there," Maria said. "I wonder how
many of these men are going to notice my mouth. Of
course they'd know if I had my bra on backwards."

Zoya tittered. She had dark patches under her
eyes and swollen lids. Her nonromance with
Amalia's brother seemed to be depressing her
more and more. Well, don't marry him in church,
then, Galia told her. Once you get to Lisbon you
can get free and go anywhere you like as a
Portuguese citizen.

"You should marry an Italian for his passport,"
Maria told Zoya. "Italians have some redeeming
virtues, like some of them dying young."

Both women stared, Galia's study particularly
intent.

"Dani died today," Maria said. "Or maybe it
was last night. He shot himself." There.

Galia said, "Come in the back room."

"I certainly won't. There's work to do here."
Amalia came up, ordered three gin-and-tonics,
and Maria set to making them up. "Marusha," said

Galia. She made Maria look at her. Those dark eyes were wells of epic sorrows. "I know you didn't love him. He's been sick in the head for a long time, you know."

"Don't say that. He loved me. I didn't know how to stop it the right way. I could have been kinder."

"Perhaps. But you outgrew him, and he stayed the same and got narrower and hung onto you. Do you want the truth? You should have sent him away years ago, before you discovered how nice it was to have a steady boyfriend."

"All right, Galia. Thank you. We're out of ice again. I wish we could buy a new fridge."

"Don't let him win, Marusha."

"You didn't see him. He was the saddest thing I've ever seen. I will never forget it until I die."

"Maybe he hoped for that," Galia said. "Also, it's quite possible he didn't. You will never know. You didn't mention a note."

"I didn't look. I wonder if I should write his wife? A sort of formal letter from an acquaintance offering condolences, with lies about the important work he was doing here. Do you know I have no idea what he has been telling her, if they even wrote to each other. I don't know how old his girls are. I guess he was considerate not to mention these trifles to me."

"He kept it his business, Marusha. As he should have."

"Yes. Well, we're about to go a complete circle, aren't we? Let's do some work around here."

Nola mumbled, "I'm awake," as Maria slipped
into bed.

"No you're not. You were grizzling like an old
bear when I came in." The wind squeezing through
the window cracks was chilling her whole head;
tomorrow she would stuff paper in the window
cracks. Bones, relax. Hands, lie open and loose.
Brain, go to sleep.

"You said you would talk to me when you got
home."

She remembered telling Nola that; she couldn't
remember what they were supposed to talk about.
Nola crying, Nola worrying about Dani. "It wasn't
your fault," she said. "You couldn't have made me
go to confession in a hundred years if I wasn't
ready to do it."

"You mean, when you promised to go, you were
ready, already?"

Was she? "I must have been. I don't know."

"You made a promise you maybe weren't going to
keep?"

"My God, what is this. Are you going to be a
lawyer one day?" Put her together with Huell, the
lawyer who didn't want to be one. The world was
full of people who followed paths they didn't
really want.

Nola persisted, "Were you?"

"Was I what? Never mind, I know what you're
drilling at me for. And keep your voice down,

you'll wake them up next door. As far as I can tell," she said, picking her words to make them come out exactly right for Nola and herself, "I must have been ready to stop with Dani, or I would have said no when you asked me to promise to go to confession."

Nola was quiet, digesting this, while chilly gusts from the windows bored into Maria's ear. She pulled the eiderdown quilt half over her head, then sat up and felt with her hand for the stack of books on the spindly side table. One by one she laid them in a row on the window sill. The task was simple, she did not have to get out of bed to do it; when one slept in a cubicle everything was within arm's length.

"People are funny," Nola said, at last. "I suppose I'm going to be the same." She turned over on her stomach and fell asleep.

Kids are heartless, Maria thought. Conscience cleared, Dani dismissed, her sister slept.

Her eyes kept fluttering open; eventually she understood she was looking for the red night light in her old room at the Greater Shanghai Funeral Home.

After breakfast, having slipped in and out of a trancelike state that passed for sleep, Maria went accompanied by her father to the funeral home. Mrs. Heller was present and on duty. Her blond hair was the same as Maria remembered it, marcelled in a pre-war style that never varied in length or number of waves. Prettily, legs

crossed and slender foot pointed, she deferred
to Poldo Conti, though it was obvious that it
was Maria who would make the decisions concerning coffins and service. Mrs. Heller said the
Italian consulate had to be notified before burial arrangements were made. One never knew, she
said to Poldo with an inclusory glance at Maria,
whether the deceased filed instructions per-
taining to the disposal of their remains.

Before coming here, Poldo had mentioned going
to the consulate afterward; neither had thought
there might be a necessity to go before.

"Then we should go there now," Poldo said.
"But first, we had better go to his room and
find what documents he had. We should have done
that before we even came here."

They took a pedicab back to Route Magy, neither saying much on the ride. Poldo kept clearing his throat and brushing his hand over his
scalp. He will miss Dani, she thought. Her
father had had no other male friend.

Maria used her key to enter the building; as
they entered, Emma opened her apartment door and
stared at Poldo.

"Emma, this is my father, Leopoldo Conti,"
Maria said. She realized she did not know if
Emma was a miss or a Mrs. She settled on intro-
ducing her simply as Emma Gavriloff, owner of
the building. Emma seemed to recollect her manners and gave him her hand to shake. "It was
terrible," she told Poldo, ignoring Maria. "I
screamed when I saw him. They brought him down

covered with a sheet, but he wasn't lying straight on the stretcher. One of my other tenants nearly fainted. This house will never be the same again." She said directly to Maria, "What do you want here?"

"I have to find some documents."

"What gives you the right? I can do that for him. I think I was his real family, in the end." Her eyes reddened, and she sobbed, her head inclined as though searching a resting place on Poldo's shoulder, "I really cared. She didn't."

Maria turned and started up the stairs, "Come on, Daddy."

He murmured, "Excuse me," and followed.

Emma darted after them, screaming, "The room is not rented to you! You may not go in!"

On a sudden thought, Maria turned and looked down at her. "Did you go in? Answer me, did you go inside his room?"

Emma said coldly, "You forget who owns this house."

"Did you touch anything?"

"How dare you!"

"Did you?" Maria turned fully and descended the stairs, past her father, to stand in front of Emma. She felt her rage mount. The thought of Emma creeping into Dani's room, touching and spying among his belongings, was not to be borne. Hardly breathing, she stared at the object that was Emma.

"I tidied up a bit, complain all you like."
Her mouth a sullen crease, Emma marched into her
apartment and shut the door.

Daniele's door was locked, and Maria fumbled
through her purse, then her pockets for the key.
She had to look through her purse again. Her
father's arm around her shoulders, intended to
comfort, felt like a huge weight. At last she
found it, at the bottom of her purse beneath her
lipstick and comb.

The smell of Jeyes' Fluid assaulted their nostrils. Emma must have used buckets of it, adul-
terated by almost no water. From baseboard to
cornice, the coal-tar, membrane-withering reek
of the disinfectant filled the room. "My God, my
God," Poldo gasped. He took six strides to the
window and flung it open. Both of them stood
there for a minute, gasping for air, before
Maria looked back into the room. Emma's hand had
been into Dani's possessions. Dani had never
stacked his books and papers that neatly.

"Why don't you leave me to this," Poldo said.
He wiped watery eyes with a handkerchief. The
long hairs in his eyebrows curled in disarray.
"I'm sure it won't take long to find his passport, and then I'll take it to the consulate.
You don't have to go there at all. Go stand outside, Maria. I mean it."

Maria obeyed, since he was already opening
drawers and rummaging through the contents of
each one. She leaned against the wall and looked

down the stairs. Emma's door was not visible but no sound came from there.

Dani's pistol had not been under the chair. Of course Ling had taken it. Take it and welcome, Maria thought.

"Here. I found it. Now, let's get out of here." Poldo emerged, handkerchief to mouth, and shut the door.

"I have to pack his things."

"You can do that another day. I left the window open. Too bad if it rains. That woman must be insane."

Yes, she could do it another day. Let Emma stop her if she dared. She glanced at the green booklet stamped with gold letters in her father's hand. "Are you sure I shouldn't come to the consulate with you? They'll want information maybe only I can give."

Poldo's hazel eyes looked pained. "What would you know that this passport can't tell them? As for the rest, he worked with me, selling Imperial Brand beverages. They don't care about anything else."

"They might, Daddy. I mustn't shirk."

Poldo started down the stairs. "If you are needed I will let you know. I want you to go home and lie down."

That sounded reasonable, too. The top of her father's bald head covered a fine, sweet mind. He did not deserve the life that his trustfulness had dealt him. On the front step, by the

laurel tree, Poldo hugged her and pointed her in
the direction of their home. "Now, go."

Nola was at school. Maria told her mother
where Poldo had gone, and then abruptly ran out
of words. I can't, she said, when her mother
urged her to eat. But she could not seem to get
up from the table and finally ate whatever was
put on her plate. She studied her mother. No
matter what was happening, her mother got up
everyday and put on one of her neat Chinese
gowns, mended stockings, and her tiny shoes. No
more than three strands of gray showed in her
black hair. Seldom did she powder her face,
which needed little artifice. Before the war she
had worn lipstick. Maria hadn't liked it, nor
had she liked the permanents Ming Chu got every
six months. Now she wished her mother would do
those frivolous things, instead of being so
somber. Those soft oval eyes often were unsee-
ing, the pretty, pale lips set and without
speech. "Mama," she started to say, and did not
go on. There was no point in asking if her
mother were unhappy. That is not what matters at
this time, Ming Chu would very likely reply. We
must stay together and live for better days.
Maria had wondered, more than once, what life
would have been like had her mother been a
rebellious woman. Perhaps that was the kind of
wife her father needed, someone restless and
demanding who drove him to action. There was no
point in that sort of speculation, either.

She realized their meal was finished. "I think I will lie down," she said.

She fell asleep at once. Though never waking, she heard the creaking swish of the door opening and closing, low voices in the dining room, the grate of a chair on the floor, the Wongs arguing in loud, clacking tones beneath her bed. When she opened her eyes, the cubicle was dark while light glinted between the crack in the curtains.

Her parents were talking as she walked through the curtains. "You look better," Ming Chu said. She rose, headed for the kitchen and what Maria knew was her strong tea elixir.

"A small complication, Maria," her father said. "The consul says he must write Daniele's family and ask if they wish to have his body returned to Italy." He looked so sorry for her, as though she might hate giving Dani back to his wife. "And if they do ask for its return…shipping is running full, these days. In the meantime…."

She knew what he was trying to tell her. As long as the living continued to flee Shanghai at the rate they were doing, dead bodies held the lowest priority over available cargo space. In the meantime, the Greater Shanghai Funeral Home would have to store Dani in the shed among the other coffins awaiting burial. "And what about the way he died," she said. One day, soon, she would explain to her father how things had stood between herself and Dani. "Did the consul want to investigate?"

"I had a feeling he wished I hadn't mentioned it," her father replied. "The man has other things on his mind. He was quite willing to accept my word on it."

The police didn't care. The consul didn't care. She felt resentful. Dani was forcing her to make up for the world's indifference to his death. He would not leave until he was ready, and he would haunt her for as long as he pleased.

13

Irene did not lament, at least out loud, their misfortunes since H.C. Ping shot Grigory. She still had her plan to get visas for herself, Babushka and Tanya, though she did not mention it these days to Tanya. Her sister was showing symptoms that worried Irene. Their plan might work for three in one family, but Grigory Gromeko could never be considered a candidate for assistance. Just looking at Prince Subarov at work in IRO convinced her that he would know at once the sort of man Grigory was. Foisting him off onto the lily-white dirt of any foreign country might be a task beyond the prince's talents. That is, if an opening for him ever came up.

Dangerous and undesirable as he might be, Grigory Gromeko was twice the man Subarov ever was in his former life of privilege. Of them all, Irene, thought, Grigory should have stayed back. He would have made an excellent Communist functionary of the Narodny Komissariat Vnutrennikh Del. The idea of it made her laugh,

Grigory Gromeko terrorizing prisoners in the cells of the NKVD.

After her bicycle was stolen, despite the various chains wound round and round it and then padlocked to a tree, she'd had to carry her new one upstairs into Grigory's room. The cost of replacement annoyed her beyond reason; money was to be hoarded more carefully than ever, now that they had lost their jobs at the club. H.C. Ping's family had thrown out the entire staff along with the sister act. Mrs. Ping had come to the club herself and screamed curses in Irene's face. The woman was a modern virago, no shy stay-at-home Chinese wife; she stamped about, wailing over the death of her stupid neckless H.C., and when Irene caught a thoughtful look on the face of the night guard, she quietly led Tanya from the premises. So far, he had not informed the family about their part in the robbery and killing.

A matter of time, she thought, if there was money to be made.

As usual, unshaven and wearing his scratchy sweater, Gromeko was sitting at the table with a glass of sirupy liqueur in front of him. He had lost perhaps ten pounds; his right arm still rested in a sling. The wounds were mending. Irene felt rather proud of her home doctoring. On the third day, the color of the holes had turned a sickly yellow, and she wondered if she would have to bring a doctor to him after all. She began using a carbolic soap, cleansing the

holes everyday. She bought a bottle of Jeyes'
Fluid and kept it handy, though she had no idea
how much water was needed to dilute half a cup
of the powerful disinfectant. The Chinese loved
Jeyes' Fluid, which came from England in metal
drums; they would drink it if they dared, to
cleanse their insides. The worse it smelled, the
better they felt about it.

Tanya treated Gromeko as though his legs had
been wounded; she brought him jars of borscht
with hunks of black bread, pelmenis with mustard
sauce, and once, an out-of-season kulich—dotted
with raisins—baked in a coffee can. Upon each
visit she laid out fresh underwear, holes and
all, and took away the dirty ones to wash. She
had taken to kissing Gromeko, like a wife coming
home from market. He did not return her kiss,
but he did not reject it, either. Tanya had
dropped a few pounds herself. Without Gromeko to
stock their larder, Babushka's culinary skills
for home consumption were restricted to an egg
or two, with plain boiled potatoes. The best
went to Gromeko.

"Can you raise that arm, yet?" Irene asked.

"You asked me that yesterday," Gromeko said,
grumpily. "I know damned well why you're so anxious, and it's not because you're worried about
my health."

Tanya said nothing, though she looked reproach-
fully at Irene.

This irritated her. Neither had shown any gratitude for her large part in Gromeko's escape from the Race Club and his recuperation.

"That is nonsense, Grigory. The timing is important, you know that too. We all need the work." Business all over the city was dwindling. Many of the tailor shops on Yates Street were shuttered. The sisters' means of livelihood—through Gromeko—were departing in herds by sea and air, their soft fists clutching British, American, and a dozen other kinds of passports.

A hint of amusement abided in Gromeko's hard, light-colored irises. "If you're that crazy to get started, go ahead. An extra month or two of honest work won't damage your dancing muscles, I'm sure. Don't mind me; just do it."

"Do you think we should?" Tanya asked later, as they mounted their bicycles. Like Irene, she did not fancy putting in any more time than needed. Unlike Irene, she wasn't bored. Nursing Gromeko had brought out maternal feelings that very soon, Irene believed, would turn truly serious. She hoped they would not culminate in a real baby; the future held no place for infant dependents.

Irene did not respond; however, she rode off in the direction of downtown, and Tanya followed.

Pedaling about on bicycles in Shanghai had become both easier and more hazardous: while there were far fewer automobiles to crowd them against the curbs, traffic lights worked fitfully or not at all. Intersections were a snarl of slow-moving, two-wheeled carts yoked to a man, and rickshaw pullers and pedicab drivers who swerved anywhere they pleased, sometimes running up on the sidewalks. Everyone ignored right-of-way rules enforced by the British-trained Sikhs, a presence whose worth everyone badly missed now that it was gone.

At the last moment, securing her bicycle to the nearest tree, Tanya began to plead that perhaps they should wait a few more weeks.

"If you're scared, I am not," declared Irene, and walked toward the doors of The Camellia Room.

"You know it's not that, Irene. I hate those people. They make me want to beat them up." Reluctantly, Tanya followed her inside.

It was early, only seven o'clock, therefore anyone they found would not be too busy to talk to them. Galia was tending bar. She offered them a cool Good Evening.

Irene said, "May I make a proposition to you? Let me speak, and then you can tell me what you think."

Galia nodded. How snooty she was! Irene thought. Upper-class bitch ending her life as a barmaid. "My sister and I have been out of work ever since the Race Club closed down." As Galia raised her carefully drawn eyebrows, Irene went on, "Forget about the club act. Take us on as waitresses. Tanya and I have done it before, and we work fast and well. We will do it for no pay if you prefer, just tips. And another thing," she said, noting the far-away speculation in

Galia's eyes, "if we earn good money, we will
pay as much as we can toward our rent on Route
Magy." She had certainly got Galia's attention
with this one.

"As much as three-quarters of it?" Galia asked.

Irene longed to smack her face. This was the
kind of social parasite who worked parlor maids
in Russia to death in exchange for one pair of
shoes per year and a straw mattress to sleep on;
well, Babushka had shown a few of them in Harbin
the back side of her hand. Beside her, Tanya
with a gusty sighing moved restlessly. Irene
said mildly, "If we earn enough to keep our-
selves alive, we will try to pay Maria's father
three-quarters, yes."

"Why don't I ask Maria about it," Galia said,
in English. "Here she is now."

She must have come in and stood behind them
for several minutes. Always slender, Maria had
become thin. Something has happened to her,
thought Irene, noting the darker skin under her
eyes. Her mouth crimped upward at the corners
but their shape seemed a fixture rather than a
momentary expression. Whether she looked at
Galia or at Irene and Tanya, the set mouth was
the same. It remained semismiling as Galia
recounted Irene's proposal. Her calm was dream-
like. Irene wasn't even sure she heard what
Galia was saying.

"She'll pay rent to my father?" Maria said, as
though Irene weren't there. "It's all rather
crazy, isn't it? She could have come downstairs

anytime to give him that bit of news. Instead, I'm hearing it from you, all the way across town."

Galia said, "They had to know we'd take them on, first. Amalia is leaving, remember, and we haven't found a single experienced girl yet."

Irene stayed out of this discussion; Galia's first words on their behalf were more valuable than anything she could say.

Maria shrugged. She walked past Irene and Tanya, past the bar, saying over her shoulder, "Do as you please, Galia, okay? I'm going to make myself a cup of tea."

"A day later," Tanya said, pedaling side by side with Irene, "and they might have found another waitress. That was a piece of luck. I'm glad you didn't grovel, though. I'd have hated that."

"I didn't have to. I just concentrated on the money. You can win over the devil with money."

At the entrance to the lane on Route Magy, they heard loud voices in altercation coming from the last building. A shrill voice cried out, "You are all miserable thieves. Shame! Shame!" As Irene and Tanya walked through the lane, a neighbor called down from his window, "You know what I wish the Communists would do when they come? Clean out the zoo in your house." Irene shrugged. The man, a Chinese dealer in properties, was apt to be the first to be cleaned out by the Reds.

The voice of their Babushka said harshly, "I wouldn't touch one of your filthy plates with

my bare hands, much less your rotten food."
More words were drowned in Ivanka's hysterical
barking.

Their bicycles held shoulder-high, Irene and
Tanya swept by the curious Wongs listening at
their open door. The Contis' amah came out on
the landing and muttered something in Chinese as
they went by. At the top Ivanka, hurling herself
to the end of her chain to greet them, was a
furball of fury twice her normal size. Babushka
and Zina Kwilecki faced each other in the
kitchen, Babushka's imposing figure impassive,
Zina leaning her slight body forward white-
faced, her black eyes glaring. Her black hair
wasn't braided today and was all mixed up with
the long knitted scarf she always wore in the
winter. Zina quiet and timid was a spectral
presence everyone was used to. A Zina sparking
anger like a long-haired cat was a novelty.

Disdainfully, Babushka said to Irene, "Tell
her we don't eat garbage, and we certainly don't
need to steal it."

"You helped yourself to kasha in my jar, I
know you did. Must I store everything in our
room to keep your hands out of it? When Leon
comes home he'll kill you! None of you deserve
to be alive. Leon will throw you all down the
stairs!" Zina screamed. Red spots sprang out on
her cheeks, her hands rose up, nails to the
fore, as if to claw Babushka's face. The nails
were blunt and the fingers thin and childish.

"Leon," Irene said, "couldn't kill the cooked food on his plate. Babushka didn't take your lousy kasha and that is the end of it. Go to your room and stop being silly."

Zina burst into tears. "We need the food. You shouldn't have done it. I need to eat! Don't you understand? I need…to…EAT!" The last was a wail, and suddenly before them Zina Kwilecki was convulsing. She seemed neither able to breathe nor utter a sound. Her cheeks collapsed as she struggled to draw in air. Then she did succeed, and the noise rushing back out was a screaming that bored from the bottom of her lungs in throat-tearing animal stridulations. Zina's delicate-lipped mouth drew back revealing sharp canine teeth; her dementia seemed to rattle the cups in their saucers. Ivanka howled, her claws flailed at the landing floor. A flurry of thuds from Conti below resounded beneath their feet.

Just as Irene was about to slap her, the red spots on Zina's cheeks disappeared, the whites of her eyes rolled up, and she dropped, but not quite to the floor. It was Babushka who caught her. The old woman supported the young one's weight comfortably, a brawny arm around her middle. "I didn't take her kasha, you know," Babushka said. "She's losing her mind." Her wrinkled yet youthful face looked puzzled, but Tanya's pockmarked one held a small, mean smile.

"Well, let's put her to bed before her hero comes home," Irene commented. She gestured to Tanya, who picked up Zina's legs, while she grasped her under the arms. They carried her limp form past Ivanka, who sniffed at it as they went by. The long scarf slithered to the floor. "Oh, bother," Irene said. She kicked it out of her way. With her elbow, Tanya manhandled the doorknob to the kwileckis' room, got it to open, and they bundled Zina inside and dumped her on the bed. Irene went back out and fetched the scarf, upon which Ivanka was gnawing, and dropped it on Zina's chest. They had been in here before performing the same task many times. There was the bed, a straw mattress supported on a crude wood-and-hemp frame, a card table on which the Kwileckis ate their meals, and two wooden boxes holding their clothes. Irene and Tanya had seen poor lodgings before, had in fact lived in a tarpaper hovel on the edge of Shanghai until they took the next, carefully planned step in their resettlement; far from sympathy, these furnishings of the Kwileckis' elicited nothing but contempt in them. A man possessed of brains and education, which Leon Kwilecki presumably did, should have done better for himself and his dependent. Gromeko, owning none of those advantages, could afford to live luxuriously if he cared to. Kwilecki, lacking guts, deserved the misery in which he and his wife lived.

Zina slept on. "Do you notice that he never thanks us?" Tanya said. "Next time we'll leave her where she drops. It certainly is a relief to

have that screeching stop. I'm starving. Wonder
what Babushka's got for dinner?"

Stirring beans on the stove, Babushka said
matter-of-factly, "She's pregnant. I felt it,
with her draped over my arm. No wonder she got
hysterical about her food."

Tanya's emotions were always as visible as a
child's momentary heartstorms. Now there was a
tinge of guilt (about the kasha, perhaps taken
as a prank), and then, in the deepened clefts
from nostrils to the corners of her mouth, there
was discontent.

Irene decided that she would not wait much
longer to implement her plan to get their visas
to another country.

14

Around about three in the morning, Thaddeus Huell, shuttling between the sixth and ninth floors of Broadway Mansions, felt his senses begin to float above their corporeal host, as though he were looking down at himself and wishing he weren't acquainted with the body. For hours now, he had walked these carpeted corridors and ridden the carpeted elevator, or stood in the sound-deadened communications room scanning Teletyped messages from the beleaguered American Embassy in Nanking. Deprived of sunlight and the simplest act of touching a natural material derived from Mother Earth, Huell knew he could soon begin to doubt his own natural existence, since even his footfalls were soundless. He wondered whether he would be shipped out to a hospital in the States or merely thrown in the brig, if he fetched his sidearm from his locker and shot out the fluorescent lights that hummed over his head day and night.

A two-man crew of Chinese workmen were installing sandbags under the windows down the end of each corridor.

We ought to cover the glass, Colonel Treadway said. That's the right way to do things. Ought to shore up every damn window for shrapnel. But the damn British would laugh us out of town if we did. Just keep your head down when you walk by. Colonel Treadway was the top Marine commander on this post. He cared more than the enlisted men did about what the British might think. Before any fighting came their way, Huell expected the red brick structure of Broadway Mansions to collapse from all the extra weight added to its beams.

One sentiment remained constant in Huell's tired, wayward thoughts: that was his fascination with Maria Conti. He dwelt on her more than his need to feel a ray of sunshine upon his depleted skin, or to sail his dinghy in the squally breezes off Piney Point. He had been homesick enough to die for the watery byways of Chesapeake Bay, where he had grown up and which he had not prized enough when he lived near them. Two weeks ago that old dinghy of his had been fixed in the heavens as the lodestar directing his course home. To complete his tour of duty, admitting that China had fulfilled his expectations far beyond an ability to appreciate them, was not dishonorable. And then, to his bemusement, Maria Conti had taken up that place.

He stepped into the elevator (usually by midnight he abandoned the stairs) and was not surprised to encounter Carlton Wisdom, the British
correspondent who worked in the upper regions of
Broadway Mansions. Wisdom was a stringer for the
Strait Courier and a half-dozen other English
language newspapers operating on the Malay
Peninsula. He fished assiduously for intelligence from the U.S. Military Advisory Group,
mainly by means of riding the elevators. In
slurred tones produced by many gin-and-bitters
partaken at the excellent bar upstairs, Wisdom
remarked, "Funny business in the wind all night,
I could tell. I heard the American Navy was told
to speed up the evacuation of citizens from
Shanghai. Do you think Chiang is going to get
his aid from Truman?"

"Beats me," said Huell, in answer to one or all
of Wisdom's comments. "Did George Vine tell you
that?" George Vine was the British assistant edi-
tor of the *North China Daily News*. He lived in one
of the three apartments on the penthouse floor,
though he was seldom seen fraternizing with the
press corps occupying the upper six floors of
Broadway Mansions. Besides his duties at the
News, he was correspondent for the American
International News Service, the *News Chronicle*,
and the *Observer* in London. Vine was busy.

Huell regretted, as soon as it was out, his
tweaking of Wisdom. The man was trying his best
to file news reports with some content in them.

There was certainly a lot, none that Huell was at liberty to reveal.

The United States Department of State had advised Americans in Nanking to leave. U.S. consular officials warned Americans of the danger of remaining in any part of China except the far south and Taiwan. And, yes, the U.S. Navy had been ordered to hurry up any civilians intending to evacuate Shanghai.

The question of aid to China was a matter of extreme delicacy. There were only so many ways of saying "no," and President Truman had used most of them. Filtered and cleansed of blunt language by official spokesmen, Truman's replies were, at their official kindest, noncommittal. Experts in Washington were said to believe that it would cost five billion dollars to rescue the Chinese Nationalists, and then only if it were certain the money would be spent wisely. The implication, undeclared orally by Truman and Secretary of State George C. Marshall, was that this would be good money thrown after bad. Marshall did say that a large U.S. aid program might involve the U.S. directly in China's civil war.

Huell believed that a pull-out by America was a betrayal of devastating proportions. He was disgusted with the American politicians whom Chiang and his wife had beguiled over the years. Their naivete about the corruption of Chiang's government was self-induced. Huell was certain of that. People knew. They did not have the courage to act. It was far easier to point to

the threat of Russian intervention and a pro-
tracted, hide-and-seek land war between
Nationalists—with their American partners—and
the Communists—with their Russian partners—
across China's vast territories. The possibility of a nuclear holocaust completed the cowing
of Congress. Even Huell had to concede the situation had got beyond remedy.

America had wrung all the juice out of China,
and now prepared to throw the husk away.

Huell, feeling sorry for Wisdom, said, "For
what it's worth, the Chinese Communists have
announced that forty-five Kuomintang leaders,
including Chiang and his wife, have been condemned as war criminals and would be punished
accordingly when captured."

Wisdom failed to perk up at this piece of
information. He sneered, openly ungrateful for
this tidbit. A cigarette seemed to burn contin-
ually between his lips. He looked as weary as,
undoubtedly, did Huell. "You're not going to
tell me there've been another hundred thousand
Nationalist casualties, and change, at Hsuchow?
Please. That's old business. I probably know
things even you don't."

"Everything but the exact date Shanghai
falls," Huell said, as he stepped out of the
elevator. He walked past the gunnery sergeant
at his desk, exchanged nods, and knocked on
Colonel Treadway's door and opened it. The
Colonel closed a folder containing classified
documents and without speaking extended a hand

for the Teletype Huell had carried upstairs. The pouches under Treadway's eyes perched there like water blisters about to burst. Treadway had been one of the 50,000 Marines who landed after V-J day to help Chiang's Nationalist troops hold ports, coal mines and railroad centers against the Communists. Treadway despised Chiang Kai-shek, while he mourned the Chinese people whom Chiang had looted. He was proud to count himself a "China Marine," a designation originally accorded any member of the Fourth Marines who had been posted in China before the war.

Treadway read the Teletype, put it down, and stared off at the far wall, where a pin-dotted map of China hung.

"Rumors, now," he said. "State Department's got nothing better to do than pass on rumors. You think he will?"

On his way up, Huell had speculated on the prospect of President Chiang Kai-shek's resigning if the Chinese Communists were willing to negotiate.

"No, sir," Huell replied. Treadway's blood-shot eyes and pale complexion disturbed him. The couch in the room was there expressly for the purpose of averting the condition the colonel was exhibiting. Huell had not caught him napping there once in thirty-six hours. "Not soon, anyway. Chiang will let things run right into the ground. But if the Reds make his arrest a condition of agreeing to negotiate, I think he will step aside pretty quick."

Treadway stood up and walked to the wall. He was a tall man who had, in the past few months, become underweight by twenty pounds. The numerals "26-12-48" were printed in the date slot above the map board.

"Look at this again," he said, tapping a pin stuck northeast of Peiping. "The Reds have bottled up 70,000 Nationalist troops in Chinchow. We know that's the main supply base for Chiang's troops in Manchuria." His bony index finger moved upward and slightly to the right. "Here. Mukden, 150,000 men cut off." The finger moved straight up. "Changchun, 50,000 under siege over a year." He stared at Huell. "He's just running on propaganda. You're the intelligence analyst. You still think Chiang won't buckle?"

This was neither question nor challenge. The colonel hated being at the final exit point of American occupation of China and seemed to hold that grudge personally against Chiang Kai-shek. He wanted the Generalissimo out of office, gone, crushed, dead, before the order came to mount a full-scale evacuation. No one but the entire Red Chinese Army was entitled to run Colonel Treadway out of town.

"I think he will, sir. When Madame Chiang comes back from the States without her three billion dollars, even he will know he's finished."

"Thirty-five years. Waste. Incredible waste."

Huell knew this was not a reference to money. Colonel Treadway was thinking of the men and resources being poured down Chiang's self-dug black hole. China's progression from the last of her imperial dynasties to the present had cost too much.

Treadway surprised him with a smile, the water blisters under his eyes nestled on his heightened cheeks. "How's Common Wisdom doing these days? Still riding the rails?"

"Yes, sir. Still getting short rations, too." Carlton Wisdom had garnered a very local fame for himself in his methods of gathering news.

Huell was anxious to be gone from this office; he didn't know about the colonel, but he had recently faced the truth that his present tour of duty was unworthy of further sacrifice. This was not the Anzio beachhead, where he had pushed to the limits of his spirit and learned a few things about himself. At this stage of the battle for China, the U.S. Military Advisory Group was as much use as a physician checking a well-turned corpse for vital signs.

On his way down, he stopped at Gunnery Sergeant Miles Hinehart's desk. Upon their first encounter, Hinehart, the Marine, had checked out the service ribbons on Huell's chest. A civilian would never have noticed it, so skillful was Hinehart's appraisal. Amused, Huell was tempted to ask, Will I do, for an Army man, Gunny?

"I'll be saying good night for the next twenty-four hours, Gunny. You know where to find me in case of need."

"Yes, sir. Glad you're getting some sleep, Captain." Hinehart wore more gray in his hair than did Colonel Treadway and seemed to have skin trouble, evidenced by a whitish patch in the shape of a caterpillar on his jaw. He was taciturn, but Huell had seen his service record. First assault wave on Guadalcanal, 7 August, 1942, with the 1st Marine Division. Wounded in arm in Japanese attempt to reinforce ground troops, 23 October, 1942. Landed Rabaul 6 November, 1943. Wounded through chest by Japanese sniper on ninth day, within five hundred yards of the beach. Awards: Silver Star, two Purple Hearts, two Bronze Stars. There was a wife, in Pennsylvania.

Reading the file, Huel thought: Another man who couldn't make much sense of civilian life. Perhaps he had a thing about China, too.

Huell took the elevator to the ground floor and in the locker room installed this year for military personnel use, changed out of his uniform. He pulled on gray slacks, found a white dress shirt that needed laundering. The valet service at the hotel took good care of his clothes and would have a stack of clean shirts and underwear put away in his room. At the entrance he signed out with the Marine guard, and finally, stepped into the open. He felt better at once. He could even make out a

star in the turgid, cloud-battered heavens.
Across the intersection The Camellia Room,
shut tight for the night, looked like a long
gray box. A black automobile with driver sat
outside the Russian consulate; tell-tale puffs
of brownish exhaust showed the engine was running. Official business at this hour? Well,
their moment of triumph was approaching. The
Chinese Reds had been good proteges.

The freshness of the approaching morning
fought with the indescribable odors of Soochow
Creek and lost. Huell smiled to himself. He had
never been happier.

He walked to the compound, recently built to
serve as a motor pool, and caught the corporal on
duty barely awake. The man curried his hair with
a swipe of the fingers and tried to look alert.

"My limousine, Nigel," Huell said. He felt
foolish as well as happy.

"Sir?"

"Just a joke, Corporal."

"Yes, sir."

Huell drove the lumpy Morris Minor over the
Garden Bridge and a mile farther along the Bund.
At Nanking Road he turned the corner and stopped
outside the Cathay Hotel. He would gladly have
walked, but he needed the car today. Viktor, a
Russian no less resplendently caparisoned than
the day man, came to him immediately and wished
him a good morning. Take care of it, please,
Viktor, Huell asked, as he always did. The
Cathay Hotel staff had laid on extra guards to

watch embassy and military staff vehicles. An experienced crew of robbers could dismantle an entire chassis in twenty minutes; in the next twenty every part would have been sold at ten times its original cost.

In his fifteenth-floor suite which faced the Bund, Huell discarded his clothing once more. The view from here in daylight could be termed interesting: Whangpo River a-bustle with shipping, tiny bobbing sampans in danger of being crushed by bigger vessels, launches crossing to Pootung and back, the Bund itself crammed with unruly vehicular traffic; Pootung a flat landscape of godowns and cultivated land receding toward the East China Sea. The islands of Japan lay on a curving line beyond, neighbor to the peninsula of Korea jutting to their north.

Separating Korea from Manchuria and the Russian-held Port of Vladivostok were two rivers, the Yalu and the Tumen. The U.S. Military Advisory Group had known for a year that the next big trouble was brewing along that boundary. Huell soon understood, after arriving in Nanking, that the Orient had only begun, not finished, with its process of rebirth.

The hot shower revived him momentarily. Girdled in one of the Cathay's good thick towels, he peeled back the bedspread, got down, and surrendered to a profound sleep.

She was there, waiting, when he rattled up in the Morris. That she did not invite him into her

home, though this was only the second time they
were meeting, crossed his awareness, but he
would be patient; he would squirm deep into her
life by his persistence and ardor. He gained one
quick insight, as she was settling into the
seat. The lane behind her was strewn with
refuse; the far end stood under minor flood
bridged by a single plank.

He saw her exquisite face clearly this morning. Already sensitive to the slightest change
in her expression, Huell wondered (selfishly, he
acknowledged) if whatever the thing was that
revealed itself in a flash of weariness would
affect his standing with her.

"Nothing the matter, I hope?"

She gave him a startled glance. "Nothing is
the matter. I'm very well, you're not to worry."

"That sounds so British."

"For some reason, we don't happen to have a
lot of Armenians in Shanghai."

Huell laughed, delighted to have her here
beside him. He'd had five hours' sack time,
could not waste another minute asleep, and had
breakfasted, dressed in clean clothes, and by
ten was calling Leonid, Viktor's day counter-
part, for the Morris Minor.

"What have you in mind today?" Maria asked. "A
jaunt to the battle zone around Nanking, perhaps? I packed my purse with an extra handkerchief, in case."

"That's very good thinking. Could you take a
few hours of boredom in the Cathay Hotel dining

room? I'm supposed to stay close to home, sort
of on a twenty-four hour basis. There's a leash
around my neck, only you can't see it."

Gravely she nodded, and seemed to withdraw
into some personal introspection for several
minutes, while Huell reflected that he was rapidly getting into trouble with himself. A lawyer
did not fling his emotions into the arena on the
strength of a single date; an army intelligence
analyst thought things through twice, and then a
third time, before committing his best judgment
to the fates. But he was neither man, really.
Huell had merely found himself pigeonholed in
those capacities without his own full consent.

On Avenue Edward VII, just as Huell began
maneuvering for a left turn onto Tibet Road, a
Chinese man crossing in front of the Morris
Minor dropped to the ground. Huell slammed his
foot on the brake; at the same instant his left
hand shot out and held Maria back from hitting
the windshield.

"Are you okay?" She nodded yes.

Huell got out of the car. The pile of rags on
the ground fluttered in the cold wind. He was
aware of people staring but no one stopped walking, pushing, pulling, or pedaling; the automobile behind his was turning out, trying to pass.
The man inside the rags was dead, starved to the
final flicker of life in his near encounter with
Huell's car. He stank of accumulated dirt and
sick bowels; the green of grass streaked his
cracked lips and a blade still protruded between

his front teeth. Huell reached down, got a grip on the rack of bone that was its shoulders, and dragged the corpse to the curb and over it. Two squatter families on the sidewalk regarded him, their hollowed expressions of resignation more upsetting than if they had protested loudly.

Huell said, apologetically, "*Mei yu fah tze*, it cannot be helped," and propped his cargo against the wall of a yardage shop, as far as it was decently possible from them. He left the near-weightless bundle there, skittish as a wind-buffeted kite about to soar off into the sky. The desire to scrub his hands on his handkerchief was urgent; Huell resisted it. He walked back to the car, got in, slammed the door. He drove on, melding with traffic that never paused. Maria said nothing, but she touched his arm for so brief a moment he doubted afterward her hand had even been there.

The Cathay Hotel, Sir Victor Sassoon's personal monument to his success in the opium trade, had never seemed so obscene to Huell, especially with Maria Conti at his side. He could not help the fact that he lived here; yet the opulence of the lobby, its grand draperies, its elaborately uniformed minions, distressed him acutely. Being the victor in war was not the triumph that people back home thought it was.

Maria Conti fitted in here. She was dressed with quiet elegance in a tailored suit of some fine navy woollen material; her feet in high-heeled pumps and lovely legs moved with graceful

assurance. When he had seated her at a table, he
excused himself and took the elevator to his
room. He threw his tweed jacket on the bed, loosened his tie, and rolled up his shirtsleeves and
scrubbed, using a nailbrush over hands and arms.
He had told Leonid, speaking softly, to disinfect
the steering wheel before allowing it to be
touched. Leonid probably had done nothing, for he
himself did not move the guests' automobiles.

Huell had been away at least fifteen minutes,
and on his return began an apology before Maria
stopped him with a motion of her hand.

At last, in the dining room of the Cathay
Hotel, he was seated before her so he could
dwell upon the delicate features, the amalgam of
East and West that had produced Maria Conti.
Those hazel eyes were downcast, hidden by black
lashes, as she perused the ornate menu. Her nose
was small and straight, her cheeks curved
sweetly to the oval chin. A strand of shiny dark
hair had loosened itself and clung to her lips.
He supposed the coral shade of her lipstick was
fashionable; he was more interested in the lips
themselves.

"You are staring," she said, and returned her
attentions to the menu.

"Sorry." He looked at the menu, which he had
come to know well during his six months of residence in the hotel. "They make a very good
Vodka Collins here, if you'd like one."

"Do you know what I would like? A bottle of
San Pellegrino water. It's much too fine and

hard to get for The Camellia Room, so this will
be a treat for me."

The name of that shoddy drinking hole coming
from her flower lips touched him with pity. He had
seen a few like it in Europe, thrown together in
deserted shops to accommodate the fighting men of
the armed forces, and always there had been one or
two bewildered and frightened girls working in
them. The first thing that had struck him about
Maria was her air of remoteness, a sort of pleasant aloofness, from the action in the bar. And the
other thing, the other was a beauty that made him
reach for comparisons and come up, lamely, with
white peony blossom. He had never seen a peony,
much less a white one. A miserable failure of a
poet was he, after all his ruminations on the
romance of China.

He ordered San Pellegrino for himself, and
then got the ordering of food out of the way.
Steak and mashed potatoes, cooked vegetables on
the side. She seemed as uninterested in choice
as he, though she commented that it was nice to
get away from rationing once in a while. The
dining room was half filled with foreigners,
most of whom were Americans out of uniform, and
British civilians. He spotted, off to the side
of a ceiling-high gilt-faced mirror, the British
Consul General, Robert Urquhart, chatting with
two civilians. Their age and style of dress
marked them as businessmen. Urquhart had been
notoriously unsuccessful at persuading the
British community to evacuate Shanghai. But this

is our home, most protested. The stubbornest
seemed to be those who had been interned in
Japanese camps during the war.

"I have to ask something," he said. "Is your
family planning to leave China? I hope you all
are, and very soon. You have Italian citizenship, don't you? So there's no problem about
getting visas to another country if you have the
right to go to Italy."

They were seated near the plate glass window
fronting the Bund. Velvet curtains the shade of
aged moss, drawn back with gilt ropes, framed a
British freighter-liner moored alongside the
wharf. Maria glanced at the ship. "We are not
going," she said, each word distinct. "We have
no plans to move."

"I don't intend to pry into your reasons. But
whatever they are, Maria, they can't come before
getting away as soon as you can. I'm deadly
serious. Pack up your toothbrush, if that's all
you can take, and don't look back."

"Thousands of foreigners aren't leaving. They
don't believe the Communists have anything
against them. My father is a businessman, a citizen of a neutral nation, and he is convinced
the new China will still need businessmen with
experience, to connect them with the outside
world." She smiled. "How do you say toothbrush
in Chinese? Let me hear you say it."

"My teacher doesn't bother with basic utility
words like that. I suspect he thinks I'm beneath
his notice, and sometimes I know I am." He drank

some water, temporizing, looking for the correct words to convey his urgency. Communists were not known to want traffic with the outside world. She had to leave; he could not go away and worry about her for the rest of his life.

"Thank you for caring about us." She asked, "Why are you still studying Chinese? You know as well as I do the American military won't be staying much longer. Do you plan to be a lawyer with Chinese clients, in Virginia?"

So much for top secret directives from the State Department, he thought.

"I have no intention of going back to law, and that is not going to be happy news to my Dad. He fought in France in the first war, but if he had doubts about taking up law when he came home, I never heard about them. It's been on my mind a lot, lately. I'm going to ask him about that when we have our brawl over my desertion of the profession." "Brawl" was simultaneously too strong and too feeble a word to describe his father's feelings. The Chinese concept of Elder Son carrying on after the father translated very well into American.

"Is being a lawyer so dull?"

"It's not dull at all. I can't even claim having the wrong temperament for the kind of practice I'd be interested in. Criminal law takes every kind of instinct you're born with plus others you acquire. But there's one other line of work…I am going to say this, at long last, out loud. I need to hear how it sounds in my own ears."

The thought struck him that any man who could cause those hazel eyes to cry tears would be the lucky winner of what appeared to be a sinewy, independent heart. "I have delusions of becoming a journalist, the foreign correspondent type, you know, roving all over the Far East, getting inside blockades. Interviewing guerilla chiefs. Have you ever heard of Edgar Snow?"

"You mean *Red Star Over China* Edgar Snow? I didn't read it, but everybody knows about him."

"That's the kind of correspondent I'd like to be. He got in to speak to Mao Tse-tung; the world had no idea what Mao was up to until that book came out. He turned Mao into a hero with his account of the Long March." In October 1934 Mao and his pregnant wife went with 85,000 troops on a retreat from Chiang's forces. Under bombardment and fighting on land, the army crossed 18 mountain ranges and 24 rivers toward the northwestern province of Shensi. One year and 6,000 miles later, 8,000 survivors reached Shensi. Among the missing were Mao's younger brother and his two small children. Huell had studied *Red Star Over China* as if he could, by so doing, learn the workings of Mao's brain.

"After they read the book people almost forgot they didn't like Communists," Huell said. "Mao sounded like a true idealist, a Galahad, when Snow rendered his talks with him into his articles."

"That wasn't objective reporting, whether or not Mao is a real patriot," she said.

"I have to agree it wasn't." That was his one reservation about Edgar Snow's style.

Their steaks arrived, beautiful T-bones sitting in puddles of beefy juice. Huell picked up his knife and fork, and put them down again. He had not intended to offer penance for being here in the Cathay Hotel; he could not bring that man in the street back to life. Nevertheless, he could not eat this meat. It would not go to waste; someone in the kitchen would benefit. Maria cut a tiny corner off her steak, stared at it, and met his eyes.

He smiled. "Do we have a problem?"

"I don't usually look round me in the streets. I'm very good at ignoring things when it doesn't suit me. But do you know what it takes to get a piece of meat like this? Of course you do, so I'm not going to excuse myself if I eat it."

Two Marine captains in civvies came in and took a table near them. They exchanged nods with Huell and gave Maria the politest of cursory glances. Huell could guess what they were saying to each other, however. Got himself a juicy number. Lucky dog, spoils of war. To Maria, they might have been invisible; she behaved as though the entire dining room were empty.

Maria ate less than a quarter of the steak before surrendering her silverware. The waiter returned to ask if they would like coffee.

"We could take it in the lounge, where I can bore you some more with my pathetic fantasies of a career in journalism," Huell said.

"I am going to ask you some questions," Maria said. She had not retouched her lipstick; her lips were lovelier without it, Huell thought, unnerved by longing. "You said before that you had to stay close to home. Do you live in this hotel?"

"Yes, ma'am, I do."

"And you have to stay here in case you are wanted by your boss?"

"That is correct."

"Are you wishing you could take me to your room?"

Oh, Maria, my honest fragrant white peony. I have been desperate to have you alone to myself. He said, "Yes. Yes. Yes."

She smiled, a blossoming of her whole face that shortened Huell's breath. "May we go there, then?"

Wordless, he rose and helped her out of her chair. The conversation of the Marine captains fell into a lull; Huell knew their necks were creaking with the effort not to turn in their direction. You both get Purple Hearts. At ease, gentlemen.

He did not touch Maria's elbow while they crossed the carpeted lobby to the elevators. She stood very straight, her gaze upon the closing doors, as they got in and he gave the uniformed operator their floor. Her regal posture touched him, made him conscious of the defenselessness of women in this man's world.

In his pocket he found the key, unlocked his door, and ushered her in.

She walked to the window and looked down at the chaotic streams of human and vehicular traffic. "It looks like complete madness. What must you think of us in Shanghai?"

"Maria," Huell said, turning her to him. At last, he was able to touch this marvelous face with his hands. Her unpowdered skin was fine and smooth as he had known it would be; palms cupping, he kissed her lips until he became dizzy. His hands moved to her back and pulled her close. She felt soft, firm, pliable wherever he stroked her. "Sorry," he muttered. "I know I'm swarming all over you." She did not seem to mind; her hands came around and wandered to his neck.

Huell groped, found the pull that lowered the venetian blinds. A hushed sort of twilight replaced the hard glare of the winter day.

Maria pressed back against his constricting arms and stepped away, dismaying him momentarily, but then he saw why. It was she who went to the bed and turned back the covers. She removed her jacket, kicked off her shoes, and held out her arms to him.

Huell was to recall moments, never the exact sequence, of making love to Maria. He could not hold her close enough, and his hands could not stop moving over her. Maria murmured something he heard dimly, so deafened was he by the hiss and charge of blood in his ears. At the touch of her hand on his stomach Huell cringed, and had to laugh at himself because of the effect it had on him. He was fifteen again, a mass of twitches any of which could have pulled the trigger and made a mess to agonize over in solitude. She must have taken pity on him, for soon he was enfolded and Huell embraced her, his lips hot upon her neck, while she held his driving back and he prayed he was pleasing her because he could not wait to make sure. I'm going to die, he thought, and he did.

After a minute of silence, he asked, "Are you all right?" He meant, Was I an animal, Did you come, and the last—Forgive me. He had forgotten to put on a rubber. Six months of abstinence tended to rust out a man's well-learned habits. He had not forgotten with that good-looking Teletype clerk in Peiping. During those episodes his brains had not shut down and deserted Thaddeus Huell.

Maria took him by the ears and lifted his head. Their eyes four inches apart, hers a glowing blur in the gloom, she whispered, "Not to worry," and laughed. She pushed him a little, and he shifted to release her. She swung her feet to the floor and got up and went to his bathroom. She was lovely naked. He had a moment to admire her before she shut the door.

He gathered her into his arms when she came back. When she was settled, the covers up and tucked around them, he said, "I usually have a little more finesse than I exhibited. I promise,

promise, promise, the very next time your pleasure will be my first and only concern."

"But I liked it," Maria said. "I liked it so much because you wanted me that much. I couldn't help going along with you; it felt like you were…melting me down, with the way you were holding and touching me, and it was very nice." She got loose of him again and lay on her back and stretched long and voluptuously; her joints gave off small clicks that sounded like crickets chirping. Huell felt her toes touching his ankles in a sharp point. "I'm hungry," she said. "Aren't you? I wish we'd brought my steak up here with us."

"We can have a fresh one. Anything you want, in ten if not five minutes. The Cathay staff lives to serve."

"Good. Then let them bring a steak sandwich with fried onions, and mustard on the side. French fries. Pelligrino water. A pear and an orange. Some cake."

"My sainted aunts," said Huell. He dialed room service and ordered two of everything.

The rattle of rain woke them. Great drops of water spotted the window pane, their glintings slanted against a darkening sky.

"Best sound in the world," Huell murmured. He realized his hand cupped Maria's hip. "I'd put on my foul weather gear and take my boat down to Mason Neck just on a bet with myself, to see if I could navigate by sense. I couldn't see the

shore, either side. Then pretty soon I'd have to
start bailing, and I'd get home soaked and
absolutely high on oxygen. My mom always said I
was a nut."

Maria's breath tickled his shoulder in tiny
spurts. "Rain is lonely," she said, at last. "It
is all by itself, and it doesn't care who it falls
on, especially the dead. It lets you know you are
not important, and doesn't remember. That is for
the living to do, whenever it rains."

The words and their thread of melancholy
infused Huell's drowsy well-being with alarm.
"What is it. Did something happen to you, Maria?"

"Things happen to everybody." She touched the
bunched scar tissue on his left thigh. "Like
that happened to you. I'm glad you weren't hit
higher up, though."

"You cannot know how lucky I feel," Huell said.

15

The festivities, part celebration, part wake, had got underway hours before Huell arrived. A Christmas tree, set up two weeks before, stood askew on the little bandstand. Its electric lights flickered sporadically, like distress signals in Morse; since eight o'clock new oddments decorated the withering branches—socks, a necktie, a rubber. Three Marines in civvies were using drinking straws as beanshooters; anyone who hit the rubber with a black bean won a kiss from red-haired Liudmila, whose expansively beaming face—slitted eyes, wide cruel mouth—looked like a fiery parody of her Tatar forebears. Gene, perched on the edge of the bandstand, a leg drawn up, cigarette in the corner of his mouth, seemed to be playing to himself; Huell could almost see flagged notes, launched in one-sixteenth time from the ukelele, collide with the din behind the smokescreen and carom back to him.

Maria greeted him with a smile. "Oh. What's this?"

"This is kind of late for Christmas, so happy new year," Huell heaped parcels in her arms. "They're all probably the wrong color or the wrong size, but I liked them. You can get them changed if you want."

"You went to Yates Road! And here's a box from Wing On! Can I look right away?" She went to the bar to open her presents behind its sheltering overhang. Her excitement made him happy; he had risked a reprimand from Treadway for disappearing from his duties to dash out for this shopping foray. It had been a mistake to go to the Wing On Department store on Nanking Road, the largest and most famous merchandise emporium in China. The store was cavernous in its depleted condition, and he had wandered for a precious twenty minutes, unable to find a store directory that might have given him clues about what gifts to buy.

Laughing, Maria held a silk blouse against herself, put it down and unwrapped a tan sweater of merino wool ("from Australia," the salesclerk said, proudly). She began to open the box covered with Santa Clauses riding rickshaws, a specialty of Wing On's gift-wrap department.

"Let me see. I want to see what he brought you," said a small voice. A minor-scale version of Maria squirmed past Huell and planted herself between them.

"This is my sister Nola," Maria said. "And Nola, this is my friend Thaddeus Huell."

"I know. Who else would give you presents? How do you do," Nola said with the suave intonation of an adult. "You are nicer looking than she said you were, but I guessed it anyway, because she doesn't always want to say everything she thinks."

Maria made a face and shut her eyes. "She's not really related to me, you know. We took her in after her own family threw her out."

"How do you do," Huell replied. "I am very, very happy to meet you." He shook hands. "And also, happy birthday. It's your twelfth, isn't it? I hope you'll like these." The parcels he had not given Maria he now placed in Nola's arms. Immediately he saw the miniature adult vanish; the child who received his gifts was open-mouthed with shock and joy. Her whispered thank you was lost in the noise, but Huell smiled and nodded. He caught Galia's wave to him from where she was seated at a table, and waved back. He was conscious of a low, tremulous contentment within himself. This night in a raucous, smoke-grimed saloon—perhaps only this moment—was worth the entire past year of wearisome emptiness in Peiping, Nanking, and until lately, here in Shanghai. "Aren't you going to open them?" he asked.

Nola shook her head. "When I get home. Maybe I'll open them tomorrow. It's nice thinking about them and have the surprise waiting for me. And maybe I won't open them at all, so I'll always have them to think about."

"Well, they're yours. Do as you please," Maria said. She held up a card she found taped to one of her packages. She read it aloud, "'If I were a stone I would still know the changings of the earth. Leaves turn and fall, and their deeds are mightier than heaven.'"

Huell felt himself blushing. "I have a book of Chinese poetry I'm trying to translate. My work is still very clumsy."

Maria leaned swiftly and kissed him and was gone away in an instant. She opened the Wing On box and before Huell could stop her lifted out a blue robe. It was not particularly flimsy in design or fabric, but Huell was embarrassed by the presence of Nola. He could hear his mother amusedly chiding: Unless you're proposing to marry Julianne, dear, earrings will do nicely.

Maria turned her back to the room and held the robe against herself. "Is it really long, Nola?"

"Right to your ankles." Nola pushed the robe against Maria's hips and measured across with her arm. "A bit tight, maybe. No, it's perfect."

Caught red-handed, thought Huell. Maria's father would come hunting for him with a shotgun.

"Galia needs me to get back to work," Maria said. But she paused, smiling at Huell, and he felt a spurt of gratitude that he was more than merely a stone. "Do you mind if I turn you over to Nola? Or join the crowd, if you like. They're getting pretty wild, maybe you aren't in the mood for that sort of thing."

Two stocky blond women who had been serving drinks came behind the bar and began to take bottles of beer from a tub filled with ice. They glanced at the three, then at the heaped parcels, but said nothing. Maria nodded, as if something had passed between her and the two women, though they were rapidly uncapping bottles and not looking at her. "Very good," Maria said. "Best behavior."

Huell did not know what she meant, but he realized her remarks were not directed at him. Nola led him to her own small table near Gene at the bandstand. She piled her presents on the table, then fetched a chair for Huell. Now he could hear Gene's music. It was nothing he could identify, except that it was Russian and melancholy.

"What would you like to drink?" Nola asked. She had to shout; they were nearly in the thick of the party. SILENT NIGHT...bellowed a Marine. He looked at Huell, recognizing him, and offered a nod. His companion, a brunette with eyes reddened from weeping, or cigarette smoke, or both, sang in a breaking voice in Russian.

Huell raised his voice a couple of notches. "What are you having?"

"Lemonade. I made it myself. I brought a big jug of it from home. There's plenty. Have a taste of mine. If you don't like it Maria will get you something else from the bar." Politely, she turned the glass for him before he drank.

The flavor had a remote connection to lemon juice; a tinge of bitterness remained in his mouth, and a heavy sweetness that was not sugar. "I like it very much," he said, stoutly. Nola looked pleased.

"It's easy, you know. Some citric acid and water, and saccharine. I didn't bother with Lemon Yellow because Daddy is low on it, and coloring wasn't important for tonight. And oh, an aspirin."

"Aspirin?"

"So it won't spoil. Acetylsalicilic acid helps keep the flavor from decomposing. I made the vodka Gene is drinking. He likes it. You put together cloves, nutmeg, cinnamon, coriander, and a little bit of oleo resin capsicum, and oil of orange, and a dash of ginger powder. Then you mix in the water and alcohol." She swung her legs and gestured with her hands, counting off the ingredients on her fingers. Her feet did not quite reach the floor. Often she smoothed the crisp taffeta skirt of her two-piece navy out-fit, an odd color for a young girl, Huell thought. Much too old if not for the white, round-collared blouse under the bolero. Her hair, parted in the middle and tied with red ribbon over her ears, bobbed and swirled with her gesturing.

"Did you really make it or did someone help you?" A seed of suspicion had begun sprouting during Nola's recital.

Nola's hands, about to describe the coalescing of the miraculous ingredients, fell to clasp together in her lap. She looked guiltily toward where Maria stood, bent over a tearful Zoya. "Well, Daddy made it, actually. But I usually help. I stick on the labels, too."

"Imperial Brand labels?" He tried to remember what he may have said to Maria that first time, when she had made him that terrible cherry brandy soda. He hoped it was not offensive.

"Yes. My father can make anything, but he hasn't much of the chemicals left. He used to get them from Bush House in London when he played with chemistry just for fun. It's very nice," she said, suddenly shy, "to get presents for my birthday. This is the Year of the Rat, you know. It lasts until the Chinese new year next February. My sister was born in the Year of the Rat, too. We're twelve years apart. Rat people are supposed to have a taste for the better things in life, only I haven't really started to cultivate that taste, yet."

"No," Huell said. "I guess you haven't had a chance, have you?"

The Marine had been necking with the brunette. Farther back, a navy rating from the HMS *Amethyst* and his girl were doing the same. The *Amethyst* was well represented tonight, though none of the 16-year-old boy-seamen from that ship was here. Huell had visited aboard. Absolutely shining with discipline and scrubbed pink complexions, the British had never impressed him so much as then, which was the point: the 1,495-ton frigate, with its puny complement (to Huell's mind) of 183 officers and men, constituted the British military presence in Shanghai.

The Marine uttered a groan, and Huell contemplated asking him to move his operations elsewhere, anywhere but in front of Nola's small nose.

"They're not very graceful, are they? I mean, one hand is holding his drink and the other is inside her neck. It's not the way I'd want my boyfriend to hold me when he's kissing me."

Huell turned to look at Nola. Her gaze upon the smooching couple was critical, like a film director's intent on setting a scene right.

Nola slipped off her chair and sat down next to Gene. He had put down the ukelele and sat bowed over it. Both hands shaded his eyes, and he nodded as she spoke into his ear. Occasionally he blew his nose on a handkerchief. His gray-flecked mustache looked neglected; a good part of it curled inside his upper lip. New Year's eve, thought Huell. Booze, sex, hysteria, and drowning in your past. He realized that he accepted this bizarre conjuncture of a 12-year-old child with said booze, sex, hysteria and a drunken sad man who was weeping over his lost Mother Russia.

Gene was just one of about thirty nationals that made Shanghai their home. Some of these others were joined in holiday fraternity within the nicotine-yellowed pink walls of The Camellia Room. The French stubbornly drank a cloudy pastis-like fluid. Their shoes were worn to the uppers. A pair of German Jews from the Wayside district nursed one Tstingtao beer between them. The Portuguese talked loudly in their blend of English-Maccanese. Four hundred years of Portuguese rule in the colony of Macau had melded Chinese, Indian and Filipino into a colorful race. The Italians resembled the French except that they chose to drink vermouth (Imperial Brand, Huell suspected). To the babble of languages the Filipinos added their singsong English, chopped in places with staccato Tagalog. And it all worked, thought Huell. They were at home here together more than if they'd had the price of admission to Eventail, the Metropole, Ciro's, the Lido, or the dance floors at the Roxy and Paramount.

The two blond waitresses seemed no part of this polyglot ebullience. They worked quickly, dispensing and clearing, their responses to bawdy comments from the men limited to automatic smiles. The shorter, prettier one approached Huell and asked if he wanted anything. She was Russian, as he had guessed. Huell said no, thank you, he had some wonderful lemonade, and was given a scornful glance that puzzled him. He looked at his watch. Forty minutes to go until midnight. For his New Year's message, President Chiang Kai-shek had offered to step aside if the Chinese Communists were willing to negotiate. Colonel

Treadway had received notice of Mao Tse-tung's
rejection within minutes of that announcement.

Nola slipped back to Huell's side. "Gene is
crying because he doesn't know if his mother is
dead or alive. He's thinking about going back to
Russia but he's scared they'll kill him. He
doesn't believe the Russians are really forgiv-
ing everybody and giving them jobs and houses."

Huell reflected, but only for a second, that
it was unsportsmanlike to worm information about
the Contis from a child. "What about yourselves,
Nola? Isn't your father going to take you all
back to Italy?"

"No. It's not that simple." She looked away
from him and sipped her lemonade.

You've done it now, you fool. You've ruined
her party. But didn't he want to know they would
be safe?

"Why not? What's the problem?" He sensed that
Maria had not told him everything concerning
their reasons for staying.

"We own the house we live in, but we can't
sell it because nobody wants to buy. Daddy says
we need capital to get started in a new country.
He thinks maybe the Communists aren't going to
be so bad when they take over. They need businessmen, don't they?" Nola looked at him, begging confirmation.

Huell, wincing inside, could not tell her what
he would have told her father: the end of all
things as they knew them was coming in the new
wave. Personal safety overrode lack of money.

"What does your mother say?"

"Mama? Mama doesn't say much."

Feeling ashamed of himself, he bored on. "Well, what do you think she thinks?"

Nola's eyes looked absently at the entwined Marine and his girl. "I think she thinks we should leave, anyhow. But Mama is Chinese, you know. This is her country, and I guess she just hopes things will come out all right. Oh!" She sat straighter, the better to see. "Look at Liudmila. She's going to sing. Galia says she used to sing in a cabaret in Harbin."

One of Liudmila's attendants had fetched Gene, who consulted with Liudmila, then went behind the bar and brought back a violin case. Galia stood up and shushed the crowd. Gene settled the instrument under his chin and raised the bow.

The first, low, moaning note from the violin brought the gooseflesh up on Huell's arms. Liudmila's voice kept them there. The texture of it was as low as any note Gene could produce on his violin; it was hoarse yet musical, rasping a dirge or a lullaby, Huell did not know. Then she smiled, and a playful rhythm crept in, and someone began a measured clapping of hands; soon everyone was clapping softly, including Huell and Nola. Liudmila sang with her eyes closed, the thin-lipped mouth producing a miraculous flow of music while Gene swayed, his tears again wetting his mustaches. Zoya sobbed loudly, and that too fitted in with the song. Across the room, Maria's eyes met

Huell's. She smiled, ruefully. Aren't we mournful tonight? Again, the only persons not partaking were the two waitresses. They stood side by side at the bar, their impassive faces somehow expressing contempt.

The song ended. Gene and Liudmila embraced; without further ado she sat down. Huell heard a sniffle and turned to Nola. "Are you all right?" He remembered asking Maria that, in the same words, in another context.

"Yes." She looked at the table, her skirt, half lifted her taffeta-sleeved arm to her nose, then dropped it.

Quickly, Huell got his handkerchief out. "Here, take this."

"Oh. Thank you."

"I wish you'd tell me whether that was supposed to be a sad song or a happy song. And if it was happy, why were all the people who understood the words crying? Did you understand the words?"

She applied the handkerchief lustily, started to give it back to him, then remembered her manners said politely, "I'll wash it and give it back to you next time."

"You keep it, okay? I wish I could take you out, sometime, you and Maria together, but I never know when I have a few hours off, so I'd hate to make a date with you and not be able to keep it."

"That's all right. I know you're pretty busy. Maria told me what you do." Delicately, she added, "Not everything, of course."

Huell laughed. Colonel Treadway's displeasure was not to be imagined; he probably had no idea how public his private operations were.

"It doesn't matter much what kind of song it was," Nola said. "Russians cry when they're happy the same as when they're sad. Especially when they've been drinking and feel homesick, and now it's Russian Christmas for them, and Gene told me he didn't even get out of bed yesterday. Once I had to stay with a Russian man I know because he didn't eat for three days. I had to hide his vodka, or I knew he'd die."

And how old was she when that occurred? Huell decided not to ask. He glanced at the two stolid waitresses. Not these Russians, he thought. They're tougher than army boots.

"Tell me about Liudmila. She's quite a lady."

"Liudmila? She's funny. She told Galia a story and Galia told Maria and Maria told me. After the war, all the American ships were coming up the Whangpo River and Liudmila was on the Bund with a lot of other girls, waiting for the sailors to come off. She met this nice one and took him to a bar and they had a few drinks, and Liudmila told him she had to go somewhere, she had an appointment. She said she wanted to exchange souvenirs to remember him by, and got twenty Chinese dollars out of her purse. So the sailor took twenty American dollars out of his pocket and gave it to her." Nola's laughter was high and delighted; the red ribbons bounced on the dark tresses over her ears. "He was so

young! Liudmila didn't give him time to find out
about Chinese money." She paused to explain.
"You couldn't buy a pin with twenty Chinese dollars. Bread cost about a million a loaf."

"I know," Huell said. "I hope she got a lot of
money that way." He meant it.

"The Chinese call her *tze lao hoo*. Yung calls
her that. It means female tiger. She's a strong
lady."

"Yung?"

"The cook. He works here, in the kitchen."

Huell knew, had learned in Peiping from an
American who called himself an old China hand,
that the term also pertained to an athletic performance in bed. He was glad Nola seemed not to
know this other meaning.

The noise settled down as Galia stood up and
tapped forcefully on a glass with a knife.
"Everybody, listen! Some of us are here tonight
for another special reason, so don't think that
you're getting your drinks at half price just
because it is new year's eve." She waited for
the hoots and whistles to die away. Galia's
brilliant red mouth smiled. Her porcelain makeup
seemed impervious to smoke or tears. "We are
also having a celebration for Zoya, who is leaving us soon." At this, Zoya let out a cry. The
small, thin man sitting next to her looked miserable. On his other side, Amalia no longer wore
her usual air of tension. Her stringy looks had
relaxed, and she had styled her gray hair in a
rather gloomy pagebob.

"We are celebrating the marriage of Zoya and Tomas, who will soon be taking her away to Portugal. They will have a new life and, Maria and I hope, very very much happiness. And we say good-bye to Amalia, who is going back with her brother Tomas and her family. I think they will always remember Shanghai as a special place, and all of us here tonight as even more special." In the midst of whistles and applause, Maria walked from the bar carrying a crystal decanter and three shot glasses. She went to Zoya, who stood up, looking dazed. A barrage of chair-scraping followed as everyone stood up. Hands clapped and voices chanted "*Piedudnat! Piedudnat! Piedudnat!*" from the Russians among them. Zoya took a shot glass of vodka and, dramatically flinging her head back, poured it down her throat in a single swallow. Maria moved to Tomas, who consumed his vodka in many small sips. "*Piedudnat! Piedudnat!*" Amalia grabbed the third glass and, workmanlike, gulped hers down. Maria moved back to Zoya and refilled the glasses. Zoya pretended horror, clutched a hand to her bosom, pleaded for mercy from Galia, Maria, and the room in general, and finally lifted her chin and tossed her vodka down as smoothly as the first time. The cheers and handclapping were frantic.

Huell watched Maria and felt a surge of erotic memory in his loins. Never more than now did he resent the futility of his assignment to Treadway's staff. The erratic hours had not bothered him before; now they barred him from

seeing Maria as often as he wished. He was conscious of time foreshortened, counting off from
weeks to perhaps days, and for all he knew suddenly cutting him dead away from her within
twenty-four hours. His parents' Christmas card,
received today, reposed folded in his pocket.
Come home soon. We miss you, son. His grandmother had written on the back, Dearest Tad,
can't wait for next Christmas when you will be
here. In a corner, his brother had scribbled Get
back before they bronze your boat.

The uproar subsided. Maria had gone to the
kitchen with her tray of decanter and shot
glasses. Within moments she reappeared carrying
another tray, loaded with a frosted chocolate
cake, plates, and silverware.

"Now this is my party," Nola said. "Mama made
that cake. Isn't it beautiful?"

"Help me clear the table, would you?" Maria
said. "Nola wouldn't have her birthday cake
until you came. Is she getting to be too much
for you? What did you used to do with your kid
brother when he was a pest?"

"Heave him into the bushes. Once I threw him
into the river." Huell smiled. "I couldn't do
that now. Last I heard, he's two inches taller
and thirty pounds heavier."

Galia detached herself from Zoya and walked
over to them; her good legs glistened in tan
nylons. "Ah, my sweet *malenki* bunny," she said,
bending to Nola and hugging her close. Resting
against Nola's cheek, her face looked nakedly

sad; Huell felt he was intruding. "I haven't given my present to you yet. Think of me whenever you wear it." She removed a ring from her pinkie finger and slipped it on Nola's thumb. "See? It's a perfect fit. Soon you will be able to wear it on the proper finger."

Nola inspected the three small pearls mounted on a slim gold band, then looked at Galia. "Did your mother and father give it to you when you were young?"

"That is correct. They did."

Maria started to utter a protest, then stopped herself.

"Well, I couldn't forget you, anyway," Nola said. "Why would I, even if you didn't give me your own ring." She hugged Galia again. When she detached herself from Galia and turned she made a startled sound; a single candle was burning in the center of the chocolate cake.

"Happy Birthday, brat," Maria said, smiling.

Outside their small group someone sang out, "It's midnight!"

Huell kissed Maria, then joined hands with her and Nola, who closed the circle by holding hands with Galia. He held Maria's hand tightly, remembering not to crush Nola's little one, and listened to the song that caused natives of the Western world to weep in their champagne and whiskies, while he imagined guns in the distance crashing, unheard, in the motley chorus of voices raised together in The Camellia Room.

16

Irene refused to allow Tanya's nervousness, betrayed to her nostrils by a sudden freshet of sweat, to distract her from what she had to say next to Prince Subarov. She felt somewhat nervous herself even though she despised Subarov. This remnant of Czarist decadence seemed to believe he was working off his debt to the Russian people by his labors at the International Refugee Organization. In actuality, he was probably enjoying a very good life in Shanghai, his housing provided at IRO expense, his entree into international society—what was left of it—guaranteed to be of the highest order, because of his rank. Not a Romanov, no, but Subarov was genuine enough. Irene had met several spurious Romanovs in Harbin; she was suprised there weren't more than five or six in Shanghai claiming blood kinship to the Czar.

"My sister and I have worked hard and saved our money." Annoyed at herself, Irene was forced to pause and clear her throat. "With our grandmother we got to Harbin with no help from anyone. We left Harbin also on our own. And the three of us have made our life in Shanghai the same way."

Subarov's blue eyes were motionless; their impersonal cordiality had not changed, though now they took on a look of waiting. Certainly he knew this preamble was leading to something.

"Therefore, when we ask for help," Irene said, "we have obviously come to the end of the line. The officials in charge of giving out visas to their countries don't know who needs them the most, and who will use them the best. We are only numbers of stateless people to them: so many Russians, so many German Jews, so many Polish Jews. Only you know which of these people should receive visas. Tanya and I are good, hard workers. We would never become a burden on the society that admits us. The Bordokoffs will be worthy citizens. It does not matter to us what country, Prince Subarov.

(But Belgium or Holland would be nice)

"The visas are put in your hands and you give them out." Irene felt a cold, rushing sensation, as if she were diving off a cliff. "The money we have saved, it is yours, Prince Subarov. Seven thousand American dollars, in cash."

The prince did not react at once. His eyes seemed glued in their sockets. He hardly blinked. Then, sighing, he sat back in his chair and contemplated the two women with a livelier expression. To Irene's dismay, he seemed amused.

"Are you attempting to bribe me?"

"Oh, no. Of course not. Never a bribe. But government is so slow, you know how officials hold meetings all the time and pass papers around for approval and stamps and seals." Irene could not tell where she stood with Subarov now; she could not read him at all. "You would know how to hurry up the process."

"With the money you are offering me."

"Yes."

"To keep for myself in its entirety if I can produce three visas for your family."

"To use as you see fit."

"I find your offer very interesting. It is certainly the first time such a one has been made to me. Refugees generally have no funds; they barely have enough to keep themselves in food."

"We have often gone without food, to save money, to save this money for an emergency." Irene felt her tone growing sullen. How she longed for the luxury of calling him a dirty Czarist parasite to his anemic, long-nosed face. He should have been eliminated by the Bolsheviks; it was a travesty to have to plead with him, to abase herself when she was the better, stronger person.

The prince looked at her as though he could read her thoughts. "I merely wished to be sure of what we were discussing, here."

You knew good and damn well, from the beginning. She glanced at Tanya, whose forehead shone with moisture, and decided to say nothing more. Let Subarov lead himself on. She had said her piece.

"The fact is. The fact is," he said, "the IRO has no visas on hand, whatsoever."

"But if you did?"

"If the IRO did have visas, Miss Bordokoff, they will be dispensed in the order applications were received. As always."

He rose to his feet, only a little man, wearing ridiculous woven-leather shoes in the middle of winter. They were almost sandals. Irene was tempted to stamp hard on one of them with her own hard-shod foot. Subarov even gave her and Tanya a smile, not a friendly one, but one tainted with pity. "I understand your position," he said. "Life is difficult. You are to be commended for having worked hard and saved your money. Keep it for a real emergency. Goodbye, Miss Tanya, Miss Irene."

When she was outside in the street Irene let her feelings go. She unlocked the chain around her bicycle, then grabbed the handlebars and thrust a vicious path through the Chinese on the sidewalk. People scattered left and right, protesting, but after a look at her grim face, decided to laugh and make comments about crazy *loo soong ning*, Russians.

"You're not planning to go to Grigory?" Tanya said, behind her.

"What would you suggest? Subarov will never give us visas now. Somebody else will always be on top of his list. He thinks he's better than us. Either that, or he gets more money from other people."

She did not believe Subarov never accepted
bribes. Irene did not look at Tanya; she could
not afford to be dissuaded by sentiment. On
January 21st, President Chiang Kai-shek had
announced his retirement and left Nanking for
Feng-hua, his native province. That was disturbing enough, then on January 31st Peiping had
fallen to the Communists. Soon afterward, the
Nationalists moved their seat of government from
Nanking to Canton. These Nationalists were liars
worse than any Irene had known in her life. This
was not a retreat, the officials said; the war
was easier to manage from a centralized location
in the south. So far south, they could practi-
cally swim across the Taiwan Strait to refuge on
the island of Taiwan. More than ever, Irene felt
the burden of caretaking on her own shoulders.
She would, and could, savage anyone who got in
her way.

She rode her bicycle grimly to Gromeko's room
on Yates Road.

He was not looking well; the new sweater knitted him by Babushka drooped at the shoulders,
where he had lost the most fat and muscle.
Despite an early healing, his arm wound had
taken an infection. A Chinese doctor said a bit
of cloth might have been left inside and was
making trouble; should he operate? Although
Gromeko told him he would think about it, Irene
wished he would do it, and quickly. She wanted
him to be able and strong. She gave no more than

a second's thought to the irony of the task she had just asked of him.

True to his personality, he gave no sign of its meaning to them all, himself, Tanya, Irene, and Babushka. Only Tanya indulged her distress, sniffing and finally weeping with hands covering her face. She rocked in her chair like a peasant woman lamenting a death, while the two talked.

"How much would it take?" Irene asked.

Gromeko drank, studying the rosy color of the liqueur through the smeary glass, the same he always used and that he seemed never to wash.

"Depends on how much you want to spend. You know the going rates. I couldn't get you English or American, or maybe I can get just one for the money you're putting up, if Tanya stayed behind." Tanya looked up; her hands fell away from her face and she clutched his good arm. Seldom comely, Tanya's looks just now were a ruin. Her pockmarks looked larger than ever, her outthrust chin massive. With rare playfulness, Gromeko wagged his arm, the one with Tanya's hand attached to it. "This girl can grip; she'll really hurt me one day." Tanya's head bent down to rest on his shoulder.

"We can spend seven thousand," Irene said. One thousand had to be kept back for expenses in the new country.

"Seven?" He nodded in approval. "Good for you. Let me look around; maybe I can find something decent for the money. Time is getting on, though. There's not much pickings left."

"Can you find Belgians? That's the best country, I hear. We wouldn't want to go to England,
anyway. I can do without living among all the
bloody snobs. Remember that Babushka will be our
dependent, or the husband's dependent. She goes
with us, Grigory, or we don't go at all."

"I know that. But that's another reason you
won't get decent pickings. Babushka will be
extra baggage, to a candidate. They'll charge
more because of her, so you won't get the full
buying power of your seven thousand."

Pressed to his shoulder, Tanya's head shook a
mute no. Gromeko looked at Irene, who shrugged.
She thought again how she would miss him as an
ally when they were gone. Gromeko always understood that hard things had to be done; he never
wasted his energy regretting having to do them.

"Are you feeling stronger?" she asked. She was
too blunt, but she was tired of locking up her
various frustrations and angers inside.

Following her drift completely, he grinned.
"Do you mean: am I strong enough to take care of
The Camellia Room?"

She nodded. She wanted him to tell her he was
going to let the Chinese doctor operate, but
dared not push him about it.

"I'm working on the arm everyday. Be patient
for a few more weeks," Gromeko said. "That job
will be my going away present to you."

Tanya would not speak to her as they bicycled
home, but that was all right; Irene was busy
hurling insults at Subarov under her breath.

He had no right to despise her money; had he ever earned a cent of his own, when the Czar was alive? She wished Gromeko would kill him. She rode her bicycle in a fury, charging at whoever got in the way and making him jump back from her.

When Ivanka leaped up in a flurry of white fur to greet them, Tanya broke into sobs, as though she had also just realized they would have to leave the dog behind. Did she think things were going to be different if they had gotten visas from Subarov? Irene thought. Either way, they could no more take Ivanka with them than they could take Gromeko. Both would die in China, Gromeko by choice.

Babushka listened to Irene without comment until she finished. Irene gave less than a full account, leaving out mention of the extra expense of including Babushka in the deal, which would get them less desirable husbands. Her grandmother, however, was too shrewd. "I am seventy-eight years old," Babushka said. "If we are all lucky, I may die soon." She removed her large self to the kitchen, where she commenced dishing out their dinner.

"We live in a lunatic asylum," Maria said, holding her head. "What an orchestra of howls and wails. Mrs. Kwilecki was crying when I met her on the stairs, and now it's the B/Ks. It sounds like Tanya is doing the honors. I almost wish they were practicing their awful cabaret numbers again."

"But the Wongs are thriving," her father said. "They stopped up the drains with bricks, did you know that, Maria? He came out and laughed at me while I was mucking them out and getting wet to my knees with filthy water. 'Wait until the Communists come,' he said. 'They'll be putting you in the drains.'" Poldo turned to his wife. "Tell me, honestly, what did I do to them to make them hate us so much?"

Ming Chu continued massaging his arm with a liniment; he had come upstairs stained and half-frozen from being immersed in icy water. She had drawn him a hot bath, but any benefit from it was depleted by the cold air blowing from the open window. Poldo had not done anything to fix the gas leak in the water heater; his dereliction in doing that one thing seemed to declare a defeat that he dared not admit in all his struggles on other fronts. She had bundled him up afterward in flannel pajamas and a sweater, and she made him wear his winter coat until he grew warmer and threw it off. The camphor in the liniment had overcome everyone's sense of taste and smell; their dinner, a dish of pheasant (pheasant was cheaper than chicken) stewed with gingko nuts, tasted of moth balls.

After four years of living above the Wongs, her husband's speculations about them had become mechanical, though the emotions they caused were always terrible, like a wasting fever.

"Their hatred is as much for me, Poldo," Ming Chu said. "I married a foreigner. The Wongs are not like so many Chinese who have been success-ful under foreign occupation. Amah says their daughter is secretly attending Communist youth cell meetings." She was not worried about the Wongs, at the moment. Nola had been very quiet since she and Maria returned from the special Mass given for Daniele. The child had been hav-ing bad dreams. For the past several nights she had stayed up later than anyone except Maria. When Maria came home from work she usually found Nola sitting over homework or finally surren-dered to sleep, her head pillowed on a book on the dining table.

Nola asked, "When is Mrs. Kwilecki going to have her baby? She doesn't look very big. It's hard to decide whether I wish she would have it soon or much later."

Her dreams are filled with unnameable terrors, thought Ming Chu. That is why she speaks a thought a child should not have in her head.

Maria glanced at her mother. What do we do here? They had talked together about Nola.

"It looks to me like she'll be having it in about five months," Maria said. "Babies get born all the time, in bad times and in good. You'd be surprised how people get by when things aren't very convenient for them. I think having a baby, giving birth, is the most inconvenient thing that happens. It's not much fun, in fact it's awful, and—" she stopped and said ruefully to

her mother, "I think I'd better shut up. Have I
made everything worse, Nola?"

"I know all about how it hurts to have a
baby," Nola said. "That's not the point."

Together, Ming Chu and Maria said, "I know."

Hours into the night, the door to her bedroom
opened. Ming Chu knew Nola was barefoot, not to
wake her father.

"Mama?"

"Come inside, quickly, or you will catch cold."

How fragile this body of her daughter was, yet
filled with a spirit so stalwart that Ming Chu
marveled she came to her at all. Every night
Ming Chu had said, quietly, Stay with me
tonight, and Nola did not say yes or no.

She tucked the eiderdown quilt under every
inch of its outer edge, tucked Nola against herself, and covered her icy feet with her bandaged
deformed ones. Poldo stirred and asked, "Are you
all right?" Ming Chu reached behind and patted
him in reassurance, then returned that arm to
its embrace around Nola.

"Mama, I don't want the silkworm eggs in bed
with me anymore. I wrapped the shoebox in a
cloth and put it on the dining table. Will they
be warm enough? Will they die?"

"The cloth will keep them warm. Silkworm eggs
are very hardy, you know. You could leave them
on the kitchen window and they would not suffer." She felt Nola's nose, which had been as
icy as her feet. The child's natural body warmth
was returning.

Nola was quiet so long Ming Chu thought she might be almost asleep. "I didn't want to go to the Mass for Daniele," Nola said. "Don't tell Maria."

Far off, a stirring in the kitchen. Amah, too, was restless. Her husband's annual visit for the New Year was approaching; there were gifts to make, special foods to prepare, though surely she was not at work on them now, at this hour? Amah took Chinese New Year very seriously; this was her own country's celebration, which lasted three days. The Western New Year, on January 1st, rolled by without affecting any Chinese except the merchants catering to Westerners.

"Last night I dreamed about Daniele in his coffin. The coffin was full of silkworm eggs, thousands and thousands. They started to hatch. All the little worms crawled over Daniele. They went up his nose and his ears, and they got into his mouth." Nola shuddered. "Daniele didn't do anything. He let them crawl into him. I didn't know if I wanted him to get up and brush them off or just lie there, dead. I thought, if he moved or did anything, I would wake myself up and jump out of bed. Even though I was asleep I knew Maria wasn't home yet, so I was going to maybe run to you or out of the house." Her trembling thrummed from head to foot, and Ming Chu found herself filled with an anger that was all the more terrible because she could not direct it anywhere. Who, what could she blame? Her husband, lying exhausted in his few hours of peaceful oblivion?

Her older daughter, who carried the true burden
of the family and would continue to do so? The
murky upper world of politicians, each side
indistinguishable from the other, who had done
their ugly work on millions of people? Or herself, because she had not spoken up to her husband
when she should have?

"Father Joseph said the Mass might not help,
because Daniele killed himself and his soul is
probably in hell. That made me feel so bad. Why
doesn't Daniele's wife write back to the consulate, Mama? I wish he could be buried. It's
not right to leave him in a shed with a lot of
other dead people. Can't Daddy ask the consulate
to write to her again?" Nola's whispers, tiny
dabs of moisture next to her cheek.

What would Father Joseph say if Ming Chu went
to him and told him that he was destined for
hell when he died? She had converted in order to
marry Poldo, but the more tales of sin and pun-
ishment Nola brought back from church, the more
Ming Chu detested the Catholic religion. These
people were confused, with their simultaneous
beliefs in God's love and the barbaric consequences of his displeasure.

"I am quite sure the Mass is saving Daniele's
soul. Will you believe your mother? And tomorrow
I will ask your father to go to the consulate,
and he shall go right away, I promise you.
Something will definitely be done before spring,
I promise you that, too."

Nature would fulfill her promise. Daniele's companions in death would be taken away, one by one, as soon as the temperature began rising. Amazing how the Chinese found astral signs mandating burial of their dead when it became imperative. Ming Chu examined the last, cynical thought, and dismissed it as unworthy of remorse. Somewhere in her life she had begun to suspect all religious beliefs, especially foreign ones. It seemed to her that those which worshipped a single God, teaching the faithful to endure their temporal miseries, usually succeeded in compounding them.

"Do you want me to give away the silkworm eggs? Amah's husband can take them back to the country." Ming Chu could just as easily destroy them, though she would not let Nola know that.

"No. They're only poor little silkworm eggs. It's not their fault. If I see them hatch and then I have to start taking care of them, maybe the bad dreams will stop. When they get big, we'll think of something to do with them, won't we?"

No mention of sending them to her aunt in Soochow.

No one had needed to tell Nola that Soochow was doomed before ever the Communist army reached Shanghai. Ming Chu cradled her daughter, warming her, providing the only comfort her powers commanded, and her anger did not abate, not for the entire comfortless night.

17

```
1    oz. Extract Catechu, liq.
5.3  oz. Acetic Acid, gla.
4.3  oz. Essence Grape
56   oz. Citric Acid
20   oz. Jet Black, liq.
10   oz. Cochineal, liq.
10   oz. Dark caramel, liq.
960  oz. Aqua
120  oz. Alcohol
```

There were degrees of desperation, Poldo thought. Anyone drinking this red wine of his either didn't care what he put in his stomach, or was committing a deliberate act of self-sabotage. Maria never told him what kind of people drank the products of his home still. She exchanged the empties for his full bottles, and the money they earned, added to rent income from the B/Ks, kept the Contis in groceries. That the B/Ks should suddenly start paying rent was a miracle he could not fathom. One day in December an envelope, marked

"Bordokoff" and containing a quantity of new gold dollars, appeared under their bedroom door. Each month after that a similar envelope was delivered in the same way. He reacted in kind; he did not speak to them. Also, he stopped his practice of meeting them on the landing to tell them he hoped they would break their necks. It lent a puny but welcome healing to his dignity.

He missed Daniele badly. As dour as Daniele could be, he was someone to whom Poldo would not have been ashamed to show his shame. Daniele, of all people, knew how a man could be made small. Poldo did not blame his daughter. She was strong and lovely and willful; in a different world, Daniele might not have withered to what he had become, his daughter's handmaiden.

His wife's coughing in the next room carried through the wall. She was not well, and Poldo fussed over her with infusions of ginger tea and hot water bottles for her feet. She had not received word from her family in Soochow in three weeks. Ming Chu hardly mentioned the war these days. After the fall of Peiping, she had drawn Nola closer to herself; often, the child slept in their bed.

If they still had Maria's old gelding, Poldo would have gladly chopped him up and served Ming Chu and Nola a nourishing broth from the meat. That would have been his contribution to his family for New Year, the Year of the Ox. In even that, Amah's husband, visiting from the country, had surpassed him.

Carrying a glass demijohn, he went to the kitchen to fill it with water. Amah and her husband were eating bowls of *poh-veh*. The scorched bottom of cooked rice was made savory by pouring hot tea over it; one ate *poh-veh* with salted vegetables or anything to hand. Amah had salted peanuts. Her husband, a wiry man of middle age and feet like corded pistons had walked, burdened with a bamboo pole slung with two heavy baskets, twenty miles in the sleety chill of February. The two baskets were filled with New Year's gifts for the Contis. He had brought salted duck eggs (dyed red for the occasion) which would taste fishy but very rich, and hen's eggs, which farmers kept in clay jars under their beds. Eggs were used on only very special occasions, and they stayed fresh for a considerable time in the porous, cooling clay jars. He had also brought two live chickens, trussed and thrust upside down in one basket. For Nola he had some lengths of sugar cane, somewhat withered since they were out of season, but sweet nonetheless. Amah would soak them in water and they would become as good as a fresh-cut harvest.

For Amah he had a quantity of tung wood shavings, and a new hair brush of pig bristle with a bone handle. He had brought her enough tung wood to dress her hair for the entire year, had he not? He said this with a hint of proud challenge. Amah remained noncommittal. She had put aside the new *py-chee*—a fine-toothed comb carved out of hardwood—as though it were of no account. Her daughter-in-law had made it, hurting her hands many times with the thin-bladed knife, he said, and sent it on with assurances of her respectful devotion.

"She doesn't say she wishes I would come back and live with her, though," Amah said.

"Why should she? It is your, our house. She cannot invite you back to live in your own house."

"And she shaved that tung wood, I know she did. She sent enough to make me a coffin." Tung, besides its use as a hair dressing, had preservative properties. The wealthy bought coffins made of tung wood.

Amah's husband, whose name was Hong, sighed in misused patience. "Instead of complaining about her character, you should be concerned that she has not yet had any children. Even a girl would be something, proof of fertility. If it weren't so expensive, our son should find another wife."

"What do you think we are, rich people?" Amah retorted. "An automobile would be a better purchase. But all that is going to change, you know." Her sparring manner fell away. "Husband, you must remain unnoticed. Look as poor as you can. Become invisible as the earth. If you cannot come next year, I will understand. But send word, somehow, so I know you are alive."

"And you? How will I know if you are alive? Can you not come home with me now, instead of always putting it off?" He looked at Poldo, laboriously filling the five-gallon demijohn through a hose from the faucet, and whispered, "What loyalty do you owe these people? If they leave, they will not take you with them. You will be out in the streets the moment they pack their things."

Poldo pretended he had not heard. The business of existing seemed to complicate itself like a chemical formula gone wild; one reagent converted one substance to another; more reagents created a dolorous soup palatable to no one. The one glimmer of hope on his horizon was a return to normal commerce after the Communists completed their conquest of China.

Amah had shushed her husband and was counting, with satisfaction, the bulbs of garlic he had brought. Poldo knew the garlic would appear in numerous guises over the spring to cure fevers and coughs, and stomach upsets. When Nola had whooping cough and their Italian doctor prescribed medicines that did not work, Amah made a paste of garlic and bound it to the soles of her feet. For twenty-four hours she sweated and cried, as the poultice burned her skin. But the terrible, barking coughs had subsided, and finally stopped. The blisters on her feet came up as big as grapes; the burns would have been worse had Amah not rubbed in mineral oil before she applied the garlic.

Poldo detached the rubber hose, and Hong leaped up to help him carry the heavy demijohn.

"No need," Poldo said. "I can manage quite well. It is nothing."

"But you must allow me, *lo-yah*," Hong insisted. "I am like a buffalo, used to hauling things."

Poldo felt it was easier to give in; between them they hustled the jug into the dining room where, at his direction, Hong set it on the floor under the window. Anyone could have seen where the demijohn virtually lived; a circular stain on the floor marked the exact spot. Poldo thanked him, and in return again received profuse thanks for gifts the Contis had given him for the New Year.

Ming Chu had taken care to uphold their honor, at a cost she would not whittle down despite the havoc wrought on their budget. There was, after all, Amah's face to consider. She had been right. The astonishment on Hong's countenance, and the pride in Amah's, had been worth it. Who gave away a whole bolt of cloth nowadays? In addition, there were twenty yards of black silk called *shang yuen soo*, noisy cloudy silk, because the material rustled as you moved. It was made with a special coating that kept the cloth from sticking to your skin, and so this silk was prized for the hot, humid summers of Shanghai. Moreover, *shang yuen soo* was washable; the more you washed it, the cooler it was to wear. The bolt of black cotton would make clothing for all seasons. But the *shang yuen soo*, the noisy cloudy silk that farmers could not afford, that would be carefully wrapped for eternity, to be shown off on special feast days if there were still a neighbor living who did not know about the magnificent gift from some townspeople of Hong's acquaintance.

To the Contis, who could not afford their rep-
utation for largesse, Hong's pleasure was grat-
ifying; it was the one pleasant thing in a year
that portended no other. The Chinese were behav-
ing as though the three festive days of the New
Year might be their last; or else they were
anticipating renewed prosperity under the
Communists. And what was New Year's without a
parade? Bubbling Well Road had been treated to a
mile-long clangor of drum and cymbal, girls
twirling silk banners, actors draped in ten-
foot-long robes and teetering on stilts, and
there was the usual serpentine dragon.

In the midst of further exchanges between Hong
and Poldo of good wishes for the New Year, a
string of explosions resounded from below-
stairs. Laughter followed, and mocking cries of
"Happy New Year!" and "Long live Mao!" Then more
explosions, a long fusillade. Even with the dining room door closed, the blasts shocked Poldo's
eardrums. He tore open the door, meeting Nola
and Amah on the landing, and looked down the
stairwell. Behind spirals of smoke, the backs of
the Wongs disappeared into their doorway. Mixed
odors of saltpeter, sulfur, and charcoal soon
enveloped everyone upstairs.

Nola said, her voice thin, "They were firecrackers, weren't they, Daddy? Not bombs?"

"Only firecrackers, Nola. A joke. These people are having their idea of fun. Don't pay
them any mind."

Hong looked at him, obviously expecting him to do something about the insult.

He was saved by Amah who said, loudly enough for the Wongs to hear behind their door, "You see, we have wonk dogs in the city too, and we treat them the same way. A kick in the arse if they get in our way is the only thing they understand. You don't do anything else with wonks and they're not worth even that much attention." With scornful laughter, she drew her husband into the kitchen.

Ming Chu's voice called for Nola. Poldo opened the door and told her the explosions had been firecrackers, courtesy of the Wongs. Pale against her pillow, she nodded wearily, unsurprised.

"Look at what they left," Nola remarked, peering at the heaps of ruptured red paper cylinders strewn on the tile floor and as far as the intermediate landing. "They won't sweep it up, ever. Why don't I make a pile outside their door and burn it all up? Shall I, Daddy?"

He wished he could let her do it. He himself had almost succeeded in destroying the house, over that matter of the crab shells. "You heard what Amah said. She handled it better than I could. Just ignore them. The Wongs are the ones who are going to have to live with that mess outside their front door."

Footsteps ascended the stairs. Leon Kwilecki's ravaged matinee-idol face, wreathed in blackish smoke, emerged at the turn of the first landing.

As Kwilecki came up the stairs, Poldo was struck by its expression of...radiance?

"Good day, Mr. Conti," Kwilecki said, smiling.

Kwilecki, smiling?

"Hello, Mr. Kwilecki. How is everything with you?"

"Most wonderful news, I am still stunned over what has happened. Something has gone right, for once. I cannot wait to tell Zina, but of course," Kwilecki said breathlessly, "I should tell you, as well. My dear, patient, sainted Mr. Conti, Zina and I have been awarded visas. To Australia!"

"*Madonna*," Poldo said, shaken. The tragic Kwileckis were to be saved. He thrust out his hand, and Kwilecki took it. Kwilecki nodded and nodded, his emotions quivering all over his face. "You see," Kwilecki said, and started again, "You see," and tears filled his eyes.

Poldo felt ready to weep, himself. It occurred to him, a second later, that with Kwilecki gone the Contis would be surrounded by hostiles, top and bottom. And a second after that Poldo realized he would have a vacant room to rent out.

Their hands had not yet separated. Kwilecki recovered first. "So, to Zina I go with this news. She will not believe me!"

"Tell her congratulations, from the Contis. Let me know if there is anything I can do to help." A grandiose offer of nothing, but it counted for sincerity, and Poldo felt Kwilecki must know that much.

"It was the usual, except for one thing," Kwilecki told his wife. "This time I decided to tell him we had no objection to going back to Poland. For you, my heart, and the baby. If I allowed our child to be born here and placed in the way of danger, then I had no right to my principles. This was what I had been thinking for months. Each week I said to myself that I would tell Subarov next week, and when that time came I put it off. What a fool I have been. A fool meddling with principles, while you grew bigger and bigger. Imagine me, my mouth open and ready to tell Subarov. He was looking so pleased, I couldn't think why, because I was preparing my speech and hadn't said anything yet. Then I heard him saying 'two visas to Australia,' and I had to ask him to repeat everything. Twice."

Zina had been crying steadily since he walked in and blurted out his news. Kwilecki noticed white strands in her hair. Besides her eyes, she looked swollen everywhere—her face, breasts, ankles. Taken with her distended abdomen, her total appearance pierced him with fear. I have almost killed her with my principles, he thought.

"Sydney, Australia," whispered Zina. "That is an island in the Pacific. What will we do there?"

"Not an island. A continent, magnificent unto itself, so large it stands between the South Pacific Ocean and the Indian Ocean. A land rich with opportunity for immigrants." He laughed a

little. "Think of it. Our child will be born an
Australian."

Five days later, he feared their child would
be born a Chinese citizen, on the spot, as they
struggled to get themselves and their possessions aboard a train bound south for the Hong
Kong border. Bodies and their bundles pushed up
the steps without cease until Kwilecki thought
he and Zina, mashed near the head of the flow,
would be suffocated. Subarov had told them to
get to the North Station at Chapei at least six
hours ahead of departure time. The advice had
been excellent. When the Kwileckis and Poldo
Conti, who had insisted on coming with them,
arrived and saw the hundreds of people sitting
and standing about on the platform, Zina wailed
a wordless cry of desolation. Their transport by
rail across Siberia had begun like this. Added
to the crush of riders and their combined
smells, the sub-zero cold had made going to the
bathroom an ordeal beyond belief. Forced by the
one broken, stinking toilet to go out on the
swaying, wind-whipped platform, Zina in frozen
shame had lowered her drawers and voided her
bowels in company with half-a-dozen men and
women. The children always kicked and cried as
their parents held their bottoms over the side.

Poldo Conti proved himself heroic. He seemed
to grow several inches in height; he spread his
arms and herded the Kwileckis within their fold,
absorbing the harshest buffeting on his back and
sides. Zina between them, Kwilecki forged ahead

while Conti pushed. People cursed in a multitude
of languages. For some reason, Conti appeared
exhilarated. Kwilecki heard him shouting, "This
is more like it! Action is the thing! I dare you
to try me! Do your worst!" and sentences in
Italian Kwilecki did not understand. In his mind
he prayed for Zina not to faint, not now.

From their seats, claimed by graceless thumps
of their bottoms, the Kwileckis waved toward the
window. Conti was invisible amongst the mob out
there, but they hoped he saw them, anyway.

By much shoving and maneuvering, Kwilecki
stowed some of their bags in the overhead rack;
the rest he and Zina squeezed in the niche
beneath their bench, guarded by their legs. The
long, upholstered bench was, unaccountably,
humped in the middle; Zina had either to perch
on its top, maintaining an uncertain balance, or
to insert her bottom in the crack at the back.
This was impossible because of her stomach.

The train did not leave for a long time.
Kwilecki hid his nervousness from Zina. His latest dreams had been nightmare sequences of long
delays in unknown terminals, while officials
approached demanding to see documents which
Kwilecki never could find, search though he
might. All his pockets were either sewn up, or
they had holes in them where his papers had
fallen through and been lost. Zina was nowhere
in these dreams; he was always beset by an
urgency to get to her.

He did not take a full breath until the train
had traveled approximately one hundred miles.
They trundled onto a long bridge, its steel,
criss-crossed girders blurring the wide brown
river below. Someone in the compartment, a
Salesian missionary priest, said they were
entering Hangchow, in Chekiang Province.
Hangchow was famous for its monasteries and gar-
dens. Its estuaries led back to the network of
canals and waterways that covered the Yangtze
River Delta area to the north.

Kwilecki relaxed a trifle; he pressed Zina's
hand and pointed at the range of handsome, tree-
decked hills framed in their window. Our luxury
tour of China, he murmured. Zina smiled and
shook her head at him.

Ming Chu Conti had given her some of Nola's
baby clothes, all they could carry. Maria Conti
had given him a mannish handshake. Go ye forth
and conquer Australia, she said, in that odd
mocking way of hers, and then kissed Zina on the
cheek. Irene and Tanya saw them off with
screamed obscenities. This was to be expected,
and Kwilecki barely registered the curses. Above
the din of the dog's barking, Irene yelled
Swine! Filthy do-nothing beggars! You took the
visas he could have given to us!

He almost stopped to point out that two visas
would have been insufficient for three persons
in her family, but decided instead to get himself and Zina out of the building.

The day before, Kwilecki went to the Wayside district to find Metzenbaum. The flat was silent and dusty; before he even stepped inside Kwilecki knew his wife was dead. The man himself had shrunk by a dozen pounds. The putrefaction of his flesh was not waiting for death; Kwilecki found himself talking on an outrush of air, not pausing to inhale. When he had to take a breath he walked away from Metzenbaum, on the pretext of looking out the dirty window. Go and see Subarov, he urged. He's not a bad sort, for a prince. He smiled, to encourage the grumbling humor in which Metzenbaum specialized.

Metzenbaum wasn't even listening. He pointed a skinny finger at the window. "See that wharf? I sweated away my life there when I worked as a stevedore. Cold or hot. But it was in the open and I breathed real air. I brought home decent wages. Wayside was prosperous back in the late thirties. We had our own people running the shops and factories. We built our rabbi a good temple. I even met a classmate from when I was fifteen, in Nurnberg. You know what I think?" He looked at Kwilecki. "A person should know when he has run out of lives. He should tell the doctor to stop treating him. Remember that, Leon."

Kwilecki had not stayed to tell him that he agreed with him. It was Zina and the child for whom he could not make that decision.

The train turned west; in answer to Kwilecki's query the knowledgeable Salesian priest said the route cut through a corner of Kiangsi Province.

Kwilecki did not like going into the interior. He wanted to keep the coast in sight and their direction due south. Zina slept inside his left arm, her stomach an awkward bulge between them. He helped her go to the toilet eight times. Each time, the Salesian guarded their places while they were gone. Zina's stomach got no sympathy from the crowd camped in the corridor.

When they cut back and went through Foochow, near the east central coast of Fukien Province, Kwilecki had not slept in forty-six hours. The sight of the sun rising on their left seemed to switch off a watch light inside of him; he fell asleep as though bludgeoned. He woke up four hours later, aching in every joint, and found Zina patiently waiting to feed him two buns she had purchased from the vendor.

"We are still going south," she said, surprising Kwilecki; he thought he had concealed his worries from her. "We are not on the wrong train; the Father said so. He is going to Hong Kong, too. All of the others in this compartment are. I think you should go back to sleep."

On the third day, Kwilecki helped Zina down the steps of the train onto the cindery ground. They stared at the long striped wooden bar separating China from Kowloon Peninsula, part of the British Crown Colony of Hong Kong. Kowloon was also on the Chinese mainland, but at that brain-numbed moment he could not begin to spell out their differences. A sentry box and a soldier in British Army uniform stood at one end of the bar, and a big Union Jack flapped in the wind above it.

The distance to the sentry box was about one hundred yards. Kwilecki and Zina gathered up their belongings and began walking.

18

The house at number 10 Dixwell Road looked familiar, as though she had once seen a picture of it
in a newspaper. The attic windows were shuttered.
The veranda below it, with its green, pot-bellied
balusters and where she had sat drinking lemonade
with her girlfriends, was cluttered with cast-off
furniture. Two bicycles were manacled to the
rail; apparently thieves were capable of removing
bicycles from second-floor verandas. The stone
walls around the garden hid from view the dia-
mond-shaped windows of the drawing room and
carved mahogany frieze over the entrance, but she
could guess at their condition; and inside, the
dark woods would no longer be polished, the
arched doorways gouged and splintered, the long,
curved banister scratched. The regular applica-
tion of her bottom had helped put a high shine on
that banister; on the night of her sixteenth
birthday party ten friends, including Bob
Madigan, had slid relay races from the attic to
the very last newel post at the bottom.

The grandfather clock, bonging away in the front hall; where had it gone to rest?

As in downtown across Garden Bridge beggars were thick on the sidewalks here. Hongkew was a district that sustained a business life all its own, a legacy of the Japanese Army occupation before and during the world war. Maria had many times complied, smiling, whenever students and Japanese housewives in kimono stopped her on the street and asked her to "make a stitch for our brave pilots." She thought she made especially neat stitches on the panels of silk offered her. The resultant messages in Japanese characters were forwarded to the home country to be given flying men to wear into battle. She never found out whether the characters were prayers or exhortations to acts of bravery; she did know the words were believed to confer powers of protection from harm. Afterward, when reports of Kamikaze missions became public, she thought of those panels. It had never occurred to her to refuse those students and housewives in kimono. She lived in the heart of the Japanese occupation; it was politic to avoid being singled out for reprisal. Italians were, after all allies of the Japanese. Dani said this, with the faintest tone of irony in his voice, as Maria plied the needle and thread on white silk.

Even odder than her sense of detachment from the house where she had grown up and where she had met Dani, was the fact that she was looking at it with Huell, instead of Dani.

"It's quite a mansion," he remarked. "Where did you keep the horse?" The gelding, Ralph, was about to be put down when her father bought it. Its British owner had been relieved and bought cocktails for everyone in the clubhouse at the Shanghai Race Course. And of course Ralph had to be put down after all when they sold the house.

Maria saw Huell did think the house rather grand, and she was pleased she brought him here; she had wanted to show Huell she did not always live above a garbage-strewn alley.

"There's a field in the back, and a barn just big enough for him. It's all fenced in. At least there used to be a fence, and there used to be a barn. Ralph shared the place with ducks, all the ones that grew up after I'd got them as babies, and he never stepped on a single one."

Dani had asked once, quite reasonably, why they couldn't eat some of the ducks when food got scarcer and scarcer in 1944. The cook made an open-palmed gesture—a Chinese shrug—and looked at Maria. Loh, the Ningpo cook, she could fight; the two of them together tested her measure of her own mettle. Go ahead and kill them all, then, she'd said. Cook must have done the deed in the night, well after bedtime. When the first duck turned up at table, braised and succulent with steaming dumplings, Maria stolidly ate a good share of it. Thank you, Maria, Dani said at the end of the meal. His smile made him handsomer than his normally sober expression allowed.

Maria had asked Huell for this little side trip, after he picked her up at Route Magy. She asked this as they were nearing the Cathay Hotel, and he had been embarrassed.

"I could apologize all day and never feel I've made it up to you," he said. "If my boss ever let go his hold of me I'd take you on a Grand Tour of China and never come by the hotel once. Would you believe me? I hate your even having to ask for a detour."

Did he realize how attractive he was? She could forgive many oversights in this trun-cated courting (destined to be limited in any case because he would soon go away). All the dancing and carefree boatings and days at the horse and dog races and the birthday parties of her set seemed frivolous; she was glad she'd had them, but they would have been nonsensical done with Huell. The war cut the meaning of life to the bone. The rare hours with him were shakingly intense ones of introspection and discovery for her.

"I wish I could at least take you dancing," he said. "Would you believe I have actually caught a glimpse of the ballroom at the Cathay? It's a grand-looking place, made for women in yards of pearls and men with slicked-back hair. Did you dance there much?"

"I was a bit young to go alone with my own date, but my parents would take me along with their friends or business groups. My mother was the one with the yards of pearls. She could do a pretty good foxtrot and I always told her it was because the ballroom floor was built on springs. All the women looked marvelous in their floating chiffons and georgettes…" Remembering, she smiled. "My father drank champagne out of my mother's satin slipper. She was quite put out at him for ruining her shoes."

"No boy friend of your own?"

"I had quite a few."

"What a stupid question. Of course you did." His fingers drummed on the hood of the Morris Minor. They were leaning against the little car, which rocked as he shifted his feet. "Where are all those guys now? Do you mind my asking?"

"They went with the war, economics, politics, more war, more politics. They grew up, but not around me."

Over lunch in the hotel dining room, which Maria assured him was very pleasant regardless of the sameness of the menu, she wondered if she were destined to be forever going to some man's living quarters rather than have him come to a place of her own. Dani often spoke of Italy, carefully avoiding mention of his home-town, Bari, in his descriptions of the beauti-ful Adriatic coast. Perhaps twice he said, If only you could see your father's country. He did not speculate upon the circumstances in which she might ever see Italy, though Maria teased him with scenarios of her making an inconvenient appearance in Bari. He did not think they were funny.

Huell talked about the waterways of Chesapeake Bay; his forays in his catboat seemed always to be undertaken alone, though sometimes his father or brother came along. His narratives caught for her whiffs of marshy-smelling spray, images of convoluted shorelines sparsely populated with hardy individuals who shunned the company of other humans. She had snippets of insights that Huell was rather like those individuals. She liked to look at him. His personableness was composed of separate attractive features: that fair complexion, the neat narrow cheekbones, the blue eyes that were capable of as much expressiveness as black. Often he forgot to mask their intense regard of her; she would see, then, that he wanted her, and again she became conscious of his clean lips. She loved his lips. She loved kissing them. They moved on hers with a tender sensuality that aroused her with sweet stirrings of moistening heat. She hated wet, hot, open mouthings and busy tongues; they were all right in themselves, but in the proper order of things were nicer when they came after the initial courting of lips to lips.

Huell's brother, he was saying, had recently committed the second desertion in the family. He wanted to become a professional baseball player.

"You mean, like Joe DiMaggio?" That was the miserly total of her knowledge of baseball. What did she and Huell have in common, really? The only two men who had been her lovers came from faraway foreign countries; newsreels and her snatched readings provided the latest information on those countries. The men didn't care, she reasoned with a clarity both sad and cynical. Sex bridged everything. For a time, at least.

And afterward, joined to Huell in his bed on the fifteenth floor, Maria was willing to acknowledge that sex was potent when it was good. He moved as though he loved her. He stroked her shoulders and kissed her breasts and murmured half-audible words that, all together, brought her hotly to climax and one more time after that.

As breathless as she, Huell lay still for several minutes, his lips against her throat.

Outside their window, a gray sky mantled Pootung. She combed his hair with her fingers. "What was it like in Italy?" What was it like in your war, while Dani was away and telling me only the pretty things in his country.

"Storytelling time? You want facts, lies, or both?"

"Anything. Whatever you remember best out of the whole affair."

"I was a raving, slobbering coward."

"Apart from that."

Huell's laugh quivered along the lengths of their bodies. "Apart from that, I don't remember much else." The covers over his back rustled as he settled to her side. "It was a bloody horror, and I wished I was anywhere but in the middle of it. Do you know how many men died in the Third Infantry Division? More than five thousand. They kept sending in replacements, so many guys died so fast. Anzio beach was just a few months near the end of the Italian campaign, but how was I to know that? It wouldn't have helped much if I did. We should have driven on over the Alban Hills to Rome as soon as we landed, but we spent so much time digging in and around, the Germans got over their surprise and gave back better than they got. That's a nice term for what they really did to us." He was quiet a moment. "But here's one thing that sticks in my mind. It summed up the action at Anzio as well as anything else I can think of. Did you ever read *Scaramouche*? He thought the world was mad, and he laughed at it."

There was this element of Huell that Maria loved. She would tell him one day, if the time left to them permitted, that he would realize his hopes of becoming a journalist. Huell often distilled his inferences in literary parables. The habit seemed to reassure him, reminded him of the unoriginality of every human thought and experience. He was self-sustaining that way but, she thought with a small tick of triumph, he still needed a woman. It was possible she might even be a special woman for him.

A sparrow lighted on the windowsill and peered inside, its head cocked as if it could see them through is own reflection in the glass.

"I was in the back of this truck, a cargo vehicle they call a six-by-six, and they were using them on this occasion to haul the wounded because there weren't any ambulances. Four other guys were in there with me, but I don't remember if they were worse off than me. Probably they were. The medic had given us all morphine before slinging us aboard. He didn't ride with us. So there was the driver, and the private sitting in the back with us. He was from the motor pool, and he was on board in case of breakdowns in the convoy, only our truck came up dead last, far behind the others. That shows you how planning can screw up in the Army.

"The private and driver were black men. Everytime we hit a bump in the road, he'd say, "Sorry, sir," as if it was his fault. He would check the other wounded men and ask if we needed anything, water from our canteens, and so on. I was drifting in and out; I didn't notice much. Then the truck stopped. I heard voices, a man's speaking Italian mixed with broken English, and a woman's, young, no English at all, just rapid-fire Italian sounding scared and pleading. The private got down and went to see what it was about, then he came back and let down the tail-gate. A woman appeared and started to climb in. The Italian man got on after her. They tried not to step on us on the floor, saying, 'Scusi, scusi.' The private loaded on some burlap sacks, big ones. He stashed them around, wherever he could. One was on the floor. It was lying right up against my cheek. The Italian man kept saying "Grazie, grazie," and thank you a lot of times in English. His accent was pretty bad. It turned out he and the girl had been to Foggia, on the Adriatic coast, to forage for food. The farmers always had food. They hid it, and sometimes they sold some at high prices.

"The Italian was trying to be polite, looking at both me and the private, but eventually he saw I wasn't concentrating, so he let me alone and talked straight at the private. He had a dictionary that he was constantly leafing through. The private helped when he got stuck. The Italian said, 'You go to Rome?' and the private came back with, 'We be goin' to Rome, yeah.' The Italian said his companion was his pupil, he was a math teacher, and their neighbors had pooled their money and sent the two of them to bring back food. It took a long time, I don't know how long, for him to get this out. I don't know if I really understood. He kept saying, ''Ow you say?' and the private said, clearly, like a teacher, 'Dey give us de cash,' and 'We be haulin' back de chow.' 'Ciao?' the Italian said. He fiddled with the dictionary but didn't know what to look up. 'No, chow, chow,' the private said, and he spelled it. The Italian was trying hard to learn. He repeated everything back the way the private said it.

"The truck hit a bump, and the private looked at me and said, "Sorry, sir." He was smiling. All the way up from Anzio he'd spoken ordinary English. I thought I should say something about the game he was playing, whatever he was doing to the Italian, but the morphine was wearing off and I was feeling sick to the stomach. Finally I just shut my eyes and tried to sleep, but I couldn't.

"It was getting dark when the truck slowed down in the city. It stopped at some street corner. The two Italians got off and the private helped unload their sacks. The Italian man said, 'I sure be grateful. I ain't never gonna forget wot dat you done, man.' And the private waved and said, 'Peace, brother.' He banged on the truck side for the driver to start up.

"I said something prissy, like, 'Private, was that quite necessary?' and he looked at me and answered, 'I don't know what you mean, Lieutenant. Can you use some water? We will be catching up with the rest of the convoy soon. There will be a medic.' He smiled, and there was something in that smile, like a wall of teeth I would never get past. I let it go."

The abrupt end to Huell's narrative disturbed Maria. "What is it? What are you thinking?"

"Home. The United States of America. Black people being kept apart from others. But they were allowed to go to war. Their draft boards got color-blind when it came to sending black men to catch equal-time bombs and bullets. They were put in all-black units, some in combat, commanded by white officers. But mostly they were mechanics and orderlies and cooks, and in the Navy they could be cooks and stewards. I'd be surprised if they regarded that as a privilege. On the other hand," Huell said, "considering their position in the white man's world, why shouldn't they stay in the rear?"

"Yes." This was not the time to mention how colonials treated the Chinese in their own country. "Did you ever meet that private again?"

"Never. I think of him and that Italian, and I hope the world isn't treating them too badly." Huell flexed his hand. "My arm has gone numb."

Maria raised her head, and when he had moved his arm from beneath it, massaged his biceps with her fingers.

"Now you have passed the story to me, and I will never forget it, either," she said. "And I have read *Scaramouche*. I thought Rafael Sabatini wrote with more flourish than Dumas ever did about his Musketeers. I checked it out of the school library so many times the sisters thought it was a dirty book."

"Did they? Did they take it off the shelves?"

"No. The mother superior read it, and let it stay. She was Irish, and she had a wonderful sense of humor." Maria put her arms around Huell; his body felt firm, the muscles in his back and sides young and resilient. She was well acquainted with death, but she could never reconcile herself to its desecrations upon healthy flesh. She shuddered.

Instantly, Huell drew the covers up over her shoulders. "Do you want to sleep?"

"No. Do you?"

"No, Maria," Huell replied.

Huell let himself out of Colonel Treadway's office and walked past Gunnery Sergeant Hinehart, who nodded and said goodnight. On impulse, Huell made a right turn and went back to Hinehart. "How are things, Gunny?" He did not particularly mean it to be a question regarding Hinehart's personal life. The Gunny had a good brain. Huell was curious to see what it made of the very general question put to it.

The whitish lesion on Hinehart's jaw looked thick and lumpy. Some tropical skin diseases never got cured; malaria also tended to linger in a man's system. Almost all the Marines and their Army reinforcements on Guadalcanal had caught malaria.

"Things, sir," Hinehart said, with no intonation in his voice. "With me, this beats retirement. It's too bad the Chinese have no choice."

"Nor anything else," Huell said. He bade a goodnight to him and took the elevator to the sixth floor. The chief Teletype clerk handed him a new message, datelined 15 April, 1949. The Chinese Communists were offering peace terms that amounted to virtual unconditional surrender from the Kuomintang government. Response was required within five days.

Five days, thought Huell. The Communist forces were reported about to cross the Yangtze River to begin a sweep into southern China. The peace term offer was a farce: the Kuomintang government would reject the terms and ask for a cease-fire and negotiations. And all the time the Communists would march on without a hitch to Shanghai.

Maria and her family had to go. Huell had never phrased it as forcefully as he had three days ago, when they were together. It's too late, she said, dully. My father goes on hoping, like the rest of the foreigners who are staying. His Italian passport has protected him before. Foreigners have come through every Chinese civil war; the Japanese invasion and occupation only made everyone more stubborn.

"But this time it's going to be different. These people are a new generation of Chinese. They're trained by Russians, and nothing stops them. They have a new creed, borrowed from Lenin. I can't even tell you what things I'm afraid might happen to you." Though Huell had not spoken of his intentions, Maria read them in him. Please don't go to my father, she said. You will only upset him, because he will know you are right, you see. He will blame himself, and he does that enough, already.

Even as he urged, he was aware that transport was uncertain. The only shipping active at the moment were British and American warships; the HMS *Amethyst* was anchored across the Whangpo river at Pootung. The HMS *Consort* was on duty guarding the British embassy in Nanking, upriver on the Yangtze. The cruiser *London* and the frigate *Black Swan* were patrolling to the east. The American naval force in the area consisted of the auxiliary communications vessel *El*

Dorado, the hospital ship *Repose*, the troop transport *Chilton*, and the destroyer *Duncan*. These would take on American civilians. A passenger liner was expected, but every berth was booked. He knew that because he had checked.

There was the Dutch ship *Boissevain*, but she wasn't due for a month at least.

The trains were leaving Chapei North Station with people piled on the roofs.

The American Navy would accept other nationals if space allowed. He decided to go to Route Magy and speak to Maria's father.

19

Business was turning bad at The Camellia Room. The British sailors disappeared for a week, and then they were back, but not for long before they were off again. The Americans dropped in less often. Irene did not bother her head about linking the rate of attendance to politics; in her experience, the health of business had always been related to politics. Her vexations stemmed from so many places that she did not know where to settle the blame for them. She had done her best, yet nothing seemed to be coming out right. It was quite possible Subarov had given the Kwileckis visas because they were due for them; but she could not stomach the sight of that cow, Zina, waddling down the stairs, going to Australia.

Gromeko, as matchmaker, had found prospects, one Dutch and one Filipino.

"Two different nationalities?" Irene could have slapped herself for not foreseeing this possibility. "Tanya and I split up? Who takes Babushka, then?"

"Whichever man is willing to have her,"
Gromeko replied. "He gets more money than the
single. Make up your minds. There isn't much
time; you should have started sooner, when the
pickings were lying around to be had."

Tanya had not helped, with her hysterics. Irene
told her coldly to take her pick, the Dutchman or
the Filipino, first choice was Tanya's.

"Neither. I don't want anyone," Tanya cried.
She looked pitifully at Gromeko.

Gromeko opened a drawer in the kitchen table
he used for every purpose and took two playing
cards from a pack inside. He found a pencil and,
shielding the cards with one hand, wrote something on each one. "Pick one," he told Tanya.
She shook her head. Patiently, he waited.
Finally she shut her eyes and extended a forefinger. It touched Gromeko's left hand. He
turned it over, revealing an eight of hearts
with the word "Dutch" scribbled across it.

Gromeko reached for a bottle, filled his glass
with absinthe to the top, and drank it down.
"Congratulations to both of you," he said.

No one had told Babushka, yet. Neither of the
sisters said one word to each other that
evening. The next morning, sitting over tea,
bread and jam, their silence ran hard and bitter
under Babushka's talking. Babushka drank her tea
the Russian way, from a glass. She liked to have
a hard candy on her tongue while she did it.
Finally, she asked if something was wrong. Tanya
whitened and shook her head; Irene shrugged. The

old woman looked carefully at these granddaughters of hers, whom she had raised since they
were four and three years old. Then she, too,
shrugged and left them to go to the bathroom,
once shared with the Kwileckis but now entirely
theirs. The girls' quarrels did not last long;
by tonight the two would be splitting a beer.

"You take her," Irene said viciously. "You're
the one who loves to eat."

Instead of snapping back, Tanya lowered her
chin and commenced to sob.

Except to relay orders to Irene at the bar in
The Camellia Room, she continued to ignore her.
She looked ill without her pancake makeup; she
flaunted the pits in her natural complexion as
though they were wounds in the hands and feet of
Jesus. Irene noticed the few men who were drinking here tonight looking with pity at Tanya. Two
of the regulars, middle-aged Europeans, wore
expressions of resentment. Tanya was not improv-
ing the particular miseries that drove them to
The Camellia Room. Galia had been appalled when
she saw Tanya, but said nothing. She would do so
tomorrow, one could count on that.

The money, seven thousand dollars, had been
paid over to Gromeko. Since he had personally
met the Dutchman and the Filipino, Irene left
the disposition of Babushka for him to decide.
Tanya was entitled to her fits. Irene wished she
had the luxury of indulging her own feelings.

The door opened and the American who was
Maria's boyfriend walked in. Leaning against the

bar, she watched him scan the room for Maria. Handsome and clean, a beauty compared to that sour Daniele. This one was obviously sick in love with her, also. She saw him glance at Tanya and quickly away.

Huell came to the bar. "Hello," he said pleasantly. "I guess Maria hasn't come in, yet."

She said nothing for a couple of seconds, then replied, "She is going to be late." A nervous excitement bloomed in her chest. "She doesn't always get to work on time, because she is so busy, you know, all the people she has to see." Since he only looked puzzled, she feared he would say Thanks, he would wait. "Maria is so beautiful that men fight over her."

"Really." He didn't like her, and he let her see it.

Why didn't he go away, then? Why keep standing there?

"The French, especially, those with some money left. You know, the last fling before they have to go home to their families in France." The heat gushed through her veins, a bright cleansing of anger that felt like a purge. "She's a lucky woman. If I were pretty, believe me I would be busier than her. Look at my poor sister Tanya, what man would want her? We need the money. A woman has to make it where she can. But she likes you best, because she is always telling us how strong and gentle you are. You are her real boyfriend, her special man."

Galia walked out of the office, saw Huell, and smiled. His eyes turned toward her, but they were blank. Galia came over and asked, "Is something wrong? What is the matter?"

If he tells her, Tanya and I will be out in the street in one minute, Irene thought. She didn't care. A lusty battle with Galia would be the sweetest medicine she had swallowed in the last three days.

Politely, as if he hadn't heard Galia, Huell said, "How are you? You're looking very nice, tonight."

"But you don't. What is it?" Galia looked at her watch. "Maria is a little late, but she always turns up. If you can wait, have a drink on the house."

"Thanks. I have to go."

"All right. But I'll tell her you were here. Do you want to leave a message?"

"No. I'll look in some other time." Without saying goodbye, he walked to the door.

Galia fixed a glare upon Irene. She switched to Russian. "What were you talking about?"

"Nothing. He just asked if Maria was here and I told him she was coming very soon."

"Are you sure that was all you said?"

Your father was the court pimp. Your mother had no father's name, Irene thought.

"Of course. He only asked the one question."

She would remember this victory over Queen Maria. Wherever she was to be, in a hovel in the Philippines or on a plantation with servants,

with or without Babushka, she would look back
and savor this moment. And there would be better
than this to come, she promised Maria that in
this hard, ungiving world.

20

Beneath the overhead lights, the bags under Colonel Treadway's eyes reflected purple. If his wife saw him now, Huell thought, she would catch a fit. He suspected the colonel's reluctance to leave China had, in the past months, acquired a different reason. He was fascinated by the progress of China's civil war; even with the aid of the Russian advisers, Mao was proving to be a tactician superior to Chiang. The United States government stood by, pouring $2.5 billion and war materiel into the ineffectual hands of Chiang's people, offering advice that was mostly ignored, and remained helpless to boost the fighting spirit of the Nationalist troops. The rot came from the top.

A cause perceived to be just had to prevail over mere money, said Colonel Treadway.

"Mao has had the Nationalists thinking he'll be coming right through Nanking, so they threw their strongest defences on the south bank of the Yangtze to keep him from crossing and coming

on to Shanghai. But he's at Angking, on the
opposite bank below Nanking. They can't hit anything
with their artillery two hundred miles
away, and they all know it."

He looked straight up at the ceiling into the
lights, without blinking. "Mao's got a problem
of his own, but he'll solve it. In all the years
fighting as a guerrilla, he has never mounted a
waterborne assault. But why hesitate now? What's
a mile or two in the river's width? He will
build boats and rafts if he has to. He will
draft anything the farmers and fishermen have
got that floats. He will give three or four logs
to each platoon and tell them to kick-swim their
way over.

"Damn," Colonel Treadway said. "Why isn't he
on our side?"

"And he has a million troops," Huell said.
"They'll be as effective as ten times that many
Nationalists. Those troops near Changchun could
have surprised Mao from the rear and done some
damage." But they hadn't. The 2,000 Nationalists
were ragtag soldiers who, cut off from their
division, had slunk away rather than fight.

"When he meets up with the rest of his people
crossing above Nanking, four field armies will
be on the march in our direction, spread across
a 400-mile front," Treadway said, his admiration
unbridled. "They can't be getting much to
eat. We haven't had any reports of looting, and
they could use every duck and chicken they come
across."

At a terrible price to his own people, Mao had been careful to keep the locals in every village enroute friendly to the new regime. Huell knew exactly what would follow, once Mao was fully in power. His mind skittered away from that; this war had become a matter so personal he felt like a refugee himself. With the proper note of interrogation in his voice, he said, "It's a two-hour drive to Lunghwa, sir."

"Of course. You'd better get going. We haven't got any official backing for your mission, and he knows that, too. Do the best you can."

"Yes, sir."

"Good luck."

Huell thanked him again and left the room. Gunnery Sergeant Miles Hinehart was waiting for him. The decorations on the left breast of his crisp greens looked more impressive than those on Huell's own left breast. Among the Gunny's campaign ribbons were his Silver Star, the Bronze Star with oak-leaf cluster, and Purple Heart with oak-leaf cluster. The oak-leaf clusters signified a second award. He wore the 1st Marine Division shoulder patch issued after the Guadalcanal campaign: a red numeral 1 on a field of blue and five white stars signifying the Southern Cross, the constellation at which the Marines gazed from their foxholes. His fore-and-aft cap bore the Marine Corps insignia.

Huell was wearing his Chinese-tailored Eisenhower jacket and trousers; the fabric was not strictly regulation, but its olive drab was close enough to

the correct shade. His ribbons included the Bronze
Star, the Purple Heart, an Army Meritorious Unit
Commendation, a WWII Victory Medal, a European-
African-Middle Eastern Campaign medal; at his
left shoulder he wore the patch for U.S. Military
Assistance Advisory Group-China; at his right
shoulder was the patch of his old unit, the 3rd
Infantry Division, diagonal blue stripes on a
white field. His infantry badge, crossed rifles
and U.S. insignia on a blue field, was pinned on
each lapel of his Ike jacket.

He had pinned his insignia on the jacket at a
fast walk; after leaving The Camellia Room he
dashed back to his locker on the ground floor at
Broadway Mansions, grabbed his gear, and
reported to Colonel Treadway on the ninth floor.
The silver captain's bars on shoulders and cap
received a quick polish on his pant leg.

Huell and the Gunnery Sergeant walked
quickly to the elevator; the ride south of the
city to Lunghwa Airfield might take two hours,
or it might require three. Getting past the
roadblocks manned by jittery Nationalist soldiers was an exercise that took all of an
assortment of official documentation plus
Huell's strained Mandarin. Hinehart was coming
along to make the visit to Ambassador John
Leighton Stuart a delegation of two.

He noticed a slight bulge near Hinehart's left
armpit.

"You wouldn't be packing a cannon under there,
would you, Gunny?"

"Only a .45 ACP, sir. No more than my Zippo lighter."

"We are on a diplomatic mission; firearms are not in our dress code on this one."

"I know. I'm not taking my rifle." Hinehart's rifle was a .30-06, M1 rifle called the Garand, the weapon that he swore saved his life in the Solomon Islands. Huell had heard he kept it slung on leather straps under his desk outside Colonel Treadway's office, though he had never seen it for himself.

They rode down in silence. From his locker, Huell withdrew a musette bag containing toilet articles, a shirt, and a change of underwear. Hinehart took a seabag from his. It was not one of the larger seabags, which could have concealed a rifle. The vehicle they drew from the motor pool was a serious-looking black Hudson. With Hinehart at the wheel and maintaining silence, Huell tried for a black hole in place of his mind. He almost resented this quiet interlude; he was not yet prepared to contemplate the gossip so casually fed to him at The Camellia Room. First came the shot, and then the sensation; for a few hours more he needed to stand off the sensation.

He felt control slipping; his heart rate accelerated, and he suppressed a sigh and tried to waylay his thoughts.

The fatal flaw in man was his penis; first he led with it, and then compounded that folly by throwing his heart in after it. Huell had done both with a will; that first sight of her had drawn him as the scent of a new blossom drew a bee. How that was possible, within the seedy environs of a serviceman's bar, he could not explain to himself.

The Reds were less than 200 miles away. This was the fact that overrode everything; why hadn't she been there for him to see, to kiss perhaps one last time? By what hopeless means could he have taken her to safety? He remembered Nola and her child's bravado. *They need businessmen, don't they?*

Quite without conscious thought, he balled up a fist and smashed himself on the scarred place on his thigh. The pain shot straight to his head, and for a second the car's twin headlights merged into one like a gunpowder flash. Better. He was back in line. Then he noticed Hinehart looking at him.

"Are you all right, Sir?"

"No problem, Gunny." He breathed silently through his mouth until the pain sank away.

Even though the Kiangwan Arsenal lay north to their southerly direction, a mile before the turnoff to the arsenal they were obliged to stop at a checkpoint. Huell performed his act, while Hinehart stared straight ahead.

They crossed a small bridge over a creek; the Whangpo River curved on their left, the railroad tracks leading to Shanghai South Station on their right. Road maintenance on the route to Lunghwa had been neglected, electric lighting sketchy. Virtually picking his way, Hinehart kept alternating his headlights from low to high beam. There was nothing to see, just weed-tufted flatness whenever the half moon chose to emerge from cloud cover. The oily, secretive odors of the Whangpo floated with them all the way.

They went through three more checkpoints, and arrived at Lunghwa with less than fifteen minutes to spare before the DC-3 took off. The DC-3 was a stripped version of the postwar, reconditioned aircraft. There were no seats. The last to arrive, Huell and Hinehart squeezed themselves and their kits against the bulkhead of the cockpit.

This flight was loaded with enlisted men; if there were any NCOs, they were not visible to Huell. The men were using their duffels as seats and backrests. Exuberance was high—they were going home. The fluorescent lights on each side worked intermittently. As the aircraft climbed, the chill increased. Some of the men gave mock groans and complained about the no-frills ride.

"What the hell, it's free," somebody said. "And it's heading in the right direction."

The level of cheer prodded Huell from all sides.

A voice near the end of the fuselage said, "I sure could use me a warm body right this minute. Vera, oh Vera, where are you when I need you?"

A corporal sitting near Huell said, "That wouldn't be the same Vera I know, would it? Tits like hot French bread loaves you could wrap around your head? Belly a man could pillow

his head and go to sleep on? Blond, but not all
the way?"

"Nope. Not my Vera," came from the back. "My
gal was kind of skinny, but she was hot as mustard. She cost me, but them Rooskies are something else when they're in the sack."

A third man said, "You ever try Chinese? In
Peiping I had me a room near post and she was
there all the time, no chasing around for tail
for me. I used to grab a pedicab any twenty minutes off I got and run up and fuck her, and she
was happy as hell to see me. She used to be an
acrobat, and she could fuck me standing on her
head, and me still in uniform. I called her the
Chink in my armor." He laughed at his own wit.

Huell listened, appalled. Did he talk that way
when he shipped out from Italy? He tried to
recall. Even with a torn leg and on crutches,
waiting for transport to the Army hospital in
Frankfurt, he had managed to connect with and
sleep with two girls. The experiences had given
him a sense of completion; a warrior fought, and
even if he did not rape or pillage, he was due
some sort of reward. Unless a man's nature sent
him to it, rape was unnecessary, not when so many
hungry women offered themselves. The first
Italian girl was Roman; her shoes were cracked,
and her sharp hipbones bruised him. The second
came from a province in the south. He had picked
each up in different bars, on successive nights.
He could not remember if he had given any thought
to what they felt about him or the condition of

their world as he talked to them in his few words of atrocious Italian. One laughed, but not meanly. He had felt like a schoolboy then; at the same time he realized the power of the American greenback.

He could not remember if he had boasted of his exploits; he hoped he had been asleep, preferably dead, when he was being flown to Germany.

Gunnery Sergeant Miles Hinehart said softly, so that only Huell heard him, "You can tell there's no one in this bunch bringing home a war bride. It's like this every time they pull out from a tour. They'll talk about pussy until you think their brains have dropped permanently into their pants. But as soon as they get close to home in the States, there's a miracle. Every man shuts his mouth. All of a sudden they've got wives and girlfriends to think of, and they're hoping nobody will rat on what they've done."

This was the most Huell had ever heard the Sergeant say in one mouthful. He did not reply. The men would not normally be talking this way in the presence of an officer. It was because of where he sat: the jumble of duffels and the bad lighting; also, he had taken off his cap to keep it from being crushed against the bulkhead.

The flight was short; he spent the rest of it staring at the black emptiness outside a window while the men filled the fuselage with images of their sexual adventures. The women were never depicted as anything more than spread legs, hot vulvas, gigantic breasts or pert, virginal ones,

billowy buttocks or neat handfuls in a man's
palms, pink or pale or yellow in color, blond,
brunet, or red-or black-haired, talented of
tongue and lip, safe or diseased, youthful or
past prime, which seemed to be thirty years of
age. One thing was a constant: the women were
always interested in money. One man said he had
an address to look up in Hong Kong, his last
chance for yellow pussy until good old Honolulu.
He had heard planes refueled in Tokyo but servicemen had to stay in the terminal.

The aircraft landed, unloaded some supplies
for the American Embassy along with Huell and
Hinehart, and taxied around almost at once for
takeoff. A civilian truck drove up and two
Chinese men began to load the supplies. The sergeant went to identify himself to the driver.

The near southwestern horizon flared with
occasional bursts of light, followed by crumps
of artillery bombardment. With each round of
light and sound, small dark shapes lifted from
unseen trees in the distance and wheeled distressed circles in the sky.

Hinehart returned, reported that their ride to
town was confirmed. He studied the flying shapes
for a moment. "They're bats. I don't think
they've got food on their minds tonight."

"About twenty-five miles off, would you say?"
Huell had no doubt the shelling was a complete
waste of ammunition.

"That's how far I make it, too."

Huell went to the entrance of the terminal and looked around. Once a hub of United States military movement, the area was deserted, littered with cigarette butts and orange peels. The staff consisted of two glum men in Nationalist uniform. They did not bother to salute Huell.

Their transport was a large U.S. Army truck used to carry cargo or troops, the kind soldiers called a deuce-and-a-half. They rode in the cab up front with the driver, a Chinese employee of the Embassy. Again, the Sergeant surprised Huell. His Chinese, a mixture of Mandarin and Shanghai, was facile if not elegant. Glum, the driver shook his head: Nanking was as good as finished; acting President Li Tsung-jen was powerless, and that coward Chiang ought to be strung up, wherever he was hiding in his "retirement." To Hinehart's question as to whether he believed any Communists had already infiltrated the city, he replied that he knew it for a fact. The men were always in civilian clothing, of course, but they were strangers, and no one dared to look at them. The driver said he would deliver the supplies but he wasn't reporting for work tomorrow; he didn't want to be caught working for the Americans when the Communists took over.

Curfew was in force, but they met no one to challenge them. The artillery barrages rocked in their ears as the truck neared the city. The driver swore. What with one worry or another, sleep was impossible.

The commanders who had plotted the gun emplacements realize their mistake by now, Huell thought. They know Mao is out of their reach. They can't split up and chase him in two different directions.

At midnight, the city of Nanking was shut down tight. Huell wondered if Chiang Kai-shek had looted the city's art treasures as he had those of Peiping. He probably had. As capital of Kiangsu Province in central eastern China, Nanking had housed a galaxy of scholars, poets, artists, and philosophers. The knowledge was common among the military flying personnel: from Peiping Chiang had ferried plane after planeload of jade and ivory carvings, tapestries, porcelains, jewels, and ancient court gowns to Taiwan. The ostensible reason, of course, was to preserve China's treasure from barbarian Communism.

The driver dropped them off at the Nanking Majestic Hotel.

Though clean, unlike the air terminal, the same atmosphere of desertion pervaded the lobby. Huell noticed pale rectangles on the walls where paintings had hung and the absence of valuable vases that were there on his last visit. The clerk apologized for the lack of food service; the hour was too late. He could, perhaps, find them something in the kitchen. The man's clothing struck Huell as odd; he wore black cotton tunic and trousers, which even under artificial light looked faded.

Huell told Hinehart he could wait for the food if he wished, but he himself was going up to his room.

"I'll meet you down here at 0800, Gunny. Good night."

The room smelled musty from lack of use. He opened the window, letting in gusts of chilly air, but he felt neither cold nor hunger. From the eighth floor he had a theater-box view: the lancings of vivid streaks into the night and red-tinged smoke rolling away from each salvo. The Nationalists were positioned close, on Nanking's outskirts. The noise did not bother him. It was something he understood and therefore could disregard.

That wall in his mind surrounding Maria yawned open and he fell in. Why hadn't he left a message with Galia? Because of what the waitress said? Was he running away? Of all times to leave Shanghai. Those men in the plane. A hundred penises looking for a warm port of call. Procreation the farthest thing from intent, more like flies leaving maggots behind on defenseless carcasses. But the women were ready, able and willing. Of course they were, you fool. Do air and water fill a belly? Much better, maggots. Try it yourself sometime.

But not Maria. Never Maria. And if it was true, what the waitress said? What then, Thaddeus Huell? Do you acknowledge your own maggots? Daddy! Don't you know us? We're yours! But

I was her own special boyfriend, the waitress told me. No money was involved.

She had been afraid, that first night he spoke to her. Don't make me sorry. Don't talk, don't tell your serviceman's jokes about me.

She knew her servicemen, did Maria.

But she heard them every night, at the bar.

Now that was true. Smoke and gossip all over her, like dirty laundry. No wonder she held herself apart from the gang at the bar. She couldn't help but expect talk about herself. Did the French boast about their conquests? Hardly conquests, if they involved money. Gossip. He recalled the smug look on the waitress's face. Something behind her chummy girl-talk there. He should have talked to Galia; instead he had run. He had a duty to perform for his colonel, couldn't spare two minutes, the good little soldier had run.

Unable to sit still any longer, Huell left the room and went downstairs. To the desk clerk he said he was going out for a walk.

"But there is curfew," the clerk protested. "It is dangerous. You must not go out."

Recollecting himself, Huell halted at the point of exit. He was in uniform, the worst sort of flag to flaunt in the dark streets at this hour, with Mao's agents skulking around. And he still had a duty to perform for his colonel. He said good night and stepped back in the elevator. The reason for the hotel clerk's clothing came to him: the man was camouflaged for any emergency; all over the city, people must be burying their U.S. currency and jewelry and trying to look poor.

He returned to his room and sat down at the window. The bombardment went on, aiming for an enemy well out of reach across the Yangtze or already making its crossing. The magnitude of the Yangtze had stunned him when back in America he first studied its importance to China. The river fed half the crops in China and times beyond count it rose and obliterated the crops. The Yangtze was the longest river in both China and Asia, and the fourth longest river in the world. Springing from its source in the west of China, the body of water coursed more than 3,400 miles, traversed twelve provinces including the autonomous region of Tibet, and fed from eight huge tributaries. It cut between mountain peaks crowned with glaciers, roared down gorges 2,000 feet high between forested bluffs, and at its northeastern angle at the North China Plain, near the cities of An-ch'ing, Wu-hsi, and Soochow, its width reached 6,000 feet. From there it chased east to its place of muster, the Yangtze Delta, before dividing into two giant arms that drained into the East China Sea.

Often, the mighty Yangtze River decreed who lived and who died. It was about to do so, again.

The drumfire was hypnotic; not calming, no, but Huell's mental alarums slowed, and he mused upon life flowing from event to inevitable event; that actions occurring centuries and

decades in the past came to fruition every second of every day. Brought about by either free
choice or abject fatalism the outcome shaped
itself and having done so, admixed with the circumstances of the day and moved on.

He knew what he felt. More than that was
beyond his ability to control.

At some point in the night Huell thought of
looking at his watch. It was nearly five. He got
up stiffly, stripped off his uniform and went
into the bathroom. Perhaps there was hot water
for a shower; if not, he would take it cold.

At six he shaved carefully, then rang downstairs for breakfast. At 0755 he stepped out of
the elevator and found Hinehart already there.

They walked to the American Embassy, which lay
in the central commercial district. Unlike
Shanghai, the traffic was orderly, past the
point of panic. Noodle vendors on street corners
were busy chopping green onions and ladling out
breakfast to customers seated on benches. The
customers were dressed as modestly as the noodle
vendors. Women toting string bags wore no rings
or watches. On servant women the ubiquitous
earstuds were missing. Distrusting banks, they
put their savings into gold and good stones.
Often all their own healthy teeth were filed
down and capped in gold.

The scenes of drabness denied the hectic prosperity that once characterized Nanking as
Shanghai's closest rival in commerce. Many store
fronts were shut down, their steel shutters

padlocked to rings set in the sidewalk. There were beggars. There were always beggars.

Gunny and I look like peacocks in a mud field, Huell thought. It was an uncomfortable feeling. He imagined the sergeant was remembering about offering a good target to snipers.

The platoon of Marines guarding the American Embassy had been reduced to six. An American flag hung from a staff above the building. The Marine sentry posted at the entrance saluted Huell and respectfully asked to see their IDs. Sir, thank you, he said, saluted again, and motioned them inside.

As they were shown into his office, Ambassador John Leighton Stuart courteously rose from his chair behind the desk. It had been Huell's decision to have Gunnery Sergeant Hinehart accompany him into the office, rather than leave him to wait in the anteroom. The idea was to show the Ambassador the colors of the U.S. Military. Hinehart's magnificent chest decorations could do no harm to Huell's case, which he was about to lay before the ambassador.

"Compliments from Colonel John Treadway, sir. He trusts notice of our call wasn't too short."

"Please sit. Could you do with some coffee? We received fresh supplies last night, but of course you'd know about it." Ambassador Stuart smiled; he was genuinely relaxed, Huell realized.

"Thank you. Coffee would be fine." Huell placed his cover on his knee; Hinehart did the same. The Ambassador's gloomy office was spare of furnishings. The only bright touch was a good Ningsia wool carpet of blue, red, and beige geometrical patttern, its design cut in relief. The usual American flag stood on its stanchion behind the desk; on the walls hung a photograph of President Harry S. Truman (signed, as far as Huell could tell). Another was a group picture on some American college campus, and a third displayed the Ambassador in the forefront of Chinese dignitaries.

"I've been reading a lot lately, you know, especially at night," the Ambassador said. He spoke slowly, as tired people will. "The literature of choice has been, for some time, the writings of Mao Tse-tung. I've been studying, you might say. There is a treatise he wrote in 1928 that lays out the core of his whole philosophy. He calls it 'The Question Of The Character Of The Revolution,' and it goes, more or less, like this: 'The program for a thorough democratic revolution in China comprises the overthrow of imperialism so as to achieve complete national liberation, and, internally, the elimination of the power and influence of the comprador class in the cities, the completion of the agrarian revolution in order to abolish feudal relations in the villages, and the overthrow of the warlords.'

"He is going to do it, Captain, and all us puny advisers with our billions of dollars have done is delay him from achieving his objective by a few months. Maybe we even speeded it up. Yes. We might have done that." Fingers laced behind his head, he leaned back in his big soft chair and regarded his visitors with eyes that reminded Huell of Colonel Treadway.

"I have read that passage, sir. And I am sure you have read his Manifesto Of The Chinese People's Liberation Army. The final one of his eight points says, 'Repudiate the traitorous foreign policy of the dictatorial Chiang Kai-shek government, abrogate all the treasonable treaties.' He wanted the U.S. troops out, and we went. He will not recognize the diplomatic corps of the United States government, either." But he knows that, Huell thought. Then why is he hanging on here?

The door opened and a white-coated houseman carried in a tray. He placed it on the desk, at the ambassador's right side. Stuart occupied several minutes pouring from a silver urn coffee steaming and very American in aroma. He asked their preferences about cream and sugar. The cups were round and deep, the coffee delicious to Huell's tongue. In China he had gotten used to evaporated milk; fresh milk was chancy, depending upon the supplier. He had scarcely noticed eating his breakfast toast and drinking some sort of dark liquid.

Gunnery Sergeant Hinehart took a few token sips, then primly set cup and saucer on the edge of the desk.

Stuart drank his own coffee in voluptuous drafts. "Americans are spoiled, wouldn't you agree? We think we are deprived of the necessities of life if we can't have butter on demand or the popcorn to go with it. For my sin of gluttony I will most probably come back in the next life as a well-digger in the Arabian desert." He smiled, displaying charm; everything else about his visage sagged with weariness. "Colonel Treadway wants—advises—me to leave Nanking as soon as possible. That's what he sent you to tell me."

"An Army Air Force courier plane will touch down in Nanking tonight at 8 P.M. Space will be made available for yourself and all of the Marines. Sir, if I may," Huell said. "In all of these evacuations, Mao has never had in his hands a high-ranking diplomat of the United States. If he does, this time, he may want to make a potent point to the American government."

"A detainment? That's hardly potent."

"Perhaps more than detainment."

"Do you know what, Captain? I intend to stay and find out precisely what he will do with me. Call me a test case. Look at these gray hairs," Stuart said, tugging at his locks. "I got them trying to talk President Chiang Kai-shek into sticking to his post instead of phoning in sick and running for Fenghua. That's his native province. Do you know what he told me? That he had a dying uncle he had to see, or maybe it was a cousin. Whichever. Since 1927 he has moved his capital three times. Now it's at Canton.

"Do you know why I am not going to move my embassy? I got tired of the Ambassador of the United States packing up, like some kind of camp

follower. Chiang may have justified his moves as
'strategic,' but they feel like shameful
retreats. It's gotten to be a personal issue
with me."

"Colonel Treadway would understand and sympa-
thize, Ambassador. He still feels responsible
for your safety." The State Department was
doubtless unhappy about the Ambassador's stub-
bornness, too. He hesitated. "Sir, I am saying
this entirely on my own initiative. Should you
be mistreated, you will be forcing the United
States into taking action they would otherwise
prefer to avoid. Colonel Treadway has not
authorized me to make this statement."

"Of course he hasn't," Stuart said, openly
skeptical. "I understand your position. I even
understand the position of the United States.
I'm very sure they will not go to war over one
man who happens to have a diplomatic title. You
may report to Colonel Treadway that I undertake
this venture on my own responsibility. My curi-
osity about Mao will not kill this cat. I trust
in the diplomatic process." He looked at
Hinehart. "What do you think, Sergeant? Did you
Marines give ground in the Pacific? My own situation is a thousand times less dangerous than
yours was."

Hinehart did not reply at once. Then, slowly,
he said, "Our unit commander was responsible
for us, sir. He tried to keep us from getting
killed at the same time we tried to hold onto
our positions."

The Ambassador seemed to be expect more, but Hinehart was done speaking. The weary flesh of Ambassador Stuart's face pinkened. "Touche," he said. "And I am responsible for the six Marines left here to guard me. I was not forgetting them, Sergeant. They are on my mind, too. Before you ever called on me I planned to send them to Shanghai. I know, I know," he said, his hand warding off Huell's reply. "Colonel Treadway would have a fit if they left me here by myself."

"They would require a direct order from him to evacuate without you. And he will not give it."

"I am, however, a personal representative of the President. I can use my clout when necessary." The gaze he directed at Huell was polite, but had become inattentive; the interview was winding down. "You have done your best, Captain Huell and Sergeant Hinehart. I will tell Colonel Treadway so. The Marines will be on the courier plane tonight." He rose, and as they did so, came around the desk and shook their hands. Huell and Hinehart saluted.

"There might be a couple of days yet," Huell said. "You can still change your mind. No government in the world will see it as a retreat."

"I will remember that, Captain. Thank you for coming. Give my regards to Colonel Treadway." He stood in the middle of the bright Ningsia carpet as they closed the door behind them.

The sentry at the gate saluted; Huell returned his salute and said, "Take care, Corporal." He was perhaps twenty years old, with dark eyes that girls might consider romantic.

They walked back toward the hotel. Neither would go outdoors until it was time to go to the airfield. Huell had failed in his objective but Colonel Treadway expected that.

"Do you want to bet, Gunny, that none of those Marines will be on the plane tonight?"

"I know it, Sir. They're Marines," Hinehart said.

Huell restrained an impulse to blurt, "Damn right, they are." Hinehart might take it as mockery. In any case, the moment had passed.

Duty done, he thought of the thing he would do as soon as he got back to Shanghai.

The date was April 20th, 1949.

21

Mao Tse-tung's men stood poised like whetted blades for the coming fight. They were massed at hundreds of camps starting opposite Anking up to Chinkiang. Ignored for the time being, the great city of Nanking crouched in between. Its Nationalist shore batteries were useless. Above Nanking the Yangtze River turned east in its run to the East China Sea, so that the shore where the Communists waited was first west, and then north. Nanking stood on the east shore, Shanghai and the sea at its back. Mao placed artillery among his camps to protect the crossing. More guns were emplaced on the north shore, closer to Shanghai. In charge was General Liu, a man known for his dedication and hot temper.

On the morning of April 19th the British frigate *Amethyst*, with her complement of 183 officers and men and sixteen-year-old seamen-cadets, sailed down the Whangpo River to Woosung. Because of its position at the mouth of the Whangpo leading to Shanghai, Woosung had

been used over time as a fort. At Woosung, the
Amethyst entered the lower arm of the Yangtze
estuary that led to the East China Sea, then
continued inward toward Nanking; she was to
relieve the HMS *Consort*, on guard duty at
Nanking. The night before, as many of the
sailors of the *Amethyst* who could get shore
leave spent it at The Camellia Room.

The ship made approximately 100 miles that
day, then anchored for the night at Kiangyin.
The captain, a man named Bernard Skinner, knew
all about Mao's gun emplacements on the north
shore. He counted on a peaceable voyage to
Nanking, since his ship was a foreign vessel and
nothing to do with China's civil war.

At 8 A.M. next day, as the crew got ready to
haul anchor, the guns on the north shore awoke.
Shells flew over the ship; more followed. All
were misses. The men on the *Amethyst* decided the
crossing was on. But it wasn't their war; they
were just spectators. The crew put on steam and
continued their journey. Ahead lay a small
island called Rose Island.

The *Amethyst* nosed into the north channel
around the island. The shore batteries at that
point opened up. Two shells hit the *Amethyst*.
Its wheelhouse in splinters, the frigate drifted
into the shallows off Rose Island. Two more
shots hit. The bridge was blasted; Captain
Skinner fell dying. More hits: dozens of men lay
scattered on deck. The *Amethyst* ground into mud,

and there she stuck, a broadside target for the shore batteries.

Someone managed to send an SOS. The radio was heard in Nanking by HMS *Consort*, which the *Amethyst* had started out to relieve. The *Consort* acknowledged the radio and relayed it to Sir Ralph Stevenson, the British Ambassador.

On the *Amethyst*, acting commander Lieutenant Geoffrey Weston ordered the one boat left intact to be lowered and the crew to jump off the ship. He still hoped the *Amethyst* might pull free of the mud; also, the *Consort* had signaled they were coming to the rescue. When the ship's company began diving overboard the Communists added machine-gun fire to their big guns. Some of the men swam for Rose Island.

There had been spectators to this massacre. Nationalist troops on the south shore sent sampans to Rose Island and took on the wounded.

Rushing from Nanking, the *Consort* arrived at Rose Island, guns blazing at General Liu's shore batteries. Almost immediately, her bridge and wheelhouse flew apart under shells. A dozen more hits killed eight men and wounded thirty, including the captain. Struggling herself, the *Consort* worried about towing the *Amethyst* free. The acting commander on the *Amethyst* told her to leave; the shore batteries would destroy her if she didn't. The *Consort* blinked a signal to the *Amethyst*: HOLD ON HELP ON WAY, and steamed back upriver toward Nanking.

For hours until late night, Lieutenant Geoffrey Weston did everything he knew to get his ship off the mud. He and a skeleton crew threw overboard their mess table, benches, bunk beds, broken equipment, pieces of the *Amethyst* herself. Finally she was light enough. The mud let go, and she labored nearly two miles upriver.

Meanwhile, from Shanghai, the frigate *Black Swan* and the 10,000-ton cruiser *London* were steaming upriver after the *Amethyst*. At 9:30 A.M. on April 21st the *London* radioed the *Amethyst*: they would soon come alongside and take her in charge. She never got there.

General Liu sent shells crashing into the *London*'s side. Fifteen men were killed, twenty wounded. Unlike the *Consort*, the 10,000-ton *London* fired not a single shot in return. They were observing the rules; this was not Britain's war. Firing back might make it theirs. The *London* turned back, signaling an apology to the *Amethyst*: SORRY WE CANNOT HELP YOU TODAY. WE SHALL KEEP ON TRYING.

Seventeen dead lay on the deck of the *Amethyst*. The wounded taken ashore by the Nationalist soldiers were put on a train to Shanghai. The frigate managed to push on up the Yangtze; she did not get far before having to drop anchor again.

Eight hundred miles away in Hong Kong, the Royal Air Force got together a medical team and sent them aboard a Sunderland flying boat to the *Amethyst*. The Sunderland barely landed before the

Communists began shooting at her. The wounded frigate lay close by. A member of the crew commandeered a sampan and ordered, then had to wave a gun at some Chinese civilians to row him out to the aircraft. Amid fire from the Communists, one medic tumbled into the sampan; the other was given no opportunity to get out or hand over his medical supplies. The pilot took off.

Soon afterward, the *Amethyst* was captured.

The Communist crossing of the Yangtze River had begun.

22

The motley flotilla crossed the Yangtze River.

Sampans, junks, rowboats, barges, rafts—soldiers holding on and being towed—landed on the opposite shore and found no resistance from the Nationalists. General Liu's troops met no resistance. Having crossed south of Nanking, General Lin Piao's soldiers met no resistance; the Nationalists fled before them. General Chen Yi crossed at Chinkiang above Nanking; they would meet up with the armies of General Lin Piao. On the north shore of the Yangtze, General Liu's artillery kept pace with them in the same easterly direction, providing cover; any Kuomintang resistance would be blasted to pieces ahead of the armies.

Shanghai was the prize.

A dream often visited can hold no more surprises in reality. The crumps of artillery fire and the tremors of the floor beneath Maria's feet were a reprise of the years she went to school under bombardment from the air. Like everyone else she

eagerly awaited liberation by the Americans from
the Japanese occupational army. It had never
occurred to her she might be killed.

The barrages sounded louder than they had an
hour ago. She went out on the sidewalk. The
crowds and automobiles bearing their rich
Chinese owners streaming across Garden Bridge
had doubled in size. They were abandoning Chapei
northwest of Shanghai and Hongkew and running
south. Odd. There was a distinct smell to their
fear, like bread left to grow sour and moldy.
She moved closer to the perfume of her mimosa
tree, in flossy bloom on this spring day. Spied
between gaps in the golden sprays the urgency of
the gray populace moved as a single mass, like a
crowd scene viewed on a tiny cinema screen; and
she could shut off the rattle and rumble of
their flight. Perhaps only the mimosa was real.
This bit of spring was her reward for adding
good dirt at the roots; in one year the tree had
grown and its reach had spread. It's not your
special soil, darlink, Galia said. It's because
of the soldiers and sailors pissing and vomiting
on it.

Another crump. A pedicab ran over a dog. Its
muzzle opened in a scream Maria could not hear
because she had turned off the sound track.

Her parents had begged her to stay home, but
there were things to salvage, those she and
Galia could hide or carry—which now would not be
very much since every pedicab or rickshaw passing was loaded with people and their belongings.

The silverware, cheap as it was, would be costly to replace; they could carry at least a hundred pieces without benefit of pedicab. Two hundred napkins made of red cotton (so that stubborn stains wouldn't show) might not weigh much but added to the metal forks and knives made up the total ability of Maria and Galia to save what they could of their assets. It was likely they would not carry away anything at all, not amongst the crowd surging past Broadway and over Garden Bridge.

To Maria's and Galia's surprise, the B/Ks had appeared for work, as Irene put it, "To save our jobs when you open for business again."

They had set to work, Maria for once grateful for Tanya's sturdiness. All the bottles of liquor were set on the floor beneath the bar counter; glassware, more than three hundred pieces of assorted sizes and shapes—Galia looked around for cover—went under a bank of tables moved edge to edge. On top of the glasses they put Galia's pillows and two crumpled bedsheets and Yung's kitchen towels. On top of those they added Galia's mattress. Around the sides they piled upended tables and chairs. It was pitiful, thought Maria, an illusion of safety. Many times she stepped outdoors and stared across at Broadway Mansions; the only word she had of Huell came yesterday via a puffing Chinese man, a janitor probably. *Cannot get away. I'll find you at Camellia or at home. Stay safe.* She had read the note so many times the paper knew how to fold itself. It was only the second time she had seen his handwriting. The letters were large and looping; the few words filled the paper with the appearance of content, if the expenditure of ink counted for something. Yes, she did expect more from him. She needed what she could never give Dani, poor Dani, unclaimed by his family and buried at last in Hungjao Cemetery.

The door opened and Grigory Gromeko strolled in.

Tanya smiled happily and went over to kiss his cheek. Maria hadn't known they were friends; were they lovers? Irene also smiled.

Maria disliked the smirking quality of it. "I'm sorry," she said. "We aren't open for business. But I can give you a cherry brandy, a quick one. We have to get out soon." She found the bottle under the counter. She hunted for a glass before remembering where all of it was now kept.

"Is Madame Galia here?" he asked. A boom then a thud; the ceiling creaked. Plaster dust sifted down on everyone's head.

"She is upstairs, packing her things. We are leaving any minute," she repeated. She wished he would go away.

Gromeko walked to the kitchen and disappeared through the door leading to the stairs.

Puzzled, Maria followed. He was starting up the stairs, his heavy tread shaking the whole flimsy structure of the stairway. "What are you doing?" Obviously, going upstairs, but "What are you doing," she said again. A tension gathered in her muscles. He turned to look down and smiled. The insides of his upper teeth were ugly, green, black. "Stop! Stop it!" she yelled. "Galia, look out, this man is up to something!" From behind, someone grabbed at her; instinctively she kicked out backward and turned to look. Glowering at her, Tanya lay sprawled at the bottom of the stairs, her skirt over her hips.

In the doorway Irene stood laughing. "Go, Grigory. Go! Go!" she shouted. She clapped her hands.

Maria sprinted up and caught Gromeko's ankle. She found she was still clutching the cherry brandy bottle. She reversed her grip on its neck and hit his ankle with it, his knee, wherever she could reach. Gromeko cursed and reached under his sweater and came out with a knife. He wagged it at her, warning her to stop. Its point looked very sharp but she kept on hitting his legs. He turned half around and swooped at her with his knife hand and Maria ducked and slammed at it with the bottle. He flinched and dropped the knife. She couldn't hear whatever his moving mouth said because of the B/Ks' shouting behind her.

At some second or other Galia had come out of her room; she stood on the landing and was pounding his face with her fists. Gromeko groped for the knife on the step. Tanya's hands on Maria's hips wrenched her down. Arms like cables enfolded her waist. She was falling, going with

Tanya, her kicking landing nowhere, her free
hand scraping on the steps. Under her, the tired
wood of the stairs crackled with multiple snap-
pings; the treads broke in a deep V and a startling pain lanced under her breasts. She flailed
the cherry brandy bottle again and hit Tanya on
the ribs or some place with bone in it.

Gromeko's left foot went through a step at the
top; helped by Galia's push he fell backward
against Maria. The snap of his ankle bone was
not loud but distinct from the grunting and
shouting of the women. His face was very close
to hers. She looked at him upside down to her,
mouthing something, his teeth bared and fetid in
her nostrils.

He was a gift she could not refuse.

She swung the bottle one more time. At last
the coarse brown glass broke; the zigzag edges
of the piece left in her hand sank into his temple, the temple itself a cavity. Blood flew up
and splashed the wall and rebounded in her face.
The spurting didn't want to stop.

Tanya's scream froze them, already frozen in a
crazy tangle on the stairs. She let go of Maria
and scrambled to Gromeko, her body half atop
Maria's on the narrow stair.

Maria heard the screaming as a roaring through
Tanya's chest, where her left cheek was buried.
She's so strong, she thought, nearly smothered.
With a final tearing groan the entire stair gave
and Maria fell through, Tanya along with her.

The sudden quiet gave up muffled patters of objects dropping onto her and the floor. Was their fighting over? Whimpering, Tanya moved with a swimming motion. Maria had no weapon but her hands left; if Tanya attacked she was dead.

Tanya! *Skazat*! *Skazat*! Say something! cried Irene.

You there, Irene, said Galia. Move yourself. Get tables and chairs. Make some kind of ladder so I can get down.

Make it yourself. Stay up here for the rest of your life.

Very well. But you take care when I have time for you.

Maria had to get air. She pushed; Tanya moaned, spread like a sack over her. Groping to brace for a lift, her hand came down on a head and recoiled. The hair on it was wet.

Marusha! Marusha! The voice persisted. I am coming down to you. Wait, I am coming. God, don't be dead, Marusha. Galia is coming for you, *malenki*. A creaking overhead going away, silence for a long time under the blackness of Tanya's body.

Tanya's chest suddenly swelled into Maria and she rolled off. "*Bol. Bol*, ay, ay. Grigory." She began to sob.

The creaking returned. Coming, Marusha, wait, wait. I am coming. Again the creaking, silence, a rumbling from some place above.

"Tanya." A spate of Russian; Irene's head silhouetted against the hole where the stairs used to be. They hadn't fallen far, since Irene

climbed down easily. Maria winced as Irene
trod on her ankle. Tanya wept grinding sobs by
the head that Maria had touched. It was not so
black down here anymore.

Irene tried to raise Tanya to her feet, and
Tanya screamed.

Be quiet, all of you, Maria said. She did not
know if she heard her own voice. She lay quiet,
herself, wondering when that other voice would
come from above.

An object like a bundle fell from above and
hit Irene. She emitted a string of furious-
sounding Russian and pounced on the bundle.

Marusha, don't let her touch it.

Why should I stop her? Go away, everybody,
Maria thought.

A flapping length of something appeared and
hung dangling. A moment later Galia scrambled
down the length and landed next to Maria. There
was the sound of a slap. More Russian, Tanya
sobbing, Irene angry.

"Marusha, where are you hurt? Can you talk?"
Galia's hands probed.

"Stomach," Maria said. She ached everywhere,
but the place under her breasts cut into each
breath she took.

Galia was busy untying the bundle. She found a
flashlight and looked down the beam at Maria's
stomach, then carefully unbuttoned her blouse.
"It is a splinter. Not a big one, but long. I can
see both ends. That's good, I think it didn't go

inside your stomach. I have to take it out and clean it, *malenki*. Be brave."

Don't be silly. You can do anything, only leave me here. I don't want to get up, ever.

Galia began taking things out of the bundle. Irene jerked at her arm and she shook it off. "*Nyet*," she said sharply. "I take care of my own, first."

Liquid splashed and drooled over her stomach; it burned icy hot.

"Don't move," Galia said. A little knife gleamed between her fingers. A lightning track of pain zipped right to left under Maria's breasts. "I am going to lift out the splinter. There. There. I am sure it is all out." Galia swabbed at the wound, then removed more articles from the bundle. "Damn," she muttered. "Why didn't I think to do this upstairs?" She got up and stood below the hole of light, squinting angrily as the thread kept escaping the eye of the needle. At last it was done.

Tanya moaned, her head in Irene's lap.

"This is not going to be bad," Galia said. "Anyway, I am very quick at this." She bent over Maria with the needle.

Not quick enough, Galia. It was very pleasant though to let Galia take charge of things.

"Say something, Marusha. I want to hear you speak. Can you sit up? You should get out of this place where I can see you better."

She knew this was coming, and she did not want to do it. But she let Galia help her sit up, and then she turned onto her sore knees, and finally she got up, with Galia's arm holding her all the way.

Irene burst out, "Bitch. You look fine. And what about Grigory, eh? You killed him. And my sister is hurt. Her leg is broken." Tanya's keening of Grigory Grigory Grigory had not paused for a second.

"Wait here, Marusha. I am going to get a chair for you." Galia pulled pieces of broken wood into a pile. It wobbled as she climbed on it and fell apart the moment she stepped to the concrete floor.

Maria stood exactly where Galia left her. The space down here was really very narrow. Gromeko's body lay in a misshapen heap, almost on top of the place where she had lain. As she stared dully, a rat with a long hairless tail darted to his head and sniffed at the cavity she had made there. Irene uttered a sound of disgust and wrenched at her shoe, but the rat was gone before she could throw it. She glared at Maria.

Galia returned, the chair in her hands. Maria saw her dilemma: the pile of broken wood where she wished to place the chair. She knew she should help remove the wood so that Galia could lower the chair. While she was pondering this, her brain languorous as a lilypad in a boggy pond, Galia scrambled down and removed the wood herself. Then she did all the things Maria could not rouse herself to do. Galia coaxed her to step onto the chair and then to the firmness of concrete above. They went through the kitchen and into the big room. The sun was shining through the gritty windows.

Galia sat her in a chair and talking in a soothing tone swabbed alcohol everywhere with a liberal hand. "Might as well take off your stockings, there is almost nothing left," she said, and did it for Maria. The old leather oxfords felt clumsy without the smoothing shield of stockings. Galia was wearing white rubber-soled shoes left over from her days as a nurse. "Now a drink. A stiff shot of vodka is what you need." She found the vodka under the bar, uncorked it, and urged Maria to drink. The liquor in her throat felt like the alcohol burning into her flesh. "Better, *malenki?*"

Poor Galia; she looked a mess, her careful hairdo hanging in shreds, her face dusty and missing streaks of pancake where she had sweated. Maria nodded and closed her eyes.

Hurry up. Irene's voice sounded as though she were in the bottom of a well.

Galia made a face. "Maybe I will break Tanya's other leg, I really want to. Do you know I never suspected they were together with that man? I could never stand him. You did a good thing, Marusha, you were brave and you should never worry about what happened. He would have killed you, that is what you should remember."

Galia, yelled Irene.

She sighed. "I have to go."

She was gone a long time. Maria didn't think of a thing while she sat in the large empty room. The automobiles honking on the street ran together like one continuous wail. Tanya was wailing too, after her first loud screams.

The din in the street suddenly got louder as the door opened. Two Chinese men peered around it. Seeing she was alone, they stepped boldly inside. Coolies, sinewy and bony from a lifetime of hard labor. On their backs were slung lumpy cloth bundles, which they put down.

"What's the matter with you?" The one who spoke omitted the honorary form of address. *Doo-tzia* was a lady who may have ridden their rickshaws or hired them to move goods; *doo-tzia* possibly was gone forever from their language. He grinned. "She's crazy," he said to his companion. "Maybe's she's been shot, look at all the blood on her." He pointed at the side room. "Maybe there's something good in there." They clomped across to the small office. The western-style leather shoes on their bare feet were too large, the laces tied with double knots. When he emerged a short time later he was wearing Maria's navy wool coat. The other man had her purse and a fistful of cigars and some pencils. "Better take it off," he said. "Someone will make you give it up if you don't." Keeping an eye on Maria, he swiftly undid their bundles and stowed away the coat, purse, cigars, and pencils. He stiffened, hearing bumping sounds from the back; in a moment the coolies were gone.

The bumping sounds beyond the kitchen grew louder, and Galia and Irene entered, supporting Tanya in the middle. Her right leg was splinted with a piece of wood and strips of cloth torn from her own skirt. Galia looked weary and dirtier than before.

Irene's eyes were swollen from crying. "I want to give you something else to think about when you run off," she said to Maria. "Killing Grigory was nothing to you, I can see that. So what about this? Your boyfriend thinks you are a whore. I told him you had dozens of men who paid you—" Galia let go of Tanya. She slapped Irene so hard that both sisters nearly went down. The slapping continued, as Irene struggled to keep the reeling Tanya on her one good foot. Irene's head rocked at each blow; saliva flew and smeared her cheeks.

Galia said, "Swine. You pig. That is what you were saying to him when I caught you." She wiped her hands on Irene's sweater, looked around for something better, and marched to the sink behind the bar to wash them.

Crying, Irene said, "How can you leave us here? How will we get home?"

Galia looked dangerous and ready to finish off Irene if she continued protesting. Irene disdained to touch her reddened cheeks. The beating seemed to calm her, as though between them they had got some necessary business accomplished. "There is food in the refrigerator," Galia said. "If you can get her upstairs there are beds to

sleep on. You may have my clothes. You have a
bicycle, so you can go for a doctor. If you
catch a pedicab you can take her to one, or a
hospital. Maybe St. John's hospital, if it is
still open. I leave it up to you; I am sure you
will survive very well. That is your profession,
isn't it?"

"There is Grigory."

"I leave him to you, also. Do as you like."
She walked into the office, and came out looking puzzled. "Where is your coat, Marusha. And
your purse?"

"They went away. Inside two very nice embroi-
dered tablecloths."

They all, even the wilted Tanya, stared at
Maria. Those coolies were right, she thought. I
am crazy. She made another effort. "Looters."

Galia looked horrified. "While I was down
there? They could have hurt you. You should have
called for me." She was already grappling with
another thought. "I have to get upstairs for
coats. It is too cold outside. But first we have
to clean you up a bit."

Yung's kitchen towels, retrieved from their
nest on top of the glassware, were filthy by
the time Galia had washed Maria and herself.
Maria had never seen Galia's real complexion
before. Her skin was quite nice; why did she
always hide it?

Galia said they had to make a platform, she
couldn't shinny up the sheets she had used to
get down. She ordered Irene to help her and

they began carrying tables and chairs out through the kitchen.

Rather than look at the discolored and soggy Tanya sitting in another chair, Maria shut her eyes. She wished she could sleep; the cannonades were soothing because they were faraway and blunt-sounding, much preferable to the shrillness of the human beings fleeing over to the Bund. Too soon Galia was back, walking purposefully in her professional nurse's shoes and bringing so much bustle and need to do things. She had to stand up while Galia put a coat on her, a much nicer one than her hundred-year-old navy coat.

Galia's voice started to sound faraway again. Her hand linked up under Maria's arm and propelled her to the door. The day's background noises crashed into her eardrums, and they were caught up in the tumult of the streets.

23

Galia held on to her fiercely with one hand and with the other fought for space to keep walking. She could do nothing to prevent bodies from caroming into Maria on her other side.

Aya aya, umah, looh-tuh, umah, ba-ba, see-ning zuh, aya, help, mama, lost, lost it, mama, father, dying, bad, automobiles blaring, a child's terrified screams over her father's shoulder, men struggling to hold precious bicycles over their heads. A flat cart piled with goods and pushed by a sweating half-naked man butted at Maria's legs.

They crested Garden Bridge and at last saw over the shoal in which they were lost. The Bund was packed with a populace moving south and obliterating all traces of counter traffic. The buildings loomed above the human current.

Galia shouted in Maria's ear, Do you want to stop anywhere? Cathay Hotel? She shook her head. She would not stop until she got home. Someone dug an elbow into her stomach and she gasped.

All her other sore places were being shoved and pummeled; she could not fall, but she could allow herself to slide under everyone's thrashing feet. The crowd pressed in, the sky pressed down. Galia pushed her, angling toward the right. Maria put out her hand, tried to make a stiff arm, and slowly they worked through. At the bottom of Garden Bridge, like two pebbles rejected by the receding surf, they fell out of the throng.

Galia released her hold on Maria. "Let's sit for awhile," she said, and placed her rump, careless of her coat, on the curb next to Maria's. Only a few dozen people walked here on the sidewalk above Soochow Creek; some did not seem to be headed anywhere and merely stood watching the stampede over the bridge and down to the Bund.

Near Maria a young woman said to an old one, "Will it be as they say? Will the Communists rape and kill the women, *Ah-bu*, Grandmother?" She was pregnant, and her tone was fearful. The grandmother was nearly bald, her few hairs clubbed in a scanty bun at the nape.

"Maybe not. But sometimes things are as bad as they say, and worse," she answered. "You were too small when the Japanese bayoneted us at Chapei near the silk factory where I worked, and I was in the middle of it. I had a knife and decided I would cut my own throat before they reached me. Your uncle in Nanking was shot for just being there. He was trying to go to work."

Her head quivered ceaselessly; age and disease
certainly got her in the end, Maria thought,
like they will get me. She moved as though to
get up, to run away from herself. The old woman
said, "I think the government wants to frighten
us about the Communists, to make us resist them.
The government takes your husband and orders him
to fight, and the rest of us can only hide, so
what difference does that kind of propaganda
make to anybody?"

"I want to go," Maria said. It was time to get
away from the sight of Broadway Mansions on the
other side of Soochow Creek. For the past ten
minutes she had been watching smoke writhing
from the highest of the three square roofs. The
emptiness that had taken over in her brain did
not try to fathom the reason for that smoke. It
veered this way and that, but did not spread
down into the building itself.

Her knees started to bleed again as she stood
up, and she felt a small spurt of warmth under
her breasts.

Galia opened her eyes; she had been very
still, as though she had used up all her
strength. "I know," she replied. "We should get
on, shouldn't we."

They struggled to their feet and started walking west. Below them on Soochow Creek the sampan
families were battened down under their oilcloth; here and there a mother performed her
unavoidable duty, the child held with its rear
end over the water. All Chinese toddlers of the

working class wore split trousers so that they could squat anywhere, anytime, without their mothers in attendance. Sampan mothers did not have that convenience.

When the sidewalk took a northerly turn, Galia said they were walking an unnecessary distance, so they cut south on Szechuan Road. The broad-shouldered pile of Broadway Mansions disappeared from view. On Peking Road they turned west again. Galia said the longer they avoided Nanking Road the better; things were probably as bad there as the Bund. The beggars and other sidewalk inhabitants evidently thought so, too. In the thousands they had taken refuge from being overrun on the main thoroughfares. None asked for money from the two foreign-dressed women.

"It's not so bad sometimes to look as bad as we do," Galia said. "The beggars are taking pity on us." Her walk had become a mechanical trudge; occasionally they bumped into each other as they threaded the obstacle course of ragged squatters. "Maybe we should go over and see if the trams are running."

They went south again, at Chekiang Road, and emerged on Nanking Road. Galia looked both ways, east and west; no sign of the green metal shield of a tram was visible. Traffic lights changed from red to green to amber and back but pedestrians and wheeled vehicles crossed anywhere they pleased, many going south.

Without a word Maria turned westward, Galia catching up to her, and they passed the plate glass windows of Wing On Department Store. Galia looked at the display of silk yardage draped on a mannequin with Caucasian features, and said, I love her purse, I wonder how much it cost? and laughed. She sounded hoarse, as though she had been up drinking all night.

On the next block stood the YMCA, where Maria had played pingpong with Bob Madigan and flirted in happy airiness with a number of infatuated boys. The lay brother who supervised youth activities would have been saddened to discover that the single ardent aspiration of these boys was not heaven but a kiss from Maria. They had been Portuguese and French and Italian, and a few Americans like Bob Madigan.

After Wing On Department Store, which occupied half the block, Nanking Road changed into Bubbling Well Road. The gates of the Shanghai Race Course across the street were padlocked. Maria thought she could hear ghostly cheering from the grandstands and the thudding of horses' hooves. She was half ghost herself. When Bubbling Well Road began curving upward they cut south again, crossing Wehaiwei Road and the broader Avenue Edward VII, on through two narrow streets, and finally coming to Avenue Joffre. They had traveled less than half the distance to Maria's home on Route Magy.

The lone shop open for business, on the corner of Rue Pere Robert, was a food shop selling

sausages, cheese, and tinned fish. All the foreigners in Frenchtown seemed to be inside pushing to get closer to the counters. A British
matron emerged, flushed and indignant, accompanied by her amah. "These people have no shame,"
she said in the approximate direction of Galia
and Maria. "Only silver dollars will do now, and
ten times yesterday's prices."

"Where in God's name have all the pedicabs
gone?" Galia said. "I have to sit."

Maria's bare feet chafing inside her oxfords
had been hurting for blocks, since their latest
turn south. Now with each step a slick wetness
rubbed along the leather. She kept walking. If
she had to she would throw away her shoes and
walk without them.

Galia pointed at two trams standing deserted
on their tracks in the middle of the street. In
there, she said; Maria did not understand what
she meant. Come on, Galia insisted. They climbed
aboard the closest tram and Galia collapsed on
the wooden bench that ran the length of the
tram. She put her feet up, then lay down on the
slatted bench. Oh, heavenly, she groaned. Sit
there and don't move, don't you go anywhere,
Marusha, she said, and fell asleep.

Maria stood up. She was halfway down the
steps, then looked back. The soles of Galia's
feet were pointed at her, the nurse shoes
scuffed and very dirty. A light snore blew out
of her friend's naked, unpainted mouth. One arm

had slipped to the floor, her hand insensible on the grimy surface.

Maria climbed back inside. She searched the unfamiliar pockets of her coat: there was a handkerchief, smelling faintly of Galia's perfume, but nothing sharp she could use to defend her with.

The sound of shattering glass swiveled her attention to the street; several Nationalist soldiers were pulling away shards of glass sticking up in the window of The Tsingtao Good Fit Shop. They worked hurriedly, though no passersby interfered. The soldiers stepped through the display window and minutes later reappeared buttoning themselves into civilian trousers and shirts. They saw Maria watching.

"*Mei yu fa tze*, it can't be helped," one of them said. He was young, no more than twenty, with the bushy eyebrows of a Fukienese. His companions told him to hurry. They crossed the street and disappeared down a side street.

The sun hid itself behind the lowest building, the hurrying pedestrians became a blur in the early spring twilight, and she sat on in the murk of the tram.

Galia awoke. Her head jerked in alarm, looking around for Maria, then she saw her and relaxed. "I dreamed of drinking from a big pitcher of ice water," she said, licking her dry lips. She pushed at strands of hair about her face and gave it up. "I was about to take a hot bath, and Eric was going to scrub my back. Then I woke up. I wonder if that was a message about whether I should marry Eric?" Stiffly she set her feet on the floor. "Did you sleep, Marusha? No, of course not, I can tell you have just been sitting there. At least you did not run away. Ah, speak to me, *malenki*, or I will never let you alone until you do. Are you worrying about that piece of vermin? Forget him. Forget Irene, too. Can you tell me at least that Irene's bad mouth isn't bothering you? No one can believe a woman like that. Galia knows people, will you believe that nothing in the world can be mistaken for quality when it is so clearly trash? Marusha, please."

Maria could not give her the embrace she needed so much; it was dangerous to yield, for she still had a distance to go and all her wit and strength would shiver into bits of broken glass if she gave in now.

She said, "Galia, don't worry. One day...." The completing thought evaporated. "Can we go, now?"

Galia sighed and got up.

Inside her shoes Maria's raw flesh had become stuck to the leather; her first steps ripped the two apart and ground a whimper from her throat but it was momentary, no more. She walked steadily for eight blocks until Galia halted outside the handsome tan facade of Gascoigne Apartments. "Where are those private guards?" She sighed. "Run off, as you would expect. Anyway, this is where Liudmila lives and where I keep most of my things. I keep our money here, too. She always took it home with her every

night. We knew nobody would dare to bother her."
Galia's smile sought to coax one from her.
"Those fools," she said. "If they asked, I would
have told them where the money was; I would have
liked to see them steal it from Liudmila." She
held Maria's hand, tugging, begging her to come
with her. "Only overnight, Marusha. Then you can
go home. We can send the porter to your parents
with a message so they will not worry."

"It's just a few blocks more. I can do it. You
have to let me," she said, fearing Galia would
trap her with both hands; she would never get
away, then.

But her friend saw her determination and surrendered. "Then I will send the porter with you."
She pressed the bell and when a small, slight man
came to the door she explained in her bad Chinese
what she wanted him to do. He nodded, willing
enough, then he stepped outside and saw Maria
under the portico light. "She not bad can walk,"
Galia said, resorting to pidgin, "you go now
quick, come back Miss Liudmila very glad." She
pushed him a little to get him started.

Maria was already walking away.

He stayed behind, her reluctant shadow and
bodyguard, for the last mile, to the entrance of
the lane on Route Magy.

First she had to endure her father's horrified
questions, and Nola's blubbering, and Amah's
noisy lamentations.

The bathroom was the only place where she and
her mother could be alone. Her feet were in a

basin of cool water and borax salts, all the
rest of her undressed and given over to Ming
Chu's careful cleansing with cotton wool soaked
in a solution of hydrogen peroxide. She was dissolving, at last she could let her bones turn to
porridge.

Her mother's face was white; tears had started
from her at first sight of Maria's exposed
injuries. All the contents of their medicine
cabinet were arrayed on a towel on the tile
floor. She took Maria's feet in her lap, dried
them with the softest thing to hand—the grayish
toilet paper that was the best quality Shanghai
people could get these days—and began gently to
apply salve to the puffed and raw toes and
heels. Amah had insisted that she use Tiger
Balm. The ointment stung; Maria's skin felt it,
not her mind.

With a few stark words, she described the
lunging, grunting savagery on the rotting
stairs. Ming Chu could not repress soft sounds
of pain as she listened.

"Mama, I didn't have to hit so hard. It was
over so fast I didn't have time to think."

Ming Chu raised her bowed head and directed a
fierce stare into her daughter's eyes. "I would
have done the same. I swear to you, no man would
live who tried to use a knife on you. If I had
been there, seeing him attack you, I would have
torn out his eyes." Unknowing that she echoed
Galia's sentiments she said, "He was no good to
anyone. People like that are better dead." She

tore open a package of gauze and wound it
loosely, ever so loosely, round and round the
wounded feet.

Maria looked at the pale skin of her mother's
smooth temples where little blue veins throbbed.

"In war people kill innocent people all the
time," Ming Chu said. "In your war, Maria, you
were given a choice to remove exactly the one
who deserved to be gone." Tears fell. "Do I
shock you? The truth is I cannot decide which
God or gods to thank for bringing you home
again. What a stupid dilemma for such a simple
feeling of gratitude."

The dissolving in Maria at last reached her
eyes; they spilled over and she cried, the sobs
tearing themselves from a well so deep that her
mother stared at her in fear.

The pressing sky had at last fallen, and Maria
wept with a passion that turned the whole world
black and blue. Her mother thought she was crying for the killing of Grigory Gromeko.

24

Broadway Mansions must look as though it had taken a hit, Huell thought. Smoke billowed from the top of the central tower. At the time the jerry-rigged incinerators had been installed, the wind was blowing from the west; then it had reversed itself and now everyone hauling stacks of records up there caught black roiling smoke full in the face. The four Marines in charge of stoking the two gasoline drums were so blackened only their NCO could guess their identities.

Setting up a military post in peacetime required merely efficient logistics; dismantling it in a hurry reduced that early vaunted efficiency to squads of ungraceful men running up and down corridors, in or out of uniform, and that uniform fouled with sweat and smoke.

Everything but the most solid hardware had to go in the fire. Colonel Treadway's edict turned the lower nine floors of the U.S. Military Advisory Group into a delirium of wrecked U.S. Government property. The Foreign Correspondents

Club of China, occupying the next six floors,
found itself an oasis of calm that could have
made a notable story for many of the journalists. The man nicknamed Common Wisdom found it
so. He had stopped Huell in the corridor and
with an ill-disguised smirk on his nicotine-dyed
face asked whether it was true that a couple of
lieutenants had put their shorts on over their
trousers.

Huell did not begrudge him his moment of
revenge. Carlton Wisdom probably had taken more
abuse in his life than most journalists who did
not work for the big papers.

"If it makes you happy to report it, feel
free," he told Wisdom. "I hear there's a real
circus over at the American consulate. They're
burning U.S. currency, you know, after they register the serial numbers. Why don't you go over
there and count how many bundles of greenbacks
are going up in smoke?" He touched Wisdom on the
shoulder to show he intended no malice, and
walked on back to the Teletype room. It made him
sad to see the guiltless machines being smashed,
the wiring cut to pieces, the disarray of the
intelligence-gathering system it had been his
job to set in place.

*The second characteristic is that our enemy is
big and powerful.*

Mao Tze-tung had said that, in his "Strategy
in China's Revolutionary War." The enemy he was
talking about was the Kuomintang, the Chinese
Nationalist Party. Since Chiang's troops were

fleeing like rabbits, what did that make the United States Armed Forces? Not much better. An undeclared enemy, at most, but heretofore respected to some degree.

A Marine private came in and relayed a message for the captain to report to Colonel Treadway.

Huell had not left Broadway Mansions for two days since his return from Nanking. He had not visited his room in the Cathay Hotel, and because he was accompanied by Gunnery Sergeant Hinehart on the drive back from Lunghwa Airfield he had not stopped at The Camellia Room either.

Colonel Treadway had heard his report on their fruitless meeting with Ambassador John Leighton Stuart and made a remark that at first dismayed Huell.

"When the commies take down that embassy, Congress will have to find somebody else to roast for that piece of embarrassment. Our ass is in the clear."

Not worthy, thought Huell, then rebuked himself for being naive. Treadway had read the repercussions exactly right; he was only speaking his mind to a man he trusted.

One of the two men he trusted, if only Treadway realized, was on the point of deserting his post.

On the morning of April 23rd Huell at last got away from Broadway Mansions. The motor pool had dwindled to three vehicles. He showed the corporal downstairs orders from Colonel Treadway that he himself had cut. Treadway's signature was easy to forge. An oversized "T" and a long tail on the "y" were the main substance of the scribble.

Yes, sir, the corporal downstairs said, the Morris Minor was still around; yes sir, fully gassed, he replied in a tone of injury to Huell's question. What do you take me for? A damned civilian?

Huell threw the little car into gear and as he drove out of the compound spotted Gunnery Sergeant Miles Hinehart standing on the corner of Broadway and Chengtu Road. He was talking to a Chinese woman, plain and not young, who was weeping and clutching Hinehart's hand. His face flashed and was gone from Huell's view in a second. The fact that Hinehart had a woman should not have surprised him, yet somehow he had never imagined Hinehart to have any other life than as the guardian of Colonel Treadway.

Huell pulled up outside The Camellia Room; yesterday he would have needed a tank to cross the street, but since then the crowds had thinned. The saloon was shut up tight, as it usually was in the morning, but he knew Galia lived there, if she hadn't moved away in a hurry.

He banged on the door, waited, banged again. He caught movement at the dusty window. "Hello? Open up!"

The door opened and he looked into the face of the blond waitress, Irene. They stared at each other. Her hair was dirty, her clothes rumpled and even dirtier, her legs bare and scratched.

Anxiety made him harsh. "What happened here? Is Galia around? Where is Maria?"

"Do you have a car? Yes! I see it. Can you take us to the hospital?"

"Take who? Who is hurt?"

"My sister. Tanya. She broke her leg."

Huell walked inside. He was not getting the answers he wanted. Tanya lay on a mattress, asleep or unconscious, her mouth open. "All right. Tanya is hurt. Who else is here?"

"Nobody."

He looked around. The room was dirty, too; it smelled like a latrine. Slowly, he repeated, "Where did Galia go? Tell me everything you know, or nobody is going anywhere." He did not fully understand why he was delivering ultimatums to a woman who obviously looked ill. He disliked her; seeing her face was the last thing he looked for at this time. He bent a knee and checked Tanya's pulse. A bit fast, from fever he supposed. The splint on her leg was a good job, whoever had done it.

"How did she break her leg?"

Irene fiddled with the splint. "An accident. She had an accident. Can we go now?"

"You'll have to help me." He doubted he could lift even half of her by himself.

Irene shook her sister's shoulder. Waking up, Tanya stared groggily at him and immediately began to cry. "Hospital," Irene said. "We are taking you to a hospital."

"Grigory," Tanya whimpered. "I don't want to leave him."

"Grigory? I thought you said nobody else was here."

"He is dead," Irene said, her voice flat. "I made a hole and buried him. Come, Tanya."

Together, they helped her up and walked, like a crutch on each side, to the Morris Minor. Irene got in the back, and he stuffed Tanya, with little cooperation from her, in the front passenger seat.

"Can we take our bicycles?" Irene asked. "We can tie them to the top of the car. There must be rope in The Camellia Room."

"I haven't time to look for rope. You'll have to get the bikes some other time."

He stepped back into the street and scanned the ugly concrete walls and tar-gravel roof of the saloon. As far as he could tell, nothing violent had happened to its exterior. He walked inside and to the rear. A pile of tables and chairs rose in the gap between the dirt flooring and the upper floor; below lay the splintered remains of the stairs. He saw a mound, covered half with cement dust, half dirt. He had never been back here before. Was Galia up there, injured, maybe dead? "GALIA!" He cupped his hands to his mouth and shouted again. Should he climb up and look for her? He looked at his watch, and walked outside and got into the car.

"What hospital do you want?" He was being churlish, he knew it. They were stealing time that he had stolen from his post.

"St. John's. Take us to St. John's."

He knew where it was: clear across town, miles from his original destination. He drove fast. The emergency entrance at St. John's, the pride of Shanghai's medical faculty, seemed deserted. He almost ran inside, found an orderly changing bedpans, and securing him by the arm made him come outside.

Tanya extracted, standing on one leg, her arms around Irene and the orderly, Huell said, "You'll be all right, now. Sorry, I have to go."

Irene said, "Tell our grandmother where we are and not to worry."

God. "Where does she live?"

Her knowing look grated on him. This woman kindled dislike by her mere presence. Case of kill the messenger? No, he felt he knew the difference between his revulsion for her personality and her blithe smearing of Maria. "You are going to Route Magy, aren't you? We live upstairs. Please tell Babushka." She gripped his arm and feeling her strength he knew she was capable of superhuman feats of persistence.

"I can do that much," Huell said. She let go.

He almost admired her. Someone that audacious deserved to be durable. The discovery that they lived above the Contis held a significance that hovered near but eluded him. A feud between neighbors? Why did Galia and Maria hire them if

they didn't get along? These were a couple of
the questions he had mulled over half the night
in Nanking; he blocked them off and concentrated
on driving.

He raced at highway speed down Lihwa Road,
shifting down instead of braking at corner
turns; the car's transmission screamed. Twice he
narrowly missed something—a runty donkey carrying basket panniers, a wooden vending stand of
some sort.

At the entrance to the alley on Route Magy he
braked with an unhappy screech from the Morris
Minor. He knew she lived in the last building—he
had seen her come from there—but which floor? He
knocked on the first door inside the entrance.
Voices behind spoke in Cantonese; the door
opened, and he said to a man with hair slicked
high on the crown of his head that he was looking for the Contis. The door slammed in his
face. Huell walked up the stairs and came upon
Nola on the next landing.

She looked shocked, but emitted a glad-sound-
ing "Oh!"

"I'm glad to see you, I really am." He bent and
scooped her in for a hug. A door opened and a tall
man came out. Huell straightened. "Mr. Conti," he
said. For months he had imagined the shape and
character of this man, wondering why Maria seemed
so defensive, even protective, of him. Maria's
father looked physically able, but he was not
fit, not by the stoop of his shoulders, or the
discouragement of his glance. Buffaloed. Huell

saw, on the alert with all his cultivated ability to observe and analyze, that shrewdness and agility were not in his nature.

"Daddy, it's Maria's boyfriend," said Nola.

"I know. It would be more polite if you called him by his name, don't you think?" He smiled, and Huell saw also that he was a kind man. There was only a slight Italian accent left; he had indeed invested his life in China.

"Thaddeus Huell, yes, sir. May I see her, please? I, ah, haven't much time. I hope she is home."

"She is, but she is ill and cannot come out to you. Let me tell her you are here. Excuse me a moment."

Nola said shyly, "I've never seen you in your uniform before. You look...."

"Funny?"

She laughed. "Sort of. It makes you different. But I've only seen you twice and each time you're different. I'm never going to know you, really, am I?" She did not make it a question. Nola knew her realities from the stories her sister said her nose was always buried in.

"Why is your sister sick? What has she got?"

"It's malaria. She gets it back now and then, and everybody thought she wasn't going to anymore. But Galia said shock can do it. She comes everyday. She's as good as a doctor."

"Mr. Huell." Conti's voice. "Would you like to go in?" He pushed open the door and told Huell to go through the curtains. "Come, Nola."

Nola looked at him and tears trembled in her eyes. "Goodbye," she said, then turned and went with her father

Huell advanced through the room, noting with distracted gaze the shelves of bottles, glass carafes, labels in a heap on the sideboard, big jugs on the floor. He parted the curtains.

She was so pale his heart lurched in fright. A purple bruise discolored her right cheekbone. A quilt covered her to the chin, and she was shivering violently, her teeth audibly chattering. A little laugh escaped her white lips. "Sorry," she said, mystifying him.

He knelt beside her bed and laid a palm on her cheek. How could skin so hot be so white? Maybe it was the anemia malaria attacks brought on.

"Listen," he said, stroking her cheek, "I have only time to tell you this: I love you. When you've got nothing else will you hang on to that? I'm going to get you out. As soon as I reach Hong Kong I'll start working on it." He could have cried with frustration. An hour had been lost carting those women around when he could have spent it with Maria. He didn't even have that hour, but he would rather be court martialed for the right reasons than the wrong ones.

"Did you hear me? I said I love you. I love you, Maria."

"Sticks and stones," she whispered, teeth clicking, "...break my bones...words are the...very devil..." Her hands came out of the depths of the quilt and pushed at her hair.

He caught them and held them still. "I don't care how you look now." A bandage on her left wrist alarmed him. "What did you do to your wrist? And why the bruise on your face?" Shock, Nola said.

"Amah's remedy. Stuff a date with pepper…twenty-four hours…guaranteed."

It took him a few moments to understand. "Good God. What about quinine?"

"Doesn't work."

"Atabrine is what you need. I'll try to send some. Dammit to hell," Huell said, angry at the minutes ticking off. For all her fever and chills, those hazel eyes were lucid and utterly incurious. How could she let him walk out without a goodbye? Even her kid sister was in tears.

"I was going to tell you when I got back from Nanking, that's where I went. So here I am like a crazy man telling you I love you. I love you, Maria, do you hear?" He stroked and stroked her face, cleared the damp hair caught under her neck, kissed her bandaged wrist, wondered again about the bruise on her cheek, suddenly noticed the quilt at her feet was raised over a boxlike frame. "If you don't want me, say so, but it won't stop me from trying to get you out of here. I will not go back to my life in Maryland and leave the other half of me in China. Do you understand?"

"…family," Maria said. "All or nobody."

"Of course your family, too. I meant everyone." He got to his feet. "If I don't get back

now, I won't be able to do anything because I'll
be in jail." Treadway was already ordering his
court martial. He kissed her dry lips. "Got to
go. Hang on. Promise me. Promise me."

She closed her eyes and tears seeped down
their corners. Huell had to be satisfied with
that, his last glimpse of Maria.

He charged through the curtains and the dining
room/bottling factory; at the instant his hand
touched the door handle he remembered his promise to tell the Babushka upstairs where her
granddaughters were. He groaned. There was no
time; he refused to give it his time. He would
send a messenger later.

On the landing stood a petite Chinese woman
with tiny pointed feet who he instantly knew was
Maria's mother.

"Mr. Huell, how do you do." His name and the
formal English words were not spoken in the flat
Shanghai accent. Maria's face with subtle differences drawn from her father.

He halted, resigned to ten years in prison.
"Yes, ma'am. I love her, you know. Will you tell
her that for me so she won't forget? Tell her
often, make her believe it." He dredged from
somewhere a proverb from his Chinese lessons and
rendered it in clumsy Mandarin: To live in
hearts we leave behind is not to die.

He had wanted to say heart, not hearts, and I,
not we, but he feared that none of it came out
right or expressed his meaning.

The DC-3 flight out of Lunghwa Airfield was a reprise of his trip to Nanking with Hinehart. Hinehart was there, sitting alongside on his seabag. Huell had nothing but his wallet containing his I.D., some American currency and Chinese gold dollars, driver's licenses of United States and Peiping municipal government issue, photographs of his family.

"I owe you my life," he said simply, to Gunnery Sergeant Miles Hinehart. Had he seen him drive off and guessed the reason? It was irrelevant.

"I was glad to do it. I think the Colonel realized I was out and out lying to him. My imagination got kind of thin after awhile, but he let me get by with it one last time just before you showed up." As though underscoring the imminent end of their association, Hinehart took an unmilitary liberty. "He's a good man, for an officer." His smile was an etching in bleakness.

Huell wanted to tell him he had seen him with his woman and to say something in comfort, but Hinehart seemed far away, his gaze on the clouds outside, or on nothing.

25

The mud-caked, wounded HMS *Amethyst* and her remaining handlers became prisoners of the Communists, while the first fifty of her crew rescued by the Nationalist troops arrived by train in Shanghai.

The British residents of Shanghai waited for the might of their government to swoop down on the Communists. Instead, only a bleat, instead of the expected roar, emanated from the Britannic lion of historic conquest. The international news services treated the *Amethyst* incident as though it were a weather report. The shelling of the *Consort* and *London* were just as sketchily treated. Great Britain's fifty dead and one hundred wounded crewmen got no laurels except among the locals.

Too many million pound sterling in too much property were at stake; the taipans had got themselves thoroughly embedded in China and they would swallow much more humiliation before venturing to antagonize the new government of China.

The foreigners were convinced that, as always before, they would rebound; after all, they were neutral in this civil war. Of the 4,000 British citizens in Shanghai, only 1,200 had left. The Danes, the Dutch, and the French also hung on to their pieces of China.

The British cruiser *Belfast* had reached Woosung, at the conjunction of the Whangpo and the Yangtze Rivers. Her mission was to replace the damaged cruiser *London*, but she held her fire at Communist gun emplacements. The nearest effective British air support consisted of a fighter squadron in Singapore, 2,250 miles away. The U.S. Navy had already warned that, once American vessels moved downriver to Woosung, they could no longer protect American citizens in Shanghai.

Nanking fell on April 24. The following day, Communist troops invaded the U.S. Embassy and pulled Ambassador John Leighton Stuart out of bed for questioning.

On May 3, General Claire L. Chennault told the Senate Armed Services Committee that the United States must defend southern China. Secretary of State Dean Acheson said that United States policy toward China would not change. She was on her own.

The American School of Shanghai made ready for Commencement Day.

Early that week the Chinese gold dollar plummeted to 35 million to one pound sterling.

The new mayor of Shanghai was General Chen Liang. He replaced the previous incumbent, who had fled to Taiwan. Soon after taking office General Chen Liang also flew to Taiwan.

After the American Navy moved out of the Glen Line Building on the corner of Peking Road and the Bund, the American consulate moved in; now they were next door to the British Consulate. The American consul, John Cabot, dug in with his staff and installed an emergency radio transmitter.

The Communists pounded the Woosung forts and the petroleum depot. Communist troops entrenched themselves on Pootung across the Whangpo River from Shanghai.

The Nationalists staged a "Victory" parade down the Bund and Nanking Road with military bands, cymbals, and a festive dragon. The Communists watched from Pootung and, perhaps in contempt, did not fire upon the parade. In the suburbs, the attack pressed forward.

Curfew was imposed. A few nightclubs—the Metropole, the Eventail on Yu Yuen Road, the Merry Widow—managed to stay open all night, as if to extract the last silver dollar, American greenback, or pound sterling to be had in this collapsing world.

On May 17, Hankow, a large city and river port in central China, fell.

On May 25, Shanghai fell.

Just as they had in Nanking, the Communist victors walked quietly into the city. They did not rape, pillage, or mistreat the citizens.

Poldo Conti went to a meeting of foreign businessmen, who got up a committee to approach the new government to discuss their future together.

The provisional governor was stern but not discourteous, Poldo reported to his wife. He said that the foreign nationals should be patient and something would be worked out. Ming Chu, whose aunt and niece had sent a message from Soochow that they were safe, took his words as reason to hope.

In celebration, the venerable and exclusive Shanghai Club held a St. Andrew's Day dinner. The British danced Scottish reels; the Americans made snide remarks about Chiang's gunboats lurking about the mouth of the Yangtze River and shooting at the *Edith Moller* bringing in mail and supplies. The *Edith Moller* was a British flag vessel, a coastal tramp steamer about 4,000 tons in size. She could and did dodge the Nationalist gunboats and docked to cheers at the Bund. By allowing her to enter, the Communists seemed to imply approval of foreigners in Shanghai.

The B/Ks above the Contis rarely showed themselves. The dog Ivanka disappeared. Eaten? wondered Maria. No, too much hair, said Nola. I didn't see any in the garbage.

The government of the Philippines agreed to offer sanctuary on Guiuan, at the southernmost tip of Samar Island, to 6,000 stateless persons.

Samar was to be a halfway house. IRO, the
International Refugee Organization, would process
the refugees for admission to other countries.

The B/Ks vanished as mysteriously as their
dog. Liudmila married an Italian, who charged
her nothing for the honor, and left for Italy.

Galia, spurning her Norwegian sea captain,
prepared to leave for Samar.

She had taken over Liudmila's apartment in
Gascoigne Apartments. The night before her
departure by train, she cooked an astonishing
dinner for Maria. The eight-foot table, laid for
two, was sparkling with crystal and silver; a
tiny porcelain vase holding a single pink carna-
tion stood between pewter candlesticks; the
damask tablecloth was virginal, down to the
folding creases Galia had not bothered to iron
out. She switched off the electric light and
they sat in semi-darkness reminding Maria of air
raids and air raid shelters, in which she had
once spent two long nights and days.

From somewhere in Liudmila's larder came
Russian caviar, which Galia served on perfect
toast points with minced egg. Of course there
was vodka to go with it. Maria drank three brim-
ming jiggers and forgot to eat.

Galia left her place at the other side of the
table and came round to feed her coq au vin
piece by piece.

"You've had as much vodka as me, so you've
been cheating," Maria said. "You ate in the
kitchen before I got here so you'd look good in

front of me. Admit it. I've seen you put away gallons with Eric, all because you sneaked in bites of *zakuska* you hid in your bra. Why didn't you marry him? What's wrong with living with his mother? He said she looks just like him, so she probably has a beard, too. Wouldn't that make you feel at home while he's sailing around on his old junk steamer?"

Galia broke off a heel of bread and chewed on it reflectively. She was wearing no makeup, only eyebrow penciling, and looked so much younger that Maria felt a pang of fear for her. She wished Galia would put on her impenetrable look again; people were usually wary of crossing Galia when she groomed herself into statuelike perfection.

"When Liudmila married I thought she was making a terrible mistake," Galia said. "She was never the type who needed a man. She had them, not the other way round. I couldn't see her being domestic, not with an Italian man from the south. Neapolitans are supposed to be soulful but Neapolitan men keep their women under their heel. I didn't want that to happen to Liudmila."

"She won't let it happen." Maria poured another vodka. "*Piedudnat, piedudnat, piedudnat,*" she muttered, and tossed it down. She grimaced at its cold bite. "Liudmila will grind up her Italian into polenta and look around for another man."

"No. She is very, very sentimental. You could not know that. She adores cooking and she probably would love having a bunch of babies. And when I realized that, I felt glad about what she did. The saddest thing I can think of to happen to Liudmila is for her to become an old woman, covered in shawls and all alone with no family."

"But that could be you!" Maria cried. "Why didn't you marry Eric!" Her heart's blood thickened with anguish for Galia; she could not look at this sumptuous apartment with its glorious rugs and curving silken couches and think of her living like a scavenger in a rotting jungle.

"But that is what I mean," Galia said. "I am not like her at all. When Eric was visiting, I was happy—for two nights. Then I wished he was gone. The moment he began to act a little bossy I wished he was gone sooner than that. Imagine me having his babies and becoming good and stuck with him." Galia made a gesture that dispensed with Eric, all men. "I am going to have a baby one day, you know, but I leave husbands for other women." She smiled. "For you, Marusha. You are not as tough as you like to think you are."

Maria did not acknowledge this. She dodged all references to Huell, the shadow man. "So you prefer a rotting jungle."

"For a little time, Marusha, that is not so bad. None of us will be condemned there for life. I may even love it and stay if they let me. Zoya might be able to visit me though I am not sure her husband will let her travel. Do you know she is pregnant? Now. I have dessert. Christmas fruit cake in a tin, United States commissary issue."

But Maria threw her arms around Galia and would not let her go. Galia laughed as if they were doing something hilarious—they were both full of vodka—and then she cried on Maria's blouse.

"I will miss you almost as much as this apartment," she said magnanimously, blowing her nose on a napkin. "Which I got into for nothing. The next person who wants it will have to pay key money to the porter…seven billion, eighty-nine trillion, forty-three quillion old old gold dollars…" she gasped, spluttering.

"…and real money, three Mexican, nineteen centavos…a fortune." Maria, laughing wildly, had to wipe her eyes. "And best of all, a sack of rice. Why the porter?"

"It seems the owner has disappeared. He ran to Taiwan or Hong Kong."

Landlords were not popular under the new regime. The cry was being heard all over the city: Death to the owners! Shoot all capitalists!

Their laughter trailed away. Galia released herself from Maria and opened the khaki-colored tin. From a cupboard she found a large painted platter and turned the cake onto it. She rummaged some more in another cupboard and brought out a dark-colored bottle with a gilt label. She waved it in triumph. "Cognac. Napoleon!"

"Only the best for Liudmila, I can tell by now. Pour it on. Pour it all over me."

Galia upended the bottle until the Christmas fruit cake sat in a deep puddle of cognac. "Stand back," she said, as she lit a match.

The fruit cake took fire as though fueled by kerosene. Both knocked over their chairs to escape the great blue flames. Then they laughed, and again jumped as the platter broke with a loud crack.

"The tablecloth! The table!" shouted Maria.

"Oh, let it all burn. Merry Christmas, Marusha," Galia said.

Maria felt tears on her cheeks. "Merry Christmas, Galia."

On July 25th, two weeks after Galia's departure, a monstrous typhoon, which the official weather people called Gloria, struck Shanghai. The Yangtze River overflowed, obliterating crops and villages. Maria could not sleep and neither did Nola under the mad battering of their window shutters. They wondered if Galia had been caught in the typhoon on her island and if she were still alive.

The Whangpo River also ran over its banks. When it receded, grisly souvenirs seeded the shores. Many of the bloated bodies were missing the backs of their heads. The shootings were attributed to farewell messages from the Kuomintang; they were attributed to Communist "cleansings"; they were accidents. The only truth lay in the reality that silence was best.

For the tenth, or perhaps it was the hundredth time, Maria asked her mother, What did you tell him? What did the two of you talk about? Tell me everything, don't leave anything out.

"He said to remind you that he loved you," Ming Chu would begin. "He said that he was leaving his heart with you, and you were to remember."

"So he wouldn't die?" Maria always said this with disbelief, but she also always persisted in her need for the fable of Huell. "And what did you say?"

"I told him that you loved him, very much, and I knew you so well that he was to understand I was speaking for you."

"How could you know I never told him?"

"Because I know you. Not after what Irene said to him. You were readier for the grave than to give him a proper sending away."

"Mama, I was."

"I knew exactly what you said, which was nothing."

"But you didn't tell him you knew about Irene telling him those things!"

Patiently, Ming Chu repeated, "I said nothing about her."

"Then what happened after that."

"He was very upset because he had to go. He became red, then quite pale, and seemed on the point of rushing back to see you. He looked at his watch and hit the wall with a fist. Then quickly he told me he had found Irene and Tanya in The Camellia Room and was forced to take them to a hospital—"

"You forgot to say he was angry. Maybe you made up the whole story, Mama."

"I do not lie, Maria. Yes, he was angry that he had to bother with a message from those two."

"And he asked...."

"He asked what kind of people they were. I said the grandmother was quiet and kept to herself—"

"Oh, Mama, to waste time over their Babushka!"

"—but that the sisters were strong and vicious. I told him they tried to rob you and nearly killed you."

"Rob Galia, Mama, not me. The man was going up to her room. You didn't mention what I did...to Gromeko?"

"That is for you to tell him. But I forgot he was going after Galia, Maria. All I could think of was what they did to you. I have wanted to go upstairs, many, many times, and your father stopped me because of that dog and because we could never win over them when they hid inside their room. Your father waited on the landing every day, but they knew he was there and never came down when he was waiting. A few quiet steps down, and they could see him."

"I don't care about them. It's just so nice not to have them over our heads. Peace is wonderful. No B/Ks to look at, I don't have to go to work, I can sleep all day."

"It is only three months since he left, Maria. Be patient, as he said."

"He is gone for good, Mama. I am not a child."

Nola came into the sleeping cubicle, where Maria and Ming Chu sat on the bed. "Can I have a Toddy?" She chewed on a fingernail. "Maybe I should save it. There are only three tins left." Her chest had lost its leanness; the faintest of twin curves mounded out her cotton dress. The dress was getting too short again, Ming Chu noticed.

At least they had some food reserves. Maria had brought home boxes of Spam, tins of powdered pea soup, chili con carne, an odd sort of tinned sausage called vienna, Cheddar cheese and butter from Liudmila's apartment. One big tin contained peanut butter, a food Nola had never tasted before and took to with delight. The two loaves of bread, some ham, eggs, and cheeses salvaged from the refrigerator at The Camellia Room were finished; Poldo had gone there as soon as pedicabs roamed the streets again. When he saw the gaping stairwell and Gromeko's grave, he told Ming Chu, he had wanted to burn the place down. I should have been there, he said bitterly. I could have protected her. Instead, he had met Chen Tai-Tai coming in to inspect her property and been accused of looting. Not stopping to argue, he walked up Garden Bridge, his arms full, until she tired of screaming and running after him.

On August 2 U.S. Ambassador John Leighton Stuart departed Nanking for the United States.

The empty rooms upstairs remained vacant. In early August two Chinese men in civilian clothes came to look at them. You own these rooms? You own the building? They looked at Poldo with a hunger that brought on a roaring in his ears that sounded like a mob cheering the guillotine.

I have collected about three months' rent in the five years since I bought it, he answered. The Wongs downstairs have not paid for a single day. Why don't you ask them? They have no shame.

The cadres smiled as though he had said something droll. The Wongs reported you. They said you were a money-gouging landlord. They are good Communists. How dare you accuse revolutionaries of dishonesty? Your wife is a Chinese citizen, therefore she is subject to a People's Tribunal for exploiting Chinese citizens.

She has an Italian passport, Poldo replied. She is not subject to the Chinese government.

They seemed not to hear but left promising action from the People's Tribunal.

The Shanghai Race Course reopened, but for a new purpose. The broad grassy field enclosed by the race track became an execution ground.

Let them try, Maria said to her mother, Let them try to take you anywhere!

Ming Chu said wearily, You cannot stop these people. It is their revolution. They will do exactly as they wish.

26

Guiuan, 15 August, 1949

Dearest Marusha, Do you remember the night
we went to see "The Hurricane" at the
Majestic? We ate those crab apples stuffed
with black bean paste and thought Jon Hall
and Dorothy Lamour together were romantic
as hell. You said it would be lovely to
wear one piece of cloth and no shoes all
year round. Well, that is me these days,
except for the shoes, especially after the
big typhoon. You can step on a nail or
splinters of wood and end up dead of blood
poisoning. I love my new hut and my room-
mates. Half the time I do not know what
language I am hearing. My God, Marusha, the
wildlife here is unbelievable. Monkeys,
squirrels, those furry things with the big
eyes? lemours, lemers, Lamours (I give up),
lots of mice, mongooses, big wild cats,
anteaters, and bats, bats, all over the sky

at night. I eat sweet potatoes and cassava and Spam and I think I am growing extra tits on my stomach. Now I know where Guiuan is—too far from civilization in Manila. There are a bunch of islands between, and there are only small boats that travel from one to the other.

Guess who I found living near me? The B/Ks. Yes.

Because of them everybody knows I am a nurse. My first patient was their Babushka. Poor old woman. The IRO infirmary did their best, but penicillin can't fix a broken heart. I think she just decided to die, so she did. Tanya acts crazy. Half the night somebody is out looking for her, she walks around and around, with a limp she will always have. Maybe she will step on a nail and finish herself off. Irene looks desperate.

I try to stay away from her.

I miss you so much. I worry about you. IRO is trying to process us as fast as possible but there are only so many visas to go around (same old problem). I do not mind it here, believe me, compared to -20 in Mukden, snow and ice almost all year. I prefer wearing a sarong. It rains so much I shampoo my hair and go to stand outside to rinse, and I get my dress washed besides! My love to your father and Mama, and kiss malenki Nola for me. love, from Galia.

It was very odd to read a letter in fluent English written in a hand that was pure Cyrillic, the letters angular and ornate and somehow incomplete because they lacked the original embellishments. The absence of Galia in her life was painful.

"Galia went from high heels and silk stockings to fighting bats out of her hair. I wonder if hell has the B/Ks living next to you? Even B/Ks with their fangs pulled. It sounds like there might be just one B/K left very soon. I wish the Wongs were over there, too." Maria folded the letter, written on lined foolscap, and stared at the exotic postage stamps. The envelope had been slit open, the cut glued together, before it reached Route Magy. Galia, the canny refugee, knew enough to omit risky comments about the regime. Russians in Mukden and Harbin were expert at writing home to their motherland. Stilted How are you's and I am fines crossing thousands of miles of Siberian tundra by train.

Ming Chu said, "I have come to believe the Wongs were in our fates from the beginning of my married life. Everything has a reason for being. We were prosperous, all the foreigners lived well on the backs of the Chinese, and so people like the Wongs were born."

"Lots of Chinese got rich, too, Mama."

"It is easier to hate foreigners than your own kind. I happen to be a convenient target."

Maria seldom left the house. She stayed close to her mother. An unknown step coming upstairs made her scalp prickle as though her hair actually moved. Several times she changed the hiding place for the American dollars she had saved up; Galia had paid back her share in The Camellia Room and insisted she take five hundred more besides, as a loan, which was the only way Maria would accept the money.

Exchanging American dollars for the new "people's currency," the jien mien piao, involved an operation that frightened Ming Chu more than the threat to herself. Poldo could not do this, for he and Yung were strangers to each other.

Maria had tracked down Yung, who did not live far from the dead hulk of The Camellia Room. He was more entrepreneur than she had suspected; in his one room he had cases of Scotch and cognac, dozens of cartons of Camels and Lucky Strikes, American cookies and cases of beer. A woman who may have been his wife left quickly when Maria entered. He was glad to buy her dollars.

She had brought twenty, and that one greenback in her pocket felt like a hot brick as she rode the tram from Frenchtown to its terminal at the Bund. None of the riders in their drab post-revolution clothes gave her more than a glance, but she knew she was conspicuous because she was not pure Chinese. People were being executed for less cause.

"I hope you prosper, Yung. If you move away, please let me know. Be careful who you do business with."

"*Hsiao-tzia*, there were always risks in what I do. Do you know who will be my customers when things cool off? Some of the big shots in the new government eventually. They will start wanting the good old days back, but only for themselves. They will need people like me. But for now—it is criminal to have fun, and everybody is trying to look poorer than his neighbor. I miss the race track, when they had horses instead of guns in there. The Communists came to rescue me, but who asked them?" He did not bother to lower his voice. Yung was Shanghai-born, and it was said that true Shanghai people outdid the southerners, the Cantonese, in business acumen.

Maria put her finger against her lips, but he said even more loudly, "Let them take me. They killed my son when they marched into Hupei province. He was a Nationalist soldier and he didn't run, like most of them. He was my only son, he was too good for even the Nationalists." A bluish tinge encircled his mouth; he shook with his emotion.

She was exhausted when she got home, battered by Yung's anger and the damp heat, then afterward the crowds surging to witness the daily public trial of capitalist exploiters. They had carried her with them for two blocks until she could stumble from their midst into an alley, where she stood shakily for minutes, she did not know how many. Her life felt as frangible as the dayfly's, and as momentary.

Her mother waited at the head of the stairs.

"I'm home, Mama, safe in my skin. Yung came through, as I knew he would. I trust him." She also feared for him. He would be caught, and she knew he did not care if he were. His recklessness made her task harder; what if he were raided while she was there? What if a spying neighbor informed the cadres of her visits? Every block throughout Shanghai and every other city, village, and community now had deputized spies called cadres.

She went to the kitchen for some cold tea, her mother hovering near, and suddenly she noticed an envelope in Ming Chu's hand.

"A messenger from the American consulate brought this," Ming Chu said.

The large envelope was plain white, bore no markings but her name written on it by hand. Inside were two smaller envelopes, each addressed to her in care of John Cabot, the American Consul General, United States Consulate, Shanghai.

She found she was sitting on her bed and that she was short of breath. She scanned the dates on the letters, her hands trembling so that she could barely read, and began on the first. It was typewritten.

Hong Kong, 27 April, 1949

Maria my Love, I've been here two days and already have a dossier going at the American consulate. The U.S. Consul General says there are dozens of cases like mine, and if this goes on Congress may have to enact legislation to handle all the petitions that seem to be flying in about fiancees left behind. I never got a chance to propose to you, so I haven't the nerve to convince myself you'll have me, that you are really my fiancee. But as far as concerns official channels, that is what you are, and your parents and your sister will somehow be covered. I don't know everything yet.

I need to talk to my father, which I've done, but all I accomplished with that first call was to assure the family I'm alive and well and on my way home. When I get there—and I can't as soon as I'd like because I am still in the Army—my Dad and I will start talking to our Congressman and State Senator and whoever else it takes to get the papers rolling. I have never been so glad that Dad is a lawyer and I at least passed a bar exam.

I love you. You can turn me down and marry the postman in our neighborhood but the fact that I love you can never change. Huell has fallen with a mighty thud that has made a crater you can see from the Milky Way. There is nothing you can do about it.

Tell your mother I am crazy about her, too. And don't forget Nola. Respects to your father. You are the sum of my life, and you cannot change that, either. Yours, Thad

The Atabrine should be clearing up the
malaria about now. I wish I could have sent
you a diamond ring with it.
    Thad.

He had signed it "yours, Thad," and Maria felt
a wave of shyness at the sight of his first name,
which she could not recall ever using. Thinking
of him as Huell had kept him at a distance of
safety. She must have been mad, believing his
inevitable disappearance would hardly move her
just because they were never on a first-name
basis. His calling her Maria was quite ordinary;
everyone called her Maria.

Having read one letter, she was content to put
off reading the second. She kicked off her sandals, piled up the pillows, lifted her hair, and
lay back, the papers in her lap. The windows
were open wide, showing nothing but the ugliness
of the concreted apartment building across the
way and a bit of sky. Below in the courtyard the
Wongs were talking amongst themselves. The
sticky heat of the day was waning.

…was it damp and hot in Maryland?

Thad. She blushed, feeling heat spread down to
her breasts. A man she knew, whose body she had
enjoyed, suddenly called Thad.

On the other side of the curtains Nola cleared
her throat with a theatrical "A-hem!"

"Come in. You live here, too."

She poked her head in. "Mama said to leave you
alone, but I had to know if…if…."

"So far it is. I haven't read the second letter yet. Come back in fifteen minutes."

"Oh. All right."

Her sister's soft footsteps—too solemn—going
away sounded like so many things that were wrong
with a child's world. How long had it been since
Nola was treated to the kindness of a lie?
Living as they did, so tightly together, no one
could hide anything from anyone. But some things
she did not know; the visit from the cadres had
been kept from her.

Maria re-read Huell's letter. It was no use,
she had lost that first flush of happiness. She
opened the second, also typewritten.

Arlington, 25 May, 1949

My Love, I know what day this is. My
mother heard it on the radio, and when Dad
and I got home she was in tears for all of
you. We'd been in Washington—every newspaper headline was the same. The U.S.
being half a day behind China helps get
the news out fast, but it isn't necessar-
ily better.

Capitol Hill is becoming as familiar as
my own home. I am always in uniform when I
visit—it gets me in where civilians get the
boot. But things are coming clearer. I am
sorry about the last letter sounding so
low. My discouragements should be kept to
myself, you don't need to hear about my
failures.

The proxy marriage
(proxy marriage? Had there been a letter in
between? These two were already months old. How
many more had been lost while she pretended
Huell was an interlude nearly forgotten?)
would have gotten you rights to a visa
but this brilliant idea got nowhere with
the State Department.

It seems a proxy marriage has to be con-
summated before a visa to the U.S. can be
issued. Ironic, isn't it? I had all the
opportunity in the world to get a ring on
you—assuming you were willing to wear it—
and I let my moment slip by me. I got
everything backwards. But I learn, and I
learn good.

I have arranged berths for you and family on the first British-flag ship that
will call at Shanghai. That could be soon,
or it could be in a few months. I have
asked the consulate to let you know which
ship and when. Your part is to get exit
visas as soon as you can, and you must
notify the Consul General of your intentions. Don't forget you need sojourn permits for Hong Kong. I will take off for
Hong Kong like a rocket the moment I hear
you have embarked. Send me word through
the U.S. consulate that you are going to
do it.

Please do it. Please, please marry me.

When I get you off the ship in Hong Kong we are going direct to the U.S. consulate, sorry, no detours (as usual), just the shortest route to a wedding ceremony. Otherwise, getting visas may take months or years, even if Dad posts bond and acts as sponsor. So you don't get a choice and I confess I am pleased about that.

I love you. Thad

The second letter was dated May 25, and here it was the end of August. More letters lost since May 25? Had her silence given him to think she didn't want him, didn't want him to do anything? What could he be thinking, with no word from her? Had a ship come and gone without the Contis because she had not seen John Cabot, the Consul General?

She looked at her watch. Nearly six, too late to go back downtown.

I love you, he had kept saying. She bit her lips, placed her hands to her head and squeezed with a ferocity she wished could smash her own skull to find oblivion.

27

She heard Nola's crying before she even entered
the alley at Route Magy. At the sight of Nola's
white, contorted face at the kitchen window and
Amah's frightened one next to hers, she broke
into a run, spinning up the stairway in a haze of
panic, middle landing, next landing.

Nola threw herself at Maria, her arms flailing.

"Mama's gone! Soldiers came and took her away
and they pushed her into a truck with a lot of
other people. They'll shoot her. I know they
will! Maybe she's dead already." Nola's body
shook; in her terror she pounded her fists
against Maria's neck.

Amah wiped her swollen eyes with a dishtowel.
"They were so rough, three men acting as if she
was dangerous! The *lo-yah* tried to fight
them...they hit him with the stocks of their guns."

The walls bore scrapes and a deep dent. The
artery in Nola's neck throbbed as if it meant to
leap through the skin.

"Where is Daddy?"

"The Italian consulate. He went…he tried to keep her behind him but they grabbed her and she couldn't walk so fast and they pushed her down the stairs. Daddy said they had no right, she's an Italian citizen, he shouted Italian citizen Italian citizen, but they never paid any attention to him." Nola's sobs chopped the words up, but Maria understood, she understood very well.

She turned, began to descend the stairs. "Amah, take care of her, I'll be back as soon as I can."

"NO!" You mustn't leave me here. You won't come back, Daddy won't come back. Nobody will ever come back!" She wrapped her arms around Maria, her feet scrambling for traction on the floor to pull her sister back.

"Oh, Nola." Maria's voice broke. Nor could she leave her here alone; the hot thin arms embodied her own hold on an earth turned upside down. "Come on, then, we'll stick together." To Amah, poor Amah with her hands shredding the forgotten dishcloth she said, "If the *lo-yah* comes home before we do, tell him we went to the American consulate. I know someone there and I am going to ask him to help me."

Nola was already dragging at her to hurry. The door of the Wong apartment stayed closed; if they were home they would have missed nothing that had happened to the Contis today.

Seated in the pedicab, whose driver pedaled with a slowness that never varied, Maria found a handkerchief and dried Nola's face, then got out her pocket comb to smooth down the hair tangled around her head. Nola allowed her to do these small things but kept asking what the American consulate could do for them. Could they make the soldiers let her go? Should they go to the Shanghai Race Course and make sure Mama wasn't already there?

They alighted on the Bund at the corner of Peking Road; this morning on her errand to the consulate she had walked here from the tram stop.

She asked the civilian American at the front desk if she could see Mr. William Dugan, who had interviewed her earlier today. The man looked at Nola, who stood visibly trembling at her side, and listened to Maria explain why she was back.

"When I went home I found my mother had been abducted by soldiers and taken away in a truck." On the way over she had thought carefully of how she would put it to this man. She would not say "arrested" because it sounded as though her mother were guilty. "My mother is an Italian citizen by marriage. They can't just take her away…Mr. Dugan knows our family's situation…we are…he has to help…" Maria's rehearsed speech evaporated; she bowed her head, her fear at last supreme. In a minute she would be just like Nola, who had begun to sob.

The civilian, a middle-aged man who had looked at her with a hint of lust the first time she walked in today, said kindly, "I'll go in and tell Mr. Dugan your trouble. I'm sure he will try to make time to see you."

Neither said anything as they waited. Nola's
hand in hers, she stared blindly at a framed
picture of President Harry S. Truman, an ashtray
on a stand, the greenish linoleum floor. The
waiting area was full; men in business suits,
some with their families, talked in low tones.
An American woman said to her husband, "How do
you expect me to cram our lives into one suit-
case each?" Oh, Mom, her teen-age daughter muttered. Maria felt the edges of their stares. A
wide hallway leading from the lobby vibrated
with activity, all men, crossing, pausing to
talk, diving for ringing telephones. Was her
father making any headway at the Italian consulate? Was her mother already dead, lying in
her own blood on the grass at the Shanghai Race
Course? Nola had leaped to that image. Maria
could not get it out of her own head.

The click of heeltaps jerked her around, as
telling as a volley of rifle fire.

It was the man returning, William Dugan behind
him. Conversation halted, heads turned toward
him. Hand outstretched to Maria, the vice consul
said, "I'm really sorry to hear what happened.
Come inside, please, try to relax, and we'll
talk about it." He took Nola's limp hand. "And
this must be your sister? How are you?" His nose
wrinkled, a grimace directed at himself. "Not
well, of course. I'm sorry, stupid of me. Come
this way."

"Those two had better have a good case," the
American woman said, as they walked by her.

Nola sat on the edge of the chair offered her, her stare fastened on Dugan.

Maria said, "My father is at the Italian consulate trying to do what he can there. Mr. Dugan, perhaps you can ask Mr. Cabot to contact the Italian Consul General. If they worked together, the Chinese authorities might listen. It is the strongest way to respond, and they will realize they can't hold her, won't they? My mother is an Italian citizen; after she married my father she took Italian citizenship, just as Nola and I were registered at birth. They can't hold her in prison for no reason. And what if they have already...." she looked aside at Nola, then at Dugan, her eyes, subdued gesture of a hand, eloquent, asking this American in the nice summer-weight worsted suit and neat haircut to jump out of his chair and act.

"Did the soldiers say why they were taking her?"

Nola burst out, "They called her a capitalist landlord. They shoot people like that, don't they?"

"The tenants downstairs who reported her have not paid rent since my father bought the building years ago," Maria said. "They hate my mother because she is married to a foreigner. They accused her of exploiting them." Beside her, Nola rustled like a leaf about to fly away into the wind. Her shock was audible. The Wongs did that?

At last, at last, Dugan rose from his chair. "Would you wait for me here? I am going to speak to Mr. Cabot. He has been over at the Philippine consulate but he may be back now."

As he opened the door the telephone on his broad mahogany desk rang. Maria nearly reached for the heavy black casing to throw it to the floor. Go, Dugan. Go. Dugan did not return to pick it up. His desk was covered with file folders and legal-size documents; passports embossed with a gilt eagle and United States of America (she read upside down) were stacked to one side. A sheaf of message slips climbed up a spindle (the first shall be last). The telephone rang again, jarring her nerves for seven or eight rings, before falling silent.

Nola stood up and wandered around the office. "You're going to marry an American and we're all going to America. Shouldn't that make the consulate do something?"

"Mr. Dugan knows about it. I told him all that this morning." But I'm not married yet, Maria thought. Intent is worth nothing on this market. "He has a letter from Huell and I brought him my passport and birth certificate to prove who I am. I showed him yours and Daddy's and Mama's papers. So the American consulate knows about us and we'll be ready to leave as soon as a ship arrives." If there are berths reserved for them; if Huell has woken up and decided he didn't love her.

Tense against the armrest of Maria's chair, Nola said, "I won't go without Mama."

"She will be with us. None of us is going anywhere without her."

If Consul General John Cabot did anything on
their behalf it would be as a gesture of kindness, or of solidarity with the consul general
of another nation. Before she left home this
morning she had told her mother that a dozen
British-flag ships may have come and gone; that
Huell would have taken her silence as refusal
and given up. Do not make up any calamities
before you know the truth, her mother had said.

I wish I'd kissed her, thought Maria. I wish I
could tell her there haven't been any British-
flag ships. The *Leong Bee* was here, Mr. Dugan
had told her, but she was Chinese-owned, based
in Hong Kong, and not safe from attack by either
Communists or Nationalists.

The telephone rang, sending a runner of tics
to her fingertips.

The door opened and Dugan walked in. He did not
answer the telephone. "Mr. Cabot put in a call to
Mr. Marino, the Italian Consul General. Your
father is in his office over there, by the way.
Mr. Marino had just sent his vice consul to the
provisional governor's office to register a
protest. He thought it would be helpful if I
joined him, and that is what I am going to do. I
might catch him there if I hurry. Do you have your
mother's passport with you, still? Okay, good,"—
Maria was already handing it to him. He looked at
Nola. "We are going to do everything we can—Nola,
is that your name?—the new government is not too

ready to offend foreign governments. There have
been one or two precedents. A French national was
arrested for owning a shortwave radio, and a
British national was taken in because his car
broke down and he was out after curfew. They were
both released."

"But neither of them was born Chinese," Maria
said.

His gaze glanced off hers and shifted to the
task of buttoning his coat. A slight stomach
swelled the second button. He patted a chest
pocket (wallet, ID, glasses?). "No. This would
be a third precedent, I expect. Miss Conti,
would you like to wait in the consulate until I
get back? Do you have a telephone at home?"

"We haven't got a telephone. Can't we come
with you?"

"That's not a good idea; it's not one I would
recommend. Let's keep this on a diplomatic level.
It's a pretty touchy stage to begin with."

And a huge favor from a disinterested party, the
United States, he did not add. Maria stood up. "We
are very grateful for anything you can do. We'll
wait outside. Please hurry, Mr. Dugan."

No one had come by for what felt like hours.
She had tried to eat the plain rice brought to
her in a chipped enamel pan and had forced half
of it down, grain by grain. After that, there
was nothing to do but sit. So this was the
inside of the police station on Foochow Road.
She had come here once to report a theft; an

amah had stolen a piece of jewelry. Their chauf-
feur, Wong (what irony, though half of China
shared that surname) had dropped her off and
gone to take care of some errands. She had been
quite exasperated at his tardiness in returning,
and stood uncomfortably at the curb for fifteen
minutes until the black Fiat reappeared.

This time she had eternity to spare.

The four walls, whitewashed in a time already
ancient, were carved (with fingernails?) with
names, dates, words in English, Chinese, many
languages Ming Chu could not read. Smudges of
a dark-colored stuff formed a crude picture of
a house with smoke spiraling from its chimney;
its artist had signed his name, Vincent van
Beri Beri.

She was so thirsty. The slop bucket in the
corner awaited her; she had not yet used it.
When that time came, she would have to tear a
piece from the bottom of her gown to use as
toilet paper.

Was it still day or was it now night? The one
light bulb screwed into the ceiling gave away
nothing; its yellowish fifteen watts reminded
her of rancid margarine which she could almost
taste. Or was it the unwashed rice, gritty with
small stones, still uneasy in her mouth?

Nola, my baby. Ming Chu could not stop reliv-
ing the sight of her child rocking frantically
between her father and the soldiers in that
scuffle on the landing. She had scratched and
pummeled, her shrieks making even the soldiers

flinch. The crunch of a riflebutt on Poldo's
shoulder had sent Nola at the soldier like a
blind, killer cyclone; had Ming Chu not caught
and held her the soldier might have caved her
head in.

...will the child grow up to be normal? Ming Chu
grieved over this more than anything that had
happened to her. An executioner's bullet to the
head or breast was a merciful finish; Nola's
agony would be a lifetime's sentence. Ming Chu
knew her husband would not recover. Since the
cadres' visit his self-reproach had worn ten
pounds from him and carved brown hollows under
his eyes.

In the end, it would be Maria's burden to hold
them all together.

At least this was summertime, she did not need
warm clothes or a blanket. But her feet, she
thought. She had to bathe them once a day and
change the wrappings or they would quickly
become foul. She decided to undo the cloths and
save them for an emergency...such as the journey
to the Shanghai Race Course. But that was stupid. What did it matter how her feet looked when
she was sent to die?

Nonetheless she bent, unlaced her right shoe
and began to unwind the wrapping on her foot.

A face appeared at the foot-square, barred cut
in the wooden door. Ming Chu thrust her bared
foot behind the other.

A key rattled and the door opened. The guard who had brought her the rice stood there for a moment, his stare on her feet.

"You know," he said, "my mother was a servant in the house of a woman with bound feet. My mother was a slave to those feet, which were smaller and more pointed than yours. They were so useless, those two stumps, that my mother had to haul her mistress everywhere, even to the toilet. She'd sit on a stool waiting for her to finish and do you know what she did as she waited? She folded toilet paper into exact squares and then she had to raise up the woman and wipe her arse." He laughed harshly. "My rice and cabbage came from her shit."

He was not young, like the soldiers who had taken her from Route Magy; this man's bitterness was gouged into him by years and memory.

Ming Chu did not answer. It was no use telling him that China had lived through three thousand years of small and monstrous cruelties and that a new flood of them had begun with Mao's regime. She had decided to speak as little as possible though she tried not to appear sullen.

"The captain wants to see you. Get up, never mind fixing your foot." All of a sudden he was enraged. "Leave the bandage!" He yanked her up and she stumbled, her high-arched, doubled-up naked foot a travesty of a normal one, exposed to a strange man. He pushed her ahead to the door and she had to go without her shoe. There are worse things, she told herself, and walked as well as she could, her bent-under toes rapping the floor in painful jolts, only her big toe and the edge of her heel anchoring her swaying weight.

He stayed behind, giving her a push every few steps. When she touched the corridor wall for support he slapped her hand down. There were so many doors like hers, their occupants silent behind them, though she could hear a man gasping as if in pain.

The guard grasped the back of her neck and thrust her into a room in which sat a young man behind a desk. He looked at her coolly as she stumbled under the guard's hand. Then he stared at her naked foot. Ming Chu found a spot under his desk, where she could see his black rubber-soled shoes and gray cotton uniform trousers, and kept her gaze there. Most of her weight rested on her left foot; its bones and crippled instep began to ache. Soon she would have to lay herself down on the very floor, or fall.

"Say good evening to the Captain!"

"Good evening, Captain."

The young man lit a cigarette. "Isn't it marvelous that you don't have to kowtow? The old days are gone forever. There is no longer a class system, although I am not certain I like being in the same class as you." He had a boy's voice, strident and not yet modulated and masculine. He was speaking in Kuo-hua, Mandarin. "I understand you claim to be a foreigner." He smiled to show her his amusement with this notion.

"I am married to an Italian citizen. I took his citizenship." Ming Chu's thirst grew; her underwear felt soaked with sweat, and she felt a sudden wave of nausea.

"I have never heard anything so ridiculous. Look at your feet. Do Italian women have feet like that? Did you look down on your Chinese people because you married a foreigner? Do you eat—" his lips widened and he laughed—"spaghetti with chopsticks?" He was very handsome, this young Communist, with large brilliant eyes and white teeth between his well-shaped lips. Ming Chu saw him through black spots floating before her eyes. She shifted to her right foot and instantly drew back; the pain in her crippled bones heaved the nausea to her throat.

"Sorry…" she whispered, turned her head just in time, and vomited. The rice she had eaten and all the vari-colored fluids left in her stomach splattered onto the floor; her legs caught a spray. The guard behind her jumped and swore.

But the captain had known it was coming and he merely watched her.

"You'd love to rinse your mouth, wouldn't you."

Ming Chu nodded. She used the back of her hand to clean her lips, hesitated, then wiped her hand on her gown. This is how it begins, she thought. Once you start sliding, the rest comes naturally. The spots increased; thirst parched her unclean mouth and the sweat on her face and body felt like ice water. Her hands and feet were freezing. A weakness like death coming for her crept up her limbs.

He was talking to her, but Ming Chu could not hear him. Her knees slowly folding, the last thing she was aware of was the hard floor and the slipperiness of her own vomit.

28

As he did yesterday, the sentry made them turn their pockets out. Poldo handed his parcel to Maria and—stiffly, because of his bruised shoulder—pulled the bottoms out of his trouser pockets. The sight of lint and bits of pipe tobacco (when he could afford the habit) collected in the seams of the old cloth hurt her like a flesh wound; today she simply did not look. When he was done, it was her turn to dig into the shallow breast pocket of her cotton dress. Her purse held nothing but their documents, an envelope, and some car fare. Without being told, she undid the string around the parcel; the half loaf of bread and small pot of jam, four boiled eggs, two chicken legs wrapped in waxed paper, and two apples made a skimpy mound on the table. She opened a second parcel and watched the sentry lift and examine cotton panties and a camisole, soap, a tube of toothpaste and a towel. Amah had bewailed the meager quantity of the food being sent to her mistress, but that was no less than the quantity Ming Chu ate at home. And they would bring her fresh food everyday, a task that gave Maria a sense of usefulness.

Nola stepped forward and stood with her arms out as though to invite the guard to pat her down, but he merely laughed and waved her inside. Her eyes narrowed and Maria, alert to her sister's newly developed fierceness, touched her shoulder and urged her along. Nola's anger flayed them all; this morning she had raged at her father for insisting that she eat a proper breakfast.

You care about all the wrong things! Why don't you ever, ever listen to Mama! So you leave ME alone! Don't tell ME what to do!

Maria's attempts to hush her had drawn fire upon her own head.

What good are you, anyway? You shut up, I'm sick of you being bigger than me. I bet I could be a better grownup than you. You let things happen, I never would have let them happen, not me, if somebody ever asked ME.

She had slammed the jug of evaporated milk on the table and run from the room. They heard her crying in the kitchen and Amah's crooning sounds of comfort. Maria could not bear the look on her father's face. She knew he had not slept all night; he had even gone out for a walk at midnight in disregard of curfew. She lay awake until finally, at three o'clock, she heard him moving about in the bedroom.

Mopping up the milk, he said, "Signor Marino told me he has telephoned the Ministero degli Esteri in Rome; they will lodge a formal protest. These things take time, Maria. There is nothing on earth so hard as waiting, is there." He looked exhausted; he had forgotten to comb the fringe of hair on his head.

"The American consulate won't stop working on it, either, Daddy. Mr. Dugan is going there again today. He has sent a message to Huell about the situation. Maybe he can do something from the States."

Her father seemed not to be listening; he continued scrubbing at the damp spot on the tablecloth. She had not mentioned Huell since she told him, two days ago, what she intended to do. I am glad for you Maria, I really am, he said, and she knew he was. He could accept Huell, not himself, as being the instrument of their escape. Through her lover they would have a new start in America under the aegis of his father. Poldo had begun drawing up names of his contacts on the West Coast of the United States; there were his friends in Hong Kong who would be invaluable in the import-export business. China was shut down, but the rest of Asia was not. Yes, a base in the United States was the ticket. Any humiliation he may have felt was hidden from Maria, but he had a limitless capacity for humiliation now.

Until her mother was taken away, he did not know he had yet to develop a limitless capacity for remorse.

We talk like children in the dark, Maria thought. No one in the world can threaten the Communists with anything, especially after the British knuckled under from the beginning. If they can shoot up British warships without reprisal they can execute a Chinese woman for no cause at all. A foreign passport had taken on the feel of the thinnest of defenses. An officer at the Foochow Road station had looked at Maria's pass bearing her Italian registration number and thrown it back at her. His contempt was the common badge of the new order; she felt it in the glances she received everywhere in the streets.

She got up and went to collect the food parcel from Amah.

Nola sat on a stool at the window. This was her new post in the household. From here she could watch the street and the entrance to the lane, in case her mother was returned home.

"You'll be late for school."

Nola did not turn her head. "I'm not going to school. I'm going with you to the jail. From now on you'll never go anywhere without me because you won't tell me what is really happening."

Maria feared, then, that Nola would insist on witnessing her mother's execution. Why should she trust anyone's word that she was dead?

At the Foochow Road jail, they were allowed to sit on a bench to wait for Signor Marino, who was to come at eleven. There were other sufferers—all Chinese—sitting or standing, their anxiety poorly hidden and plucked out in plain view each time a prisoner was hustled through the room. The cells that must be in the back could not be seen. Like everyone else keeping vigil— one of them a woman with child at breast, another a man holding a paper with his son's name written on it—the Contis could not help staring at the gloomy corridor that angled off to the right.

At one minute to eleven an officer switched on a radio mounted on a shelf. A blare of martial music, then a voice announcing a public address by Chairman Mao: "A People's Revolution." All over the room, men in uniform stopped what they were doing.

Poldo rose and went after Nola, who had gone to the door near the sentry. He bent down, whispered, and brought her back. "Do not move, talk, or make any faces," he said softly.

The speech lasted twenty minutes. Heads up, barely breathing, the men listened to their leader. In agony, Maria glanced surreptitiously at her watch. No one went in or out. She couldn't see Signor Marino beyond the sentry.

Another blast of music. The speech was over. Released, the troops dispersed. Maria went to the door and met Signor Marino arriving. He waved his pass at the sentry and entered the station house.

"Buon giorno, buon giorno. I waited until the last minute in case a call came through." A gentleman from Florence, was how Poldo described him years ago. He was leaner than he used to be and did not look well. Maria remembered his long bony nose from the few times he had come to dinner at their house. When he asked them to take Daniele in Poldo was honored to do so. She had been a schoolgirl, flattered to death by his compliments on her grace and charm.

"Did it?" she asked roughly. "Did you hear from Rome?"

"Yes, the Ministro's secretary telephoned." He looked from Maria to Poldo, who had stood up. "There was no answer to their protest. The main problem is the new government has not yet been formed. Until the People's Republic of China has been ratified by the Chinese People's Political Consultative Conference (how the words rolled in Italian, Maria thought, mad with impatience at the ponderousness of the words) there is only a vague roster of officials working in the provisional government. Not one will accept delegations from foreign powers. They are very difficult, Signor Conti," he said, distress dragging down his voice—he was nearly mumbling. "No one can reach them until they agree to be reached."

Maria had already secured Nola to her side; she felt her trembling. The Americans will do no better, she thought.

She was correct. Vice Consul William Dugan informed them of the same situation in slightly different words. But Captain Huell had sent a message back telling the Contis to hold fast, he was talking to his congressman and senator. Dugan delivered these facts with his arms slightly held out from his sides, as though to catch anyone who might be fainting.

"We will be in touch with you daily," he said. "Even if we have nothing to report, someone will be in touch. You'll be here in this station about the same time everyday, won't you?"

Maria looked at him. "Yes."

Her father had taken Nola to the bench where he held her in the circle of his arms.

Dugan watched the tableau. "Why didn't you leave when you could?"

"Why didn't thousands of other nationals leave?" she said evenly. He knew as well as she the rejoinder was weak. Her mother was the one in peril, not the foreign nationals.

"Have you any message for Captain Huell? We can do at least that much, be your couriers to him and back. It's too bad his mail took so long to get to you. Nonessential mail gets lowest priority in the diplomatic pouch."

"Tell him," Maria said. She could not hold back the wetness in her eyes. "Tell him we will be on that ship when my mother is released.

I...don't know what else there is to say." She opened her purse and gave him the envelope. "If you could send him this, I would be grateful." She was always telling Dugan she was grateful, and she was, far beyond what the trite word could convey.

"Of course. Glad to do it. Glad I can do anything." Dugan lifted his shoulders, expressing ruefulness, and took his leave.

Next day Maria found a clipping from the People's Liberation News pasted on the wall of their landing. When she saw her mother's photograph on the clipping she knew the Wongs had crept upstairs in the night and put it up. Suddenly short of breath, Maria ripped it off the wall and stared at her mother's picture and thanked God she had found it before Nola. But she couldn't read it. She had never learned to read Chinese. Amah was no use, she had never learned to read or write. She had to show it to her father. The full-face speckled newsprint likeness gave not a clue to her mother's condition. It looked like an obit picture.

While Nola was in the bathroom Maria unfolded the clipping and without a word gave it to her father. Poldo's color changed. Frightened, Maria watched his lips, straining to understand the difficult intonations of written Chinese as laboriously he read aloud the characters. The story was brief. It was about her crime in overcharging the tenants in her apartment building. "This woman is married to an Italian and hopes to escape

justice. The Revolution shed rivers of blood to
correct the crimes of the rich. A confession is
expected to be forthcoming."

Maria wondered if their parcels were being
given to her mother. No used underthings ever
were returned. A note Poldo had written and
enclosed with the food was confiscated and
torn up.

The evening silences at home were torturous.
They received no news from the Voice of America
or the BBC, for Poldo had dismantled his shortwave radio. Maria visited Yung twice after their
daily vigils at Foochow Road station. His recklessness had redoubled. He seemed not to care
how visible his operations were. A new woman
occupied his room amongst all the crates and
boxes.

"Yung, be careful," Maria said, and he replied,
"For what? A quick death is the best way to go. In
fact I am planning my speech when I face the firing squad."

"Then find me another currency dealer. I cannot afford to be caught with you."

"My cousin. He lives at number 638 Yangtzepoo
Road, but I can't guarantee how far you can
trust him. It's because of his wife. She gets
too frightened. One day she may report him to
save herself. His ten-year-old son is getting
brain-washed in school. He may turn in his
father. The children get big red paper "hero"
medals for doing it, did you hear about that? Do
you see the advantage of not having children or

wives?" Yung tipped his head in the direction of the woman sitting on the bed. "This one has nowhere else to go. With me she gets her food and a place to sleep. If she reports me, I wish her nothing but good luck."

The woman was comely and perhaps in her thirties. She sat with the pale quietude of contained tragedy. She looked at her folded hands when Yung spoke of her.

At home Maria counted her money. Thank God there was still the five hundred dollars Galia made her take. Since May prices had risen sixty times. Mao Tse-tung's economists initiated a device for quelling inflation: wages, bank deposits, some government payments, and bond issues were to be expressed in terms of commodity units called commodity basket values. One unit equaled six catties of rice, one and one-half catties of flour, sixteen catties of coal, four feet of white shirting. By dealing in this unit, a person was protected against further inflation. The comedy was that the Contis could not deal in the legitimate market.

One day Maria found her sister standing before a large pot of boiling water and dropping her silkworm cocoons into it.

"Oh, Nola."

"It can't be helped," she said, like a grandmother explaining the facts of life to a child. "The moths were about due to come out. It's better to get rid of them before they start laying eggs. And if I let the eggs hatch I can't be running out all the time picking mulberry leaves for the silkworms." In the early summer she had done that, monitoring each stage of growth until the fourth and last one, when the four-inch, pearly-white worms with horns on their tails began to weave their cocoons. Nola dropped a handful containing a shimmering golden one into the pot. "Maybe they'll let me send a yellow one in to Mama."

"Maybe they will." Maria watched them bobbing in the steaming water. "They're pretty, aren't they." The naturally gold cocoons were rare and prized by silk manufacturers. Such perfect ovals, never to give birth to the fat, bumbling moths that would mate, the females to lay hundreds of pinhead-size yellow eggs.

"They're okay," Nola said. "I don't care if they're pretty or not."

"Don't throw them all in the pot. Couldn't you give some to Elizabeth?"

"She left."

"What do you mean, 'she left'? Left for where, when?"

"She left for Denmark last week. She dropped in to say goodbye, but we were out."

"Oh, Nola. Your best friend."

Steadily Nola threw cocoons into the boiling water. Her hair stuck damply to her cheeks. "I suppose. I don't care so much about her leaving."

"I know," said Maria. She went to their sleeping cubicle and looked at her wall calendar. She put a tiny circular dot, rather like a silkworm egg, at the lower corner of the box for September 12. This was the fourteenth day since her mother had disappeared into Foochow Road jail.

29

On September 21 the People's Republic of China was ratified. Peiping was renamed Peking, which became the capital of the new government. Three days later, Mao was elected chairman of the government.

The Foochow Road jail was decked with red bunting inside and out. Large framed photographs of Mao Tze-tung were hung on every wall. The soldiers and officers manning the station house were jubilant; news bulletins proclaiming the greatest day in the history of China trumpeted from the radio at 15-minute intervals. A parade, half military and half civilian, marched to band music. Banners of red cloth blazoned with Mao's round beaming face and crescent hairline called forth roars of acclamation from spectators. Since the banners swept by in the hundreds, the shouting was a continuous roaring. The parade took an hour to pass the entrance to Foochow Road jail.

Because of the noise, the Contis did not at first hear themselves being addressed. A young captain, someone they had seen walking to and from the corridor, was speaking to them.

Poldo got to his feet. "I beg your pardon. I missed what you said."

The captain's luminous eyes and thick eyebrows were striking and he was over six feet tall, as northerners often were. The Contis remembered him especially. He said, "You speak Shanghai very well. I'd never heard of foreigners doing that."

"I have lived more than half my life in China. My wife...." He had been about to say "My wife is Chinese," but realized in time what a blunder that might have been. Their entire premise for the release of Ming Chu was based on her Italian citizenship.

"I am quite aware that your wife is Chinese. But is she also Italian?"

Beside Poldo, Maria was utterly still. She had Nola's hand in hers.

The captain said briskly, "I am releasing her. You may take her home today."

"*Madonna*," Poldo whispered. Blood rose to his head and pumped madly. He looked at Maria, but it was Nola who spoke.

"Now? Please, when? Daddy, he said today."

"Captain," Poldo said. "I cannot thank you...we all thank you..."

The captain said. "You should thank Chairman Mao. Such a great day as this should be observed with acts of mercy. Therefore I have declared amnesty for your wife." He lifted an admonishing forefinger. "Take her home and think about the new order in force today. China for China. Foreigners will no longer live off my country like leeches."

Barely hearing him over the radio and the parade, Poldo nodded.

"Yes," Maria said. She cleared her throat and said again, firmly, "Yes, we will. We thank you as well as Chairman Mao."

The captain jerked his head once, sternly, and strode away.

"Daddy, he didn't say what time today…" Nola began, then looked down the corridor and shrieked "Mama!"

Ming Chu slept. Nola made a nest for herself on the bed, ready to bring her tea and food when she awakened. Maria had stopped at the Italian consulate to take the news to Signor Marino and after him to William Dugan. Amah was weeping quietly over the stew she was cooking for their dinner.

All of Poldo's strength seemed to have left his limbs. He sat at the dining table unable to move, his hands hanging because he lacked the strength to hold them in his lap. His blood pressure still beat in his ears. With a huge effort, he got up and fetched his list from the sideboard, then made himself scan his overseas names and addresses, the European names swimming together with the Anglo and Hong Kong ones. He found he was weeping. He dug out his handkerchief and mopped his cheeks but the tears continued, beyond his control. The flood of his tears ran into the grooves in his cheeks and dripped off his chin. He could not recall when he had last wept, not when he was young and whetting his ambitions in China, never when he was intent on realizing those ambitions. He had worked so gladly that he felt he deserved to recoup his fortunes, convincing himself that China's foibles would readjust to suit. Thousands of others like him had believed it. Because of his delusion he had nearly lost Ming Chu.

Fool. Fool. Worse than that, a coward. He realized why he had held on. The world outside was too hard, too unfamiliar for him in his middle age. China was all he knew. When his freighters had been bombed to the bottom of the Whangpo his guts had gone down with them.

For twenty-three days in the Foochow Road station house he had had time to study the caliber of the new guard. Rumors said these young, hardy northerners spoke Russian, that their mentors were elite members of the Marxist regime. Amongst these men in the station, the deference toward foreigners that he had accepted without question was missing. The young captain had dismissed him as though he were an insect.

He knew past doubting that it was time to get out. Afterward he could maneuver again in the free markets, look up these old contacts on his list. He would not stay long under the protection of his daughter and her new family; the very prospect of it made him wish for death.

What was this? Pride resurfacing? Take care, Poldo. Watch your next steps.

He began to make notes. He had to visit his godown office and clear it out, burn the useless files; then he had to find a buyer for this building.

He stopped writing. There were the damned Wongs. Those curs would sabotage any attempt at a sale. And these days to display wealth enough to purchase an apartment building begged for death by execution. Each day these people were paraded in the streets, forced to wear placards denouncing their crimes against the people.

Exhausted, Poldo covered his face with his hands.

"No one mistreated me," Ming Chu told them. It was true. After the first day the young captain had been indifferent to her. He sent for her five times more but barely looked at her as he worked at his desk. She decided that the summonings were a formality intended to remind that her fate was still in his hands. He could have had her beaten, she saw enough streaks of blood and splashes of it on the floor and walls. She did not tell her family of the terrifying screams she heard from the corridor and the beatings sounding like dull crunchings of bone breaking. In the passageway between cells she had walked by an old man being kicked by a guard shouting Get up, dirty old sod! The man kept trying to get to his feet, and each time was kicked back down. His lips were torn and blood spewed forth at each kick. Ming Chu stepped on a pebble, looked down and saw it was a tooth.

On the fourth day (a reckoning that was only approximate because she had no window in her cell) her guard opened the door and threw a string-tied parcel on the floor and shut the door again. Imagine her joy, she told her family, Nola clamped against her side, when she opened it. She had not disappeared; they knew where she was and were allowed to reach her in some way. How she wanted to thank the captain, but she dared to speak unless given permission. Sometimes he read to her a passage from Mao's writings; once he told her that her older daughter had become too Westernized.

That remark delivered, he ignored her as she stood dazed and mulling over and over what he had said about Maria. It meant he had met her, perhaps all of them, and they must have visited this very station to deliver the parcel. These speculations comforted her throughout the long hours in her cell.

More parcels were delivered. Some of the food was spoiled but for her idled body the remainder was enough. The best part of it was knowing her family knew where she was.

"The underwear, Mama," Nola said from under her arm. "Didn't you get the underwear? We brought some everyday."

"I received three parcels of underwear. Perhaps they thought one change a day was spoiling me." The garments felt like Christmas gifts. She had ripped two camisoles into strips with which to bind her feet. She asked her guard if she might wash. The next day he gave her a small basin of water, an enormous concession, she realized by then.

That was when she began to suspect she would be set free, that perhaps her Italian citizenship was protecting her. Also, she never saw anyone superior in rank to the captain. Was this significant? Did a mere captain have authority sufficient to condemn to death someone with a foreign passport?

"But he let you suffer," Maria said. "He made you stay in that hole and he made us wait and worry."

"He let me go. It is the only thing that counts." She looked down and stroked Nola's cheek, wondering about the child. Her eyes were perpetually widened, the dark irises rimmed with alarm like a feral cat's.

Saying nothing, Poldo took her hand and raised it to his lips, something he had never done before the girls. Ming Chu felt Nola tense, as if she resented her father intruding upon her territory. Yes. There were wounds yet healing. She would have to be vigilant to help her daughter find her childhood again.

Washington, 22 September, 1949

Maria my Peony, I feared because I didn't get word from you. When the consulate notified me what had happened I went crazy and charged over to Capitol Hill. Dad couldn't meet me there but he made plenty of calls from Arlington which preceded me.

Nobody gave me any hope. It's what the consulate must have told you. Politics do NOT make allowances for individual cases. These people were ready to sacrifice their ambassador in Nanking. He and I knew it but at that time it was just academic for me. Now it's personal in a way that serves me right for all my sins.

All I got out of my banging on doors was a promise to "look into it." I felt like a dot on the world map. That's all one person is worth in world politics. Maria, how I wished I could fly in and snatch your mother out of there. I've never felt more useless in my life. All the things I've learned have been worthless where I need them.

My discharge is coming up. Soon I won't even be able to flaunt the old Good Conduct Medal.

Thank God your mother is safe. Keep her close to you and get on that ship so I can grab you all and take you home with me. Do

you know what else makes me a happy man?
That your not answering was only because of
the mails. It feels like, how can I put it?
like a reprieve from my idiocy.

Your
Thad

30

In mid-January the fogs enveloped the sampan families and drifted inland. Icy winds shrieked between the books lining the windowsills of Maria's and Nora's sleeping closet.

For six weeks Maria had been dealing with Yung's cousin. Yung's splintered door half off its hinge, the empty room, looted bedding, dark stains on the wood floor—Maria saw enough in less than a minute before she fled the premises. The cousin, a middle-aged man full of nervous mannerisms, had nearly fainted with fright when Maria turned up on his doorstep. He gave her a rate well below the current black market exchange, but she was forced to accept it. Until she found someone else she had to use him. The cousin refused to talk about Yung. She felt a sort of incomplete grief for him though he had made it clear he looked forward to the end of his life.

The public trials went on. The Chinese civilian population attended them with a zest that

made Poldo think of the French Revolution. *Sha!*
Sha! Kill! Kill! screamed the men and women at
People's Park, behind the Shanghai Race Course.

Despite official proclamations, Shanghailanders
operated by feel and by rumor. Newspapers did not
tally the numbers of landlords and businessmen
executed; private estimates had the total at one
million throughout China.

Arlington, 15 December, 1949

My Maria, When I received your letter,
my very first from you and the most important of my life, I had to go out to my
boat to read it. There was no other place
in the world that seemed right for such an
occasion. And when I finally opened and
read it my old boat could have been sinking and I wouldn't have noticed. That was
where you said that even if you never left
China you would love me until you died.

My God, My God. You love me. You actually
said it. Coming out of my reserved Maria it
has to be the declaration for the ages.
Mine. Can I say that? Mine those eyebrows I
wanted to kiss everytime you raised them,
Not to worry. My girl.

My mule-natured, lion-hearted independent warrior woman. There is nothing you
have to do to prove to me that you can
take care of yourself. You can.

Only God's little jokes and governments
can ever beat you down.

I think I am delirious. My mother says I've been falling over things since your letter came.

My brother says I make him sick to his stomach.

He's jealous. Wait until he sees you!

And I can't wait until you are in front of me and I make you say, "I love you, Thad."

Now I realize you never called me that. You never called me anything. Quite an admission from you. Keep tumbling those walls, I need to know everything that goes on behind them. No, don't run off, I didn't mean that. I'll let you keep as much of yourself to yourself as you need.

I'll just sneak behind your back and ask your Mom.

At least she recognized my sterling character and trusted me.

Some small things happened here. When I got back I ran some errands for the guys in the Foreign Correspondents Club in Broadway Mansions—delivered letters, visited family, things like that—and I got to know some of the people at the Overseas Press Club. I have a job with the Washington Post when I report back as a civilian.

It pays six peanut shells a week, but what the heck, it's a beginning. Then there's the School of Journalism at George Washington U. I'll be a thirty-year-old freshman. Could you stand it?

My Dad doesn't mind anything I do anymore.

He's even pleased my brother will be a pitcher in the minor leagues. He is just so glad he has us both alive and well at home. What happened to you has given him a perspective like a new sort of religion. My mother says she could stand getting used to the peace around here. She sends her love.

You love a man, Maria, who is so awfully humble about his good luck someone has to take pity on him.

> Your Thad

Maria folded the letter and put it high on the top of the closet with the others. She had received the letters that had been missing. There were no other hiding places she could think of, but if Nola climbed on a chair and took them down to read she was welcome to do it.

She put on her coat, a pair of old rubber boots she used to wear mucking out Ralph's stable at Dixwell Road, a mackintosh over her coat, and a floppy oilskin hat on her head. Her hair reached below her shoulders and she never pinned it up anymore. There was no Camellia Room to primp for, though the reason she let it grow was Huell. He loved her hair and preferred it down.

She went down the stairs, passing the Wongs' door, and stepped into the alley. Even in this semisheltered place a cold sleety gust chilled her through mackintosh and coat. Several inches of water stood in the alley. The gutter hardly ever drained properly; her father had given up trying to make it and instead poured gallons of Jeyes' Fluid into the standing water to prevent mosquitos from breeding.

She decided to walk down Rue Maresca. Her hands deep in the mackintosh pockets, she smiled up into the rain, which hit hard as pellets. After the horrible summer the air was clean and refreshing. She drew it deep into her lungs, and hummed a bit. The beggars huddled against the peeling POST NO BILLS looked at her as though she were mad.

In her pocket she held a card, the one taped to a box he had given her at Christmas in The Camellia Room, fourteen months ago. "If I were a stone I would still know the changings of the earth. Leaves turn and fall, and their deeds are mightier than heaven."

31

The message read, "You are booked on the *Elsie Moller*, due in a few days. She sails on January 20th. Sorry you can't take much with you, she will be fully loaded. Congratulations and Godspeed. William Dugan, Vice Consul, United States Consulate General."

The Contis had been nearly ready for months. They procured their exit visas immediately after Ming Chu was released. Poldo sold his demijohns and carafes, the remaining chemicals, the sideboard, the dining room furniture, most of their dishware, three new damask tablecloths and silver and crystal, the chandelier, extra clothing and bedding and a quilt, old shoes, a silk Persian carpet rolled up for years and stored under the big bed inside layers of butcher paper, the big range on which Loh the Ningpo cook prepared five-course banquets and the even bigger Westinghouse refrigerator—old and clanking—and everything else they could not take or Amah could not use. Ming Chu insisted that Poldo sell the inlaid rosewood chairs and matching table that had belonged to her parents. Their beds went at the very last. Found through Amah and Yung's cousin, the buyers took away the things in small lots they hoped would not attract the attention of the cadres.

Smiling, the Wongs watched the dispersal of the Conti household. Poldo realized to them it signified the final degradation of the Contis; they were starving, or leaving China. Either was quite satisfactory to the Wongs.

Her golden teeth hidden behind compressed lips, Amah was nevertheless glad to see them go. At least the family would be safe, and it was time for her to return to the country and confront her daughter-in-law. Nola said her farewells to the nuns and her schoolmates, and the priests at St. Columban's with a hardihood Maria recognized from her own dawning progression toward self-reliance. But Nola cried when it came to parting with Amah. The woman who had cared for her from infancy blew her nose for the last time and pushed her away; the sooner her mother was aboard ship the better.

The *Elsie Moller* looked like anything but the instrument of their deliverance. Although a Union Jack flew at her mast, the rest of her appeared every inch the worn-down, coal-burning, rusty coastal tramp steamer that seldom put in anywhere long enough for painting and refitting. Accommodations for the Contis did not exist; that is, the passenger berths that slept

four to six in the main housing were long ago
reserved, but quarters had been added on below,
'tween decks. Bamboo matting provided parti-
tions between units; the common mess table was
bolted down in the center. For lighting there
were portholes; nothing else had been arranged
yet. The Contis were fortunate. Other latecomers
had to sleep on deck. The toilets were topside,
however, though chamber pots had been placed
beneath their bunks.

"It's funny having a floor made of steel. How
long does it take to get to Hong Kong?" Nola
asked. Her bunk was a canvas cot. When she sat
on it her bottom slid to the center and her feet
pointed up.

"About six days," Poldo said. "Twelve days if
we row."

They all looked at him. He had made a joke.

The clang of shoes clambering down the ladder
brought into view the families who were to share
their quarters. They were a Dutch couple and
their two sons, about nine and ten years old;
and a British man and his dark-haired Russian
wife, whose name was Lila. They shook hands all
round, wished each other good luck. The boys
seemed paralyzed by the presence of Nola, a girl
virtually in their bedroom.

"I'm going outside," Maria said, and began
climbing.

On deck she stared at the Bund. How odd it
was to be standing on the wrong side of it.
Tomorrow and long after she was gone from here,

everyone would continue pushing carts and pedaling pedicabs and hawking food on the Bund. On
Nanking Road the trams were running once more.
The refugee beggars would continue to die
until Mao's regime did something for them. Or
to them. The great buildings of commerce lined
up in a row all the way to Garden Bridge would
endure to serve one government function or
another. The Cathay Hotel which was also
Sassoon House would be left intact; somehow
she didn't doubt it. The Communists, when they
got tired of reforming China, would find a
lucrative use for its luxurious trappings.
Everything eventually settled down. China had
always seethed, experienced a revolution, and
found its feet. The soft, vulnerable bodies of
human beings did not fare so well.

The Contis had walked out of their house at
Route Magy leaving no ownership papers anywhere near it. The Wongs could swarm upstairs
and claim the entire three floors as theirs if
they liked.

The Chinese crewmen passing behind Maria made
soft sucking sounds, the noises expressing what
they dared not say in case they were reported to
the British officers.

Maria ignored them.

She was thinking about Dani, sleeping to the
west in Hungjao Cemetery, and the irony that she
was leaving her native land and he was to remain
far from his. As far as she knew, Gromeko was
still buried in his shallow, cement-dirt grave

under The Camellia Room. Did Yung rest in a
decent grave? Probably not. After execution the
bodies were carted in trucks to vast holes dug
on the edges of the city.

But Galia was alive, and someday she would
see her.

How smelly the Whangpo River was, how alive
even while the dead floated on their way to the
sea. It became the lifeline of Shanghai from the
moment the British warships steamed upriver to
start a colony on nothing but mud flats. The
taipans had lived like kings, their clerks like
minor princes. The staffs hired from home
enjoyed entree into private clubs, had tennis
memberships and servants, luxuries beyond the
reach of their brethren in England. Here was the
pinnacle of colonial privilege built upon territories wrested from China a century ago. All
gone: the might and money of the East India
Company, the war to force China to import Indian
opium and ending in China's humiliating defeat.
Great Britain demanded and got huge pieces of
China, but the star of all was to be Shanghai,
the legend of the Far East.

No wonder it was so hard to give up.

Bobbing in their sampans at the stern, the
wind-chapped grandmothers and the children they
were left to watch eyed her but none asked for
money. They knew she was finished with China.

She noticed her father standing at the rail
farther up the ship; then she saw her mother

standing even farther along, Nola at her side. All of them were staring out at the city.

Every one of the passengers was on deck, commenting and exclaiming on the changing landscapes ashore. The Bund was far behind, not even the tip of the Cathay Hotel visible, and any buildings to be seen were godowns or factories.

Finally, everything smoothed out and became clusters of farming hamlets. The land was flat and green, misty with the morning's rain. Shallow boats rocked as the *Elsie Moller* passed; the men in them were fishing with nets. The fishermen were both young and old, but when they gathered in the nets their arms always bulged with muscle. They flung the nets out with graceful sweeps so dexterous the nets puckered the water in a perfect circle before sinking. A few boats carried big-beaked cormorants. Bands around their necks prevented them from swallowing any fish they caught. The catch belonged to the master, but to the delight of the children aboard the ship a fisherman removed the band on his bird and allowed it to dive in and come up with a fish. A few seconds of wet scales glistening in the sunlight, and then one could see its shape sliding down the cormorant's long neck.

The youngest of the passengers had never seen any of these things before. The Whangpo had curved east and then due west as though retreating back into China. Upon reaching Woosung, the

Elsie Moller's bow pointed true north, on the point of nosing into the Yangtze River. The water was darker and running fast.

"Now we turn right," Poldo said to Nola, "And soon we will be in the biggest water you have ever seen, the East China Sea." He tipped his head into the breeze and inhaled deeply. "Try. You can smell it already." After a moment he said in a puzzled voice, "We are not going east."

The *Elsie Moller* was steaming straight ahead; several islands lay in its path.

Looking over the side, Maria said, "The water is awfully choppy."

"It gets very shallow toward the center," Poldo said. That is why that sailor is casting the lead, to gauge the water's depth. See that man on the bridge with the captain? He is the Yangtze estuary pilot. But why are we crossing to the north channel when we could easily sail east on the main channel? The main channel is the deep one." As he said this, the ship jolted under their feet. "We just bumped over a sandbar."

Other people were asking the same question. An American, one of those who had a bunk in the main housing, climbed to the bridge to ask the captain what was happening. In a few minutes he returned to the main deck and began circulating among the passengers and speaking to them, apparently passing on a message. He had hair the color of a blood orange, and Maria watched it move toward where they stood by the rail.

"Captain says we are taking the north channel in the estuary to the sea," he told Poldo. "And I don't think he liked telling me this, but it's best you know it." He glanced at Maria as though she might become alarmed and start fainting. "He said it might be necessary to order everyone to go below deck. I don't think it'll be bad, whatever might turn up, but we'll just be ready, won't we. He doesn't want us to panic; just that I should pass the word quietly." He nodded and made his way aft.

She and her father exchanged glances and both looked round for Ming Chu and Nola.

In the wheelhouse someone gave a shout. Minutes later, the ship's speed picked up and at the same time the deck jarred again, and again, as though the ship were trying to jump obstacles. Poldo ran to the bow, where he had spotted Ming Chu and Nola.

"Everybody below!" the captain shouted through a megaphone. "Go 'tween decks, everyone!" He bellowed more orders but they were lost in a loud crash. A plume of water flew up to the south behind the ship.

Maria scanned Woosung behind them for the source of the shot, looked at the islands ahead, and at the instant she spotted a low shape racing toward them from seaward smoke burst from the low shape and more water kicked into the air.

Poldo was back, Ming Chu and Nola under each arm. The deck jumped, and he swerved and almost lost his footing. Maria steadied him, took Nola

and pushed her to the ladder. Other passengers
were scrambling down the opening. At another
jolt of the ship, the Russian woman named Lila
lost her grip on the ladder and fell to the
steel plating below. Her husband stood behind
Poldo and Ming Chu and had not seen his wife
fall. Poldo stepped back, shielding Ming Chu
with his body, and gestured at the man to go
before them. Puzzled, he thanked Poldo and got
his feet on the ladder.

"Nola, you go ahead of me," Maria said. "Mama,
you come behind between me and Daddy." She meant
to place her mother's feet on each rung as they
climbed down. No one was pushing. That was a
good thing, as the ship shuddered and hitched
her way over the sandbars.

Their 'tween decks quarters were packed with
people. Lila was sitting up, fingering bruised
places on her shoulder and knees as her husband
supported her from the back. The little boys of
the Dutch family looked white-faced in the dim
light allowed in by the portholes.

Another salvo blasted the air and water, the
impacts punching through the plating like metallic blows.

Amidst the breathless murmurings and bewildered comments, the red-haired American said,
"Shouldn't we all get down on our faces? Less of
a target that way."

"Good thinking. Down we go," Lila's husband said.

Poldo helped Ming Chu to lie down. Maria pulled Nola under her and tried to cover her mother as well.

The invader kept firing, and suddenly a heavy rumble of fire entered the invisible scene above. The new gun boomed; compared to these cannonades the first salvos sounded like pistol shots. Under their feet the *Elsie Moller* vibrated and strained and leaped like a greyhound.

Maria clutched Nola and her mother; her father held onto them all. What a stupid way to die after everything, she thought. What a dirty trick on Huell, who will wait and wait on the docks in Hong Kong until someone gives him the news. The booming and crashing went on over their heads, while the steel plating seized their bodies and eardrums with the ship's pounding, grinding, thudding, and twice the hull yawed as if it wanted to fall on its side.

"What the hell is this all about?" a man said, his voice muffled. "A small ship fires on us, then apparently some big ship starts firing too. It's not our ship, we haven't got a gun aboard."

"The heavy gun is firing back," Poldo said. "It must be a warship, and British, because the Communists haven't anything like it."

"It is British." The voice of the red-haired American held a tone of certainty. "She must have come up from Hong Kong to escort us. And that small ship attacking us is probably a Nationalist gunboat. They've been hanging around the mouth of the estuary attacking any

shipping that passes up this way. They captured the *Edith Moller*, you know."

"The sister ship of this one," Poldo said. "So
that is why we were avoiding the main channel."

"That's it. But I wasn't authorized to say so.
The captain said he thought the Nationalists
wouldn't expect us to take the shallow route."
As if to remind them they were taking the shallow route the *Elsie Moller* jerked and wallowed
in a sea-sickening motion.

Uneasily, Maria remembered the *Amethyst*, stuck
in sand and mud, punctured by shell and bullets
and eventually captured. It took her a moment to
sort out the sides and loyalties. The British
had caved in to the Communists and recognized
the new government; Chiang was feeling vengeful
and attacked, like a rabid dog, British-flag
shipping entering and leaving Shanghai. What if
her family had been booked on the sister ship?
Would they have landed in Taiwan? Would they
have been released to go to Hong Kong?

Boots clattered on the ladder. White trousers
followed, white tunic; finally, as Maria looked
up, the pink face of the captain. He was a large
man; his presence towered over the prone bodies.

"It is over," he announced. "Saved by the
bell. You can come topside if you like."

They had been rescued by the HMS *Cossack*. Even
at a distance she looked dangerous and reassur-
ing as she came about in the main channel, cutting a curving wake behind her rear. She stayed

on the south side of the estuary, waiting for the *Elsie Moller*, which had at last floundered over the last of the sandbars and made it to deeper water.

By evening all the passengers knew the HMS *Cossack* had indeed been sent to escort them to Hong Kong. Chiang's gunboat had run away under fire from the *Cossack*. Discreetly, the explanation for the near-foundering of the *Elsie Moller* became known. The ship was behind schedule and a rapidly outgoing tide had left the estuary a perilous place to cross.

That done, they had clear sailing.

Temperatures rose as they went south. A cold day fell no lower than 55 degrees. On the night before they were to arrive at Hong Kong, Maria could not sleep. Her watch face was invisible but she knew it must be long past midnight. She rose from her cot, put her coat on over her pajamas and slipped on her shoes. Quietly she climbed the ladder to the main deck. There was an arc of moon, and many stars, not at all put out by the running lights of the ship. She looked at her watch; nearly three in the morning. Yesterday afternoon they had sailed through the Taiwan Strait between Fukien Province and Taiwan. With the *Cossack* as escort, the *Elsie Moller* saw no more Nationalist gunboats, even though the ship was passing right under the nose of Chiang Kai-shek's refuge.

Maria lifted her gaze to the stars. Were they thick and dense enough to be the Milky Way? They weren't; there wasn't that sweep of white, truly like a swath of milk that somehow managed to sparkle.

She did not move, forgot about time, the only sound in her world the rumble of engines and the swish of the stern wash.

"I couldn't sleep, either." Nola's voice sounded sleepy. Ming Chu had said to Maria yesterday, Do you think she is getting better? Maria thought so. She had sung

Nola, Nola,
Not a capi-to-la
Just a little town

teasing, a test, and Nola stuck out her tongue and answered that one day she was going to be a big town and watch out.

And you, Mama? Maria asked. Do you mind leaving China?

She did not have to be told. Ming Chu's grief was a luxury she had put aside. It was enough for the present that her family were to be safe.

"Have I ever been to Hong Kong?" Nola asked.

"When you were very small, and I was thirteen."

"Did I like it?"

Maria laughed. "You didn't seem to. You cried all the time. You were a terrible pest."

"America is awfully big, isn't it," Nola remarked. The dark sea rushing by beneath them glinted off the tops of its waves, perhaps reflecting the stars.

"Not as big as China. But it's bigger than you can ever imagine than Shanghai."

In the early morning Maria was back on deck as the ship entered Hong Kong Harbour. Two tugboats approached to take her in hand. The *Elsie Moller* seemed only a little bigger than the junks littering the harbour and the ferry boats filled with people. The ship seemed terribly slow, but presently Maria could see the water frontage of Victoria, as Hong Kong island was called. The Peak with its mansions and the villas down its slope shone in the sun. The streets downtown between the big office buildings were already bustling with tiny cars and buses and people on foot. She gave all of that part of Hong Kong the merest glance, then kept her gaze focused on the long wharf, where an oceanliner and an American and a British navy warship were moored.

The tugboats herded the *Elsie Moller*, guiding her to the berth allotted her. Now Maria could see vehicles parked behind a barrier; she could make out people standing on the pier itself. Somehow she knew which one to look at. His clear fresh skin grew clearer in her sight, then his nice eyebrows that one day would be handsome bushy ones. His hands were on his lean hips, his fair hair whisking about in the cool breeze; he was smiling and speaking to her, saying things she understood without hearing. He raised an arm to wave, and she waved back. Now she could see his blue eyes, the only thing she saw, really; her entire body flushed and was joined into those happy eyes.

THE END

About the Author

Lucille Bellucci grew up in Shanghai during a period of turbulence extending from the Sino-Japanese war in 1937 until World War II encompassed China. She remained there with her family until 1952, after spending three years under the Communist regime. She has lived five years in Italy, 15 years in Brazil, and is the author of *The Snake Woman of Ipanema* and *A Rare Passion*.

Bibliography

CHINA Yesterday and Today, Edited by Molly Joel Coye, Jon Livingston, and Jean Highland, Bantam Books, 1975-84

China And United States Far East Policy 1945-1966 (a Chronology), Congressional Quarterly, Inc., Washington DC, 1967

How the Far East was Lost, Congressional Quarterly Service, Washington, DC, 1967

Order of Battle, U.S. Army, World War II, Shelby L. Stanton, U.S. Army Military History Institute, Carlisle Barracks, Carlisle, PA 17013-5008

    a. Input from MHI Volunteer Layton Pennington on Uniforms and Combat Decorations

Selected Military Writings of Mao Tse-tung, Foreign Languages Press, Peking, 1968

Shanghai, Harriet Sergeant, Crown Publishers, Inc., 1990.

Stillwell and the American Experience in China 1911-45, Barbara W. Tuchman, The Macmillan Company, New York, 1970

The Fall of Shanghai, Noel Barber, Coward, McCann And Geoghegan, New York, 1979.

###